# "I can't do this alone anymore,"

she said to the blank sky. "I need someone to help me."

"Helen!" a deep, unfamiliar voice called out.

It was the first time Helen had heard another voice in the Underworld, and at first she assumed she was hallucinating. Her face was still tilted up, and she couldn't move it to look or she'd be sucked under.

"Reach toward me, if you can," the young man said in a strained voice, like he was struggling at the edge of the pit to get to her. "Come on, *try*, damn it! Give me your hand!"

At that moment her ears filled, and she could no longer hear what he shouted at her. All she could see was a flash of gold—a bright glimmer that pierced through the dull, defeated light of the Underworld like the lifesaving beacon of a lighthouse. She caught the barest glimpse of an angular chin and a full, sculpted mouth at the very edge of her vision. Then, under the surface of the quicksand, Helen felt a warm, strong hand take hers and pull.

# DREAMLESS

A STARCROSSED NOVEL

JOSEPHINE ANGELINI

An Imprint of HarperCollinsPublishers

HarperTeen is an imprint of HarperCollins Publishers.

Dreamless

Library of Congress Cataloging-in-Publication Data
Angelini, Josephine.
    Dreamless : a Starcrossed novel / by Josephine Angelini. — 1st ed.
        p.    cm.
    Summary: With help from her new friend Orion, seventeen-year-
old Helen Hamilton descends into the Underworld in search of a way
to break the Furies' blood curse and prevent the start of another Trojan
War.
    ISBN 978-0-06-201202-9 (pbk.)
    [1. Supernatural—Fiction.   2. Mythology, Greek—Fiction.   3.
Nantucket Island (Mass.)—Fiction.]   I. Title.
PZ7.A58239Dr   2012                                        2011022938
[Fic]—dc23                                                          CIP
                                                                     AC

Typography by Erin Fitzsimmons
13  14  15  16  17   LP/RRDH   10 9 8 7 6 5 4 3 2 1

First paperback edition, 2013

*For my husband, with all of my love*

# PROLOGUE

On Monday morning, school was canceled. Power still hadn't been restored to certain parts of the island, and several streets in the center of town were impassable due to damage done by the storm.

*Yeah, right,* Zach thought, as he walked out his front door. *It was the "storm" that demolished half the town, not the freaky new family that can outrun cars.*

He jogged for a few blocks, just to put some distance between himself and his dad. He couldn't bear to stay at home and listen to his father complain about the team missing football practice when all he was really complaining about was spending another day separated from his three star athletes—the amazing Delos boys.

Zach went down to India Street to look at the ruined Atheneum steps along with dozens of other gawkers.

Everyone was saying that an electrical wire had shorted out in the middle of the street the night before and that it had gotten so hot it melted the pavement. Zach saw the hole in the ground and he saw the downed power wires, but he knew the wires hadn't caused all that damage.

Just like he knew the exit sign over the door by the girls' locker room hadn't burned a huge patch of grass *fifteen feet* away from it.

Why was everyone so stupid? Were they so blinded by the Delos kids that they were willing to overlook the fact that the marble steps of the library couldn't possibly have been cracked by the frigging wind? Didn't anyone else see there was something more going on? It was so obvious to Zach. He'd tried to warn Helen, but she was too wrapped up in Lucas to see straight. Zach knew she was similar to them somehow, but he'd tried, anyway. She was like the whole island was about them, just like his dad was, too. Blinded.

Zach was walking through town, glowering at all the fools milling around, oohing and aahing over the melted asphalt, when Matt saw him and waved him over.

"Check it out," Matt said when Zach joined him by the edge of the police tape. "They're saying it must have been the main line to the island that did that. Pretty incredible, huh?"

"Wow. A hole. How incredible," Zach said sarcastically.

"You don't think it's interesting?" Matt asked, raising an eyebrow.

"I just don't think a downed power wire did all that."

"What else could it've been?" Matt asked in his usual, analytical way, gesturing to the scene of destruction in front of them.

Zach smiled cautiously. Matt was smarter than most people gave him credit for. He was handsome, he wore all the right clothes, he captained the all-state golf team, and he was from an old and respected family. On top of that, he knew how to play it cool around people who mattered and talk about interesting things, like sports. In fact, Zach always suspected that Matt could have been one of the most popular kids in school if he wanted, but for some reason, Matt had given up his spot on the popular team and chosen to be the Geek King instead. It had to have something to do with Helen.

Zach still hadn't figured out why Helen chose to hang out with geeks herself, considering she was more beautiful than any movie star or supermodel he had ever seen. Her decision to be the wallflower was another part of her mystery, and her attraction. She was the kind of woman that men *did* things for. Things like sacrifice their social standing, or steal for, or even fight for . . .

"I wasn't here," Zach replied, finally answering Matt's question. "But it looks to me like somebody did this on purpose. Like they thought they could get away with it."

"You think someone . . . What? Smashed the library, ripped down a ten-thousand-volt power line with their bare hands, and then melted a four-foot hole in the street . . . as a prank?" Matt asked evenly. He narrowed his eyes and gave

Zach a small, closed-lipped smile.

"I don't know," Zach finally answered. Then a thought occurred to him. "But maybe you do. You've been hanging out with Ariadne a lot lately."

"Yeah, and?" Matt said calmly. "I don't see your point."

Did Matt know? Had the Delos kids told him what was going on while they left Zach out of it? Zach studied Matt for a moment and decided he was probably just sticking up for the Delos family like everyone else did whenever Zach mentioned how odd they were.

"Who says I have to have a point? I'm just saying that I've never seen a downed power line do that before. Have you?"

"So the police, water and power, all the people that are trained to deal with natural disasters, they're wrong and you're right?"

The way Matt put it made Zach feel a little silly. He couldn't come right out and say that a family of supermen was trying to take over his island. That would sound crazy. Feigning disinterest, Zach looked out across the street to the demolished steps of the Atheneum and shrugged.

That's when he noticed someone, someone special, like Helen—like those frigging Delos kids. Only this guy was different. There was something inhuman about him. When this guy moved he sort of looked like an insect.

"Whatever. I don't really care what happened," Zach said, acting like he was bored. "Have fun staring down that hole."

He walked away, not wanting to waste any more time on someone so obviously on the Deloses' side. He wanted to see where that freak was going, and maybe figure out what they were all hiding from him.

He followed the stranger down to the docks, and spotted a beautiful yacht. It was something right out of a storybook. Tall masts, teak deck, fiberglass hull, and red sails. Zach walked toward it with his mouth open. The yacht was the most beautiful thing he'd ever seen, except for one face. . . . Her face.

Zach felt someone tap him on the back of his shoulder and, as he turned around, the world went dark.

# ONE

**R**ed blood bloomed from underneath Helen's torn finger-
nails, pooled in the crescents of her cuticles, and trailed
down her knuckles in little rivers. Despite the pain, she
gripped the ledge more tightly with her left hand so she could try to
slide her right hand forward. There was grit and blood under her
fingers, making her slip, and her hands were cramping so badly
that the center of her palm was starting to spasm. She reached
with her right, but didn't have the strength to pull herself any farther forward.

Helen slid back with a gasp until she was dangling from her
rigid fingertips. Six stories beneath her kicking feet was a dead
flowerbed, littered with moldy bricks and slates that had slid off
the roof of the dilapidated mansion and broken into bits. She didn't
have to look down to know that the same would happen to her if
she lost her grasp on the crumbling window ledge. She tried again

to swing a leg up and catch it on the windowsill, but the more she kicked the less secure her grip became.

A sob escaped from between her bitten lips. She had been hanging from this ledge since she descended into the Underworld that night. It felt to her like hours, maybe days had passed, and her endurance was flagging. Helen cried out in frustration. She had to get off this ledge and go find the Furies. She was the Descender—this was her task. Find the Furies in the Underworld, defeat them somehow, and free the Scions from the Furies' influence. She was supposed to be ending the cycle of vengeance that compelled Scions to kill each other off, but instead here she was, hanging from a ledge.

She didn't want to fall, but she knew that she would get no closer to finding the Furies if she went on clinging here for an eternity. And in the Underworld, every night lasted forever. She knew she needed to end this night and start the next anew, in some other, hopefully more productive, infinity. If she couldn't pull herself up, that left only one option.

The fingers of Helen's left hand began twitching and her grip gave way. She tried to tell herself not to fight it, that it would be better to fall because at least it would be over. But still she clung to the ledge with every bit of strength remaining in her right hand. Helen was too afraid to let herself go. She bit down on her bloody lip in concentration, but the fingers of her right hand slid across the grit and finally came away from the edge. She couldn't hold on.

When she hit the ground she heard her left leg snap.

Helen slapped a hand over her mouth to keep the scream from erupting across her quiet Nantucket bedroom. She could taste the flinty grit of the Underworld on her cramped fingers. In the pewter-blue light of predawn, she listened intently to the sound down the hall of her father getting ready for the day. Thankfully, he didn't seem to hear anything out of the ordinary, and he went downstairs to start cooking breakfast as if nothing were wrong.

Lying in bed, trembling with the pain of her broken leg and her pulled muscles, Helen waited for her body to heal itself. Tears slid down either side of her face, leaving hot tracks across her chilled skin. It was icy cold in her bedroom.

Helen knew she had to eat to heal properly, but she couldn't go downstairs with a broken leg. She told herself to stay calm and wait. In time, her body would be strong enough to move, then stand, and then walk. She would lie and say she'd overslept. She'd hide her sore leg from her father as best as she could, smiling and making small talk as they ate. Then, with a little food in her, she would heal the rest of the way.

She would feel better soon, she told herself, crying as quietly as she could. She just had to hold on.

Someone was waving a hand in Helen's face.

"What?" she asked, startled. She turned to look at Matt, who was signaling her back to earth.

"I'm sorry, Lennie, but I still don't get it. What's a Rogue Scion?" he asked, his brow wrinkled with worry.

"I'm a Rogue," she answered a bit too loudly. She'd faded

for a second there, and still hadn't caught up to the conversation.

Helen straightened her slumped shoulders and looked around at the rest of the room to find that everyone was staring at her. Everyone except Lucas. He was studying his hands in his lap, his mouth tight.

Helen, Lucas, Ariadne, and Jason were sitting around the Delos kitchen table after school, trying to catch Matt and Claire up on all things demigod. Matt and Claire were Helen's best mortal friends, and they were both incredibly smart, but some things about Helen and her past were too complicated to be taken for granted. After everything they'd gone through, Matt and Claire deserved answers. They'd put their lives on the line to help Helen and the rest of the Delos family seven days ago.

*Seven days*, Helen thought, counting on her fingers to make sure. *All that time in the Underworld makes it feel like seven weeks. Maybe it has been seven weeks for me.*

"It sounds confusing, but it's not," Ariadne said when she realized that Helen wasn't going to continue. "There are Four Houses, and all Four Houses owe each other a blood debt from the Trojan War. That's why the Furies make us want to kill someone from another House. Vengeance."

"A billion years ago someone from the House of Atreus killed someone from the House of Thebes and *you* are expected to pay that blood debt?" Matt asked dubiously.

"Pretty much, except it was a lot more than just one death. We're talking about the Trojan War, here. *A lot of* people died, both demigod Scions and full mortals like you," Ariadne said with an apologetic grimace.

"I *know* a lot of people died, but how does this blood-for-blood thing get you anywhere?" Matt persisted. "It never ends. It's insane."

Lucas laughed mirthlessly and lifted his eyes from his lap to meet Matt's. "You're right. The Furies drive us mad, Matt," he said quietly, patiently. "They haunt us until we break."

Helen remembered that tone. She thought of it as Lucas's professor voice. She could listen to it all day, except she knew she shouldn't want to.

"They make us want to kill each other in order to fulfill some twisted sort of justice," Lucas continued in his measured tone. "Someone from another House kills a person in our House. We kill one from theirs in retaliation, and on it goes for three and a half thousand years. And if a Scion kills someone from his own House, he becomes an Outcast."

"Like Hector," Matt said tentatively. Even saying the name of their brother and cousin set off the Furies' curse, angering the Delos clan. Matt only risked it now for the sake of being clear. "He killed your cousin Creon because Creon killed your aunt Pandora, and now you all feel an irresistible urge to kill him, even though you still love him. I'm sorry. I'm still not seeing how that's even remotely like justice."

Helen looked around and saw Ariadne, Jason, and Lucas gritting their teeth. Jason was the first to calm himself.

"That's why what Helen is doing is so important," he replied. "She's in the Underworld to defeat the Furies, and stop all this senseless killing."

Matt gave up reluctantly. It was hard for him to accept the Furies, but he could see that no one at the table was any happier about their existence than he was. Claire still seemed like she needed to clarify a few things.

"Okay. That's an Outcast. But *Rogues* like Lennie are Scions who have parents from two different Houses, but only one House can *claim* them, right? So they still owe a blood debt to the other House," Claire spoke carefully, like she knew what she was saying was difficult for Helen to hear but she had to say it, anyway. "You were claimed by your mother, Daphne. Or by her House, rather."

"The House of Atreus," Helen said dully, remembering how her long-lost mother had returned to ruin her life nine days ago with some very unwelcome news.

"But your real father—not Jerry—even though, Lennie, I have to say, Jerry will always be your real dad to me," Claire amended passionately before getting back on track. "Your biological father, who you never knew and who died before you were born . . ."

"Was from the House of Thebes." For a moment Helen met Lucas's eyes, then quickly looked away. "Ajax Delos."

"Our uncle," Jason said, including Ariadne and Lucas in his glance.

"Right," Claire said uncomfortably. She looked between Helen and Lucas who refused to meet her eyes. "And since you were both claimed by enemy Houses you two wanted each other dead at first. Until you . . ." She trailed off.

"Before Helen and I paid our blood debts to each other's Houses by nearly dying for each other," Lucas finished in a leaden tone, daring anyone to comment on the bond he and Helen shared.

Helen wanted to dig a hole straight down through the tiled floor of the Delos kitchen and disappear. She could feel the weight of everyone's unasked questions.

They were all wondering: How far did Helen and Lucas go with each other before they found out they were first cousins? Was it just a little kissing, or did it get "scarred for life" serious?

And: Do they still *want to* with each other, even though they know they're cousins?

And: I wonder if they still do it sometimes. It wouldn't be hard for them because they can both fly. Maybe they sneak off every night and . . .

"Helen? We need to get back to work," Cassandra said with bossy edge in her voice. She stood in the kitchen doorway with a fist planted on her slim, boyish hip.

As Helen stood up from the table, Lucas caught her eyes and gave her the tiniest of smiles, encouraging her. Smiling back ever so slightly, Helen followed Cassandra down to the Delos library feeling calmer, more self-assured. Cassandra shut the door, and the two girls continued their search for some bit of knowledge that might help Helen in her quest.

*Helen turned the corner and saw that the way was blocked by a rainbow of rust. A skyscraper had been bent across the street as if* a giant hand had pressed it down like a stalk of corn.

Helen wiped the itchy sweat off her brow and tried to find the safest route over the cracked concrete and twisted iron. It would be hard to climb over, but most of the buildings in this abandoned city were crumbling into dust as the desert around it encroached. There was no point going another way. One obstruction or another blocked all the streets, and besides, Helen didn't know which way she was supposed to go in the first place. The only thing she could do was to keep moving forward.

Scrambling over a jagged lattice, surrounded by the tangy smell of decaying metal, Helen heard a deep, mournful groaning. A bolt shook loose from its joint, and a girder above her broke free in a shower of rust and sand. Instinctively, Helen held her hands up and tried to deflect it, but down here in the Underworld, her arms didn't have Scion strength. She slammed painfully on her back, stretched out over the crisscrossing bars beneath her. The heavy girder lay across her stomach, pinning her down across her middle.

Helen tried to wiggle out from underneath it, but she couldn't move her legs without excruciating pain radiating out from her hips. Something was certainly broken—her hip, her back, maybe both.

Helen squinted and tried to shade her eyes with a hand, swallowing around her thirst. She was exposed, trapped, like a turtle turned over onto its back. The blank sky held no cloud to provide even a moment of relief.

Just blinding light and relentless heat . . .

Helen wandered out of Miss Bee's social studies class, stifling a yawn. Her head felt stuffed up and hot, like a

Thanksgiving turkey on slow roast. It was nearly the end of the school day, but that was no comfort. Helen looked down at her feet and thought about what awaited her. Every night she descended into the Underworld and encountered yet another horrendous landscape. She had no idea why she'd end up in some places a few times, and other places only once, but she thought it had something to do with her mood. The worse the mood she was in when she went to sleep, the worse her experience in the Underworld.

Still focused on her shuffling feet, Helen felt warm fingers brush against hers in the hustle of the hallway. Glancing up, she saw Lucas's jewel-blue eyes seeking hers. She pulled in a breath, a quick inward sigh of surprise, and locked eyes with him.

Lucas's gaze was soft and playful, and the corners of his mouth tilted up in a secret smile. Still moving in opposite directions, they turned their heads to maintain eye contact as they walked on, their identical smiles growing with each passing moment. With a teasing flick of her hair, Helen abruptly faced forward and ended the stare, a grin plastered on her face.

One look from Lucas and she felt stronger. Alive again. She could hear him chuckling to himself as he walked on, almost smug, like he knew exactly how much he affected her. She chuckled, too, shaking her head at herself. Then she saw Jason.

Walking a few paces behind Lucas with Claire at his side, Jason had watched the whole exchange. His mouth was a worried line, and his eyes were sad. He shook his head at Helen in disapproval and she looked down, blushing furiously.

They were cousins, Helen knew that. Flirting was wrong. But it made her feel *better* when nothing else could. Was she supposed to go through all of this without even the comfort of Lucas's smile? Helen went to her last class and sat behind her desk, fighting back tears as she unpacked her notebook.

*Long splinters enveloped Helen, forcing her to remain completely still or risk impaling herself on one of them. She was trapped inside the trunk of a tree that sat alone in the middle of a dry, dead scrubland. If she breathed too deeply, the long splinters pricked her. Her arms were twisted behind her and her legs folded up uncomfortably underneath her, tilting her torso forward. One long splinter was lined up directly with her right eye. If her head moved forward while she struggled to break free—if she even let it sag a little with fatigue—her eye would be stabbed out.*

*"What do you expect me to do?" she whimpered to no one. Helen knew she was completely alone.*

*"What am I supposed to do?" she suddenly screamed, her chest and back stinging with a dozen little puncture wounds.*

*Screaming didn't help, but getting angry did. It helped steel her enough to accept the inevitable. She'd put herself here, even if it was unintentional, and she knew how to get herself out. Pain usually triggered her release from the Underworld. As long as she didn't die, Helen was pretty sure she would leave the Underworld and wake up in her bed. She'd be injured and in pain, but at least she'd be out.*

*She stared at the long splinter in front of her eye, knowing what the situation demanded she do, but not sure she was capable of doing it. As the anger fueling her seeped away, desperate tears welled up and spilled down her cheeks. She heard her own constricted, choked-off sobs pressing close to her in the claustrophobic prison of the tree trunk. Minutes passed, and Helen's arms and legs began to cry out, twisted as they were into unnatural shapes.*

*Time would not change the situation. Tears would not change the situation. She had one choice, and she knew she could either make it now or hours of suffering from now. Helen was a Scion, and as such a target for the Fates. She'd never had any choice but one. With that thought, the anger returned.*

*In one sure movement, she jerked her head forward.*

Lucas couldn't take his eyes off Helen. Even from across the kitchen he could see that the translucent skin across her high cheekbones was so pale it was stained blue by the lacy veins running below the surface. He could have sworn that when she first came over to study with Cassandra at the Delos house that morning, her forearms were covered in fading bruises.

She had a spooked, hunted look to her now. She looked more frightened than she had a few weeks ago when they all thought that Tantalus and the fanatical Hundred Cousins were after her. Cassandra had recently foreseen that the Hundred were focusing nearly all their energy on finding

Hector and Daphne, and that Helen had nothing to fear. But if it wasn't the Hundred frightening Helen, then it had to be something in the Underworld. Lucas wondered if she was being chased, maybe even tortured down there.

The thought tore him up inside, like there was a wild animal climbing up the inside of his rib cage, gnawing on his bones as it went. He had to grit his teeth together to stop the growl that was trying to grind out of him. He was so *angry* all the time now, and his anger worried him. But worse than the anger was how worried he was about Helen.

Watching her jump at the slightest sound, or tense into herself with wide, staring eyes, pushed him almost to the point of panic. Lucas felt a physical need to protect Helen. It was like a whole body tic that made him want to throw himself between her and harm. But he couldn't help her with this. He couldn't get into the Underworld without dying.

Lucas was still working on that problem. There weren't many individuals who could physically go down into the Underworld like Helen could and survive—just a handful in the entire history of Greek mythology. But he wasn't going to stop trying. Lucas had always been good at solving problems—good at solving "unsolvable" puzzles in particular. Which was probably why seeing Helen like this hurt him in such a nagging, hateful way.

He couldn't solve this for her. She was on her own down there, and there was nothing he could do about it.

"Son. Why don't you sit next to me?" Castor suggested, startling Lucas out of his thoughts. His father motioned to the chair on his right as they all sat down at the table for Sunday supper.

"That's Cassandra's seat," Lucas replied with a sharp shake of his head, but really what Lucas was thinking was that it was *Hector's*. Lucas couldn't bear to take a seat that never should have been vacated. Instead, he took his place on his father's left at the end of the community bench.

"Yeah, Dad," Cassandra joked as she took the seat that she had automatically inherited when Hector became an Outcast for killing Tantalus's only son, Creon. "Are you try-ing to demote me or something?"

"Wouldn't you know it if I was? What kind of an oracle are you, anyway?" Castor teased, poking Cassandra in the belly until she shrieked.

Lucas could see that his father was seizing this rare oppor-tunity to play with Cassandra, because those opportunities were nearly over. As the Oracle, Lucas's little sister was pulling away from her family, from all of humanity. Soon, she would drift away from all people and become the cold instrument of the Fates, no matter how much she was loved by those closest to her.

Castor usually took any chance he could to joke around with his daughter, but Lucas could tell that this time he was only partly focused on taunting Cassandra. His mind was elsewhere. For some reason Lucas couldn't immediately see, Castor really didn't want Lucas to sit in his usual seat.

He understood a moment later when Helen sat down next to him, in the place that had, through time and use, become *her* spot at the table. As she stepped over the bench and slid down next to him, Lucas watched his father's brow furrow.

Lucas shook off his father's disapproval and let himself enjoy the feel of Helen next to him. Even though she was obviously hurt by whatever was happening to her in the Underworld, her presence filled Lucas with strength. The shape of her, the softness of her arm as it brushed against his while they passed plates around the table, the clear, bright tone of her voice as she joined in the conversation—everything about Helen reached inside of him and soothed the wild animal in his rib cage.

He wished he could do the same for her. Throughout dinner, Lucas wondered what was happening to Helen in the Underworld, but he knew he would have to wait until they were alone to ask. She would lie to the family, but she couldn't lie to him.

"Hey," he called out later, stopping Helen in the dim corridor between the powder room and his father's study. She tensed momentarily and then turned toward him, her features softening.

"Hey," she breathed, moving closer to him.

"Bad night?"

She nodded, angling herself even closer until he could smell the almond-scented soap she had just used to wash her hands. Lucas knew she probably wasn't aware of how they always moved toward each other, but he was.

"Tell me about it."

"It's just hard," she said shrugging, trying to dodge his questions.

"Describe it."

"There was this boulder." She stopped speaking, rubbed her wrists, and shook her head with a pinched expression. "I can't. I don't want to think about it any more than I have to. I'm sorry, Lucas. I don't mean to make you angry," she said, responding to his huff of frustration.

He stared at her for a moment, wondering how she could be so wrong about how she made him feel. He tried to stay calm while he asked her the next question, but still, it came out rougher than he would have liked.

"Is someone hurting you down there?"

"There's no one down there but me," she replied. By the way she said it, Lucas knew that her solitude was even worse somehow than torture.

"You've been injured." He reached out across the few feet separating them and briefly ran a finger across her wrist, tracing the shape of the fading bruises he had seen there.

Her face was closed. "I don't have my powers in the Underworld. But I heal when I wake up."

"Talk to me," he coaxed. "You know you can tell me anything."

"I know I can, but if I do, I'll pay for it later," she groaned, but with a touch of humor. Lucas pressed on, sensing her lightening mood, and wanting so much to see her smile once more.

"What? Just tell me!" he said with a grin. "How painful

could it be to talk to me about it?"

Her laugher died and she looked up at him, her mouth parting slightly, just enough so Lucas could see the glassy inner rim of her lower lip. He remembered the feel of it when he kissed her and he tensed—stopping himself before he dipped his head down to feel it again.

"Excruciating," she whispered.

"Helen! How long does it take to use the powder—" Cassandra cut off abruptly when she saw Lucas's back moving away down the hall, and Helen blushing furiously as she darted toward the library.

*Helen hurried through the room with the peeling petunia wallpaper, avoiding the rotted floorboards by the soggy, mold-infested couch. It seemed to glare at her as she ran past. She'd already come this way a dozen times, maybe more. Instead of taking the door on the right or the door on the left, both of which she knew led nowhere, she decided she had nothing to lose and went into the closet.*

*A mossy wool overcoat loomed in the corner. There was dandruff on the collar and it smelled like a sick old man. It crowded her, like it was trying to shoo her out of its lair. Helen ignored the cantankerous coat and searched until she found another door, hidden in one of the side panels of the closet. The opening was only tall enough to permit a small child to pass through. She knelt down, suddenly creeped out by the wool coat that seemed to watch her bend over, like it was trying to peek down her shirt, and hurried through the child-sized door.*

The next room was a dusty boudoir, caked with centuries of heavy perfume, yellow stains, and disappointment. But at least there was a window. Helen hurried to it, hoping to jump out and free herself from this terrible trap. She pushed the lurid peach taffeta curtains aside with something approaching hope.

The window was bricked up. She hit the bricks with her fists, just jabs at first, but with increasing anger until her knuckles were raw. Everything was rotted and crumbling in this labyrinth of rooms—everything except the exits. Those were as solid as Fort Knox.

Helen had been trapped for what felt to her like days. She'd become so desperate she'd even closed her eyes and tried to fall asleep, hoping to wake up in her bed. It didn't work. Helen still hadn't figured out how to control her entrances and exits from the Underworld without half killing herself. She was frightened that she was actually going to die this time, and didn't want to think about what she would have to do to herself to get out.

White spots crowded her vision, and several times now she had almost passed out from thirst and fatigue. She hadn't had any water in so long that even the sluggish goo that spattered reluctantly out of the taps in this hell-house was starting to look appealing.

The strange thing was that Helen was more frightened in this part of the Underworld than she had ever been, even though she wasn't in any imminent danger. She wasn't hanging from a ledge, or trapped in the trunk of a tree, or chained by the wrists to a boulder that was dragging her down a hill and toward a cliff.

She was just in a house, an endless house with no exits.

These visits to the parts of the Underworld where she was in no

*immediate danger lasted the longest and ended up being the hard-*
*est in the long run. Thirst, hunger, and the crushing loneliness*
*she suffered—these were the worst kind of punishment. Hell didn't*
*need lakes of fire to torment. Time and solitude were enough.*

*Helen sat down under the bricked-up window, thinking about*
*having to spend the rest of her life in a House where she wasn't*
*welcome.*

It started pouring rain right in the middle of football practice, and then everything went sideways. All the guys started
throwing each other around, sliding in the mud, really
tearing up the turf. Coach Brant finally gave up and sent
everyone home. Lucas watched Coach as they all packed it
in, and could tell he wasn't really into the practice to begin
with. His son, Zach, had quit the team the day before. From
what everyone said, Coach hadn't taken it well, and Lucas
wondered how bad the fight had gotten. Zach hadn't been
in school that day.

Lucas sympathized with Zach. He knew what it was like
to have a father who was disappointed in you.

"Luke! Let's go! I'm freezing," Jason hollered. He was
already stripping off his gear on his way to the locker room,
and Lucas ran to catch up.

They rushed to get home, both of them hungry and wet,
and walked right into the kitchen. Helen and Claire were
in there with Lucas's mom. The girls' track uniforms were
soaked through, and they hovered expectantly by Noel with
excited looks on their faces while they dabbed at themselves

with towels. At first, all Lucas could see was Helen. Her hair was tangled and her long, bare legs glistened with rain.

Then he heard a whispering in his ear, and a flare of hate flashed through him. His mother was on the phone. The voice on the other end was Hector's.

"No, Lucas. Don't," Helen said in a quavering voice. "Noel, hang up!"

Lucas and Jason rushed toward the source of the Outcast's voice, compelled by the Furies. Helen stepped in front of Noel. All she did was hold out her hands in a "stop" gesture, and the cousins ran into her hands like they were running into a solid wall. They were thrown back onto the floor, gasping for air. Helen didn't budge an inch.

"I'm so sorry!" Helen said, crouching over them with an anxious look on her face. "But I couldn't let you tackle Noel."

"Don't apologize," Lucas groaned, rubbing his chest. He had no idea Helen was *that* strong, but he couldn't have been happier that she was. His mother had a shocked look on her face, but both she and Claire were fine. That was all that mattered.

"Uuuhh," Jason added, agreeing with Lucas. Claire crouched down next to him and patted him sympathetically while he rolled around, trying to get his breath back.

"I wasn't expecting you boys home so soon," Noel stammered. "He usually calls when he knows you'll be at practice. . . ."

"It's not your fault, Mom," Lucas said, cutting her off. He hauled Jason to his feet. "You okay, bro?"

"No," Jason replied honestly. He took a few more breaths and finally stood all the way up, the blow to his chest no longer the thing hurting him. "I *hate* this."

The cousins shared a pained look. They both missed Hector and couldn't stand what the Furies did to them. Jason suddenly turned and walked out the door, out into the rain.

"Jason, wait," Claire called, hurrying to follow him.

"I didn't think you'd be home this early," Noel repeated, more to herself than anyone else, like she couldn't let it go. Lucas went to his mother and gave her a kiss on the forehead.

"Don't worry. It'll be fine," he told her in a choked voice.

He had to get out of there. Still wrestling with the knot in his throat, he went upstairs to change. Halfway down the hall to his room and half out of his clothes, he heard Helen's voice behind him.

"I used to think you were a good liar," she said softly. "But not even I bought it when you said 'it'll be fine.'"

Lucas dropped his sodden shirt on the floor and turned back to Helen, too wrung out to resist. He pulled her to him and let his face rest against her neck. She fitted herself against him, taking his weight as his big shoulders curved over and around her, and held him until he was calm enough to speak.

"A part of me wants to go find him. Hunt him down," he confided, not able to tell this to anyone but Helen. "Every night I dream about how I tried to kill him with my bare hands on the steps of the library. I can see myself hitting him over and over, and I wake up thinking maybe this time I *have* killed him. And I feel relieved. . . ."

"Shh-shh." Helen ran her hand across his wet hair, smoothing it down and gripping his neck, his shoulders, the bunched muscles of his back—tucking him closer to her. "I'll fix it," she vowed. "I swear to you, Lucas, I'll find the Furies and stop them."

Lucas pulled back so he could look at Helen, shaking his head. "No, I didn't mean to put more pressure on you. It kills me that this is all on you."

"I know."

That was it. No blame, no "pity me." Just acceptance. Lucas stared at her, running his fingers over her perfect face.

He loved her eyes. They were always changing, and Lucas liked to catalogue all their different colors in his mind. When she laughed, her eyes were pale amber, like honey sitting in a glass jar on a sunny window. When he kissed her, they darkened until they were the rich color of mahogany leather, but with strips of red and gold thread shot through. Right now they were turning dark—inviting him to lower his lips to hers.

"Lucas!" his father barked. Helen and Lucas sprang apart and turned to see Castor at the top of the stairs, his face white and his body stiff. "Put a shirt on and come to my study. Helen, go home."

"Dad, she didn't . . ."

"Now!" Castor yelled. Lucas couldn't remember ever

seeing his father this angry.

Helen fled. She squeezed past Castor with her head bowed and ran out of the house before Noel could ask what had happened.

"Sit."

"It was my fault. She was worried about me," Lucas began, his stance defiant.

"I don't care," Castor said, his eyes burning into Lucas's. "I don't care how innocently it started. It ended with you half naked, your arms around her, and the two of you just steps away from your bed."

"I wasn't going to—" Lucas couldn't even finish that lie. He *was* going to kiss her, and he knew if he kissed her he would have kept going until either Helen or a cataclysm stopped him. The truth was, it didn't really bother Lucas anymore that some uncle he never met was Helen's father. He loved her, and that wasn't going to change no matter how wrong everyone said it was.

"Let me explain something to you."

"We're cousins. I know," Lucas interrupted. "Don't you think I realize that she's as closely related to me as Ariadne? It doesn't *feel* like that."

"Don't lie to yourself," Castor said darkly. "Scions have been plagued with incest since Oedipus. And there have been others in this House who have fallen in love with their first cousins, like you and Helen have."

"What happened to them?" Lucas asked cautiously. He could already tell that he wasn't going to like his father's answer.

"The outcome is always the same." Castor stared intensely at Lucas. "Just like Oedipus's daughter, Electra, the children born to related Scions always suffer our greatest curse. Insanity."

Lucas sat down while his mind raced, trying to find a way around this impasse. "We—we don't have to have children."

There was no warning, no notice that Lucas had pushed too far. Without a sound, his father rushed him like a bull. Lucas jumped back up to his feet but didn't know what to do next. He was twice as strong as his father, but his hands stayed passively at his sides while Castor grabbed him by the shoulders and pushed him back until he was pinned against the wall. Castor glared into his son's eyes, and for a moment Lucas believed his father hated him.

"How can you be so selfish?" Castor growled, his voice seething with disgust. "There aren't enough Scions *left* for either one of you to just decide you don't want to have kids. We're talking about our *species*, Lucas!" As if to drive home his point, Castor slammed Lucas into the wall so hard it began to crumble behind him. "The Four Houses must survive and stay separate to maintain the Truce and keep the gods imprisoned on Olympus, or every mortal on this planet will suffer!"

"I know that!" Lucas yelled. Plaster from the shattered wall rained down on them, filling the air with dust as Lucas struggled under his father's grip. "But there are other Scions to do that! What does it matter if Helen and I don't have children?"

"Because Helen and her mother are the last of their line! Helen must produce an Heir to preserve the House of Atreus and keep the Houses separate—not just for this generation—but for the ones yet to come!"

Castor was shouting. He seemed blind to the white dust and breaking masonry. It was as if everything his father had ever believed was tumbling down on top of Lucas's head, smothering him.

"The Truce has lasted for thousands of years, and it must last for thousands more or the Olympians will turn the mortals and the Scions into playthings again—starting wars and raping women and casting horrendous curses as it amuses them," Castor continued relentlessly. "You think a few hundred of us are enough to preserve our race and keep the Truce, but that's not enough to outlast the gods. We must endure, and to do that every single one of us must procreate."

"What do you want from us?" Lucas suddenly shouted back, shoving his father off of him and rising up out of the bowed and breaking wall. "I'll do what I have to for my House, and so will she. We'll have kids with other people if that's what it takes— we'll find a way to deal with it! But don't ask me to stay away from Helen because I can't. We can handle anything but that."

They glared at each other, both of them panting with

emotion and covered in white dust grown pasty with sweat.

"It's so easy for you to decide what Helen can and can't handle, is it? Have you looked at her lately?" Castor asked harshly, releasing his son with a disgusted look on his face. "She's suffering, Lucas."

"I know that! Don't you think I'd do *anything* to help her?"

"Anything? Then stay away from her."

It was like all the anger had rushed out of Castor in a flash. Instead of yelling, he was now pleading.

"Have you considered that what she's trying to do in the Underworld could not only bring peace between the Houses, but also bring Hector back to this family? We've lost so much. Ajax, Aileen, Pandora." Castor's voice broke when he said his little sister's name. Her death was still too fresh for both of them. "Helen is facing something none of us can imagine, and she needs every ounce of strength she has to make it through. For all our sakes."

"But I can help her," Lucas pleaded back, needing his father on his side. "I can't follow her down into the Underworld, but I can listen to her and support her."

"You think you're helping, but you're killing her," Castor said, shaking his head sadly. "You may have made peace with how you feel for her, but she can't cope with her feelings for you. You're her cousin, and the guilt is tearing her apart. Why are you the only one who can't see that? There are a thousand reasons you need to stay away, but if none of them matter to you, at the very least stay away from Helen because it's the best thing for *her*."

Lucas wanted to argue, but he couldn't. He remembered how Helen had told him that she would "pay for it later" if she talked with him about the Underworld. His father was right. The closer the two of them got, the more he hurt Helen. Of all the arguments his father had made, this one cut Lucas the deepest. He shuffled to the couch and sat down again so his father wouldn't see his legs shake.

"What should I do?" Lucas was completely lost. "It's like water running downhill. She just flows toward me. And I can't push her away."

"Then build a dam." Castor sighed and sat down across from Lucas, rubbing plaster from his face with his hands. He looked smaller. Like he had just lost the fight, even though he'd won, taking everything from Lucas. "You have to be the one to stop this. No confiding in each other, no flirting at school, and no quiet talks in dark hallways. You have to make her hate you, son."

Helen and Cassandra were working in the library, trying to find something—anything—that could help Helen in the Underworld. It was a frustrating afternoon. The more the two girls read, the more they were convinced that half the stuff about Hades was written by medieval scribes on serious drugs.

"Ever see any talking-skeletal-death-horses in Hades?" Cassandra asked skeptically.

"Nope. No talking skeletons. Horses included," Helen responded, rubbing her eyes.

"I think we can put this one on the 'he was definitely high' pile." Cassandra put the scroll down and stared at Helen for a few moments. "How are you feeling?"

Helen shrugged and shook her head, unwilling to talk about it. Since Castor had caught her and Lucas outside his bedroom, she'd been tiptoeing around the Delos house when she had to come over to study, and stuck inside the hell-house each night.

Usually in the Underworld, Helen could count on at least one or two nights a week where she was walking down an endless beach that never led to an ocean. The endless beach was annoying because she knew she wasn't getting anywhere, but compared to being trapped inside the hell-house it was like a holiday. She didn't know how much longer she could take it, and she couldn't talk about it with anyone. How could she possibly explain the perverted wool coat and lurid peach curtains without sounding ridiculous?

"I think I should go home and eat something," Helen said, trying not to think about the night that awaited her.

"But it's Sunday. You're eating here, right?"

"Um. I don't think your dad wants me hanging out here anymore." *I don't think Lucas does, either*, she thought. He hadn't looked at her since the day Castor had caught them with their arms around each other, even though Helen had tried several times to smile at him in the hallway at school. He'd just walked by like she wasn't there.

"That's nonsense," Cassandra answered firmly. "You are a part of this family. And if you don't come to dinner, my mom will be offended."

She walked around the table and took Helen's hand, leading her out of the study. Helen was so surprised by Cassandra's uncharacteristically warm gesture that she followed quietly.

It was later than the girls had thought, and dinner was starting. Jason, Ariadne, Pallas, Noel, Castor, and Lucas were already seated. Cassandra took her customary place next to her father, and the only spot left was on the bench, between Ariadne and Lucas.

As Helen stepped over the bench, she accidentally jostled Lucas, running her arm down the length of his as she sat down.

Lucas stiffened and tried to pull away from her.

"Sorry," Helen stammered, trying to shrug her arm away from his, but there was no room to move over on the crowded bench. She felt him bristle, and she reached under the table and squeezed his hand as if to ask, "What's wrong?"

He snatched his hand out of hers. The look he gave her was so full of hatred it froze the blood in her veins. The room went silent and the chitchat died. All eyes turned to Helen and Lucas.

Without warning, Lucas threw the bench back, knocking Helen, Ariadne, and Jason onto the floor. Lucas stood over Helen, glaring down on her. His face was contorted with rage.

Even when they were possessed by the Furies, and Helen and Lucas had fought bitterly, she had never been afraid of him. But now his eyes looked black and strange—like he wasn't even *in there* anymore. Helen knew it wasn't just a trick of the light. A shadow had blossomed inside of Lucas and snuffed out the light of his bright blue eyes.

"We don't hold hands. You don't talk to me. You don't even LOOK at me, do you understand?" he continued mercilessly. His voice rose from a grating whisper to a hoarse shout as Helen scrambled away from him in shock.

"Lucas, enough!" Noel's horrified voice was tinged with dismay. She didn't recognize her son any more than Helen did.

"We're not friends," Lucas growled, ignoring his mother and continuing to move threateningly toward Helen. She pushed her shaking body away from him with her heels, her sneakers making pathetic squeaking noises as she scuffed them against the tile, looking for purchase.

"Luke, what the hell?" Jason shouted, but Lucas ignored him, too.

"We don't hang out, or joke around, or share things with each other anymore. And if you EVER think you have the RIGHT to sit next to me again . . ."

Lucas reached down to grab Helen, but his father gripped his upper arms from behind—stopping him from hurting her. Then Helen saw Lucas do something she'd never once dreamed he'd do.

He spun around and hit his father. The blow was so heavy it sent Castor flying halfway across the kitchen and into the cabinet of glasses and mugs over the sink.

Noel screamed, covering her face as shards of broken dishes went flying in every direction. She was the only full mortal in a room of fighting Scions, and in serious danger of getting hurt.

Ariadne ran to Noel and used her body to protect her, while Jason and Pallas jumped on Lucas and tried to wrestle him down.

Knowing her presence would only enrage Lucas more, Helen scrambled up onto her knees, slipping across a bit of broken crockery as she stumbled to the door, and jumped into the sky.

As she flew home, she tried to listen for the sound of her own body in the high, thin air. Bodies are noisy. Take them into soundless spaces like the Underworld or the atmosphere and you can hear all kind of huffs and thumps and gurgles. But Helen's body was as silent as a grave. She couldn't even hear her own heart beating. After what she had just been through, it should have been thundering away, but all she felt was an intolerable pressure, like a giant knee was grinding into her chest.

Perhaps it wasn't beating because it had broken clean through and stopped.

"Is this what you wanted?" Lucas shouted at his father while he fought to break free. "Do you think she hates me now?"

"Just let him go!" Castor yelled to Pallas and Jason.

They paused, but didn't let go right away. First they looked over at Castor, to make sure *he* was sure. Castor stood and nodded his head once before passing judgment.

"Get out, Lucas. Get out of this house and don't come back until you can control your strength around your mother."

Lucas went still. His head turned in time to see Ariadne brush a drop of blood from Noel's face, her glowing hands healing the cut instantly.

An old memory, formed of images before he had words, came back to Lucas in a rush. Even as a toddler he'd been stronger than his mother, and once during a tantrum he'd pushed against her face while she was tenderly trying to kiss him quiet. He'd made her lip bleed.

Lucas remembered the hurt sound she'd made—a sound that still filled him with shame. He'd regretted that moment his entire life and since then he hadn't once touched his mother any harder than he would touch a rose petal. But now she was bleeding again. Because of him.

Lucas pulled his arms away from his uncle and cousin, threw the back door open, and hurled himself into the dark night sky. He didn't care where the winds took him.

# TWO

Helen took tiny, gasping breaths. This was the fifth night in a row she'd descended into this same spot in the Underworld, and she knew that the less she moved, the slower she sank into the quicksand. Even breathing too deeply edged her farther into the pit.

She was prolonging the torture, but she just couldn't bear the thought of drowning in filth again. Quicksand isn't clean. It's stuffed with the dead and decaying bodies of all its former victims. Helen could feel the moldering remains of all kinds of creatures bumping up against her as she was slowly dragged down. Last night her hand had skimmed across a face—a human face—somewhere under the tainted sand.

A pocket of gas bubbled to the surface, sending up a plume of stench. Helen vomited, unable to control herself. When she eventually drowned, the putrid dirt would rush into her nose, her eyes, and fill her mouth. Even though Helen was only up to her waist, she knew it was coming. She began to cry. She couldn't take it anymore.

"What else can I do?" she screamed, and sank lower.

She knew thrashing didn't work, but maybe this one time she would reach the dry reeds on the side of the pool and be able to grab them before the heavy muck swallowed her. She waded forward, but for every inch of progress she paid with an inch of depth. When she was up to her chest she had to stop moving. The weight of the quicksand was pressing the air out her, like a great weight settling on her chest—like a giant knee was pressing down on her.

"I get it, okay?" she cried. "I put myself here by being upset when I fall asleep. But how am I supposed to change the way I feel?"

The quicksand was up to her neck. Helen tilted her head back and thrust up her chin, trying to will herself higher.

"I can't do this alone anymore," she said to the blank sky. "I need someone to help me."

"Helen!" a deep, unfamiliar voice called out.

It was the first time Helen had heard another voice in the Underworld, and at first she assumed she was hallucinating. Her face was still tilted up, and she couldn't move it to look or she'd be sucked under.

"Reach toward me, if you can," the young man said in a strained voice, like he was struggling at the edge of the pit to get to her. "Come on, try, damn it! Give me your hand!"

At that moment her ears filled, and she could no longer hear what he shouted at her. All she could see was a flash of gold—a bright glimmer that pierced through the dull, defeated light of the Underworld like the lifesaving beacon of a lighthouse. She caught the barest glimpse of an angular chin and a full, sculpted mouth at the very edge of her vision. Then, under the surface of the quicksand, Helen felt a warm, strong hand take hers and pull.

Helen woke up in her bed and pitched forward, frantically scraping the muck out of her ears. Her body was still racing with adrenaline, but she forced herself to stay very still and listen.

She heard Jerry make a cawing sound downstairs in the kitchen—a high-pitched "WHOOP-WHOOP" siren noise that was more suited to the middle of a crowded dance floor than it was to Helen's snug Nantucket home. Jerry was *singing*. Well, sort of.

A burst of relieved laughter jumped out of Helen. She was safe at home, and this time she hadn't broken anything, stabbed herself, or drowned in a festering bog. Someone had saved her.

Or was it all in her head?

She thought about the deep voice and the warm hand that had pulled her from the pit. Healers like Jason and Ariadne could go down around the edge of the Underworld in spirit, but no one except Helen could physically get into the Underworld with his or her body still attached to the soul. It was supposed to be impossible. And Helen had been in Tartarus—the lowest of the low. Even farther down in the Underworld than Hades itself. Not even the strongest

Healers had ever come close to it. Was she so desperate for help that she had hallucinated?

Confused about whether or not she had imagined the whole thing, Helen sat in her sodden bed for a few moments and listened to her father mangle Prince's "Kiss" while he made breakfast.

Jerry was getting half the lyrics wrong—which meant he was in a great mood. Things between him and Kate were going very well: so well that Helen hadn't seen much of her father the past three weeks. Even their timeworn system of trading weeks cooking for each other was all thrown out of whack, but that was okay with Helen. She wanted her father to be happy.

Jerry repeated the line "you don't have to be beautiful" four times in row, probably because he couldn't remember any of the other words. Helen smiled and shook her head, thanking her lucky stars she had a father like Jerry to wake up to, even if he was a terrible singer. She had no idea why he could never get the words to songs right, but she suspected it had something to do with being a parent. Nobody's parents were supposed to sing Prince well. It would be disturbing if they did.

Throwing back her covers, Helen launched into cleaning mode. Two weeks ago, Claire had taken Helen to the mainland to get the special plastic sheets that moms use if they have a kid who wets the bed, making a thousand cracks about the Princess and the "Pee" along the way. Helen didn't mind. The sheets were uncomfortable and super-embarrassing to buy, but a necessity since every night she came back from the Underworld either bleeding or covered in yuck.

She stood up and started stripping her bed as fast as she could. In the laundry room, she took off her muddy boxer shorts and threw out her ripped T-shirt, putting everything that could be salvaged into the wash. She took a quick shower, and then retraced her path with a rag to clean up the dirty footprints she had tracked across the floor.

A few days ago she had considered using her superfast Scion speed to get through this new and annoying morning cleaning ritual, but she decided that it would probably scare her dad to death if he ever caught her doing it. Instead, Helen had to either get up at the crack of dawn or run around frantically at normal human speed to cover her tracks, like she was doing that morning. Out of time, Helen wiggled into some jeans before she had completely dried off while trying to pull a sweater over her damp hair. It was so cold in her room that the tips of her ears were beginning to go numb.

"Lennie! Your breakfast is getting cold!" Jerry shouted up the stairs.

"Oh, for crying out . . . Crap!" Helen cussed as she stumbled over her book bag. Her sweater wasn't all the way on yet, and it was still covering her face and pinning her arms over her head.

After a moment of flailing around like a muppet, Helen regained her footing and paused to laugh at herself, wondering how a demigod could be such a damn klutz. She assumed it had to have something to do with the fact that she was so tired. Helen righted her clothing, grabbed her school things, and ran down the stairs before her dad could start singing "Kiss" again.

Jerry had gone hog wild on breakfast. There were eggs, bacon, sausage, oatmeal with nuts and dried cherries, and of course, pumpkin pancakes. Pumpkin pancakes were a favorite of Jerry's and Helen's, but around Halloween, which was only about a week and a half away, anything with pumpkin in it was on the menu. It was sort of a competition between the two of them. It started with roasted pumpkin seeds and went all the way to soups and gnocchi. Whoever found a way to sneak pumpkin into a dish without getting caught was the winner.

The whole pumpkin thing had started when Helen was a little girl. One October she'd complained to her dad that pumpkins only got used as decoration, and although she loved jack-o'-lanterns, it was still a big waste of food. Jerry had agreed, and the two of them resolved to start eating pumpkins instead of just carving them up and then throwing them out.

Unfortunately, they found that pumpkins on their own are so bland they're practically inedible. If they hadn't gotten creative with the cooking, they would have given up on their Save the Pumpkins crusade after the first year.

There were a lot of nauseating creations, of which the pumpkin popsicles were by far the worst, but the pancakes stood out as the biggest success. They instantly became as large a part of the Hamilton family tradition in late October as turkey was on Thanksgiving. Helen noticed that Jerry had even made fresh whipped cream to put on top, and that made her feel so guilty she could barely look at him. He was worried about her.

"Finally! What were you doing up there? Quilting?" Jerry joked, trying to make light of his worry, as he looked her up and down.

For a moment, his eyes widened with fear and his lips pressed together in a harsh line, then he turned back to the stove and started serving. Jerry wasn't a nag, but Helen had gotten skinny over the past three weeks—really scary skinny—and this humongous breakfast was his way of trying to remedy that without having to go into a big, boring lecture. Helen loved the way her dad handled stuff. He didn't pester her the way other parents would if they saw their daughter turn into a scarecrow, but he still cared enough to try to do something about it.

Helen tried to smile bravely at her dad, took a plate, and started stuffing the food down her throat. Everything tasted like sawdust, but she pushed the calories in, anyway. The last thing Helen wanted was to make her dad anxious about her health, although to be honest, even she was starting to feel a bit worried.

She healed quickly from any overt injury she sustained in the Underworld, but every day she felt weaker. Still, she had no choice—she had to keep going until she found the Furies, no matter how ill the Underworld was making her. She'd made a promise. Even if Lucas hated her now, she would fulfill it.

"You have to *chew* bacon, Lennie," her dad said sarcastically. "It doesn't just dissolve in your mouth."

"Is that how it works?" Realizing she had been sitting there stock-still, she forced herself to act normal and crack a joke. "Now he tells me."

While her dad chuckled, she wrenched her thoughts away from Lucas and considered all the homework she hadn't done. She hadn't even finished reading the *Odyssey* yet, not because she didn't want to read it, but because she hadn't had time.

It seemed like everything on Helen's to-do list needed to be done yesterday. On top of that, her favorite teacher, Hergie, kept trying to pressure her into joining the AP classes. Like she needed to expand her reading list.

Claire cruised up the driveway in the new hybrid car her parents had bought her and yelled, "Honk-honk!" out the window rather than actually honking the horn. As Jerry tried, and failed, not to hover, Helen stuffed the remaining pancake down her throat, nearly choked, and ran out the door with her shoelaces still untied.

She hurried down the steps, taking a glance back at the widow's walk on her roof, but she knew it would be empty.

Lucas had made it painfully clear to Helen that he would not sit on her widow's walk again. She didn't know why she bothered to look up there, except that she couldn't seem to stop herself.

"Button your coat, it's cold out," Claire admonished as soon as Helen got in the car. "Lennie? You're a frigging mess," she continued as she put the car in gear.

"Ah . . . good morning?" Helen said with wide eyes. Claire had been Helen's best friend since birth, and was therefore entitled to yell at Helen whenever she felt like it. But did she have to start so early? Helen opened her mouth to explain, but Claire would not be deterred.

"Your clothes are falling off your body, your nails are bitten down to nothing, and your lips are chapped," Claire ranted, plowing right through Helen's weak protests as she tore out of the driveway. "And the bags under your eyes are so god-awful it looks like someone punched you in the face! Are you even *attempting* to take care of yourself?"

"Yes, I'm trying," Helen sputtered, still trying to button up the front of her coat, which had suddenly become harder to figure out than Chinese algebra. She gave up on the buttons and faced Claire, throwing up her hands in frustration. "I'm eating *up here*, but there's no food in the Underworld and I can't seem to stuff enough down when I'm in the real world to compensate. Trust me, I'm trying. My dad just fed me enough breakfast to choke a linebacker."

"Well, you could at least put on some blush or something. You're white as a sheet."

"I know I look awful. But I've got other things on my mind. This whole descending thing isn't exactly easy, you know."

"Then don't descend every night!" Claire exclaimed like

it was obvious. "Take a break when you need it! Obviously, you're not going to solve this in a few weeks!"

"You think I should treat the Furies like a part-time job?" Helen yelled back, finally finding her voice.

"Yes!" Claire shouted back, and since she was naturally better at shouting than just about anybody, Helen shrank back into her seat, cowed by her itty-bitty friend. "Three weeks I've put up with this and I've had enough! You're never going to find the Furies if you're so tired you can't even see your own big, stupid feet!"

After a slight pause, Helen burst out laughing. Claire tried to keep a straight face, but eventually she gave up and laughed her amazing laugh as they pulled into the parking lot at school.

"No one would think any less of you if you decided to limit your trips down there to once or twice a week, you know," Claire said gently as they got out of the car and started toward the front door of the school. "I can't believe you can force yourself to go down there at all. I don't think I could do it." Claire shuddered, remembering her own recent brush with death when Matt hit Lucas with his car. Claire had almost died in the accident, and her soul had traveled down to the dry lands—the outskirts of the Underworld. The memories of that place still frightened her, weeks later.

"You would if you had to, Gig. But it doesn't work like that, anyway. It's not something I decide to do." Helen threw an arm over Claire's shoulders to pull her out of her disturbing recollections of the thirst and loneliness of the dry lands. "I just go to sleep and end up there. I don't know how to control it yet."

"Why doesn't Cassandra know? She's so smart and she's been doing a lot of research," Claire said archly. Helen shook her head, wondering if she really wanted to get in the middle of the feud between Claire and Cassandra.

"Don't blame Cassandra," she said carefully. "There isn't exactly a manual for descending. At least Cassandra and I haven't found one in that pile of ancient Greek and Latin the Delos family calls archives. She's doing her best."

"Then that settles it," Claire said, crossing her arms and narrowing her eyes with conviction.

"Settles what?" Helen asked in a worried tone as she turned the dial on her locker.

"You and Cassandra can't do this alone. You need help. Whether Cassandra wants me to or not, I'm helping." Claire shrugged as if the matter was settled, which it most certainly was not.

Cassandra insisted the archives were for Oracles and the priestesses and priests of Apollo *only*, despite the fact that there hadn't been any real priests or priestesses of Apollo in about three and a half thousand years. Matt, Claire, Jason, and Ariadne had offered to help Cassandra a bunch of times, but she wouldn't accept because that would go against tradition, and for a Scion, going against tradition was nothing to sneeze at.

The Fates had a thing against Scions in general, but Scions who broke tradition usually found themselves on the Fates' extra-special hate list. Plus, most of those archives were hexed against the uninitiated. The only reason Cassandra let Helen in the library at all was because no one could think of a hex that could harm her. Helen was protected by the cestus. In the real world she was impervious to practically everything. But Claire most certainly was not.

Helen followed her stubborn friend down the hallway, feeling her shoulders slump more with every step. She hated the thought of going against Cassandra, but when Claire set her mind to something there was no point in arguing with her. Helen just hoped that whatever Claire was planning didn't get her permanently cursed with boils or lice or something equally horrid. Claire could get seriously hurt.

The bell rang just as Helen and Claire scooted into homeroom. Mr. Hergesheimer, or "Hergie" as he was called behind his back, gave them one of his most disapproving glares. It was almost like he could smell the trouble brewing inside Claire's head. Hergie assigned both of them two words of the day for the next morning as preemptive punishment for whatever it was they were so obviously up to. From that moment on, Helen's day got progressively worse.

Helen had never been the most attentive student, and now that she was spending her nights slogging through the Underworld, she had even less interest in school. She was scolded in every class, but at least one of her peers was doing even worse than she was.

As their physics teacher tore into Zach for not writing up his lab, Helen wondered what had happened. Zach had always been one of those guys who looked awake and alert no matter what time it was. Usually, he was a bit too alert, sticking his nose where it didn't belong. Helen had never seen Zach looking so washed out and disconnected. She tried to catch his eye and smile at him in solidarity, but he turned away.

Helen sat staring at his blank face until it finally sank into her sleep-deprived brain that about a week ago she had heard someone say that Zach had quit the football team. Zach's dad, Mr. Brant, was the football coach, and Helen knew that he pushed Zach to be perfect in everything he did. There was no way Mr. Brant would allow his son to quit without a fight. Helen wondered what had happened between them. Whatever it was, it couldn't have been good. Zach looked horrible.

When the bell rang at the end of class Helen tried to touch Zach's arm and ask him if he was okay, but he acted like she wasn't even there and walked out of the room. There was a time in their lives when Helen and Zach had been friends—he used to share his animal crackers with her on the playground—but now he wouldn't even look at her.

Helen had just resolved to ask Claire about Zach and his mysterious condition at track when she caught a glimpse of Lucas from afar. Everything else dissolved like a chalk drawing in the rain.

He was holding a door open over someone's head, politely making a bridge so that a smaller underclassman could walk beneath his arm. He glanced back down the hallway at nothing in particular and spotted her. His eyes narrowed in anger.

Helen froze. It felt like someone was kneeling on her chest again. *That's not Lucas,* she thought, unable to breathe or move.

As Lucas disappeared in the throngs of rushing students, Helen made her way down to the locker room to change for track, her mind wiped clean, like the sky after a thunderstorm.

When Claire showed up, Helen immediately started asking her questions. She'd stumbled across this trick a few weeks back when she realized that if she peppered her best friend with questions, Claire wouldn't have time to ask how she herself was doing. This time, Claire really did need to talk. Jason was having a bad day and Claire was worried about him.

Jason and Claire weren't officially dating, but ever since Jason had healed her they were obviously more than just friends. They had become very close very quickly, and now she was Jason's closest confidante.

"Are you going over to his house after track?" Helen asked quietly.

"Yeah, I don't want to leave him alone right now. Especially since Lucas is still MIA."

"What do you mean?" Helen asked, alarmed. "He hasn't been home at all since . . ." *Since he told me to go to hell, hit his father, endangered his mother, and got thrown out of his house?* Helen finished in her mind.

Claire seemed to know exactly what Helen was thinking, and she squeezed Helen's hand in support as she explained.

"No, he's been home a few times since then. He apologized to his parents and they forgave him, of course. But he's never around anymore. No one knows where he's been going or what he's been doing, and honestly? Everyone's too afraid of him to ask. He's changed, Lennie. He doesn't talk to anyone, except maybe Cassandra. He vanishes right after school, and sometimes he doesn't come home until one or two o'clock in the morning, if he comes home at all. His parents are letting him go because, well, without Hector around, no one can really *stop* him. Jason is worried," Claire said before glancing sideways at Helen. "You haven't seen him lately, have you?"

"Today. But only for a second, way down the hall," Helen said, ending the line of questions before Claire could ask her how she felt. "Look, I gotta pick up the pace. Are you okay, or do you want to talk some more?"

"You go ahead," Claire said with a troubled frown.

Helen gave Claire a little smile to let her know she was okay, even though she kind of wasn't, and then sped up to finish her run in a time that Coach Tar would think showed initiative.

Lucas saw Helen at the end of the hallway, and forced his face into an angry shape, willing her to hate him or fear him—whatever it took to get her the hell away from him. For her own good.

But Lucas didn't see hate or fear in her eyes. She didn't turn away from him like she was supposed to. She just looked lost.

It felt like chewing glass, but Lucas forced himself to turn his back on her and continue down the hallway.

All he had intended was to push Helen away.

But then things got out of hand: striking his father; his mother, bleeding; the blind rage he felt. Lucas knew what anger felt like. He and Hector had been fighting tooth and nail since they were big enough to stand. But this was like nothing he had experienced before. He'd woken something up inside of himself, something that he'd had no idea existed in him.

The genie was out of the bottle and it wouldn't fit back in.

Finishing her run long before Claire, Helen decided that she wanted to walk to work so she could think. She sent Claire a text explaining that she didn't need a ride to the News Store that afternoon and stifled the suspicion that Claire would probably be pleased with Helen's decision to go it alone.

They had never avoided each other before, but things had changed. Their lives were pulling them in different directions, and Helen was beginning to wonder if their friendship would ever be the same again. The thought made her want to cry.

The temperature started to plummet as Helen walked up Surfside Road toward the center of town. Her jacket was unbuttoned and the straps from the book bag over one shoulder and the gym bag over the other pulled the two sides of her jacket apart so she couldn't close the front properly. With an exasperated cluck of her tongue, Helen unslung her bags. As she bent over to put them down on the ground, she experienced a strange vertigo. It seemed for a moment that the sidewalk didn't quite match up to the street, like there was something terribly wrong with her depth perception.

Straightening up with a gasp, Helen put an arm out to the side in case she fell over, waiting for the rush of blood to her head to end. The vertigo was gone in a moment but an even more disturbing sensation replaced it. Helen felt like she was being watched, like someone was standing right in front of her, staring directly into her eyes.

She took a step back and reached out, but touched nothing but thin air. Glancing around nervously, Helen spun on her heel, grabbed her bags, and jogged into the town center. Cassandra had foreseen that Helen was safe from attack for the next few days at least, but she'd never promised that Helen would be left in peace. Helen knew someone from the Hundred Cousins was most likely watching her, she just hadn't expected to feel so paranoid about it. Suddenly, Helen imagined that she could feel someone's breath on her neck. The thought made her bolt into the News Store like she was being chased.

"What is it?" Kate asked. She looked behind Helen for whatever had spooked her. "Is someone following you?"

"It's nothing," Helen replied with a phony smile. "The cold gave me the shivers."

Kate gave Helen a skeptical look, but Helen ducked around her and deposited her things behind the register before Kate could get into it.

"Did you eat after track?" Kate asked. "Go to the back and make yourself a sandwich," she ordered when Helen didn't respond right away.

"I'm not really hungry," Helen began, but Kate cut her off angrily.

"Is that your final answer? Think carefully," Kate warned as she planted a flour-dusted fist on her curvy hip.

Helen shut her mouth and went into the back. She felt like Kate and Jerry were both blaming her for getting so thin. But she couldn't explain what was really going on to either of them.

Helen smeared some peanut butter on a hunk of bread and drizzled honey over it before she took a giant, angry bite. She chewed mechanically, hardly noticing the sticky ball of bread and nutty-sweet paste sealing up her mouth. She felt like she was choking on something most of the time, any-way—like there was a wad of words lodged permanently in the back of her throat. What was a little peanut butter compared to that?

She gulped down a glass of milk and shuffled back out front, still feeling like she was being blamed for something that wasn't her fault. She avoided Kate for the rest of the night to punish her.

After an uncomfortable few hours walking on eggshells at the News Store, Helen lied and said that Claire was picking her up. Outside in the dark, sure that no one could see her, Helen jumped up into the night sky and flew toward home. She soared high, pushing herself to go up to where the rarified air tugged at her eardrums and dug at her lungs.

She had promised Lucas once that she wouldn't leave the island without more training in transoceanic travel, and technically, she'd kept that promise. She was still over Nantucket, just very *high* over it. Helen reached up and up until she could see the bright web of night-lights that connected the whole continent underneath her. She flew until her eyes watered and the tears froze on her cheek.

She stretched out and let her body float until her mind emptied. This must be what it was like to swim unafraid in the ocean, but Helen preferred to swim in an ocean of stars. She floated until the cold and the loneliness became intolerable, and then she drifted back down to earth.

Helen landed in her yard and ran in the front door, hoping her dad wouldn't notice that there hadn't been a car in the driveway to drop her off, but Jerry wasn't in the kitchen. She poked her head into her dad's room just to make sure, but he wasn't there, either. Helen reminded herself that it was Friday night. He and Kate probably had plans. Since she and Kate hadn't spoken for most of the evening, Helen hadn't thought to ask if Jerry would be spending the night at Kate's place or not. Now she regretted holding a grudge. The house was too empty, and the silence seemed to press painfully on her ears.

Helen washed her face, brushed her teeth, and went to

bed. She kept her eyes open for as long as she could, willing herself to stay awake despite the fact that she was so tired she was near tears.

If she fell asleep, she knew she would descend into the Underworld and plunge herself into a loneliness that was even more complete than the loneliness she felt in the real world. But the longer she lay in bed, the closer her thoughts drifted toward Lucas. Helen rubbed her hands over her face and tried to push the stinging tears back into her eyes. The unbearable weight began to settle on her chest again.

She couldn't allow herself to wallow, or in a few moments she'd be wallowing in the filth of the pit. Then a thought crossed her mind.

Maybe this time she wouldn't be alone in the Underworld.

She knew that her savior was probably a mirage, but Helen was desperate. Even talking to a mirage was preferable to wandering through hell alone.

As she focused her thoughts on the deep voice she'd heard, Helen allowed herself to fall asleep. She pictured the flash of gold, the beautiful mouth, and the sound of him saying her name as he held out his hand for her to take. . . .

Helen was on a prairie-like plain with lots of dead grass and undulating hills. She'd been to this part of the Underworld before, but something had changed. She couldn't quite put her finger on it, but everything felt a little bit different. For one thing, there was noise. Helen couldn't remember ever hearing any sound in the Underworld that she hadn't made herself—not even the sound of wind on the grass.

Somehow, the Underworld felt *real*, and not just part of a terrible nightmare. Helen had experienced this before, if only briefly, when she was miraculously pulled from the pit. As jarring as this new perspective on the Underworld was, it was also a relief at the same time. Hades seemed less hellish for some reason. Looking around now, Helen was reminded of that moment in *The Wizard of Oz* when Dorothy sees in color for the first time.

She squinted into the distance and saw dancing flashes of gold, coupled with the sound of shrieks, grunts, and clangs. There was a fight going on, and it sounded like a brutal one. At least Helen could be certain of one thing. The guy with the warm hands wasn't a mirage.

She ran as fast as she could toward the commotion.

When she crested a small rise she saw a big guy with an overgrown mop of loose chestnut curls using a long dagger to hack away at the tattered vulture-bat thing that was flapping around his head. As Helen ran closer, she heard the harpy snarl and cuss, trying to rip at the young man with her talons. Even though he was fighting for his life, Helen couldn't stop herself from noticing that he really needed a haircut.

"Haircut" got the upper hand for a moment, and Helen saw him grin in a half-surprised, half–self-congratulatory way. Then, as he realized that he was still losing, Helen watched the grin quickly turn into a self-deprecating grimace. Even though he was battling away, he seemed to maintain a good sense of humor.

"Hey!" Helen shouted as she neared the struggling pair.

Haircut and the harpy paused awkwardly in the middle of the fight, each of them still clutching the other's throat. Half of Haircut's mouth lifted up in a surprised smile.

"Helen," he managed to croak out, as if he always had a pair of talons wrapped around his neck. Helen was so taken aback by his nonchalance she almost laughed. Then everything changed again.

The world started to slow down and thicken around her, and Helen knew that meant that in the regular world her body was waking up. A part of her brain was beginning to register an annoying bleating noise coming from a universe away, and she knew that she would never make it to Haircut before waking. Helen looked around frantically, then bent down and picked up a rock at her feet, straightened up, and chucked it at the monster . . .

. . . and the rock from the Underworld went right through her bedroom window, breaking it into about a hundred pieces.

# THREE

Helen sat up in bed, listening to the annoying blare of her alarm clock. The one night she actually wanted to stay in the Underworld, and she'd woken up. It was still dark, but even in the predawn gloom she could see the mess she'd made.

Jerry was going to kill her. No matter how much Kate pleaded with him that Helen had a rare "sleep disorder," this time Jerry was actually going to murder her.

Her dad had this thing with conserving heat—like the house's thermostat had a direct line to his psyche—and chilly gusts were already blasting directly through the gigantic hole she'd made in her window. Helen smacked herself on the forehead and fell back onto her mattress.

She was as good as grounded, that flying monstrosity had probably eaten Haircut, and it was all because Helen had to wake up at ugly-o'clock-in-the-morning to get to a track meet on the mainland.

High school sports are complicated for people who live on tiny islands. In order for island athletes to compete with other schools they have to travel by boat or by plane, and for Helen and the rest of her teammates, that meant getting up before the crack of dawn. Sometimes she really hated living on Nantucket.

Stifling a yawn and trying to push the image of Haircut dying a vicious death from her mind, Helen pulled herself out of bed. She duct-taped a blanket over her broken window, gulped down some instant oatmeal, and left for the island's airport. Ironically, she flew there. But of course she couldn't fly all the way to the mainland. Missing the plane and then showing up at the meet on time would raise all kinds of questions, so she did the responsible thing.

Landing a cautious distance away, she started jogging toward the tarmac just as the sky turned a shy pink. She saw Claire parking her car in the lot and ran over so they could go together to the waiting prop plane. Helen was excited to tell Claire about Haircut, but before she could open her mouth, Claire was rolling her eyes and grabbing Helen by the shoulders.

"Oh, for crying out loud!" Claire mumbled in exasperation as she undid the misaligned buttons on Helen's pesky jacket and then redid them correctly. "You look like a dyslexic five-year-old. Am I going to have to come over every morning and dress you now?"

"Hamilton!" Coach Tar shouted before Helen had a chance to think up a reply, let alone tell Claire what had happened the night before. "You're sitting with me. We need to talk strategy."

"I have something to tell you," Helen blurted out to Claire as she backpedaled toward Coach. "I saw someone there, you know, *last night*." Claire's eyes widened hopefully as Helen got dragged away.

The rest of the flight, Coach blabbed excitedly about how Helen should draft this runner and then pull out in front of that runner—all useless advice considering that if she wanted to she could break the sound barrier. Helen half listened and tried to not worry too much about Haircut.

He was big, tall, and powerfully built, and he looked like he knew what he was doing with that long dagger he had been using to defend himself. Helen tried to convince herself that he was probably fine, but she wasn't entirely convinced.

Whoever Haircut was, he certainly looked like a Scion. But maybe he was just a six-foot-four, muscle-y, unbelievably good-looking mortal with a great smile. And if that was the case, the poor thing was definitely dead. No mortal could fight off that harpy.

All morning, Helen tried to find an opportunity to talk to Claire, but she didn't have a chance. She ran her first race, trying not to win it outright, but she was distracted, wondering whether or not it was possible to get killed in the land of the dead. The useless internal debate ruined her concentration, and she ended up running way too fast. Helen

pretended to pant when she realized that all of the specta-
tors were staring at her with their mouths hanging open. All
except one.

Zach Brant didn't look the slightest bit surprised as Helen
ran past at jackrabbit speed. In fact, he looked almost bored.
Helen had no idea what Zach was doing at the meet—he'd
never come to one before. From the way his eyes seemed to
be glued to her, Helen could only assume he had come to
watch her, but she had no idea why. There had been a time
when Helen would have assumed Zach was watching her
because he had a crush on her, but that time was long gone.
Lately, it seemed like he wanted nothing to do with her.

Helen won her race, then she cheered while Claire finished one of her own before they finally met up by the
triple-jump sand strip.

"So what happened?" Claire puffed, still winded from
running.

"I saw . . ." Helen broke off. "Let's go over there," she continued, pointing to an empty expanse of field at the edge of
the track. There were a lot of people milling around, and
Zach was standing a bit too close.

By this point, Helen was nearly bursting to tell Claire
what she had seen. While they walked she whispered under
her breath, "I saw a person. A *living* person."

"But, I thought you were the only one who can go down
there in your body—not just as a spirit."

"Me too! But last night there was this boy. Well, not a *boy*.

I mean he was ginormous. A guy, around our age, I guess."

"What was he doing down there?" Claire asked. She didn't sound convinced that Helen had really seen someone.

"Getting his ass handed to him by a harpy?" Helen said. "But the night before last, he pulled me out of the quick-sand. One of his arms is all shiny, like it's covered in gold." Claire looked at her dubiously, and Helen realized just how nuts she sounded. "Do you think I'm going crazy? Sounds crazy, right? And it's not even supposed to be possible."

"Do you mind?" Claire said suddenly. She glared over Helen's shoulder at Zach, who was following them. "Private conversation here."

Zach shrugged, but he didn't walk away. Claire took his defiance as a challenge. She yelled at him to go away in her most authoritative voice, but he wouldn't budge. Eventually, she had to take Helen's hand and steer her toward the edge of the open field where the woods began. Zach couldn't very well follow them without Claire causing a scene about it, but he didn't turn away, either. He just kept staring at them as Claire dragged Helen into the scrub.

"Is this necessary?" Helen asked as she straddled a scratchy bush and untangled the end of her braid from the brittle, lichen-covered branch of a small birch tree.

"Zach's been acting really weird lately, and I just don't want him to see us," Claire said with narrowed eyes.

"You mean he didn't go away when you ordered him to, and you dragged me in here because you don't want him to win," Helen corrected with a chuckle.

"That too. Now tell me exactly what happened," Claire urged, but they were interrupted again, this time by the sound of rustling leaves. It came from deeper inside the woods.

A large man stepped out of the undergrowth. Helen shoved Claire behind her and stepped toward the intruder, ready for a fight.

"Don't you knuckleheads know that some seriously sketchy men hang out in the woods around high school track meets?" the blond giant said testily.

"Hector!" Helen gasped with relief and jumped into his open arms.

"What's up, cuz?" he said with a laugh and hugged her tight. Claire joined them and gave Hector a big squeeze before she pulled back and punched him on the chest.

"What are you doing here?" Claire demanded disapprovingly. "It's too dangerous."

"Relax, Five-Two," Hector said as he broke eye contact and looked down, the smile on his face fading fast. "I spoke to Aunt Noel this morning. She told me none of the family would be here."

"They aren't, and we're really glad to see you," Helen said quickly, giving Claire a little pinch for being so insensitive.

"Of course we're glad to see you!" Claire exclaimed as she rubbed her pinched arm. "I didn't mean it like that, Hector, you know that. How've you been?"

"Not important," he said with a shake of his head. "I want to know how you are. And how Luke is doing after last week," he asked in a low voice.

Helen tried not to flinch, but it was impossible.

"It's bad," Claire said sadly.

"Yeah, I know. I talked to Aunt Noel. I still can't believe Luke would do something like that." Hector's voice was harsh, but he looked at Helen sympathetically.

Helen tried to concentrate on Hector's pain instead of her own. She had lost Lucas, but Hector had lost his whole family. He was so worried about them that he was willing to wait all day crouched in the bushes outside a stupid track meet just to make contact with someone relatively close to them.

Apart from Daphne, whom he barely knew, Hector was alone. Helen realized that of all the people in her life, Hector most likely had the best idea of what she was going through, which was strange since they'd only recently stopped disliking each other.

"How's my mother?" Helen blurted out, needing to end the sad silence they had all fallen into. Hector gave Helen a cagey look.

"She's . . . busy" was all he would say about Daphne before he turned back to Claire and changed the subject.

Hector normally told everyone what he thought, whether they wanted to hear it or not. The way he'd dodged Helen's question made her wonder exactly what her shady mother was up to. Helen had tried to get in touch with Daphne a few times in the past three weeks, but she hadn't gotten a response. Maybe her mother was purposely avoiding her? Helen didn't get a chance to dig deeper. Hector was too occupied teasing Claire about how she seemed to be getting shorter. But just as the two of them began to shove each other playfully, an ominous darkness enveloped the woods.

Helen shivered involuntarily and looked all around in a panic. Even though she knew he was dead, she could almost feel Creon reaching up from the grave to try to pull her down into that horrible darkness.

Hector noticed the change in the light just as Helen did. He put out a hand and grabbed Claire protectively by the shoulder. Helen caught Hector's eye. They both recognized this eerie phenomenon.

"A Shadowmaster?" Helen whispered. "I thought Creon was the only one!"

"So did I," Hector whispered back, his eyes darting all over the place, looking for a target. But the darkness was like a curtain, closing them in. They couldn't see farther than a few feet in front of them. "Take Claire and run."

"I won't leave you—" Helen began.

"RUN!" Hector screamed as a flashing sword cut through the black curtain and arced down on top of him.

Hector knocked Claire out of the way as he bent backward and to the side like a gymnast in midleap. The bronze blade whistled past his chest and buried itself a full foot into the half-frozen forest floor. Hector kicked savagely into the encroaching shadows, sending his attacker flying through the air and leaving the sword lodged in the ground.

In one fluid motion, Hector raised his torso back to vertical and claimed the sword for himself. As he yanked it out of the ground he used the grip-stop-go momentum of the freed blade to slash across the chest the next figure that appeared out of the gloom, all the while moving faster than the beat of a hummingbird's heart.

Helen felt metal shatter against her cheek, and in the crippled light she saw the bright fragments of an arrowhead bursting into a dandelion shape under her right eye. She recoiled instinctively from the impact even though she was completely unhurt, and backpedaled until she bumped up against Claire's leg with her heels.

Helen stood guard in front of her mortal friend. Stunned and breathless, Claire couldn't stand yet, and she certainly couldn't run. Helen planted her feet in between Claire and the attackers and called up her lightning.

The sound of a bullwhip snapping and the stale taste of ozone filled the air as light branched out from Helen's hands, creating a latticed wall of electricity that protected her and Claire. The unnatural darkness created by the Shadowmaster fell back in the blue blaze and no fewer than a dozen armed Scions were revealed. *Where had they all come from?* Helen wondered frantically. *How had so many crept up on them?*

At the center and to the back of the phalanx, in the place Hector had taught Helen was reserved for infantry officers, Helen caught a brief glimpse of a terrifying, alien face. *It*, whatever it was, had red eyes. It looked directly at her and then fell back until it was again covered in the Shadowmaster's gloom.

"Too many!" Hector grunted as he fought off two more men.

"Behind us!" Helen yelled as she spun around and saw that four fighters were flanking them. She sent out a bolt of weak lightning—just enough to stun and not to kill them. Unfortunately for Helen, holding back her power required way more energy than just letting the bolts go.

Helen felt dizzy. She forced her eyes to focus as three of the four men fell convulsing to the ground. The fourth kept coming toward her. She had used up most of the water in her body, which was already slightly dehydrated from running a distance race, and she didn't have enough left to create another controlled bolt. She could still create one that would kill them all, but she couldn't bring herself to do that.

Jumping over Claire, who was still struggling to get her wind back, Helen threw a punch at the remaining Scion. Helen had never been good at striking, and her punch barely got his attention. He hit her back hard, knocking her down to the ground on top of Claire and making her ears ring.

A dark shape streaked down from the sky, landed on top of Helen's attacker, and sent him careening into the trees. It was Lucas. Helen's breath caught at the sight of him. How could he have gotten here so quickly? she wondered frantically. Lucas looked down at Helen, his face impassive, and then threw himself against the main group of attacking Scions.

Helen heard Hector bellow, and saw that several men were trying to fit chains and thick metal cuffs onto his arms and legs. She scrambled over to help him wrestle the bindings off while Lucas dealt with the fighters who were left standing. In a blinding blur of movements, Lucas had disarmed and injured two men before Helen even made it to Hector's side.

Seeing that his small army was no match for Helen, Hector, and Lucas, the creepy leader of the phalanx made a shrill chittering noise, and the onslaught ended as quickly as it began. The wounded were hiked up onto shoulders, weapons were retrieved, and the band of hit men dissolved into the trees before Helen could even brush the hair off her sweaty face.

Helen saw Lucas turn his back on them and stiffen. Hector put his hands to his temples and dug the heels of his hands into the sides of his head, as if he was trying to keep his skull from splitting in half.

"No, Hector! Don't!" Claire yelled as she threw herself on top of him. She put her hands over his eyes and tried to block his sight so he wouldn't see Lucas. Even with Claire nearly smothering him, Helen could see Hector's face redden with rage.

Lucas was shaking with the effort to hold back, but finally, he gave in. He had a crazed look in his eyes as he spun around to face Hector. The Furies had him, and they were telling him to kill his cousin or die trying.

"Please, Lucas, go! Go!" Helen rasped through her parched throat. She knew he had ordered her never to touch him again, but she didn't care. She jumped up and put her hands on his shoulders, shoving him away from Claire and Hector.

Helen pounded on his chest, but Lucas couldn't tear his eyes away from Hector. In his urgency to kill the Outcast, Lucas threw Helen to the ground hard, and she cried out as she twisted her wrist on the uneven underbrush.

Hearing her shout of pain seemed to shock Lucas out of his frenzy. He looked down to see Helen on her knees, cradling her injured wrist.

"I'm sorry," he whispered. Before Helen could get to her feet, he jumped into the air and was gone from sight.

She stared after Lucas, his name hanging in the back of her throat, pinching it closed. She wanted to call him back to her and demand some kind of explanation. If Lucas hated her, why apologize? Why protect her in the first place?

"Len, snap out of it!" Claire yelled as she tugged on Helen's arm. "There's a fire!"

Helen dragged her eyes away from the bit of sky that Lucas had disappeared into and looked around while Claire hauled her to her feet. There was smoke billowing up from the dry brush and she could hear the first shouts of alarm as people made their way from the track meet over to the edge of the woods.

"Your lightning started it," Hector explained briefly. "I have to go. I'm not supposed to be here."

"What was that?" Helen asked, raising her voice to stop Hector from leaving.

"A battalion of the Hundred Cousins. Our dear uncle Tantalus wants revenge for Creon, and he won't stop until I'm captured. I have no idea how they found me," he replied, adding a foul curse at the end. "Stay safe, little cousin. I'll be in touch."

"Wait!" Helen yelled after him, but just then several witnesses pushed through the trees to see to the fire, and Hector had to run away. "I was talking about that thing that was giving the orders . . ." She trailed off lamely as Hector's back melted into the distance.

Helen let Claire make up the cover story. It was almost too easy for Claire to convince everyone that there had been a freak storm. Lots of witnesses had seen lightning flashes and "dark clouds" mysteriously covering the woods. All Claire needed to do was cast herself and Helen as innocent bystanders who just happened to be the first to arrive at the scene. Helen couldn't be sure, but she thought she saw Zach grimace when Claire told her tall tale. She wondered whether Zach had seen the whole thing. But if he had, why didn't he say anything?

On the flight home, Helen and Claire had plenty of time to get freaked out about what had happened. They couldn't risk being overheard by one of the teammates, but they kept glancing over at each other with worried eyes. Neither of them wanted to be alone that night so they made plans for Claire to come and sleep over at Helen's house.

As soon as Claire disembarked, she and Jason rushed to meet. He looked pale and tense, and they regarded each other with such obvious devotion it made Helen's heart pinch.

"Luke didn't know if you'd been injured or not," Jason choked out as he reached inside Claire's jacket. Under the cover of her coat, he ran his softly glowing Healer's hands lightly over Claire's arms and ribs, checking her for broken bones or internal bleeding. "He said you got knocked down by a Scion. . . ."

"She's fine," Helen said soothingly.

"Of course *you'd* think she's fine. You don't have any concept of how easy it is for her to get hurt. *You're* impervious," Jason snapped back at Helen, his voice rising slightly with every sentence.

"I'd never let anything happen . . ." Helen began incredulously, but Claire touched Helen's arm and silenced her.

"I'm okay, Jason," Claire said patiently as she reached toward him with her other hand. She held on to both Jason and Helen, as if she was trying to use her arms to bridge the gap between them.

It seemed that Jason put down a heavy burden as he nodded, finally accepting that Claire was safe, but as they turned to walk to Claire's car, he glared at Helen, almost as if he didn't trust her.

On the way to the parking lot, Claire repeated the conversation they'd had with Hector, but she couldn't give Jason much information.

"I spent most of the time knocked on my ass. It was over really fast, though," she finished sheepishly.

"There was this creepy commander," Helen told Jason. "He didn't look right."

"Luke never said anything about that," Jason said with a shake of his head.

"Maybe he didn't see him," Helen said, unable to bring herself to say Lucas's name. "There was also a Shadowmaster there."

"We know," Jason said with a worried glance over at Claire. "Lucas mentioned that."

"What was Lucas doing there, anyway?" Claire asked.

"He didn't say," Jason replied with a tired shrug. "Luke doesn't seem to think he needs to explain himself to anyone anymore."

"Is he okay?" Helen asked quietly. Jason pursed his lips.

"Sure," he said, throwing up his hands like there was nothing else he *could* say, even if they both knew it wasn't the literal truth.

"Are you going to be all right getting home alone?" Claire asked Helen when Jason left to go get his car. It took a moment for Helen to catch on, and when she did, she was stunned. Claire was ditching her for Jason.

"Hector said they were after him, not me. I'm not in any

73

danger," Helen said in a cold voice.

"Not exactly what I meant," Claire said with raised eyebrows. Then she made Helen face her. "Hector is being hunted, and Jason's going out of his head about it. He needs to talk to someone right now."

Helen didn't respond. She wasn't about to say she was fine with Claire blowing off their plans when she wasn't. She knew she was being childish, but she couldn't stop herself. A big part of her wanted to say that she needed someone right now, too. Helen waited with Claire until Jason pulled up next to Claire's car, but she didn't say anything else. When they were gone she trotted toward a secluded area, looked around to make sure no one was watching her, and then took off and flew home.

Helen circled her house a few times, looking down at the empty widow's walk. For just a moment, Helen let herself hope that Lucas would be up there, waiting for her to come home. It was almost as if she could feel him there, like his ghost was walking back and forth, scanning the horizon for her. Looking for the mast of her ship . . .

But as usual lately, she was all alone.

Helen landed in her yard, and went into the house. Jerry had left her a note and a rapidly cooling casserole. He and Kate were working late. It was delivery night, and that meant they would spend hours restocking the shelves and doing inventory. Helen stood in the middle of the kitchen with only one light on in the hall and listened to the house be empty. The silence was overwhelming.

Helen looked around at the dark kitchen and thought about the ambush that she had survived just hours earlier. It reminded her of the time she had been ambushed by Creon, right where she was standing. Lucas had come and saved her life. Then, afterward, he'd sat her on the counter and fed her honey. Helen pinched her eyes with her fingers until she saw pale blue spots and told herself that they hadn't known *then* that they were cousins, so it was okay that she'd felt what she had. But she knew they were cousins *now*, so it wasn't okay to relive it.

Helen couldn't allow herself to stand around and think about Lucas. Standing still would lead to more thinking, more thinking would lead to hysterical crying, and Helen could not allow herself to cry before she slept or she would suffer for it in the Underworld.

Shutting off her memories, Helen marched upstairs and got ready for bed. All she wanted was someone to talk to before she laid her head down, but it seemed like no one was around anymore, not even Jerry and Kate.

Helen saw that her dad had replaced the blanket she had put over the hole in her window with a blue tarp and smiled to herself. He might not be around for Helen to talk to every moment of the day, but at least her father loved her enough to try to fix her messes. She checked the seal on the tape holding it down. It was on tight, but the room was still so cold Helen could see her breath. She climbed reluctantly into bed and pulled the miserable bed-wetter sheets up to her chin to keep in the heat.

Helen glanced around her room. The silence pounded in her ears and the walls spiraled in on her. She didn't want to be the Descender anymore. For all her suffering she had learned nothing, and she was no closer to freeing the Rogues and the Outcasts from the Furies than she had been when she first descended. She was a failure.

Helen was at the end of her endurance. She was beyond tired, but she couldn't let herself fall asleep in this condition. If she did, she didn't know if she would ever have the strength to wake up again. She needed something, anything, to look forward to.

A fragment of a thought flashed across her mind's eye—the sweet image of a strong hand that was open and ready to take hers. Behind that helping hand was a mouth that smiled as it said her name.

Helen didn't just want a friend, she needed one. And she didn't care if she had to go to hell to find him.


Automedon saw the Heir to the House of Atreus circle her house twice, staying high in the night sky before she landed in her yard. At first, he thought she stayed aloft because she had spotted him. He sank back into the neighbor's bushes and took on the preternatural stillness that only a creature of nonhuman lineage could achieve. He knew the Heir was powerful and should not be underestimated. He hadn't seen lightning like she had made during the battle in the woods in many years.

But like most modern Scions, she was oblivious to her true potential. None of these gifted infants knew that power was meant to be wielded. The strong *should* rule. That was what nature intended, from smallest microbe to the great leviathan. The weak die, and the strongest becomes queen of the nest.

Automedon willed the chitin in his skin to harden and hold fast until he realized that the Heir's focus was not on him, and that he could relax his rigid outer camouflage.

The Heir was taking her time to land so she could look at the fenced-in platform on her roof. Strange, he thought, it was almost as if she expected someone to be up there, and yet he had never seen anyone use that platform in the three weeks he had been watching her. He made a mental note of her interest in the widow's walk, trusting in his instinct that there was more to that place than met the eye.

She landed in the yard and looked over her shoulder, the moonlight catching her smooth cheek. Many years ago in a faraway country, Automedon had seen that same exquisite face, kissed by the same adoring moon, as it looked back over the ocean of blood that had been spilled to possess it.

The Heir went inside her house but turned on no lights. Automedon heard her pause and stand very still just inside the kitchen at the front. Her strange behavior made him wonder if one of the Hundred Cousins had been incited by their failure to seize the Outcast that afternoon to disobey Tantalus's orders. Was one in the house? Automedon rose out of the bushes. The Heir was not to be touched, not yet. He took a step forward and heard her go upstairs. She went into the bathroom, turned on a light, and started washing up as if nothing was wrong. Automedon retreated back into his nest and listened.

He could hear the Heir lay down in her bed. Her breathing was elevated, almost as if she were frightened. Automedon extended the proboscis that lay under his human-looking tongue, sliding it out to taste her pheromones on the air. She was afraid, but there was more than just fear in her chemical signature. There were many conflicted emotions bubbling to the surface, changing her chemistry too quickly for Automedon to identify them clearly. The burden of her task was weighing heavily on her. He heard her sniff a few times, then finally she relaxed, and he heard her breathing turn into the slow rhythm of sleep. As she unlocked the portal, the unearthly cold of the Void sucked the last vestiges of warmth out of her room.

For a millisecond, her body vanished from this world altogether, but Automedon knew that it would reappear, like all the other Descenders' had, alive and functioning and covered with the sterile dust of another world. She would lie unnaturally still then, and open her eyes hours later, only remembering that she had been in the Underworld for what, from her perspective, could have been ages.

The Heir might lie in the posture of sleep for hours, but

after weeks of study, Automedon had learned that this Descender never truly rested. He had crept in, hung from her ceiling, and waited for the telltale movement of the eyes under the lids that signaled the deep, healing sleep that mortals need. But it never came.

Without true rest, each night she would grow weaker and weaker until the time came for his master to strike.

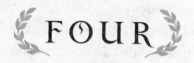

# FOUR

elen felt the stale air of the Underworld envelop her. She flinched and looked around, half worried that her attempt to think positively had failed, and that she was going to find herself in the pit.

"Do you always wander around hell in your pajamas?" asked a sardonic voice. Helen whirled around and saw Haircut, standing just a few feet away.

"What?" Helen stammered, looking down at herself. She was wearing a nightshirt and shorts with gap-toothed pumpkins and hissing black cats all over them.

"Don't get me wrong, I like the short shorts, and the Halloween motif is hilarious, but I'm getting cold just looking at you."

Haircut took off his jacket and started stuffing Helen into it without even asking if she was cold. She thought for a moment that she should refuse, but as soon as she felt how cozy his jacket was, she realized that she was freezing her butt off, and decided she'd better not complain.

"I'm wearing what I wore to bed," Helen explained defensively as she tugged her hair out from under the coat's collar. She hadn't given any thought to what she wore when she descended. "So . . . do you always fall asleep with that stupid gold shrubbery on your arm?"

He looked down at his arm and chuckled to himself. Helen couldn't remember ever hearing laughter in the Underworld, and she almost didn't believe she was hearing it now.

"A bit too much bling, huh? How 'bout this?" The tree branch that snaked around his forearm shrank until it was no more than a thick gold bracelet. Embossed with a leaf design, it circled his wrist like a cuff. Helen had only seen one other object magically transform like that: the cestus of Aphrodite, which she wore around her neck in the guise of a heart necklace.

"Who *are* you?"

"I'm Orion Evander. Head of the House of Rome, Heir to the House of Athens, Third Leader of the Rogue Scions, and bearer of the Golden Bough of Aeneas," he said in a deep and impressive voice.

"Ooh," Helen hooted sarcastically. "Am I supposed to bow or something?"

To her surprise Orion laughed again. For all his high-and-mighty titles, this guy was definitely not stuck-up.

"Daphne said you were powerful, but she never mentioned you were such a wiseass," Orion said. Helen's amused face dropped immediately.

"How do you know my . . . Daphne?" she demanded, awkwardly avoiding the use of the word *mother*.

"I've known her my whole life," Orion replied, concerned. He took a step closer to Helen and looked her in the eyes, like he wanted to make it clear that he wasn't joking around anymore. "Daphne took a big risk to help me get here so I could help you. Didn't she tell you I was coming?"

Helen shook her head and looked down, thinking of all the unreturned messages she had left on Daphne's voice mail.

"We don't talk much," Helen mumbled. She was embarrassed to admit it to a stranger, but Orion didn't look at her like he thought she was horrible daughter or anything. In fact, he smiled sadly to himself and nodded, as though he knew exactly what Helen was feeling. He looked back at her with kind eyes.

"Well, even though you two aren't close, Daphne wanted you to . . . DUCK!" He suddenly screamed as he grabbed Helen's head and pushed it down.

A snarling black dog sailed over Helen and hit Orion directly on the chest. Orion absorbed the blow and fell back, his long dagger already in one hand as the other hand held the dog back by its throat. Unsure what she should do, Helen scrambled up to her knees and saw Orion slashing at the snapping head of the creature. He was on his back and he couldn't get the momentum required to deliver a killing stab. Helen hauled herself up to her feet, but had no idea how to jump into the fight. The beast's claws raked at Orion's chest, leaving jagged, bloody scratches.

"This is not a spectator sport!" Orion shouted from the ground. "Kick it in the ribs!"

Helen stowed her shock, planted her left foot, and booted the monster with all her might. It didn't seem to hurt the hellhound at all. Instead, all the kick managed to do was get the beast's attention. Helen stumbled back. The monster turned its glowing red eyes on her. She squeaked in terror as the beast dove at her.

"Helen!" Orion said fearfully, snatching the monster by the tail and pulling it away.

The salivating jaws closed just inches away from Helen's face and, as she covered her head with her arms to protect herself, she heard the hellhound shriek in surprised pain as Orion drove his blade into the back of its skull.

Helen shook herself awake, her arms reaching out and her legs kicking as if she were trying to crest a great wave. She was back in her bedroom.

"No way!" she shouted into the dark.

Helen couldn't believe it had happened again. She *had* to learn how to control her passage into and out of the Underworld, or she was never going to be of any use in the fight against the Furies. Especially now that she had found Orion. She couldn't just disappear on him whenever there was danger.

Helen didn't waste a second. She called her mother immediately, intending to ask about Orion, but as usual, she was sent to voice mail after two rings. She left her mother a message, but instead of telling her about Orion, Helen got so annoyed she wound up asking if Daphne was avoiding her. She hung up, disgusted by the whiny tone in her voice. Daphne had never been there for Helen. She didn't know why she had even bothered to call.

Helen scrubbed her hands over her face. She was okay, but she couldn't say the same for Orion. She would never forgive herself if something had happened to him. Helen wanted to climb under her covers and send herself back into the Underworld, but she knew that it would be a wasted effort. Time and space moved differently down there, and even if she descended immediately, she wouldn't arrive in the same place or the same time as when she had left.

She folded her arms in consternation, and as she did so, she realized that she was still wearing Orion's jacket. She patted the pockets and found his wallet. After about half a second of moral quibbling, Helen opened it and riffled through, curious.

Orion had two driver's licenses—one from Canada and one from Massachusetts. Both said that said he was eighteen years old and legally allowed to operate heavy machinery, but neither of his licenses listed his last name as Evander, the name he had given her. His American driver's license said his last name was Tiber, and in Canada his last name was listed as Attica. He also had a student ID from Milton

Academy, a well-known prep school on the south shore of Massachusetts, that said his name was Ryan Smith.

Smith. Yeah, right. Helen wondered if all Scions were creativity impaired when it came to aliases, or if "Smith" was the running joke among demigods.

She looked for any other bit of information she could find in the remaining pockets of his jacket, but all she came up with was four dollars and an old paper clip. She paced around her icebox of a bedroom, thinking of her options. She was desperate to know if Orion was okay, but she wasn't too sure it was a good idea to go poking around in his life. With four different last names, Orion was obviously a secretive guy. Helen couldn't go looking for him without blowing whatever cover he was trying to create for himself.

She briefly wondered why he needed all the aliases, then almost immediately answered her own question. The Hundred Cousins had tried to kill off all the other Houses, and until they discovered Helen and her mother, they'd believed that they were the only Scions left in the world. As Head of the House of Rome and Heir to the House of Athens, Orion had probably spent his whole life on the run, hiding from the Hundred Cousins, the largest faction of the House of Thebes. They made it their mission to hunt down Scions from the other three Houses and kill them. If Helen went looking for Orion, she knew that she would only give him away. Like she had Hector, she realized suddenly.

It hadn't occurred to her before, but now Helen was

certain that it was her fault that Hector had been found. Cassandra had foreseen that the Hundred weren't actively trying to kill her at the moment, but Cassandra had also said they were still keeping tabs on her—probably watching her every move. And Hector had been discovered as soon as he made contact with her. If Helen went looking for Orion, she would lead the Hundred straight to him.

Helen shivered, partly from the cold and partly from fear. She wrapped Orion's jacket a little tighter around her shoulders and decided that she was not going to be able to fall back to sleep right away. She went downstairs and heated up some of the casserole her dad had left her and then sat down at the kitchen table to eat, get warm, and think about what she should do next.

When she had finished her late meal she went back up to bed, still debating whether or not she should tell the Delos clan about Orion. A part of her was starting to believe that the farther she kept herself away from Orion, the better off he would be.

"Kneel, slave," Automedon said, and faced the rising sun.

Zach did as he was told. He heard his master mumbling something in Greek and saw him take a beautiful, jeweled dagger out of the sheath on his hip. Automedon finished speaking, kissed the blade, and turned to face Zach.

"Which is your strong hand?" he asked almost pleasantly. That frightened Zach.

"My left."

"The mark of Ares," Automedon said with surprised approval.

Zach didn't know how to respond to that. He hadn't had any say in which hand was stronger, so how could it be a compliment? He decided to hold his tongue. His master usually preferred it when Zach was silent.

"Hold it out," Automedon ordered.

Zach extended his left hand, trying to keep it from shaking too much. His master hated any signs of weakness.

"Do you see this dagger?" Automedon asked, not expecting a reply. "This was my blood brother's dagger. His mother gave it to him before he went to war. Pretty, isn't it?"

Zach nodded solemnly, his outstretched hand trembling underneath the beautiful blade in the cold dawn.

"Did you know that a part of a warrior's soul is kept inside his weapons and his armor? And when you are killed in battle, and your opponent takes your armor and your sword, he owns a bit of your soul?"

Zach nodded. In the *Iliad* there were several heated fights about who got whose armor. More than one of the great heroes died in dishonor over armor. He knew it was a really big deal.

"That is because we all swear on our arms. It's the *oath* that puts our souls inside the metal," Automedon explained intensely. Zach nodded to show he understood. "I swore my loyalty on this dagger once, as did my brother before me. I swore to serve or die."

Zach felt a burning sensation across the palm of his hand,

like a needle of fire had just been shot through it. He looked down and saw that he was bleeding freely, but that it was only a flesh wound and it wouldn't cause him any permanent harm. Automedon grabbed his wrist and directed the blood to flow across the blade of the dagger, until both sides and all the edges were bathed in Zach's blood.

"Swear on your blood, spilled over this blade, that you will serve or die."

What choice did he have?

"I swear it."

The next morning, Helen sat with Cassandra in the Delos library for another session of what she secretly thought of as "Sundays with Sibyl." She still hadn't decided whether to tell the Delos family about Orion or not. Twice she'd opened her mouth to ask if Cassandra could "see" whether or not Orion was still alive, and both times she'd closed it again. The third time she was spared, because Claire came barging into the library, closely followed by Matt, Jason, and Ariadne. All four were demanding that they be allowed to join in on the research.

"We've been through this before," Cassandra said firmly. "We can't risk it. Some of these scrolls have curses imbedded in them that could harm the uninitiated."

The other three turned to Claire expectantly.

"So initiate us," Claire said, crossing her arms and narrowing her eyes in challenge. "Make us priests and priestesses of Apollo."

"Say that again," Jason said, turning to Claire. He was so stunned there was almost no expression on his face.

"That's the plan you've been working on for the past two days? The one you told us *not to worry* about?" Matt asked in an increasingly high-pitched voice.

"Yup," Claire responded, completely unfazed.

"Oh, honey. There is no way I'm becoming a priestess," Ariadne said. She shook her head definitely. "Don't get me wrong, I'd risk my life to help Helen, but join the clergy? Uh-uh. Sorry."

"Why not? Do you even know what it means to become a priestess?" Claire asked. "Well, I've done some reading and I can tell you, it's not what you're all thinking."

Claire explained that the ancient Greeks were much more relaxed about the whole priest thing than any modern-day religion. They had to remain childless while they served the god Apollo, but no one was expected to be a priest or a priestess forever. You could leave whenever you wanted. Then there were a few little rules about keeping various parts of your body clean, making regular burnt offerings accompanied by some basic chanting, and observing a day of fasting once every new moon to honor Apollo's twin sister, Artemis. That was about it.

"Oh. Well, sign me up then," Ariadne with a grin and a shrug. "I can totally handle making sure that the creases between my toes are cleansed before joining others at table, just don't ask me to give up—"

"We get it, Ari," Jason interrupted, not wanting to hear

what his sister was about to say. "So, how would we go about this?"

"There's bound to be some kind of test we have to pass," Matt added, intrigued. He seemed to be warming up to the idea of becoming a priest of Apollo.

"The Fates decide who gets to join. Then the Oracle performs the ritual of initiation," Claire replied, looking pointedly at Cassandra.

"Me?" Cassandra said, taken aback. "I don't know how to . . ."

Cassandra broke off when Claire sheepishly handed her an old parchment. It had obviously been stolen out of the Delos library, which meant that for days now, Claire had been breaking into the library and searching through potentially cursed scrolls before she had found it. There was a moment of silence as it sunk in for everyone just how dangerous Claire's actions had been.

"I had to do something!" Claire protested to no one in particular. "Helen's been putting herself through hell, literally *through hell*, every night. . . ."

"And what makes you think Helen is more important than you are?" Jason asked, his face turning bright red with anger. "You could have been killed by some of the stuff written in those scrolls!"

"I can't just sit back and watch my best friend suffer! I won't do it, even if I am *only mortal*," Claire shouted back at him, like she was quoting something he had said to her.

"That wasn't what I meant, and you know it," he said as he

threw up his hands and made a frustrated noise.

"Guys," Helen said as she tried to step between them, tapping her hands together in the universal sign for "time out."

"Just stay out of this!" Jason yelled. He brushed past Helen on his way to the door. "You're not the center of *everyone's* universe, you know."

The door slammed behind him, and an uncomfortable pause followed. After a moment, Claire whirled around to face Cassandra.

"Can you do it?" Claire demanded. Helen was surprised to see tears sparkling in her eyes. "Can you initiate us, or not?"

Cassandra looked up from the scrolls she had been studying since Claire had handed them to her, and paused to gather her thoughts.

To Helen, it looked like Cassandra was as unconcerned with the emotional quarrel between Jason and Claire as she would be with a TV show that happened to be on in the background while she was trying to read. In a way, this was more disheartening than anything that had been said during the fight. Jason obviously held some kind of grudge against Helen, but at least they all cared about each other. Helen didn't know if the same was true of Cassandra anymore.

"Yes I *can*," Cassandra said. "But that's not the right question to ask me."

"*Should* Cassandra initiate us, Sibyl?" Matt asked, his eyes narrowed like he was testing a dangerous theory that could blow up in his face.

The room got cold. The eerie, glowing aura of the Oracle

overtook Cassandra's girlish frame, bowing her shoulders until she was stooped over and shadowing her face until she looked like an old woman. When she spoke again her voice was a chorus as the Three Fates spoke through her.

"You all are found worthy and shall suffer no injury from the knowledge you seek. But be warned. For suffering awaits you all."

The acid-purple glow of the Oracle's aura snuffed out, and Cassandra fell to the ground in a heap.

Before anyone could recover from the shock of witnessing the paralyzing presence of the *Moirai*, somehow Lucas appeared at his sister's side, already gently lifting her up off the floor and into his arms.

"When did you come in?" Ariadne asked him, looking over her shoulder at the door, and then back at Lucas with wide eyes. He didn't bother to respond. His focus stayed entirely on his little sister.

Cassandra's eyes fluttered open and her head twitched as she regained consciousness. Lucas steadied her as she flailed slightly with the shock of coming around to find herself being held up in the air. He smiled at her and she smiled back, neither of them needing to talk to be able to communicate. Helen would have given everything she had to see Lucas smile at her like that. His face was so beautiful when he smiled. She wanted to touch it.

Lucas brushed past Matt as he carried Cassandra out of the library, and as he did so, Helen noticed that he made no sound as he walked. Somehow over the past few weeks

Lucas had learned how to use his ability to manipulate the air to create a soundless vacuum. It was almost like he wasn't really there anymore. Helen's heart squeezed so tightly in her chest that she thought for a minute that she would choke. Lucas was erasing himself, and he was probably doing it so he didn't have to suffer actually *being* in the same room as her. He hated her that much.

Claire told everyone that they couldn't safely read the scrolls without a proper initiation first. They'd have to wait until Cassandra was able to perform the ritual. Everyone else filed out silently, engrossed in thought, but Helen stayed behind in the library for a few seconds in order to collect herself.

Every time she saw Lucas it got worse. He was changing, but not for the better. Something *wrong* was happening to Lucas.

Blinking her stinging eyes, Helen scolded herself. She didn't have the right to worry about him anymore. She wasn't his girlfriend. She wasn't even supposed to look at him.

Helen defiantly shook off the thought before it could suck her in. She had to keep busy. Motion. Action. That was the key.

As Helen walked out of the library, she came across Claire and Jason sitting on one of the many back staircases in the sprawling Delos house. From what Helen could gather, they had already worked past the angry phase of their argument and were moving steadily to an understanding. They held hands as they talked. Claire sat on a slightly higher step to compensate for her small stature, and both of them were leaning toward each other so close it was like they were trying to climb into each other's eyes.

Helen ducked out the back door before she had to witness any more of the emotional exchange. There were some clacking and huffing sounds coming from the tennis-courts-turned-arena, and she wandered toward it, wondering who was training. Her first thought was that Castor and Pallas were working out together, but when she went inside she saw Ariadne and Matt going at it like a couple of gladiators with wooden practice swords. Matt fell back on his ass, and Helen cringed for him. She knew exactly what he was going through.

"Good, Matt," Ariadne said as she bent over to lend him a hand. "But you're still dropping your guard too much when you . . ." Ariadne trailed off when she saw Helen was watching her.

"I didn't know you were teaching Matt to fight," Helen said awkwardly when she realized that the two of them were blushing. They shot each other nervous glances and then looked back at Helen with cornered looks on their faces.

"Guys? What's going on?" Helen finally asked when she couldn't figure out why they were acting so guilty.

"My dad doesn't want mortals involved in any of the fighting," Ariadne admitted. "He sort of forbade us to teach Matt how to use a sword."

"Then why are you doing it?" Helen asked, but neither of them answered her. Helen tried to picture Matt fighting someone like Creon, and the image truly frightened her. She had to say something. "Matt, I know you're a good athlete, but even with training it would be suicide for you to take on a Scion."

"I know that!" he said in a strangled voice. "But what am I supposed to do if I get caught in the middle of a brawl or hit one of you with my car again? Just stand around and wait for someone to come rescue me? I'd be dead if I did that. At least this gives me something of a shot."

"Scions don't usually attack mortals. No offense, but we think it's dishonorable," Helen responded sheepishly. She didn't want to put Matt down, but it was the truth.

"Matt doesn't have to be attacked to end up getting hurt. Or killed," Ariadne said in a wavering voice.

"I know he doesn't, but . . ." Helen began gently and then broke off. She couldn't help but think that after a few weeks of training Matt might start believing he could handle himself against one of the Hundred, which was madness. "This is a really bad idea, you guys."

"I can't just stand around and do nothing! I'm not afraid!" Matt yelled at her. Ariadne stepped forward and touched Matt's arm to calm him down.

"You're not helping," she said gently to him before she turned to Helen with a steely look in her eyes. "I don't think it's right for him to be around Scions and not even know how to hold a sword. I honestly don't care if no one else in this family agrees with me. I'm going to teach him. So now the only question is, are you going to tell my father or not?"

"Of course I won't!" Helen said in an exasperated voice before she turned to Matt to plead with him. "Just, Matt, *please* don't try to fight a Scion unless you absolutely have to do it to defend yourself!"

"Right," he responded with a bitter tilt to his lips. "You know, I may not be able to lift a car over my head, but that doesn't mean I'm useless."

Helen couldn't remember Matt ever being so bitter about anything. She tried to explain what she meant, but got strangely tongue-tied. Honestly, she wished he were a little more cowardly. He'd probably live longer that way, but she couldn't very well say that to him.

When Helen didn't respond right away, Matt left the arena with Ariadne following close behind. As they got a few paces out of the enclosed area, Helen heard Ariadne saying something conciliatory, and Matt cutting her off in frustration. They continued talking as they moved away, but Helen didn't even try to eavesdrop. She was just too damn tired.

Helen sat down on the sand with her head in her hands. There wasn't one person she could turn to, even just to chat for a few minutes before she had to face her seemingly impossible task in the Underworld.

The sun started to set. Another day was ending, and another night in the Underworld awaited her. Helen lifted her head and attempted to find the energy to fly home, but she was so wrung out she could barely focus her eyes. If she stayed there any longer, she would fall asleep, and she didn't want to descend while she was in the Deloses' backyard.

She hauled herself to her feet, and as she did, she felt that strange vertigo again. It was as if a part of the world broke off and turned into a picture while her body moved around it. Helen fell back down onto a knee and tried not to vomit. She saw the sand swim in front of her eyes, and for a moment, she thought she saw it actually move. She held very still and closed her eyes.

She could hear a heartbeat. And it wasn't hers.

"Who's there?" she whispered, her eyes darting all over the place. She summoned a globe of electricity and held it in the palm of her hand. "Come any closer, and I will kill you."

Helen waited a few more moments, but there was no response. In fact, there was nothing but perfectly still air. It was actually quite peaceful. Flexing her hand, she allowed the electricity to dissipate, and a shower of sparks fell between her fingers and bounced harmlessly on the sand. She shook her head and laughed at herself, unable to stop a note of hysteria from creeping in. She was cracking up and she knew it.

When Helen got home she started cooking dinner for herself and her dad, but halfway through she got a call from Jerry. Helen could tell from the stiff tone of his voice that he really wanted to yell at her for breaking her bedroom window, but since he was calling to tell her that there was a terrible mix-up involving a shipment of spider-shaped balloons at the store and he would be leaving her alone another night, he felt guilty enough to let the whole window thing go. Helen tried not to sound too sullen when she told him she was sorry he had to work late, then she hung up and stared at the half-prepared meal that she no longer felt like finishing or eating. She repackaged what she could and ate a bowl of cereal standing up by the kitchen sink before she went up to get ready for bed.

Throwing Orion's jacket over her shoulders, Helen opened her bedroom door. She was about to step inside but her feet stopped where they were. Her bedroom used to be her sanctuary, her place of retreat, but it wasn't anymore. It was a place where she suffered every single night. And on top of that, it was Eskimo cold. Standing on the threshold, Helen took a deep breath and then let it go, sending a big cloud of steam out in front of her as she did so.

"Well, Orion whatever-your-last-name-is," she said to her empty room as she stepped inside, shut the door, and slipped her feet into a pair of rubber boots. "I hope you were serious about wanting to help me, because I've never needed help more than I do right now."

Of course, Orion didn't show. Helen spent what felt like a day's worth of time wandering around the periphery of the Fields of Asphodel. She paced through the slippery mud of the flats around that meadow of creepy flowers, hoping he would appear at any moment, but he never did.

Helen didn't go into the Fields because the flowers

depressed her. Asphodels were pale, scentless blossoms that stuck up out of the ground, stiff and evenly spaced, like gravestones. She had read that asphodel flowers were the only nourishment for the hungry ghosts in the Underworld, and although Helen had yet to see any ghosts, she could feel them all around her, sense their eyes in the still air.

She'd focused on Orion before she went to sleep, hoping that by doing so she would appear next to him. She didn't have the Underworld figured out by any stretch of the imagination, but she knew enough to know she would only see him if he had descended into the Underworld the same night. She paced back and forth, hoping he would appear, but she sensed that if she didn't appear in front of him when she descended she wouldn't see him, even if she waited forever.

And the more she thought about it, the more Helen had to admit that she wasn't sure Orion would join her the next night, either. Maybe he'd decided that he'd had enough of the Underworld altogether.

She tried to look on the bright side. At least he'd given her the tip about dressing better before she went to sleep, and although it would be impossible to explain to Jerry why she was wearing a pair of galoshes to bed, it was still better than walking barefoot through all that nasty mud.

On Monday morning, Helen awoke and sighed, saddened by the fact that she would have nothing to look forward to when she went to sleep that night. She reminded herself that Orion had never been a part of the bargain. She'd always thought she would have to do this alone. Reluctantly, she hauled herself out of bed to clean up the night's mess and get ready for school.

# FIVE

**Sleep well?** read the text from the unknown number. Helen plowed into Claire's back and practically knocked her down.

"What the hell, Lennie!" Claire complained loudly. Helen reeled off to the side and tried to regain her footing without stepping all over her tiny friend.

"Sorry, Gig . . ." Helen mumbled distractedly while she typed: **Who is this?**

"Who are you texting?" Claire asked curiously.

**4-get me already? I'm 4-lorn,** read the reply. Clever, Helen thought. So clever she decided to take a chance.

**4-lorn? B-cuz you have 4 last names?** Helen asked back, a faint smile creeping up her face and an oddly large butterfly flapping away in her tummy.

"Lennie? What's going on?" Claire took Helen's upper

arm and pulled her along the corridor toward lunch.

"I think this might be that Orion guy—the guy I met in the Underworld. I just don't know *how*. I never gave him my number," Helen mumbled.

Claire steered Helen safely through the cafeteria while Helen stared with single-minded determination at the screen on her phone. If this was a trick, Helen knew she could possibly be outing Orion, but she had to test her mystery texter and find out for sure. If some unknown person had her number, it might not be safe for her, either. Finally, a reply came.

**Ha! 4 names, but only 1 coat. Freezing! Meet me 2-night?** Orion wrote, and now Helen was certain that it was Orion on the other end of the thread. No one else could possibly know about the coat she had accidentally stolen from him, and then slept in since, except Orion. Helen hadn't even had a chance to tell Claire about it.

**4-sure. 2-night. I won't ditch you, at least,** she replied. She realized that last line was snotty as she sent it, and desperately wished she could snatch it out of the air before it reached him. Helen had waited for hours. It wasn't that she considered meeting Orion a date. It was just that it was the first time she'd ever been expecting a boy who didn't show. It hadn't felt great.

**Hey, no fair. Couldn't go to the caves last night. Exam today** came Orion's delayed reply.

*Caves?* Helen wondered. She was a little more relieved than she should have been that he had such a good excuse, but rather than stop and examine why, she decided to stick to the most important things first. Like how Orion had found her.

**How'd you get my #?** Helen wrote while Claire pushed her down into her usual seat and started unpacking Helen's lunch for her.

**Daphne.**

**What! When?** Helen's thumbs were pressing down so hard she had to remind herself to ease up before she snapped her phone in half.

**Uh . . . 5 minutes ago? Got 2 go.**

**Did you TALK to her?**

Helen waited, staring at the screen with her mouth hanging open, but when she didn't get an immediate response she knew the conversation was over.

"So. Orion, huh?" Claire said through pursed lips. "You didn't tell me you'd gotten his name."

"Well, you never asked about him again."

"Sorry," Claire said, knowing she messed that one up. "I was preoccupied—dodging Cassandra and Jason, looking for that scroll. So what happened?"

"We talked." Helen took a distracted bite out of the sandwich that Claire had put in her hand.

She had a dozen questions to ask Orion, but she knew that she would have to wait until that night to get any answers. The first question she was going to ask him was why Daphne would take his calls and not hers. Orion had said that he'd known Daphne his whole life. Maybe the two of them were really close. Closer than Daphne was to her own daughter? Helen had no idea how she felt about that.

"Are you going to tell me about this Orion guy or am I just supposed to sit here and watch you chew?" Claire asked with raised eyebrows. "And why are you so grouchy?"

"I'm not grouchy!"

"Then why are you scowling?"

"I just don't know what to think about all this!"

"All *what*?" Claire nearly shouted with frustration.

Again, Helen was confronted with the fact that there was a lot that she and Claire didn't share with each other anymore.

Speaking as quickly and as quietly as she could so she could get the whole story in before the end of lunch, Helen told Claire all about how he had tried to pull her out of quicksand the first time. Then she described the gold branch on Orion's arm, the fact that twice now he'd seemed to be fending off some kind of attack from hellish monsters when she had never seen anything like that down there, and how he had protected her during one of those attacks.

"I don't want you to tell Jason about this just yet, okay? Because apart from texting just now, I've only spoken to Orion once, so I don't know what to think about him. He said Daphne sent him down there to help me," Helen said with a confused shake of her head. "And honestly, Gig, I don't know what she's up to. I feel like she's always scheming."

"That doesn't mean Orion is. You don't have your powers in the Underworld, right?" Claire asked with shrewd eyes.

"And he's a good fighter?"

"He's an amazing fighter, and from what I've seen, he doesn't need extra powers to take care of himself. He killed the thing that was on top of me with his bare hands, practically."

"Then maybe Daphne's only scheme is to try to keep you alive. The first time you two met, he did save you," Claire said with an indulgent smile.

Helen wanted to argue but, as always, Claire had a really good point. Daphne wanted to get rid of the Furies and, according to Cassandra, Helen was the only one who could do it. On top of that, Helen was Daphne's daughter and her only heir. But even so, Helen doubted that Daphne was just trying to protect her.

After a few moments of biting her lip, trying to find a hole in Claire's argument, Helen had to admit to herself that the only reason she disagreed was because Daphne had abandoned her as a baby. She simply didn't trust her. Maybe she was being too harsh. Maybe this time Daphne was only trying to help.

"Okay, you're right . . . I have major issues about Beth or Daphne or whatever she's calling herself this decade. But I wouldn't be so suspicious if she'd just answer the damn phone when I called once in a while," Helen said with exasperation. "I don't expect her to tell me everything she's doing, but it would nice to know what country she's in, at least."

"Have you ever considered that maybe it's safer for you if

you don't know where she is or what she's doing?" Claire asked gently. Helen opened her mouth to argue and shut it again, knowing she wouldn't win that point, either. But she still wished she knew where the hell Daphne was.

Daphne held her breath and stayed very, very still. She'd managed to convince her lungs that they only needed a fraction of the air they were used to, but there wasn't much she could do about her hammering heart. The man she had taken a blood oath to kill was in the next room. She had to find a way to calm herself, or all her sacrifice would be in vain.

From her hiding place in his bedroom she could hear him in the adjoining study. He was at his desk, writing the legion of letters that he used to direct his cult, the Hundred Cousins. She could almost picture his once-chiseled face, his faded blond hair, and her teeth tingled with the thought of tearing him apart. After so many years, Daphne was just yards away from Tantalus, the Head of the House of Thebes and the murderer of her beloved husband, Ajax.

Hours passed, and Tantalus was still scribbling away. Daphne knew that each of the letters Tantalus was laboring over would be taken by separate couriers and mailed from different post offices scattered up and down the coast. He was meticulous about disguising his location, and because of that, it had taken her nineteen years to track him down. She'd been obliged to follow the body of his only son back to Portugal, never once letting the corpse out of her sight no matter how many times she had to shape-shift. She knew that even Tantalus would surface long enough to put the ritual coin in his only son's mouth, and she had been right.

Finally, she heard Tantalus put down his pen and stand. He called in the mortal porter to take the letters to the couriers. Then he poured himself a glass of something from the well-stocked bar. It took a moment for the scent to waft in to where she was standing, but she knew what he was drinking immediately. Bourbon. Not cognac, not expensive whiskey, but sweet bourbon straight out of Kentucky. He took a few sips, savoring the flavor, then stepped into his bedroom. He shut the door behind him and spoke.

"You should know, Daphne, that one of those letters was to the Myrmidon I have nested outside your daughter's charming little house on Nantucket. If he doesn't hear from me personally, she's as good as dead."

Daphne nearly moaned aloud. She knew Tantalus wasn't lying about the Myrmidon. It had led a phalanx to attack Hector at Helen's track meet. If that *thing* was watching Helen and not chasing Hector as she had assumed, Daphne knew she had no choice. She swallowed her heart and stepped out from her hiding place.

Tantalus stared at her like a starving man at a feast, his eyes skipping all over her face and body. Even though his gaze made her skin crawl, she tolerated it and focused instead on the small measure of bourbon she had smelled that remained in his glass. That was how he had known she was there.

"You *smelled* me, didn't you?" she asked, her voice catching on the bitter lump in her throat.

"Yes," he breathed desperately, almost apologetically. "Even after all these years, I still remember the smell of your hair."

Daphne summoned a spark in the palm of her hand, just to warn him. "If you yell for your guards, I'll kill you where you stand and take my chances of beating that letter back to my daughter."

"And if you manage to beat my letter back to Nantucket, then what? Do you honestly think you can kill a five-thousand-year-old Myrmidon? One who fought beside Achilles himself?"

"Not alone," Daphne responded coldly, shaking her head once. "But with your brothers and their children? It's possible we could take the monster down together."

"But not probable," Tantalus said heavily. "And it would end up costing us both. You know Hector would be first into the fight, and first to die. And I wonder if you could stand to lose him again . . . He looks so *much* like Ajax. But I'm curious, does he feel the same?"

"You filthy-minded animal!" Daphne sparked and crackled, but eventually controlled herself.

This was his plan. Make her use up all her bolts on useless anger until she was left without a bargaining chip. That's what had happened the night she had lost Ajax, but she was older and wiser now.

It took many times more energy to withhold a bolt to stun

a target and not kill, but after years of practice, Daphne had managed to figure out that aspect of her modest power over lightning. She sent a small, baby-blue bolt across the room and put Tantalus on his knees.

"You have a Myrmidon, *not* a Scion, nested outside my daughter's window. Why?" she asked calmly. When he didn't answer, she crossed the room and touched him with her glowing hand. Tantalus sighed with pleasure, until she sent a charge through her fingertips.

"She's protected . . . by the only living Heir to my House," he huffed, his whole body twitching with electric pain. "Can't allow more . . . Outcasts. Atlantis . . . too far away already."

He still didn't know about the Rogues, Daphne thought.

"The insect isn't in any Scion House, and wouldn't become an Outcast if it killed Helen and all the Deloses on Nantucket combined. Which, by the way, would save you a lot of trouble," Daphne continued, amping up the voltage. "So why haven't you ordered it to attack yet?"

"How could I . . . stop you . . . from killing me . . . if I had no collateral?" he huffed. Daphne cut off the current so he could speak clearly. "I want to rule Atlantis, not just survive to see it. I must become part of my House again to do that."

His chest squeezed tight, and he rolled onto his back in pain. A moment later, Tantalus took a deep breath and smiled up into Daphne's hypnotically beautiful face.

"I knew you'd find me someday and that you'd come to me."

There was an insistent knock on the door, followed by a tense inquiry in Portuguese. Tantalus glanced at the door, and then up at Daphne. She shook her head to let him know to keep his mouth shut. Daphne didn't understand Portuguese and she couldn't risk letting Tantalus speak, even if his silence was the thing that would give her presence away. She heard the guard at the door hesitate, and then rush off, most likely to get reinforcements. She grabbed Tantalus by the shirt and bared her teeth at him.

"I will *always* be behind the door, under the bed, or around the next corner—waiting for my chance to kill you. It's in my blood now," she whispered viciously into his ear.

He understood her meaning and smiled. Daphne had taken an oath that was more binding than any human contract ever contrived. Someday she would have to kill him, or *not* killing him would kill her.

"You hate me that much?" he asked, almost awed that Daphne would tie her life to his, even if it was to the death. More guards arrived and began pounding on the door, but Tantalus took little notice of them.

"No. I loved Ajax that much, and I still do." She noticed with pleasure how deeply it hurt Tantalus to hear her say that she still loved another more than him. "Now tell me, what do you want from Helen?"

"What *you* want, my love, my goddess, my future queen in Atlantis," Tantalus chanted, helpless as he fell yet again under the spell of that Face. The guards began to knock down the steel-and-concrete-reinforced door, and Daphne was forced to back away from Tantalus.

"And what do I want?" she asked, her eyes darting over the two-foot-thick stone walls of the chamber, looking for an alternate escape route. There was none.

Daphne looked out the recessed casement behind her at the sheer drop to the ocean. She looked up, hoping to find a way up and over the parapet top of the citadel, but the overhang prevented her. She couldn't fly like Helen could. She also couldn't swim. Daphne was out of time, but she needed to hear what else Tantalus had to say before she jumped out the window and tried, somehow, not to drown. She glared at Tantalus and summoned the last of her sparks to threaten him into talking. He smiled up at her sadly, like he was more hurt to see that she was about to leave him than he was that she was threatening his life.

"I want Helen to succeed in the Underworld, and rid us all of the Furies," he finally replied, gesturing to the plush prison that he was forced to live in as an Outcast. "She is my only hope."

"Son of a bitch!" Orion swore at the top of his voice as he ducked instinctively and stumbled to the side. "When you descend, you just appear out of thin air?"

They were standing on some blah part of the salt flats that rimmed a sea Helen had never been able to get to, and therefore suspected didn't really exist. Just another charming aspect of hell—it promised landscape that it never delivered. Helen looked at Orion's panicky face and realized that she had practically materialized in his back pocket.

"I'm sorry!" she exclaimed sheepishly. "I didn't mean to come in so close."

"That is really unnerving! Is there any way to *warn* me first?" Orion was still clutching his chest, but he had also started to laugh a bit as well, and the sound was infectious.

"I don't think so," Helen chuckled through her words. It was a nervous chuckle, and Helen tried to ignore that fact. She had been really worried he wouldn't show, and a bit happier than she would have anticipated that he had.

"Hey, I may have scared the crap out of you, but at least I remembered to bring your jacket." She shrugged her shoulders out from under the collar, tilting her face down to hide an overexcited blush.

"Yeah? And what are you going to wear?" he asked, eyeing her bare arms skeptically. Helen paused in midmotion. She'd forgotten to put her own jacket on under his, and she was only wearing a T-shirt.

"Um . . . Whoops?"

"Just keep it for now," he said, shaking his head like he had expected this. "Better give me my wallet, though."

"I'll give you your jacket back at the end of the night," she promised, handing over his wallet.

"Sure you will."

"I will!"

"Look, do you really want to argue all night about whether or not girls *ever* return clothes they borrow from guys? Because from what I've noticed, one night can be an actual eternity down here."

Helen grinned. She had to remind herself that she didn't know much of anything about this guy because she was starting to feel like they had been hanging out for years.

"Who *are* you?" she asked, trying not to sound too over-awed. She'd never met anyone like Orion before. He was obviously just as tough as the Delos boys, but Orion was so different. Sometimes the Delos boys acted a little full of themselves, but Orion was down-to-earth, even humble. "Where'd you come from?"

Orion groaned. "We're going to need that eternity after all. Originally? I'm from Newfoundland. Look, my life story is really complicated, so first we'd better head toward some cover before something ugly finds us."

"About that," Helen interjected as they turned their backs on the nonexistent sea and made their way to a thick patch of raggedy marsh grass. "Why is it that every time we're together you're getting chewed on by some horrendous monster?"

"The Bough of Aeneas," he said, and pointed to the bright golden cuff around his wrist. "It was made by one of my ancestors from a very magical tree that grows at the edge of the Underworld, and unfortunately for me, monsters are drawn to it like insects to a barbecue."

"Then why don't you take it off?" Helen asked, like that was a no-brainer.

"Because you, Your Chosen Oneness, can come and go down here as you please." He held apart some tall reeds for her to step between. Helen was about to argue that point, but she didn't get the chance. "I need the Bough to open the gates between the worlds. If I didn't have it with me, I'd just be wandering around inside a cave system in Massachusetts right now. Totally lost."

"Cave?" Helen asked as she remembered Orion mentioning this before. "The gate to the Underworld is in a cave in *Massachusetts*?" she asked incredulously. Orion smiled at her and explained.

"There are hundreds, maybe thousands of gates to the Underworld scattered all over the world. Most of them are in these really cold spots at the bottom of caves. They're 'in between' places that don't *become* gates to the Underworld without some kind of key. As far as I know, the Bough is the only relic left that can do it, and because I'm Aeneas's Heir, I'm pretty much the only person who can use it."

That made sense to Helen. She wore the cestus, an ancient relic from the goddess Aphrodite, and only women born to the House of Atreus could wield it.

"But I thought magic didn't work down here," Helen said as she automatically touched her heart necklace. She knew the magic of the cestus didn't work in the Underworld or she wouldn't have ever been injured down here, and she got injured almost every time she descended.

"Only Underworld magic works in the Underworld," Orion replied. "This is a different universe from ours, and it has its own rules. You must have noticed it. We don't even have our Scion powers down here."

"Yeah, *that* I've noticed," Helen said. Intrigued by her leading inflection, Orion looked over at her as he stamped down the high vegetation to make a path. He paused in thought, and then laughed when he figured out what Helen meant.

"The hellhound! You just stood there with your eyes crossed!"

Helen's shoulders started shaking with embarrassed laughter. "I didn't know what to do! I don't know how to fight without my lightning!"

"You froze up like you were having an asthma attack or something," he chuckled. "For a second I thought I needed to have a chat with Daphne about whether I should carry a spare inhaler. . . ."

He broke off when he noticed how quickly Helen's mood changed at the mention of her mother. She hated how he could just call her "Daphne" like that, like they were best friends or something.

"That bad, huh?" he asked quietly after a moment of tense silence.

"I don't know what you mean," Helen replied in an angry monotone. She turned, intending to blaze her own trail through the tall reeds, but Orion laid a hand on her shoulder and turned her back around.

"I'm a Rogue, too," he said softly. "I know what it's like to hate your family."

Helen's anger evaporated at the sight of his sad eyes. One of her hands reached out to touch him, and she had to snatch it back at the last second. She had forgotten for a moment that Rogues like her could only be claimed by one House. Half of Orion's family would be compelled to kill him if they ever encountered him, which they were sure to do. The Furies worked like magnets, drawing opposite sides together until they eventually collided. Helen had been hidden on a tiny island, and the House of Thebes had still found her; she could only assume that something similar had happened to Orion.

"Did you and your family ever find a way around the Furies? You know, like I did with the Deloses?" she asked softly. Helen didn't want to specifically say Lucas's name or talk about how the two of them had fallen and saved each other, she just hoped that Daphne had filled Orion in on some parts of her history.

"No," he said in a tight voice, understanding Helen's meaning immediately. "I still owe my blood debt to my mother's House, the House of Rome."

"But you can be with her at least, right?" Helen asked tentatively.

"No, I can't," he said in a final way. Helen recalled that he was the *Head* of the House of Rome, and not the *Heir*. He must have inherited his mother's title when she died.

"So you were claimed by your father's side? The House of Athens?" she asked, making an effort to move the conversation away from his mother.

"That's right," he said, turning away from Helen to end the line of questions.

"Hey, I'm sorry, but I'm just trying to get this straight. You were the one who brought up the whole family thing in the first place. Asking about my mother."

"You're right, I brought it up." Orion held up his hands and made a frustrated sound. "I'm good at listening, not talking, and I have no idea what you're feeling right now because I don't have my powers. I can't read your heart, and it's driving me bananas." He shook his head at a thought. "I guess this is the way normal guys feel it, huh? It's really scary, so just give me a second, okay?"

"Okay." Helen couldn't look at him. She didn't entirely trust herself with Orion.

"I'm going to start over," he said, almost like he was warning her. Helen nodded and found herself laughing nervously again.

"All right. Start at the start this time." Helen steadied her voice, trying not to sound so giggly. It was *annoying.*

"Right. Here goes. I'm Head of the House of Rome, but because I was claimed by the House of Athens, the House of Rome has been hunting me since the day I was born. But for other very complicated reasons, the House of Athens has never accepted me, either." Orion looked at Helen like he was forcing himself to jump off a cliff. "When I was ten my father, Daedalus, became an Outcast defending me from my cousins. He had to kill one of his own brother's sons to protect me. Since then I haven't been able to go anywhere near him. The Furies make us try to kill—"

"Yeah." Helen cut him off quickly so he wouldn't have to spell out what he'd tried to do. Orion nodded at her, silently thanking her for stopping him.

The image of trying to kill Jerry flashed through Helen's mind and she pushed it away, unable to bear the thought of attacking her own father.

"Everyone I'm related to wants me dead for one reason or another, and because of that I've been in hiding for most of my life. So, I'm sorry I got all aggro with you, but it isn't easy for me to open up like this, because . . . well, it's usually fatal for me to get close to anyone."

"You've been completely on your own since you were ten, haven't you?" Helen asked in a hushed voice, still unable to wrap her head around everything he had told her. "Running from both sides of your family?"

"And hiding the fact that I exist from the Hundred." Orion looked at the ground to conceal the dark look in his eyes. "Daphne's helped me out when she could. She was there the first time the House of Athens came to kill me. She tried to help my dad, and she saved my life. That paid her side of the blood debt to my House, even though I still owe the House of Atreus. Didn't Daphne tell you any of this?"

"Like I said, my mother and I don't talk much." Was it too much to think that Daphne should have given her a heads-up about this? Something still bothered Helen. "How did she find you and your dad to begin with?"

"Daphne's been on a mission to help the Rogues and the Outcasts for, like, twenty years now. She's traveled all over the world, and because the Furies draw Scions together, whenever she finds a Scion she finds a confrontation. She has a ton of *amazing* stories. I can't believe she never told you any of this."

But, of course, Helen didn't know what Orion was talking about. She barely knew anything about Beth Smith-Hamilton, her supposed mother, but she knew even less about Daphne Atreus.

"Anyway, she's saved a lot of lives, mine included, and now your mother can be with any member of any House. That's why she's the leader of the Rogues and Outcasts."

Helen's jaw dropped. Her mother was a hero? Her shady, unreliable, *deadbeat* mom—the one Helen couldn't even remember—was some kind of Scion savior? If that was true, then something was either not right in the universe, or not right with the way Helen understood it.

"Listen, part of the reason I told you all of this was because I thought it might make it easier for you to forgive Daphne if I did. And please trust me on this one—you have to forgive your mother, Helen. Not for her sake, but for your own."

"Why are you defending Daphne?" Helen asked him suspiciously. She thought about the influence of the cestus and wondered if Daphne was controlling him. "Did she ask you to say all this stuff to me?"

"No! You're misunderstanding what I . . . Daphne never asked me to say anything," he stammered. Helen made a derisive sound that kept him from continuing. She was angry again, but she didn't exactly know why. Not knowing made her even angrier. She stomped past him and started marching out of the weeds.

Helen broke through the tall grass and started climbing a steep hill that was lousy with the remains of some tumbled-down medieval castle. As she stomped past a stone stairway that broke off in midair, Helen asked herself why she was so angry. She realized that it wasn't just one thing. Several things were ticking her off simultaneously, and she was now facing them at the same time.

First, Daphne had sent Orion into the Underworld without bothering to mention it. Second, Cassandra was keeping Claire and Matt from helping her when it was her butt that was dragging through the Underworld every night, not Cassandra's. And Lucas . . . how could he treat her that horribly? Even if he hated her, how could he do that to her? For the first time, Helen felt angry about what he had done, rather than devastated.

As she stomped along, taking her feelings out on the ground, Helen realized that, most of all, she was angry with herself. She had been so paralyzed with sadness that she had stopped making choices. She had allowed herself to drift along like a helpless bit of fluff. That had to end.

When she was out of breath from hiking up the steep incline at a breakneck pace, Helen braced herself against a massive, mossy block of granite that had once been part of the moldering castle's outer wall. She whirled around to grill Orion, who was struggling to keep up with her.

"Do you even know why you're here?" she snapped.

"I'm here to help," he said through panting breaths.

"You told me my mother sent you. Do you know what the cestus is?"

"Son of Aphrodite, by the way," he said pointing to himself. "The cestus doesn't work on me. Daphne can only influence hearts. I can *control* them."

"Oh, wow. That's a pretty terrifying power," Helen mumbled, momentarily sidetracked. "But you still seem awfully willing to do whatever Daphne tells you to do. Does she have something on you?"

"No! I'm not here because of *Daphne*, you lunatic! I'm here because I think that what *you're* trying to do is amazing, and probably the most important thing any Scion has done since the Trojan War! The Furies destroyed my family, and there is nothing I want more than to stop them from doing that to anyone else. You're the Descender, and this is your task, but you are an *embarrassingly* bad fighter without your powers. I'm here to pull you out of whatever smelly hole you fall into so that you actually live long enough to do what you're meant to do!"

Helen closed her mouth with a snap. It was obvious that Orion was being honest. He had no hidden agenda, even if she still suspected that Daphne did. In fact, the deeper Helen looked into his eyes, the more convinced she became that he would do anything to help her stop the Furies.

The Bough of Aeneas was a monster magnet, but she could see that Orion needed to help her in any way that he could or he would go crazy sitting on the sidelines. And Helen knew that she would go crazy with sadness if she had to do this alone. *She* needed help, and *Orion* needed to give it—in a way, it was perfect.

"I'm sorry, Orion. What I said was unfair. It's just that I feel like so many people are trying to tell me what to do right now, but no one is actually *telling* me anything. . . ." Helen stopped, struggling to find the right words.

"I get it. You're so crucial that everyone's afraid of saying the wrong thing to you." He sat down and rested for a moment on the grass. "But I'm not afraid, Helen. I'll tell you everything I know, if you want me to."

An ominous howl echoed through the valley. Orion jumped up and his head snapped around, seeking the source. He reached under his shirt to draw the long knife that was concealed underneath as he took a hold of Helen's shoulder and began pushing her in front of him as he moved.

"Uphill," he ordered in a tight voice.

Helen craned her head to look back and caught a glimpse of a distant patch of reeds being mowed down in a swath. The threat was steamrolling its way toward them. Helen had seen enough to know that whatever it was that was making its way through the marshland was *gigantic*.

Without her Scion strength and speed, she felt like she was barely going faster than a walk. Orion forced her up the steep hill, one hand on his knife and one hand on the small of her back to keep her from losing her footing. The thing in the grass was gaining on them.

"Go!" Orion barked into her ear.

"What do you mean, go? Go where?" she screeched, not understanding. Orion pushed her as hard as he could toward higher ground, and she stumbled forward onto her hands and knees.

She looked back over her shoulder at Orion who stood a few paces away, facing the thing that Helen could hear scrabbling toward them but still couldn't see. Orion looked back over his shoulder at her, his green eyes so intense they nearly glowed. Helen had seen that look before and she knew what it meant. It meant that he was digging in. She couldn't run off and let him fight that thing on his own. She slid back downhill to make her stand with him.

"Get out of here!" he screamed.

"And where the hell am I supposed to . . ."

## SIX

The sun was just starting to come up. Helen woke in her bed, freezing cold and reaching out to grab on to a boy who had never been in her bedroom.

"No!" she exclaimed in a ragged voice. Her breath puffed out of her mouth like smoke in the subzero room. "Oh, no no no, this can't be happening!"

Helen scrambled out of bed and staggered to her dresser on numb legs to get her phone. The message light was blinking. She went into her messages and read:

**That sucked. I'm going to bed now. Text me later.**

She sat down on the edge of her bed. Relieved laughter bubbled out from between her chattering teeth as she shivered in her freezing-cold bedroom. She checked the time; Orion had texted her at 4:22 a.m. It was 6:30-ish now, and Helen wondered if that was late enough. Deciding that it was silly not to try to get in touch with him she sent back:

**R U still in 1 piece?**

She waited a few minutes but didn't get a reply. Helen wanted to fly to the mainland and check on Orion at Milton Academy, but the last thing she needed was to get into trouble for skipping. Finally, she had to let it go and start getting ready for school.

Helen stood up, and as she did, she saw that she was still wearing Orion's jacket. She could already hear him teasing her about that one, even though this time, stealing his jacket hadn't been her fault. She tilted her face down, slowly brushing her cheek and lower lip across the collar. It smelled like him—fresh and a little wild, but still safe somehow.

Shrugging impatiently out of the sleeves and telling herself not to be so foolish, Helen went into the bathroom to take a shower. She took her phone with her, in case Orion tried to contact her, and reminded herself to wash her hair. She even took time to condition it.

As she toweled off and brushed her teeth she thought about how she needed to stop being at the mercy of the Underworld. She had been wandering around aimlessly for . . . well, for a lot longer than real-world time reflected. She owed it to Orion to make a better plan.

At school, the first thing Helen did was track down Cassandra.

"We need to meet this evening," Helen told her.

"Okay," Cassandra replied calmly. "Did something happen last night?"

"There's something I need to tell the whole family. And I'm inviting everyone. Claire, Jason, Matt, Ari," Helen added as she backpedaled down the crowded hallway.

"They're not ready," Cassandra called out in protest, but Helen cut her off.

"Then *make* them ready. I'm done wasting time." Helen didn't give Cassandra a chance to argue.

"You up for a little ancient Greek tonight?" Helen asked Matt and Claire in homeroom.

"Yeah!" Matt responded excitedly, like the über-geek he was. "Do we need to bring anything?"

"Claire?" Helen asked with a shrug, understanding that Matt was asking about what was required for them to become ordained. "You're the one who found the scroll."

"I wouldn't know," she said. "I didn't read the whole damn thing. I'm not actively suicidal."

"I'm sure Cassandra will know. We'll figure it out tonight," Helen said confidently.

"Why the big switch?" Matt asked. "Last time I checked, you were on the fence about us joining the 'study group.'"

"And look how great that's worked out for me," Helen said. "Let's face it, Matt, you and Claire have been helping me prepare for tests since we were in kindergarten. Last night I realized that I've been trying to take this test on my own, and that's probably why I keep failing it."

She would have told Matt about Orion, but she noticed Zach staring at her, and decided to wait until that night to tell everyone together. The bell rang and ended the conversation. Helen left for her first class wondering what Zach had heard, and how much of it he would be able to understand.

Orion didn't contact Helen again until lunch, and when he did all he sent were little word-bursts like *zzz* and *taco* and *H2O*. Helen could relate. She didn't know how long she and Orion had spent in the Underworld the night before, but as usual it had left her tired, hungry, and unbelievably thirsty. At least now there was someone in her life who knew what she was really going through down there. She asked him how he managed to make it out of hell with all his body parts still attached, but his reply was "It'll give me a thumb cramp." After that, Helen figured he was either planning to tell her in person, or that he wanted to avoid a rehash altogether, so she let it go.

That evening Cassandra agreed to ordain Matt, Claire, Jason, and Ariadne in the arena with Castor, Pallas, Helen, and Lucas as witnesses. She recited a few things in ancient Greek while she burned some resinous logs in a bronze disk thingy that Jason told her was called a brazier. Then Castor took out a cage full of small birds that started tweeting away as soon as they were uncovered.

"Wait, what are those for?" Claire said in a voice that edged dangerously close to a screech.

"Just be glad the ceremony didn't call for something big,

like a horse or a cow," Jason said as an aside to Claire. He wasn't kidding.

Cassandra bowed gravely to her father and held out her hands like a platter. Castor took a tiny blade from his belt and laid it on Cassandra's palms. As he did so, she started glowing bright green, purple, and blue with the icy hues of the incalculably old, tri-part aura of the Oracle. Possessed by the Three Fates, Cassandra turned to Matt and offered the blade to him first.

"Cut off the offering's head and throw the carcass in the fire, mortal. You have been found worthy," the three voices chimed with creepy harmonic beauty.

After a moment's hesitation, Matt reached into the cage and grasped a struggling bird in one hand and took the little knife in the other. In the firelight, Helen could see that Matt's face was a mask of disgust, and his hands were shaking terribly as he cut.

Thankfully, he didn't falter, and the sacrifice was over quickly. Ariadne and Jason followed Matt efficiently, like they had done this sort of thing before, which Helen assumed they probably had. Claire was the only one who balked, and Jason had to steady her hands the whole way through it.

When all four had been initiated, the Fates left Cassandra in a rush, and the fire went out as if it had been doused with a bucket of water. Cassandra staggered for a moment, balanced herself on Lucas, and then finally managed to stand up straight.

As they all made their way back into the library, Claire started to cry a little, shaken by what she had done. Helen wanted to run up and comfort her, but Jason pulled Claire close and bent down to whisper something reassuring in her ear. For a moment, Claire hid her face against Jason's chest and let him guide her as she walked along blindly.

At such a show of tenderness, Helen couldn't help but look over toward Lucas, who was walking on the other side of the group. He was as far from her as he could get, and he never once glanced up at any of them. Helen looked away. She felt the weight settling on her chest again, but this time the crushing feeling that she was becoming so familiar with was coupled with something else. Frustration. She had to stop falling apart every time she looked at Lucas, and focus. Too much was at stake.

When they all got back into the library, Matt was still a little green around the edges. Helen started talking immediately to divert any well-meant but probably embarrassing questions about whether or not he needed to puke.

She told everyone about Orion, his fights in the Underworld, and his connection with her mother. There were a few questions about how he got into the Underworld, and more than one disbelieving outburst that anyone but her could survive down there. Helen explained that Orion had the Bough of Aeneas, and it allowed him to travel between the worlds.

"And he's definitely not just a spirit," Helen said with certainty. "He loaned me his jacket, and it was still on me when I woke up in the morning."

"That break-in at the Met?" Castor said urgently to his brother as soon as Helen mentioned the Bough.

"Had to have been. All that was stolen was a piece of ancient metalwork. A *golden leaf*," Pallas replied. "And it was stolen by an unknown woman who walked right in, smashed her hand through plate glass, and walked out. A woman who didn't bother to wear a mask, didn't use anything but her bare hands, and apparently didn't shed one drop of blood."

"Let me guess," Helen said heavily. "My mother, right?"

"But why would Daphne steal the Bough, and then just hand it over to Orion?" Jason asked. "It's such a *powerful* object."

"Orion told me he's descended from Aeneas, so he's the only one that can get it to work," Helen answered.

"Then he's Heir to the House of Rome," Castor said in a slightly awed voice.

"He's actually the Head of *that* House. How'd you know?" Helen asked.

"You haven't read the *Aeneid* yet, have you?" Castor said, without reproof. "Aeneas was Hector's best general in the Trojan War, and one of the few survivors when Troy fell. He was also the founder of Rome, and the founder of the Scion House of Rome."

"*And* he was the son of Aphrodite." Ariadne grinned suggestively at Helen. "So is this Orion guy as hot as . . . Ouch!"

Jason had kicked his tactless twin under the table. When she looked over at him he shook his head at her to make sure she didn't keep going. As it was, Helen felt like her face was trying to burst into flames, though she didn't know exactly why. She hadn't done anything to be ashamed of.

"You said 'that' House a moment ago, almost as if he were connected to more than one," Lucas said without raising his eyes to meet Helen's.

"He is," Helen stammered, looking anywhere but at Lucas. "Orion is Head of the House of Rome, but he's also Heir to the House of Athens."

The room erupted into several conversations at once. Apparently, Orion was the first Scion ever to inherit two Houses, which made sense once Helen thought about it since the Furies worked so hard to keep the Houses separate. As Helen picked snippets of conversation out of the turmoil, it became clear that there was a prophecy concerning Orion, and it wasn't a good one.

"Wait! Hold up," Helen interrupted as she started to hear people talk about Orion in a way that she didn't like. "Will somebody please explain this to me?"

"There's not much to explain," Cassandra said briskly. "There was a prophecy made before the Trojan War by Cassandra of Troy. She foresaw that there would be a Multiple Heir—we think that means a Scion who inherits more than one House. This Multiple Heir, or the 'Vessel Where Royal Scion Blood Has Mixed' to be exact, is one of a trinity of Scions that we think are supposed to replace the three major gods—Zeus, Poseidon, and Hades. The Three Scions are to rule the sky, the oceans, and the land of the dead, if they manage to overthrow the gods and take their places, that is. The existence of the Multiple Heir is a sign that the End Times are coming to a close. The final battle is about to begin."

"He's known as the Tyrant," Lucas said quietly, and all eyes turned to him in the otherwise motionless room. "He's described as being 'born to bitterness' and he's supposed to be capable of 'reducing all mortal cities to rubble.'"

"Like a Scion Antichrist?" Claire whispered to Jason, but in such a hushed room, everyone heard her desperate question.

"No, dear, it's not exactly the same," Pallas said soothingly as he reached out to Claire and briefly squeezed her hand. "In our understanding, this is when we Scions get the chance to fight for our immortality. It's not intended to be the end of the world. That said, if the Final Battle goes badly, most mortals won't survive it. The coming of the Tyrant is one of the signs that it's all beginning."

"The prophecy says that the choices the Tyrant makes leading up to the Final Battle may decide all our fates, god, Scion, and mortal alike. That's really all we know," Castor added.

"Remember, this is just one section of a very long and very complicated prophecy. Most of which is *missing*," Ariadne explained to Helen, Matt, and Claire. "And there's quite a bit of debate about whether what we have was taken down verbatim, or if parts are just poetry, like in the *Iliad*."

"So this prophecy could be nothing more than a bunch of pretty words, but you've already decided that Orion is this Tyrant guy?" Helen asked in disbelief. When no one spoke up to deny it, Helen continued. "That's so unfair."

Lucas shrugged, his jaw clenched, but kept his eyes trained on the floor. The rest of the Delos clan shot each other looks. Helen glanced from face to face, and then threw her hands up in frustration.

"You don't know him," she announced defensively to everyone.

"Neither do you," Lucas countered harshly. He looked up and met her eye to eye for the first time in a week, and the force of his glare knocked the air right out of Helen's lungs. There was a tense moment, and everyone stiffened, watching Lucas. He dropped his gaze.

"But he's not like that," Helen said barely above a whisper, and shook her head. "Orion could never be a tyrant. He's really sweet and, well, *compassionate*."

"So is Hades," Cassandra said, almost as if she were talking about a long-lost friend. "Of all the gods, Hades is the most compassionate. After all, he's said to be the one who's watching with you when your life flashes before your eyes. Maybe it's Orion's compassion that makes him the right replacement for Hades."

Helen didn't have a clue how to argue with that, but she knew in her heart that it was wrong of Cassandra to compare

Orion to Hades, or to call him a tyrant. Orion was so full of vitality and optimism—he'd even made her laugh *in hell*. How could a guy like that ever take the place of Hades and become the Scion version of the god of the dead? It didn't fit.

"None of this is set in stone, Helen," Ariadne said when she saw how upset Helen was getting. "If you say Orion is a good guy, I believe you."

"Orion's been through a lot because of the Furies, and he's willing to risk his life to help me get rid of them, so that no one else suffers like he has. That's not something a bad person would do," Helen insisted.

"Sounds like you know him better than you've said," Lucas said stiffly.

"I've only talked with him twice, but time is different down there. It was like days passed. I'm not saying I know everything about him, because I don't. But I do trust him."

Helen could feel waves of irritation radiating out from Lucas, but he didn't say another word. In a way, she would have preferred it if he had starting shouting at her again. At least then she would know what he was thinking.

"Let's hope you're right, Helen. For all our sakes," Cassandra said pensively. Then she stood up and went to the scrolls, essentially dismissing everyone. Taking the hint, they all filed out of the library and headed toward the kitchen.

Noel had prepared a mini-feast to celebrate the ordination of the first new priests and priestesses of Apollo in probably about a jillion years. Helen had to smile at the spread, appreciating the fact that the Delos family did pretty much everything with food. Fights, celebrations, convalescences—every major turning point and sometimes just Sunday mornings, merited a major sit-down. It made their house a home. Helen knew she was a cousin and that she was a part of this family, but she didn't feel welcome anymore. If she stayed, she knew Lucas would go. Helen hung back, unwilling to enter the kitchen.

"Get in there and eat!" Claire ordered cheerfully, coming up behind her.

"Ha! Do I look that thin?"

"Thinner."

"I can't do it, Claire," Helen said hoarsely.

"He's already left, you know. He just took off. But I get it." Claire shrugged. "It sucks you won't stay and celebrate, but I can't say I blame you. I wouldn't feel comfortable, either."

"This was really brave of you, you know," Helen told her seriously. "It took a lot of guts to join the priesthood."

"I should have done it sooner," Claire said quietly. "I let you wander around down there without any help for too long, and . . . well, *look* at you. I'm so sorry, Lennie."

"That bad, huh?"

"Yeah," Claire said bluntly. "You look really sad."

Helen nodded acceptingly. She knew that her friend wasn't being cruel, just honest. She gave Claire a hug and snuck out the back before anyone else could tell her to come in and sit down. Helen was just about to fly off when she heard someone approaching from the side, moving across the lawn toward her.

"Just tell me you're not letting him call the shots down there," Lucas said in a low voice. He stopped while he was about ten feet away from her, but she still edged away from him. There was something combative about his stance that Helen didn't like.

"I'm not," she said. "Orion isn't what you think. I told you, he just wants to help me."

"Right. I'm sure that's all he wants." Lucas kept his voice flat and cold. "You can fool around with him as much as you want, but you know you can't really be with him, don't you?"

Helen's jaw dropped. "I'm not *with* him," she huffed, nearly breathless with shock.

"The whole point is to keep the Houses *separate*," Lucas said bitterly, ignoring her denial. "No matter how charming this Orion guy is or how many times he lends you his jacket, don't forget that he is the Heir to two Houses and you are the Heir to another. You can never commit yourselves to each other."

"Okay. I'll try to resist *marrying* him at that cute little chapel in hell. You know, the one right next to the festering pit of dead bodies?" Helen seethed. She wanted to scream at him, but forced herself to keep her voice down. "This is ridiculous! Why are you even saying all this to me?"

"Because I don't want you getting sidetracked by some trashy piece of Roman eye candy."

"Don't talk about Orion like that," Helen said in a low, cautioning voice. "He's my friend."

Helen had seen Lucas get angry plenty of times before, but she'd never heard him put anyone down so callously. It was beneath him. He seemed to sense her disappointment and had to look away for a moment, like he was disappointed in himself, too.

"Fine. Have your friend," Lucas said calmly, his face controlled again. "Just remember that this is *your* task. The Oracle said you were the one who has to complete it. Don't get confused. What you're attempting to do in the Underworld is so difficult that the Tyrant might not need to fight you to get you to fail. Maybe all he needs to do is distract you."

Suddenly, Helen was sick of getting lectured by Lucas. He didn't have the right to tell her how to behave, and he certainly didn't have to remind her what her duty was. She took a step closer to him.

"I'm not distracted, and I know this is my task. But I'm not *getting anywhere* on my own. You have no idea what it feels like to be down there!"

"Yes I do," he whispered harshly, almost before Helen had stopped speaking. Then Helen remembered. Lucas had been in the Underworld, too, the night they fell. She was close enough to him now to see his eyes, and they were so dark blue they were nearly black and sunken. His face looked thinner and much too pale, like he hadn't seen the sun in weeks.

"Then you should know it's almost impossible to make it through that place without someone there to help you," Helen said, her voice catching slightly at the thought of how sick he looked. But she didn't back down. "And Orion is helping me—not distracting me. He's taken a lot of risks to be there for me, and I know in my heart he wants to stop the Furies just as much, maybe even *more* than we do. I don't believe he's this evil Tyrant everyone is talking about. And I'm not going to judge my friend based on some ancient prophecy that may or may not be a bunch of poetic nonsense."

"That's very fair of you, Helen, but remember there's always a grain of truth in the prophecies, no matter how much poetry has been frosted on top."

"What's *wrong* with you? You never used to talk like this!" Helen exclaimed, raising her voice to a shout for the first time. She didn't care if the whole household came running and saw them alone together. She took another step toward him, and this time, he was the one to take a step back. "You used to laugh at all that 'inevitable fate' crap!"

"Exactly."

He didn't have to finish his thought aloud. She knew he was talking about the two of them. Tears started to heat up Helen's eyes. Helen knew she couldn't get emotional in front of him or she would truly lose it. Before she could start crying, she jumped into the night sky and flew home.

Dawn was near. The sky began to fade from deepest black to a midnight blue, and soon it would brighten with the color-rush of sunrise. Daphne didn't know if that was a good thing or not. She had stopped shivering hours ago, which meant that she was becoming hypothermic. The sun would warm her, but it would also dehydrate her further. She had used up most of the water in her body generating nonlethal bolts to use on Tantalus, and that was before she had thrown herself into the ocean, over twenty-seven hours ago.

She shifted on the patch of flotsam that she had latched on to after hurling her body out the window. She had fallen well over a hundred feet into the churning waves, and then smashed repeatedly against the rocks. The gash on her forehead had closed, and three of her four broken ribs were mended, but the fourth would heal no further until she ate and drank. Her left wrist was still broken, too, but her ribs had tormented her the most. Every breath, every rise and fall of the water, almost felt like her last.

But not quite.

Daphne raised her head and craned it around painfully to find land. The tide was changing. It would bring her back in closer to shore, like it had the previous morning. She could only hope that Tantalus's guards had either abandoned their search for her up and down the beach, or that she had been swept far enough away that she could allow her pathetic collection of discarded fishing net, Styrofoam, and twigs to drift ashore. She knew she couldn't last forever in the water. Her raft was beginning to sink. Guards or no, Daphne would have to go ashore soon or drown.

She stayed low, glancing at the beach every time the swells allowed. She saw a large man running toward the water's edge, faster than a mortal's eyes could see. He stripped to the waist as he charged through the sand, his blond curls glinting gold in the first flashing rays of the dawn.

Her beloved Ajax, a true son of the sun, had come with the dawn to rescue her.

Daphne tried to cry out with joy and found that she could do no more than wheeze through her swollen throat. Though it made her cracked lips bleed, she smiled at the sight of her beautiful husband, who was just about to take her in his arms and carry her far away from all danger. Just like he always did, before he was murdered.

If Daphne could have cried then, she would have. Ajax was dead, she remembered anew, and it hurt as much as it had that first moment. Why struggle so hard to live when her beloved was waiting for her by the River Styx? She thought of the terrible lie she had told her daughter and for a moment she regretted leaving Helen to believe she was Lucas's cousin, now that she was going to die. Her wounded body relaxed, her eyes still locked on her husband's twin.

The man's thick thighs hit the water, somehow resisting the normal drag. Slipping beneath the surface, she saw him jackknifing through the waves. As her ears became submerged, Daphne heard Hector, son of Pallas, call out to the sea and ask it to support her surrendering body.

Daphne felt her face tilted back toward the air, and took a ragged, choking breath. She hacked at the vile salt water bubbling up out of her lungs, trying and failing to say the words *Myrmidon* and *Helen*. But all she could see was Hector's worried face. At the end of her endurance, Daphne finally lost consciousness.

# SEVEN

Helen didn't see Orion for the next few days. She had to descend each night whether she wanted to or not, but she told him not to waste his time meeting her there until they had a plan.

**I'm better off alone for now,** she texted while Claire drove to school. **After all, the monsters think you're the delicious one.**

**Smart monsters. I am tasty.**

**Says who?**

**Don't believe me? See for yourself.**

**Yeah? How?**

**Bite me.**

Helen burst out laughing. Claire looked over at her as they walked across the parking lot.

"What are you two texting about?" Claire asked.

"Nothing important," Helen mumbled, hiding her phone in her bag.

As she and Orion texted throughout the day, cracking jokes about how exhausting it was to lead a double life, Helen started to get the feeling that he was a little *too* relieved to be given a break.

**You don't have to jump for joy at the thought of NOT seeing me tonight, you know,** she typed testily on her way to lunch.

**NOT happy I won't see you. Happy b/c I need to study. Can't pay my board w/o full scholarship, and my broke ass has no place else to go. Bad grades=homeless Orion.** ☹

Helen stared at his text, her brow pinched together. She could tell he had put the frowny face at the end to make light of what he wrote, but it didn't work. She thought about what it meant to have no place to live but boarding school.

**Where do you go over summer break? Christmas vacation? Do you just stay in the dorms by yourself?**

**Oh boy. Can of worms . . .** he texted after a long pause. **Summers I work. Christmas I volunteer.**

**What about when you were a little kid? When you were only 10?** Helen remembered that he'd told her he'd been on his own since then. **You couldn't have had a job that young.**

**Not in this country. Look, just drop it, okay? Class is starting.**

"Helen?" Matt asked, repressing a smile. "Are you going to text with Orion all through lunch?"

"Sorry," Helen said with a grim expression. She put her phone away, wondering what country Orion meant. She pictured him as a little boy, having to work in some hor-rendous sweatshop that condoned the use of child labor, and started to get angry.

"Did something happen between you two?" Ariadne asked. "You seem upset."

"Nope. Everything's fine," Helen said as cheerfully as she could. Everyone was staring at her like they didn't believe her, but she couldn't tell them what the text was about. It was private.

Orion sent her a "good luck in the Underworld" text that night, but he sent it so late that Helen didn't get it until the next morning. It was obvious he was dodging her—probably because he didn't want to talk about his childhood. Helen decided to let it go until he trusted her better. This was not something she could rush, but she was surprised to find that she didn't mind waiting. So what if she had to work a bit harder to gain his confidence? He was worth the extra effort.

"Is that Orion?" Claire asked, her eyes narrowing when Helen jumped to pull out her vibrating phone.

"He said he found something," Helen said, ignoring Claire's disquiet.

Her best friend shot her a concerned look, and Helen hoped Claire would let it go. She didn't have the energy to deal with a "Do you like this boy, or *like* this boy?" cross-examination by her best friend, especially not when so much was at stake.

"What is it?" Cassandra asked.

"A scroll from the private diary of Marc Antony that talks a lot about the afterlife. He wants to know if you want him to scan and email it to you."

Cassandra rubbed her eyes. They had been locked in the Delos library every day after school for three nights in a row, looking for some kind of clue that could lead them to a plan. So far nothing had come up.

"Wait, Marc Antony? As in Antony and *Cleopatra*?" Ariadne asked with stars in her eyes. "She was such a badass."

Helen grinned in agreement and typed the question to Orion. She paused to read his response. "Yup, same Roman. I guess he's a relative on his mother's cousin's side. It looks really convoluted, but Orion's mother was related to both Marc Antony and Julius Caesar if you go back far enough."

"Yeah, but go back far enough and even you and me could be related, Len," Claire said wryly. She fluffed her inky black hair to point out how genetically different she and blonde Helen were.

"Huh. I've never thought of it like that, but you're probably right, Gig," Helen mused. A disturbing idea started to bud in her mind, but Cassandra interrupted Helen's half-formed thought.

"Helen, tell Orion not to bother. Marc Antony was trying to become Pharaoh, so he would only have been interested in the Egyptian afterlife." Cassandra's mounting frustration was obvious.

Helen began to type in Cassandra's reply, adding the

"thank-you" that Cassandra so glaringly omitted.

"Wait a sec, Len," Matt said before she could send it. "Just because Orion's information is from a different culture doesn't make it incorrect."

"I agree with Matt," Jason said, perking up from his study stupor. "The Egyptians were obsessed with the afterlife. It's possible they knew more about the Underworld than the Greeks did. They could have exactly the information Helen needs to navigate down there. We could overlook it if we're biased to favor the Greeks."

"Sure, it's possible that the Egyptians had a three-dimensional map of the Underworld complete with magic passwords!" Cassandra responded sarcastically as her frustration boiled over. "But Marc Antony was a *Roman* invader. An Egyptian priest initiated to the level of knowledge that Helen needs would have died before telling a *conqueror* even one of the sacred secrets of the Underworld!"

Everyone knew that Cassandra was reminding them that the same level of devotion was expected from the newly ordained priests and priestesses of Apollo. Jason and Ariadne had been raised to deal with these kinds of expectations. Matt and Claire paused to think about it. Helen watched her two oldest friends give each other worried looks. When they both seemed to steel themselves, she couldn't help but feel proud.

Helen glanced around the room, thinking to herself how freaking awesome her friends were, when her eyes landed on Jason. He was looking at Claire like she had just canceled

Christmas. When he saw that Helen was watching him, he looked away quickly, but he still looked pale to Helen.

"What we really need are the Lost Prophecies." Cassandra started pacing.

"Wouldn't that make them the 'Found' Prophecies?" Matt quipped.

"Okay, I'll bite," Claire said, ignoring the bad pun. "What are the Lost Prophecies?"

"It's a mystery," Jason answered with a shake of his head. "They're supposed to be a collection of the prophecies that Cassandra of Troy made right before and during the ten years of the Trojan War. But no one knows what's in them."

"That's big. How'd they get lost?" Claire asked.

"Cassandra of Troy was cursed by Apollo to always prophesy with perfect clarity—not easy by the way—but to never be believed," Cassandra said distractedly.

Helen remembered the story, even though it was just a small part of the *Iliad*. Apollo fell in love with Cassandra of Troy right before the war. When she told him that she wanted to remain a virgin and rejected his advances, he cursed her. A dickhead move if ever there was one.

"Apollo's curse made everyone think Cassandra was crazy. The priests still kept records of what she foresaw during the war, but they didn't think they were very important. Most of them got misplaced or only parts of them survived," Ariadne said with downcast eyes as if her ancestors embarrassed her. "That's why all the prophecies about the Tyrant are so spotty. No modern Scion has been able to find them all."

"What a waste," Matt said darkly. "I wonder how many times the gods have gotten away with something criminal like that, just because they *could*."

Ariadne's head snapped around at Matt's sharp tone. She was surprised to hear him speak so passionately, but Helen had seen this side of Matt before. He had always hated bullies. He'd had a thing about tough guys throwing their weight around for as long as Helen could remember. It was one of the main reasons he wanted to be lawyer. Matt thought powerful people should protect the weak, not beat up on them, and Helen could see the same childhood anger against injustice seething in Matt again at the thought of Apollo cursing a young girl because she wouldn't have sex with him.

Helen had to admit that Matt had a point. Most of the time, the gods seemed like big, supernatural bullies. Helen wondered why humans had ever worshiped them at all. As she puzzled over this, her phone buzzed again.

"Orion says he figured the diary was a long shot because it's really stupid," Helen read aloud. His next text made her burst out laughing. "He just called Marc Antony a flaming twit."

"Aw, really? That's too bad," Ariadne said, flapping her incredibly long eyelashes in disappointment. "Antony always seemed so romantic on paper."

"Shakespeare can make anyone look good," Matt said, smiling to see that Ariadne's budding crush on a dead guy had been quashed. He turned to Helen. "You know, it's really nice to see you laugh, Lennie."

"Well, it *is* Friday night. I figured, what the heck?" Helen joked, but no one laughed. Everyone but Cassandra was staring at her expectantly. "What?" she finally demanded when the silence dragged on too long.

"Nothing," Claire answered, slightly annoyed. She stood and stretched, signaling that the night was over as far as she was concerned. Taking her cue, Cassandra left the room without even saying good-bye. Everyone else stood and started to gather their things.

"Do you want to stay and watch a movie?" Jason asked Claire hopefully. He looked around to include everyone in his invitation. "It *is* Friday."

Matt glanced over at Ariadne. She smiled and encouraged him to stay, and then everyone looked at Helen. She didn't want to go home alone, but she knew she couldn't bear to sit in a dark room with two hormonally fraught not-quite couples.

"I'll be asleep before the popcorn is out of the microwave," Helen lied, and forced a laugh. "You guys have fun, but I think I should rest."

No one argued with her or tried to convince her to stay. As Helen walked outside, she wondered if they didn't put up a bigger fight because they knew she needed to sleep, or because they didn't want her around. She couldn't blame them if they wanted her gone— no one likes a fifth wheel, and a heartbroken fifth wheel is even worse.

Taking in a lungful of the crisp autumn air, she turned

her face to the clear night sky with the intention of taking flight. Her eyes were drawn to the three bright stars of Orion's Belt, and she smiled at the constellation, thinking, "Hey, dude" in her mind.

She had the sudden urge to walk home instead of fly. It was far, nearly the entire length of the island from 'Sconset to her house, but these days she was used to spending hours wandering around in the dark. Helen stuffed her fists into her pockets and started trudging down the road without a second thought. Glancing at the sky, she realized that what she really wanted was to be with Orion, even if *this* Orion was just a bunch of chilly stars. She missed him.

Helen was halfway down Milestone Road, wondering if anyone would think she was crazy if they caught her out walking clear across the dark interior of the island in the middle of the night, when her phone buzzed. The number was blocked. For a moment she wondered if it was Orion. She answered quickly, hoping it was him. When she heard Hector's voice on the other end she was so startled that she could barely stammer out a greeting.

"Helen? Shut up and listen to me," Hector interrupted with his usual directness. "Where are you?"

"Well, I'm walking home right now. Why, what's up?" she asked, more curious than offended by his abrupt tone.

"Walking? From where?"

"Your house. I mean, your old house." She bit her lower lip, hoping she hadn't said something stupid.

"Why aren't you *flying*?" He was practically shouting at her.

"Because I wanted to take a . . . Wait, what the hell is going on?"

Hector quickly explained that Daphne had confronted Tantalus and then been injured and lost at sea for over a day. He told her how it had taken Daphne three days to recover enough to be able to tell Hector about the Myrmidon parked outside Helen's front door.

Helen knew she should have been worried about her mother, but she heard the word *mur-ma-don* and had to stop Hector to ask what that was.

"Did you even read the *Iliad*? You didn't, did you?" Hector admonished, his voice rising again. Helen could picture Hector's face turning purple with frustration.

"Of course I read it!" she insisted.

Hector cussed loudly and then explained as calmly as he could that the Myrmidons were the elite warriors that fought with Achilles during the Trojan War, and Helen put it together. She was familiar with Achilles' special squad of nightmare soldiers; she had just never heard the word pronounced properly before. Myrmidons weren't human, but *ants* transformed into men by Zeus.

"The creepy guy that attacked us at my track meet!" Helen exclaimed, covering her mouth with a hand. She finally understood why the leader of the group, the *captain* Helen suddenly realized, had bothered her so much— because he was really an *it*. "I thought soldier ants were all female," Helen added, confused.

"Yeah, and I thought ants looked like ants and humans looked like humans," Hector said drily. "Don't be fooled, Helen. That thing isn't a man, and it definitely doesn't have the same feelings we do. Not to mention the fact that it's enormously strong and it has thousands of years of battle experience."

Helen thought about a program she'd seen on TV about ants. They could march for days, lift loads hundreds of times their weight, and some of them were unbelievably aggressive.

Looking up and down the dark, cold road, Helen suddenly wished that Hector was with her, even if he was a grouchy pain in the ass 90 percent of the time. She also wished she had paid better attention to him when he was punching her in the face. At least then she'd know how to fight.

"So what do I do?" Helen asked as she tried to look everywhere at once.

"Get airborne. It can't fly. You're usually safer in the air, Helen. Try to remember that from now on, okay?" he coached. "Go back to the family and tell them what I told you. Then *stay* there with Ariadne. She'll keep you safe. Lucas and Jason will find the nest, and my father and uncle will probably have to go to New York to bring this issue before the Hundred. After that, Cassandra will make the decisions. You should be fine."

Like the great general he was always meant to be, Hector could plan every moment of a confrontation. Still, Helen didn't think he sounded very convincing when he promised her safety.

"You're really afraid of this Myrmidon, aren't you?" Helen asked as she got airborne.

The thought that Hector was afraid of anything frightened Helen more than the empty road in front of her. She heard him sigh heavily.

"Myrmidons have been used as contract killers for Scions for thousands of years. Apart from the House of Rome, which has its own loophole for kin-killing, if a Scion wants to kill a relative without becoming Outcast, he or she goes to a Myrmidon. Of course, this isn't something we like to talk about. Myrmidons are a part of our world, and not all of them are dishonorable killers. But some are. They're physically stronger than we are, and they don't have the Furies to worry about. Using one to spy on your own family is a red flag that someone is about to get assassinated, and it gives my father and uncle the right to call for a formal, closed meeting of the Hundred. Something called a Conclave."

"But that's good, right?" Helen asked nervously. "Castor and Pallas can call for this Conclave thingy and get rid of it, right?"

"*If* they can prove you're Ajax's daughter and part of the family, the Hundred would make Tantalus get rid of the Myrmidon. If they can't, well, then you're just a member of the House of Atreus to the Hundred, and in their minds you're a target. But I don't know what they'll do. I'm not there, am I?" He sounded more sorry than bitter, like he felt he needed to apologize to Helen for leaving her alone when she was in danger, which was totally insane. He was in *exile*. Before she could argue, Hector continued in a hassled voice. "Just do exactly what I tell you, and then I'll be less afraid. All right?"

"All right," she promised, already feeling guilty because she knew she wasn't going to keep that promise.

She and Hector spoke briefly about Daphne, although he wouldn't tell her where they were. He assured Helen that her mother was going to make a full recovery and then promised to get in touch again when he could.

After disconnecting the call, Helen flew to her side of the island to look for the "nest" on her own. She wanted to at least locate it and make sure that her dad was okay. Then she wanted to be the one to decide if it was dangerous or not. Helen wasn't five. She was competent enough to scout out the situation and decide for herself if it was worth raising the alarm. Besides, she wasn't exactly helpless. She had the cestus to keep her from harm and her lightning to knock it out if it got feisty. If that Ant-man came anywhere near her or Jerry, she'd toast it first and think up an excuse to tell her dad later.

Scouring the neighborhood, Helen pictured the nest as a big, webby structure, and assumed it would stick out easily. Nothing caught her eye. She was just about to give up when she noticed that halfway up the side of her neighbor's house and partly obscured behind a gigantic rhododendron bush, there seemed to be a tiny bulge, like the wall was ever so slightly ballooning out.

It was so subtle Helen knew that her mortal neighbors wouldn't be able to see the difference. The nest was perfectly camouflaged to look exactly like a large patch of shingle siding on the house, right down to the texture and color. The Myrmidon had even masked the bulge it made by spacing the fake shingling to create an optical illusion.

Helen stared at the nest for a few moments, her pulse pounding in her ears, waiting to see if it moved. When she didn't hear even the slight sound of an occupant breathing inside the slim pocket, she decided it was safe to check it out. She blew on her sweaty palms to dry them, told herself to stop being a baby, and soared close, until she was right alongside it. The nest was made out of some kind of cement-like material that was designed with lots of little peepholes. As she suspected, most of those holes faced her house directly. From that angle, she could even see part of the way inside her bedroom.

The hairs on the back of her neck were starting to prickle with the thought of some giant bug watching her undress, when she heard a chittering noise below her.

Helen soared feetfirst to a safer height. Like an arrow flying backward, she gained altitude while keeping her eyes glued to ground, to see where the noise had come from. Staring up at her from her neighbor's lawn was the same skeletal face and red, bulging eyes she had seen in the battle in the woods. Its head twitched blindingly fast, like it swiveled atop a stalk instead of on a neck, and that slight but startling motion was enough to break Helen's nerve. She flew across the island and landed at the Delos compound a moment later.

Walking quickly to the dark front door, Helen realized how late it was. Everyone had gone to sleep. She looked in the silent windows and shifted from foot to foot, feeling strange about ringing the bell and waking up the whole house at two o'clock in the morning. After all, she wasn't in any immediate danger. From what Hector had said, the Myrmidon had been watching her for weeks and it hadn't attacked yet. Helen wondered if she shouldn't just go home, deal with the nest on her own, and tell her cousins about it in the morning.

She heard a thud behind her and spun around, her heart in her throat.

"What are you doing out here?" Lucas asked in a harsh whisper, adjusting the pull of gravity on his body as he transitioned states. He immediately began walking toward her forcefully. His face changed into a frozen mask of surprise as he registered Helen's anxious state. From the way she was glancing around, wringing her hands, he could tell it had nothing to do with him. "What happened?" he demanded.

"I . . ." she began breathlessly, then broke off when a disturbing thought distracted her. "Are you just getting home *now*? Where were you?"

"I was out," he said tersely. Lucas took a few more steps toward her until he was close enough that she had to tilt her head up to look at him, but she refused to give him any ground. She was done with being afraid of him. "Now answer *my* question. What happened to you?"

"Hector called. Daphne learned that Tantalus sent a Myrmidon to watch me. The thing just caught me snooping around its nest, like, two seconds ago."

Without warning, Lucas reached out and grabbed Helen by the waist, and threw her straight up into the air. She released herself from gravity as a reflex, and on the momentum of Lucas's toss, she soared twenty, then thirty, then forty feet up. Lucas rocketed past, catching her by the hand. He pulled her behind him at an unbelievable speed. Helen's ears popped with the pressure of the mini-sonic boom that she and Lucas created.

"Where's the nest? Near my house?" he yelled frantically over the rushing wind.

"At my neighbor's. Lucas, stop!" Helen was frightened, not of him, but that they were moving so fast. He slowed and faced her, but he didn't stop entirely or let go of her hand. Flying in close, he looked her directly in the eye, searching for a lie.

"Did it sting you?"

"No."

"Did Hector tell you to go look for its nest on your own?" His words came so quickly she barely had time to process what he was saying.

Helen's head hurt and her vision swam. They were up so high the air was dangerously thin. Not even demigods could survive space, and Lucas had brought Helen right to the edge.

"Hector said not to go near it . . . but I wanted to see for myself before I made everyone panic. Lucas, we have to get lower!" she pleaded.

Lucas looked down at Helen's chest and saw it bellowing in and out as she struggled for oxygen. He drifted nearer, and she felt him share the slip of air he had wrapped around himself with her. A gust of oxygen brushed gently past her face. She inhaled, and instantly felt better.

"We can call more breathable air to ourselves, but you need to relax first," Lucas said. He sounded like himself again.

"How high are we?" She stared at him, shocked that he was being kind to her. She didn't know what else to say.

"Look down, Helen."

Overwhelmed, she followed his gaze to the view beneath them.

For a moment, she and Lucas floated weightless above the slowly spinning Earth, just looking at it. Black sky edged the white-and-blue haze of atmosphere swaddling the planet. The silence and the bleakness of space only served to emphasize how precious, how miraculous their little island of life truly was.

It was the most beautiful thing Helen had ever seen, but she couldn't fully enjoy it. If ever she came this high again, she knew would always recall that Lucas had brought her here *first*. Now this, too, was something they shared. She was so confused she wanted to cry. Entirely by chance, Lucas had claimed yet another piece of real estate in her mind, and *he* was the one who had ordered *her* to stay away from him.

"Why bother to show me this? Or teach me anything at all?" Helen said, choking on the words. "You hate me."

"I never said that." His voice held no emotion.

"We should go down," she said, forcing her eyes away from his face. This wasn't fair. She couldn't let him toy with her like this.

Lucas nodded and gripped Helen's hand tightly. She tried to pull it away but Lucas resisted.

"Don't, Helen," he said. "I know you don't want to touch me, but you could still pass out up here."

Helen wanted to scream that he couldn't be more wrong. Pretty much the *only* thing she wanted was to touch him, and it was eating her up inside. At that moment, she imagined herself drifting closer and brushing against him until she could feel his body heat leaking out through the gaps in his clothes. She pictured how the scent of him would hit her in a wave, riding the tide of that heat. She knew thoughts like that shouldn't even cross her mind, but they did. Right or wrong, whether she was allowed to act on it or not, it was what she truly wanted.

What she didn't want was to be pushed and pulled in so many different directions that she didn't know how to behave. She didn't even know who she was supposed to *be* around him anymore. She resented him for it, but worse, she was disappointed in herself for wanting him even after he had treated her so badly.

Ashamed of her own thoughts, Helen didn't allow herself to look at Lucas as they flew to a lower altitude. When she could breathe easily outside his slip of air, Helen noticed that they were over some dark part of the continent. She searched for the familiar glowing nets that she recognized as Boston, Manhattan, and DC at night, and couldn't believe it when she found them. By Helen's estimation they were *hundreds* of miles away.

"How fast are we?" she asked Lucas in awe.

"Well, I haven't been able to beat light . . . yet," he said with a mischievous glint in his eyes. Helen turned her head and stared at him, amazed that he was acting like himself again. This felt right. This was the Lucas she knew. He smiled for a moment, then seemed to stop himself. Still staring at her, his lips slowly slackened and dropped.

Helen felt like she was falling toward him. She realized that Lucas was an emotional black hole for her. If she was anywhere near him, her heart simply *couldn't* get away. Helen dropped Lucas's hand and drifted ahead of him. She needed a moment to get a hold of herself.

She turned her attention back to the situation, forcing herself to focus and take control. She had to keep her mind busy or she was lost.

"I gather from both your reactions that this Myrmidon is a really big problem," she said.

"Yeah, it's big, Helen. Myrmidons are faster and stronger than Scions, but worse than that, they don't feel emotions like we do. Having one spying on you is a very big deal. And I never even knew it was there." He sighed, like this was somehow his fault.

"But how could you have possibly known? We haven't been anywhere near each other in over a week."

"Come on," he said. Lucas began drifting toward the East Coast, brushing off Helen's last comment. "We need to get back and tell the family."

She nodded and took the lead. They didn't hold hands on the way down, but Helen could still feel Lucas near to her, disturbingly warm and solid. She kept telling herself that she was only imagining that they were in sync, but her actions proved her wrong. They touched down in unison, transitioned, and continued on into the house without ever breaking stride with each other.

Lucas walked in the front door loudly, flicked on the lights in the hallway, and began calling out to the rest of the family. Moments later, everyone was in the kitchen, and Helen was repeating everything that had happened to her that night, minus the bit about visiting the outer atmosphere with Lucas.

"This is cause for a Conclave," Castor said to his brother. "Bringing a Myrmidon into the equation could be considered an act of war within the House."

"Did you get a good look at the Myrmidon's face?" Cassandra asked. Helen nodded and tried not to shudder at the thought of how his head had flicked around like something alien.

"It had red eyes," Helen answered squeamishly.

"Did Hector happen to mention the Myrmidon's name?" Pallas asked Helen quietly. "It would help if we knew which one we're dealing with."

"No. But next time he calls, I can ask," Helen replied gently, aware that even saying Hector's name upset Pallas. Helen could tell that Pallas wished for nothing more than to be able to talk to his son directly. It wasn't right that Hector couldn't be there, she thought angrily. They needed him.

Cassandra led everyone into the library. She went directly to a book that was so fragile Castor and Pallas had dismantled it and put each individual page in a separate plastic covering. Helen approached Cassandra as she gently leafed through the stack of pages, and noticed that the book was really old—like King Arthur old.

"This is a codex from the time of the Crusades," Cassandra said, holding up a painted page of a knight in black armor. Like the Myrmidon, he had bulging red eyes and a skeletal face.

"It looks a lot like him," Helen said as she peered at the page. It was a beautiful work of art, but it was still a painting, not a photo. Helen shrugged. "I can't tell for sure from this. Do all Myrmidons look about the same?"

"No, some of them had black, faceted eyes, and some had slightly red skin. A few were rumored to have had antennae that they hid under their helmets," Castor answered pensively. "Helen, are you sure the one you saw had *red eyes*?"

"Oh, yeah, no doubt about that," Helen said positively.

"They were really shiny, too."

"Automedon," Pallas said, looking at Castor. For the first time Helen could remember, Castor used an English curse word, and a foul one at that, as he nodded in agreement with his brother.

"Makes sense," Cassandra said. "No Scion ever claimed to have killed him."

"Because no one could." Lucas looked over at Helen, shaking his head slowly as if he couldn't believe this was happening. "He's immortal."

"Okay, see, *that* I don't get," Helen said nervously. She was looking for a flaw, something logical that would make the situation seem a little less dire. "If Myrmidons are immortal, then why isn't the world crawling with them?"

"Oh, they can be killed in battle. And most of them were killed at some point in history. But, see, that's sort of the catch with Automedon," Ariadne said with wide, apologetic eyes. "There are stories of soldiers literally cutting Automedon's head off, and he just picked it up, put it back on, and kept fighting."

"You've got to be kidding me," Helen said with a raised eyebrow. "How can that even be possible? He's not a god. Wait, is he a god?" she asked Ariadne in a hurried aside, in case she had missed something.

"No, he's not a god," Cassandra answered for her. "But he might have shared blood with one. This is just my guess, but if Automedon became blood brothers with one of the immortals thousands of years ago, *before* they were all locked away on Olympus, then Automedon *can't* be killed, not even in battle."

"Blood brothers? Are you serious?" Helen asked dubiously. She pictured two kids in a tree house pricking their fingers with a safety pin.

"To Scions, becoming blood brothers is a sacred rite, and it's pretty hard to do outside of combat," Jason said with a smile, seeming to understand Helen's misinterpretation. "You have to be willing to die for someone, and that person has to be willing to die for you. Then you have to exchange blood while you are in the process of saving each other's lives."

Helen's eyes darted over to Lucas. She couldn't help but think of how they had broken out of the Furies' curse by nearly dying for each other. From the look in Lucas's eyes, Helen knew he was thinking exactly the same thing. They hadn't exchanged blood the night they fell, but they had both saved each other's lives and that had bound them together forever.

"You can't make it happen or plan it. It's something that comes out of an extreme situation," Lucas said directly to Helen. "And if the two brothers live, sometimes they share a few of each other's Scion powers. Now imagine doing that with a god. Theoretically, it could make you immortal."

"But you don't know *for sure* if that's the case with Automedon," Helen challenged. "Cassandra said she was just guessing."

"Yeah, but Cassandra's guesses are usually pretty close to

the mark," he snapped, his temper rising quickly.

"You've been blowing this out of proportion since the second I told you! The more I think about it, the more I doubt I'm in any real danger," she continued defensively.

Lucas's face blanched with anger.

"Enough!" Noel yelled from the doorway. "Lucas, go upstairs and go to bed." Lucas whirled around to face his mother, but Noel didn't give him the chance to start with her. "I'm sick to death of watching the two of you fight! You're both so tired you're not even making sense anymore. Helen, go upstairs with Ariadne. You're sleeping over."

"I can't leave my father alone with that *thing* practically next door," Helen said, slumping down on the edge of Castor's desk. Noel was right. All the endless running around, coupled with the emotional minefield she had to navigate whenever Lucas was near, suddenly hit her like a brick. She was *exhausted*.

"Trust me, if you're here, then that creature won't be far away. I know it's going to be hard for you to accept this, but both your father and Kate will be safer if you keep your distance from now on." Noel said it as kindly as she could, but her words were still harsh. "Lucas, I want you to go with your father and uncle to Conclave. I think it would be best for you to spend a little time in New York."

"Noel! He's not eighteen yet," Castor began to argue.

"But he is Heir to the House of Thebes, Caz," Pallas countered gently. "Creon is dead. After Tantalus, you're next in line. That makes your eldest the Heir. Lucas has every right to attend Conclave before he comes of age."

"Tantalus could have another child," Castor said impatiently.

"The Outcast, marked for death, will bear no more children," Cassandra chanted in multiple voices from the corner of the room.

The sound made Helen's spine recoil and bunch up, like someone had poured cold water down her back. As one, the room turned to see the eerie aura of the Oracle flicker across Cassandra's face and purple, blue, and green lights trace like spirits along the edges of her body. Her usually pretty face was puckered like an old woman's.

"Lucas, son of the sun, has always been the intended Heir to the House of Thebes. So it has come to pass." The Oracle cackled, and her body convulsed violently.

The light suddenly went out and Cassandra shrank. She glanced around with terrified eyes and clasped her arms around her body, cowering inside her clothes. Helen wanted to comfort Cassandra, but there was a chill around her that Helen couldn't ignore. She just couldn't force herself to take a step closer to the frightened girl.

"Now, all of you, go to bed," Noel said in a shaky voice, breaking the silence.

She pushed everyone toward the door and corralled the small herd toward the stairs, leaving Cassandra in the library by herself. Helen dragged herself upstairs and collapsed onto the guest bed without undressing or even pulling the covers down first.

When she woke the next morning she was covered in dried slime. Helen had fallen asleep in such a foul mood that when she got to the Underworld, she'd found herself chest deep in a prehistoric swamp. It wasn't the quicksand pit, which was an enormous relief, but it still *stank*. It took every ounce of effort to keep the muddy water out her mouth as she waded through it, always just one wrong footfall away from drowning. After a night of half panic, Helen awoke to find herself even more tired than she had been the day before.

She hauled herself out of bed and noticed that her shirt was nearly torn off, there were odd sticks and dead leaves tangled in her hair, and she'd lost a shoe. Of course, she ran into Lucas on her way to the bathroom. He stared at her for a moment, his eyes ticking up and down her bedraggled frame while the rest of his body remained rigid.

"What? You going to yell at me again?" Helen challenged, too tired to be careful.

"No." His voice broke. "I'm done fighting with you. It obviously isn't helping."

"Then *what*?"

"I can't do this," he said, more to himself than Helen. "My father was wrong."

Her bleary brain was still processing his words when he opened the nearest window and jumped out of it.

Helen watched him fly away, too tired to be surprised. She continued on to the bathroom, sprinkling nastiness all over the floor with every step. She looked down at the mess she was making and thought about how much worse it would get when she undressed. The only solution her partially paralyzed thought process came up with was to step into the shower, still fully clothed. As she rubbed a lemony-smelling bar of soap over her torn shirt she started to laugh. It was an unstable laugh, the kind that threatens to tip into a sob.

Ariadne knocked on the door. Helen stuffed a hand over her mouth, but it was too late. Ariadne took Helen's silence as a signal that something bad was happening, and barged into the bathroom.

"Helen! Are you . . . Oh, wow." Ariadne's tone changed from concerned to dumbstruck in a second. She saw Helen was still completely dressed through the glass door of the shower. "Um, you know you forgot a step, right?"

Helen burst out laughing again. The situation was so ridiculous that there was nothing to do *but* laugh.

"Are you still wearing a *shoe*?" Ariadne choked out.

"I woke . . . up . . . with only one on!" Helen lifted up her bare foot and pointed at it. Both of the girls laughed hysterically at Helen's wiggling toes.

Ariadne helped Helen clean up, and together they dragged the dirty bedding and soggy clothes to the washroom. By the time they made it down for breakfast, everyone else was nearly finished.

"Where's Lucas?" Noel asked, craning her head anxiously to look behind Helen.

"Jumped out a window," Helen answered. She got a mug and poured herself some coffee. Lifting her head, she noticed that everyone was staring at her. "I'm not kidding. We bumped into each other in the hallway and when he saw me, he literally jumped out a window. Anyone want coffee?"

"Did he say where he was going?" Jason asked with obvious concern.

"Nope," she said evenly.

Helen's hands were shaking, but she stirred some cream into her mug and took a drink, anyway. In the state she was in, she figured it might actually steady her. She felt like her whole body was hot and cold at the same time.

"Helen? Are you feeling ill?" Noel asked with narrowed eyes.

Helen shook her head uncertainly. It was impossible for a Scion to come down with a mortal sickness, yet when she ran a hand across her forehead, it came back wet with sweat. Still staring at her hand, Helen heard an electric car cruise quietly up to the house and stop.

"Lennie! Get your butt out here and help us with these books!" Claire yelled from the driveway.

Helen turned to look out the window behind her and saw Claire and Matt getting out of Claire's car. Grateful for the interruption, Helen scurried out from under Noel's piercing look to help them.

"We hear you have an ant problem," Claire said through a grin, and started stacking books on Helen's outstretched arms.

"Because that's exactly what I need, right?" Helen laughed ruefully. "More problems."

"Don't worry, Len. We'll split up into groups and tackle this in shifts. We'll figure it out." Matt sounded so certain. He shouldered a backpack full of books, closed the trunk, and put an arm over Helen's shoulders as they walked together toward the house. "Claire and I didn't join PETA's most wanted list for nothing, you know."

As Helen, Claire, and Matt were just about to go back inside, they heard Castor and Pallas saying their good-byes and decided to let the Delos family have a moment alone. From what Helen could gather, Conclave was a big deal, like a Supreme Court trial and an international summit meeting combined. Once it started, no one was allowed to leave until a course of action was decided upon, so sometimes these meetings could take weeks.

Helen tried not to listen in too much while they hugged and said their good-byes, but she couldn't help herself when she overheard Castor privately pulling Noel aside to ask if Lucas was coming or not.

"I don't know where he went. He could be in Tibet by now," Noel replied, sounding like she was on her last nerve. "I was hoping he'd go with you to New York for a few weeks. Get him out of here and give him a chance to . . ."

"A chance to what?" Castor asked sadly when Noel ran out of things to say. "Just leave him be."

"I have left him be, and it's obviously not helping!" Noel said. "He's so angry all the time now, Caz, and I think it's getting worse—not better."

"I know. He's changed, Noel, and I think we're going to

have to accept that it might be permanent. I was hoping he'd just hate *me*, but it seems like he hates the whole world," Castor said heavily. "And I honestly don't blame him. Could you imagine if someone had separated us like I separated them?"

"You had no choice. They're cousins. That's not something that's going to change," Noel said emphatically. "Still, if your father did to us what you did to Lucas—"

"I don't know what I would have done to him," Castor said as if he couldn't even think about it. Helen heard them kiss and immediately switched off her Scion hearing.

"Let's go to the library and get to work!" she suggested loudly to Claire and Matt, and started walking around the house to use another entrance. Her mind was racing.

Had Castor really separated her and Lucas, and if so, how? Helen thought back over the outburst at dinner, and realized that Lucas had been just as angry with Castor as he was with her—maybe more. Had Lucas hurt her because his father had *ordered* him to?

"Len? You know I love you, but you really need to stop spacing," Claire said with a cute grimace. Helen looked around and realized that she had paused in the middle of the hallway on the way to the library, like her legs had just quit or something.

"Sorry!" she said, and rushed to keep up with her friends.

Lucas circled the Getty Museum, a gleaming white building elegantly perched on top of one of Los Angeles's more scruffy hills. The white stone structure capping the dry, rocky hill was strikingly similar to the Parthenon. The Parthenon was originally a treasury, so Lucas felt it was fitting that he was coming to the Getty to make a withdrawal of coins.

He was searching for a spot that would hide him for the one moment of his landing when he would have to slow down enough that he could be seen. Lucas moved in faster than a human could see, settling too lightly on the ground to leave any footprints. The instant he touched down, Lucas half ran, half flew to the door so quickly that all a security camera picked up would be a faint blur. Stopping right next to the door, Lucas froze and disappeared.

In the last few weeks, he had learned that if he didn't move around too much he could scatter light so that the surface of his body looked like whatever was *behind* it. In the beginning, before he had perfected his invisibility cloak, it was still possible for a Scion to make out a faint fracture between the picture he created and his surroundings. Luckily, only one Scion had ever noticed it, and that had been Lucas's own damn fault.

After a half an hour wait, a maintenance man finally came out the door with a rake in one hand and his early morning thermos of coffee in the other. Lucas simply slipped around him and walked in without tripping a single alarm. He could have ripped the door off its hinges, but he didn't want to attract too much attention to himself. Lucas didn't know whether his plan would work, but he didn't want his family to get suspicious and interfere.

He'd always been taught that museums were sacred places because they housed so many Scion relics, but he never imagined that one day he'd be pushed to a point where he'd consider breaking into one. Now he was desperate. He had to do something to help Helen.

His father had been wrong. All it took was one look at Helen—her clothes torn and covered in that black mud from the Underworld—and Lucas knew for sure that *he* wasn't Helen's problem. He had done as his father had ordered, but she was still suffering. Staying away from her was not enough.

Lucas knew Helen was strong, and he trusted her to make good decisions even when he disagreed with her. She had insisted that Orion was helping her, so no matter how much it ate him up inside to think of the two of them alone together, Lucas had stepped back.

He'd promised himself after the night Pandora died as he watched the dawn break from Helen's widow's walk that he would suffer anything as long as Helen moved on and lived a full and meaningful life. He'd turned himself into something twisted in an attempt to break things off between them. Yet that morning she'd looked sicker than she had before Lucas had pushed her away.

Whatever was happening to her went far beyond her feelings about their doomed relationship.

Lucas moved so quickly down the hallways of the museum that his face couldn't be recorded. Even though his surroundings changed by the nanosecond, Lucas knew where he was going. There were plenty of signs to point him in the right direction. THE TREASURES OF ANCIENT GREECE was a huge crowd pleaser, and this famous exhibit of recently unearthed gold artifacts had already traveled all over the world. This month it was the Getty's turn, and they had plastered the place with bright silk banners in celebration.

They'd also put a lot of pictures of the artifacts online. In true Southern California style, the smaller, less impressive pieces of gold that had been left out of other museums' promotional pictures were clumped together in huge, sparkling group shots. Los Angeles just loved to get as much dazzle as it could into one frame, and after over two weeks of flying all over the world, searching every museum, that was how Lucas had finally found what he was looking for. On the internet.

Compared to the other pieces in the collection, the small handful of gold coins was hardly worth displaying. He had to go to one of the back cases to find them, but when he did, he didn't waste any time. As far as he knew these three coins—each with a poppy flower engraved on one side— were the last remaining obols that had been forged in honor of Morpheus, the god of dreams.

Lucas stole them all.

"We're going around in circles!" Helen moaned to the unsympathetic library ceiling. "I know it doesn't make much sense, but trust me, there's no such thing as geographical progress down there. Did I mention the beach that doesn't lead to an ocean? It's just wet sand like a beach at low tide, except there's no ocean. Ever. It's just a beach!"

She was so tired she felt like she was starting to crack up, and every now and again she'd shiver unexpectedly, which was beginning to worry her. She couldn't get sick. It was both impossible and annoying. Helen's phone buzzed, interrupting her scattered thoughts. Orion was asking if the "Greek Geeks" had come up with anything yet. She smiled at his nickname for her study group and texted back that they hadn't. She asked him what he was reading on the Roman end.

**War, orgy, rinse, repeat. Getting boring,** he texted. **Almost ;)**

"Is that Orion again?" Ariadne asked with a pinched face. Helen glanced up at her and nodded in a hassled way while she typed.

She understood why everyone was concerned—they had to make sure the Houses stayed separate—but sometimes Helen felt insulted. Sure, Orion was gorgeous. And brave. And hilarious. But that didn't mean they were dating or anything.

"Wait! You can find Orion!" Claire exclaimed, derailing Helen's wandering thoughts.

"Yeah, I told you already. I concentrate on his face and I appear right next to him, just like Jason and Ariadne do when they bring people back from the edge of the Underworld. But I can only find him if he's in my same infinity," Helen answered. "Because if he isn't, I won't ever find him, even if he descends the next . . . Oh, forget it."

"Helen, I understand all that," Claire groused in frustration. "What I don't know is if Orion is the only person you can find just by *thinking* about him."

"I've already tried to find the Furies that way, Gig—a bunch of times. It never works."

"They're not *people*," Claire said very clearly, trying to contain her excitement. "What if you focused on someone who lives down there? Do you think you could use that person as a kind of beacon?"

"It's the land of the dead, Gig. Looking for someone who *lives* down there is kind of an oxymoron, isn't it?" Helen asked, getting lost in Claire's logic.

"Not if she was kidnapped, *body and soul*, by the boss himself," Claire said. She folded her arms across her chest and smiled like she knew a secret.

Jason made a surprised sound in the back of his throat. "How'd you get so smart?" he asked, gazing admiringly at Claire.

"Just lucky for you, I guess," she answered with a grin.

Ariadne, Helen, and Matt shared confused looks while Jason and Claire smiled at each other, forgetting that there were other people in the room.

"Um, guys? Hate to interrupt, but what are you talking about?" Matt asked.

Jason stood up and went to the stacks. He brought back an old book and laid it open in front of Helen. She saw a painting of a young black woman, walking away from the viewer, but looking back over her shoulder like she didn't want to go. She was dressed in a gown of flowers and wore a crown that sparkled with jewels as big as grapes. Her body was as graceful as a ballet dancer's, and even in the profile view her face was stunningly beautiful. Yet despite her great beauty and wealth, she radiated a crushing sadness.

"Oh, yes," Ariadne said quietly. "I remember now."

"Who is she?" Helen asked, awed by the image of this sad, beautiful woman.

"Persephone, goddess of flowers, and the queen of the Underworld," Jason answered. "She's actually a Scion. The only daughter of the Olympian Demeter, the goddess of the earth. Hades kidnapped Persephone and tricked her into marrying him. Now she's forced to spend the fall and winter months in the Underworld. They say Hades built her a night garden next to his palace. Persephone's Garden."

"She's only allowed to leave the Underworld to visit her mother in spring and summer. When she comes back to earth she makes the flowers bloom everywhere she goes." Ariadne sounded dreamy, like she was enchanted by the thought of Persephone making the world blossom.

"It's October. She'd be down there now," Matt added with cautious hope.

"And you're sure she's not an immortal?" Helen pinched her eyebrows together in doubt. "How can she still be alive?"

"Hades struck a deal with Thanatos, the god of death. Persephone can't die until Hades lets her," Cassandra spoke from across the room, making Helen jump.

She'd forgotten Cassandra was sitting there, writing a

letter to her father, who was still in New York City. Castor and Pallas were only allowed to receive written messages while in Conclave, and they had asked for some specific information on the Myrmidon. Cassandra had always had the disturbing ability to remain as still as a statue, and lately that ability had become so pronounced it was getting downright spooky. She joined the rest of the group and stared at Persephone's picture with a frown.

"So she's trapped down there," Helen said, directing her focus back to Persephone's sorrowful figure.

"But she could still help you," Cassandra said. "She knows everything about the Underworld."

"She's a prisoner," Helen replied with an angry scowl. "*We* should be helping *her*. Orion and I should, I mean."

"Impossible," Cassandra said. "Not even Zeus could get Hades to part with Persephone when Demeter demanded her daughter back. Demeter sent the world into an ice age, nearly killing off humanity over it."

"He's a kidnapper!" Matt exclaimed, outraged. "Why isn't Hades locked up on Olympus with the rest of them? He's one of the three major gods. Shouldn't he be part of the Truce?"

"Hades is the eldest brother of the Big Three, so I guess that technically he is an Olympian, but he was always different. I can't remember any literature that says he's even *been* to Mount Olympus," Cassandra said with a quizzical little grimace. "The Underworld is also called 'Hades' because it is entirely his realm. It's not part of the Truce, or even part of this world for that matter."

"The Underworld has its own rules," Helen said. She understood this bit better than anyone. "And I'm guessing you all think that Persephone might be willing to break a few of them?"

"I don't want to promise anything, but if anyone would even be able to help you down there, it would probably be her," Jason said. "She is the queen."

Helen's phone buzzed.

**Want to know Julius Caesar's favorite dirty joke?** Orion texted.

**Meet me tonight,** Helen texted back. **I think we're onto something.**

# EIGHT

Helen stared at the croissant and wished that one of her talents was X-ray vision. She very much wanted to know what was under that flakey crust. If it was spinach, it had to go on the tray at the end of the case. If it was ham and cheese, well then, it had to go in her belly.

"Lennie? You've been staring at that pastry for ten minutes," Kate said in a matter-of-fact way. "Any longer and it'll get stale before you get it into your mouth."

Helen straightened up and focused her eyes, trying to laugh like nothing was wrong. The laugh came out so forced and delayed that it sounded almost creepy. Kate gave her an odd look and stared pointedly at the croissant. Helen took the expected bite and regretted it. Spinach. Still, it gave her something to do so she would stay awake, and Helen *had* to stay awake for the rest of her shift, no matter what she had to put in her mouth.

Her vision had been blurring in and out every few minutes all night, and if she accidentally fell asleep and descended without Orion's face in her mind she knew she wouldn't meet up with him in the Underworld like they had planned. But even more important, she couldn't allow herself to nod off and a microsecond later appear in the News Store, covered in crazy gunk from the Underworld.

The last few days Helen had been scared stiff that she might fall asleep in class or at work, descend, and wake up in front of everyone she knew covered in unexplainable filth. Especially *this* evening. She was more tired than she had ever been in her life, and Zach was bogarting a table at the back of the News Store, in the Kate's Cakes section. Where Helen was stationed.

Several times Helen had tried to strike up a conversation, trying to find out what he was doing there all by himself on a Saturday night, but he barely even acknowledged her. He just kept ordering food and coffee, and typing on his laptop in a distracted way, almost as if he were just doodling. Never once did he make eye contact. When she did catch him staring at her, which happened more than Helen liked, he usually had a disgusted look on his face, as if he had just caught her picking her nose or something.

Wiping down the countertop for the thousandth time to keep herself awake, Helen heard the bells on the front door jingle as someone walked in. She wanted to scream. It was so late, so tantalizingly close to closing. The only thing she wanted was for the night to end so she could count her drawer, go home, and flop into bed. She could tell Zach to scram at ten o'clock sharp, but a new customer could take forever. She heard Kate squeal with happy surprise.

"Hector!"

Helen was out front, jumping into Hector's arms along with Kate, in about half a second.

Hector picked up both of them easily, one girl to an arm. Although it usually took Hector about five minutes to say something that annoyed the bejeezus out of Helen, when he smiled and held out his arms for a hug she forgot how much of a pain in the ass he usually was. Hanging from Hector's neck was like reaching up and hugging the sun—nothing but nurturing warmth and light.

"I could get used to this!" Hector chuckled, holding them both up in the air and squeezing them until they were breathless.

"But Noel and I just talked a few hours ago! She told me you were still in Europe, studying. What are you doing on Nantucket?" Kate asked when Hector put them down.

"I got homesick," he said with a shrug. Helen knew he was telling the truth, even if the whole cover story about studying in Europe was a lie. "It's just a quick visit. I'm not staying long."

The three of them chatted pleasantly for another few minutes, although Hector kept shooting Helen worried looks. If Hector was concerned for her, then Helen knew she must be a scary sight. Excusing herself, she went into the back to throw some water on her face.

When Helen returned to the Kate's Cakes section, Zach wasn't in his seat, but hurrying *back* to it. He gathered up his things in a rush and bolted out of the café, his eyes glued to the floor. Helen followed him hesitantly to the front, watching him plow past Hector and out the door. Hector raised his eyebrows at the strange behavior.

"We'll miss him horribly," Kate said sarcastically. Then she checked the time. "You know what? If I hurry, I can make a drop at the bank before the last pickup. Can you close up alone, Lennie?"

"I'll help her," Hector offered, making Kate smile.

"Are you sure? You know I can only pay you in food, right?" Kate warned playfully.

"Deal."

"You're the best! Be sure to box up as many leftovers as you want for your family, too," Kate said as she gathered her things and headed for the door.

"I'll do that," Hector called as she jogged out the door. He sounded cheery enough as he shouted good-bye, but his face fell as soon as Kate was gone.

No matter how much he would have loved to do as Kate asked, there was no way Hector could bring his family anything. Helen touched his arm consolingly and then pulled him into a hug when she saw him shake his head.

"I couldn't stay away. I had to see someone related to me." He squeezed Helen tight, like he could hug his whole family through her. "I'm glad I can be with you at least, Princess."

As Helen hugged him back, a black anger started to rise up out of the tenderness she felt, and it had nothing to do with the fact that he was still calling her "Princess" even though she'd asked him a million times not to. How dare the Furies separate Hector from the people he loved? He was more committed to family than anyone Helen had met. Now, more than ever, the Delos family needed Hector's strength to carry them through, but he was an Outcast. Helen had to find Persephone and beg her to help. She needed to end this.

"So you just stopped by because you needed a hug?" Helen asked sardonically when they pulled apart, trying to lighten the mood.

"No," he said seriously. "Not that a hug from you isn't worth it, but there's something else. Did you hear anything about a break-in at the Getty?"

Helen shook her head, and Hector pulled a piece of paper out of his jacket pocket and showed it to Helen.

"It was obviously a Scion," Helen said as she read the description of the impossible break-in and the stolen artifacts. "Who did it?"

"We don't know. Daphne's asked all the Rogues and Outcasts she knows, but so far no one's admitted to it." Hector rubbed his lower lip with his thumb. It was a gesture Helen had seen his father make when he was thinking. "We can't figure out why these gold coins, and *only* these coins, were stolen. As far as we know, they have no magic that's particular to any one of the Four Houses."

"I'll ask the family," Helen said, taking the piece of paper and tucking it into the back pocket of her jeans. Then she covered her mouth as a giant yawn escaped. "Excuse me, Hector. But I can barely keep my eyes open."

"I came here feeling all sorry for myself, but you know what? Now that I'm here, I'm more worried about you. You look pretty beat-up."

"Yeah, yeah, I'm a total disaster." Helen laughed ruefully as she tried to smooth her hair and straighten her clothes. "The Underworld is, well, it's *exactly* as bad as you'd think. But at least I'm not alone down there anymore—that's something."

"Orion. He's solid," Hector said with a serious nod. Helen gave him a surprised look, and he continued, "I've never met him in person, of course. The Furies. But Daphne put the two of us in touch right after I had to leave here. We text each other occasionally, and he's really been there for me. He's had a rough life, and he knows what I'm going through. I feel like I can talk to him."

"Orion is really easy to talk to," Helen agreed thoughtfully. She wondered if Hector knew more about Orion's childhood than she did. The thought bothered her. *She* wanted to be the one to listen to Orion's secrets, and she had no idea what that meant.

"And he's reliable. He helped me find Daphne when she was lost at sea. He's a powerful Scion, Helen. But I think he's an even better friend."

"Wow. You're *gushing*," Helen said, flustered by all the high praise coming from Hector, of all people. "What's going on? Have you got a little man-crush on Orion?"

"Whatever." Hector brushed off Helen's teasing. "Look, I'm just saying I like him. That's it."

"Well, so do I," Helen said softly, not certain what else Hector wanted her to say.

"And I don't see a reason why you wouldn't. In fact, I don't see a reason why you wouldn't do more than just *like* him. And that's fine," Hector said. "But he's Heir to both Athens and Rome, and you are the Heir to the House of Atreus. You know what that means?"

"The two of us together unite three of the four Houses," Helen said, frowning.

She had secretly hoped it was jealousy that had turned Lucas against Orion, but now that she considered it, she wasn't so sure. Maybe he didn't care if Helen was with another guy or not. Maybe all he cared about was keeping the Houses separate.

"Not that the two of you couldn't get cozy for a while," Hector said quickly, misinterpreting Helen's pained look. "But you couldn't really . . ."

"Really *what*, exactly?" Helen looked at Hector sharply and crossed her arms. "No, go on. I'm dying to hear what the Scion rule book says I can and can't do with Orion."

"You can have fun—you can have *a lot* of fun if you want. Not for nothing, but I hear that Scions from the House of Rome are particularly good at that. But don't get too close to him emotionally, Helen," he said seriously. "No children, no long-term commitment, and for gods' sake don't fall in love with him. The Houses must stay separate."

It was almost too weird to talk about this with Hector, but at the same time it wasn't. Helen knew he wasn't judging her or giving her an empty lecture; he only wanted what was best for everyone.

"We're just friends," Helen replied with a certainly she didn't entirely feel. "Neither of us wants anything else."

Hector studied her for a moment, almost like he pitied her.

"The whole world could be in love with you and you wouldn't even notice, would you? Like that weird kid, sitting here so he can stare at you for hours on end."

"You mean Zach?" Helen shook her head. "Maybe two years ago I would have agreed with you, but not anymore. Zach *hates* me."

"Then why was he camping out here on a Saturday night?" Hector asked dubiously.

A thought occurred to him and his eyes started scanning around until they finally landed on the counter. His face froze.

"He knows," Hector whispered.

"That's impossible. I never told him anything."

"You always leave your phone out like that?"

Hector gestured to the countertop, and sure enough, Helen's phone was sitting next to the rag she had been using. She *never* left her phone laying out at work, especially not since Orion had started texting her.

Helen stormed over and snatched it up, scrolling through

the first screen that lit up. It was the entire thread of texts with Orion, including their plan to meet in the Underworld.

Zach must have stolen her phone out of her bag and gone through her messages. Helen stared at the screen, her mind frozen with disbelief. How could Zach betray her like that?

"He was at that track meet, too, wasn't he?" Hector's face was grim and his eyes were two shrewd slits. "I saw him on the edge of the forest, following you and Claire. Right before the Hundred 'mysteriously' appeared out of the trees."

"Yeah, he was there," she mumbled, still dumbstruck. "I trusted him! Not enough to tell him about my powers, but I never thought he'd do anything to hurt me."

"Well, he knows, and he's got to be giving information to the Hundred. That's the only way they could have found me." Hector looked over the text thread and sighed heavily. "And now the Hundred will know about Orion as well."

The thought hadn't occurred to Helen, but now that Hector brought it up, she felt a surge of panic. As a Rogue, Orion had spent his whole life hiding his existence from the House of Thebes, and Helen had unwittingly led them right to him. She started typing a frantic text.

"Make sure you tell him to ditch his phone," Hector added as he began moving around the News Store, checking for any sign of an impending attack. Helen explained the situation to Orion as quickly as her thumbs would allow.

Orion didn't seem at all surprised.

**Before I ever even got in touch with you I knew they'd find out**

**about me eventually. Don't panic. I've prepared for this.**

Helen couldn't believe he was so calm. She relayed the compromised text thread to him, but he responded that everything that they had texted was indecipherable to others. He pointed out that there was no way for anyone to trace the phone number he was using back to his location and told her several times that he was safe.

**They're fanatics. They'll kill you,** she typed, unable to believe that he wasn't already packing a bag.

**Look, I don't have 4 last names (that you know of) for nothing. Trust me, K? C u 2nite as planned.**

Helen smiled at her phone, relieved that he was still willing to help her. Then she got angry. Orion had barely even flinched when she told him that he had been discovered. Didn't he know how dangerous the Hundred Cousins were?

"What's the matter?" Hector asked when he returned from checking the back alley and saw her stormy expression.

"He says he has it all taken care of."

"Then don't worry about him. Orion's been outmaneuvering murder plots since he was old enough to walk. If he says he took the proper precautions, then he did." Hector spoke with such perfect faith in Orion's abilities to protect himself that Helen was left speechless. "You just focus on what you need to do," he said over his shoulder as he glanced up and down the empty street. "I have to get back to Daphne and tell her about this."

"You're going out *there*?" Helen shouted in disbelief, jumping up to stop him. "But they could be hiding! There's a new Shadowmaster, you know."

"Think strategically, Helen. If the Hundred didn't make their move minutes ago when I was unaware and vulnerable, that means they won't strike tonight. The real question a good general would ask herself is, why aren't they coming for me when they know I'm right here?" He eyed her thoughtfully.

"Why are you looking at me like that?" she asked, pointing a finger at Hector and narrowing her eyes suspiciously. "What do you know that I don't?"

Hector smiled and shook his head, like Helen had entirely missed his point.

"I know that there are a lot of people counting on your success. It's so important, they're willing to let me go without a fight to make sure your descent tonight isn't disrupted." He opened the back alley door and kissed her on the forehead. "Just don't forget that the people who really love you need *you* much more than they need your *success*. Whatever you and Orion are planning for tonight, be careful in the Underworld, Princess."

"Damn it!" Helen yelled.

"Was something supposed to happen?" Orion asked expectantly.

She had just tried to picture Persephone's face and teleport herself and Orion into the queen's presence. They hadn't moved a millimeter. Helen paced around in a circle, kicking at little twigs until she realized they were actually tiny, yellowed bones.

"Why can't it just *work*?" she moaned. "Just *once* I want to come up with a plan and have it work. Is that too much to ask?"

Orion opened his mouth, about to say something to calm Helen down.

"Of course it isn't!" Helen interrupted, her rant picking up steam. "But nothing works down here! Not our talents, not even the geography works. That lake over there is tilted on a slope! It should become a *river*, but oh, no, not down here! That would make too much sense!"

"Okay, okay! You win! It's ridiculous," Orion said, chuckling. He put his hands on her upper arms, making her hold still and face him. "Don't worry. We'll think of something else."

"It's just that everyone's counting on me. And I really thought we had a plan, you know?" Helen sighed, her anger spent. She let her head fall forward and thud against Orion's chest. She was so tired. Orion let her lean against him while he stroked her back comfortingly.

"Tell you the truth? I never thought it was going to work," Orion said cautiously.

"Really?" Helen looked at him, deflated. "Why not?"

"Well, you haven't seen Persephone's face, just a picture of it."

"But that first time I appeared near you I never saw your

whole face, either. All I pictured was your voice and your hands and your . . . mouth." Helen stumbled over that last bit, her eyes dropping down to admire his lips involuntarily.

"Well, those are still real pieces of me—not just pictures," Orion said quietly, looking away. "Anyway, you don't even know for sure if that picture you saw of Persephone is accurate."

"And you were going to mention this . . . when?" Helen said, punching his shoulder to dispel the tension with some humor. "Why didn't you say something?"

"Because what the hell do I know?" he said, like it was obvious. "Look, until we find what works, I say no ideas should be taken off the table. We'll figure this out, but only if we don't get narrow-minded."

Helen felt her heart grow a little lighter. Orion knew exactly how to handle her sleep-deprived mood swings. Somehow, it was okay for her to be herself with him no matter how cranky she felt.

"Thanks." She smiled up at him gratefully.

Helen could feel his heart under her hand, beating hard. His breathing sped up, each breath staying high and tight in his lungs. Helen was suddenly very conscious of the fact that he was holding her, and the small of her back tightened with sensitivity under the weight of his hands. An intense moment passed. Helen had the feeling that Orion was waiting for *her* in some way. She laughed nervously to cover the fact that she was breathing just as fast as he was and eased out of his arms.

"You're right. We should stay open to all ideas," she said as she moved a step away.

*What the hell am I doing?* she thought, clenching her fists until her nails dug into the palms of her hand.

What she was doing was *trying* not to think too much about what Hector had said about how she could have "a lot of fun" with a Scion from the House of Rome. What did that mean, exactly? It was the House of Aphrodite, after all. . . .

"You wouldn't happen to have any, would you? Ideas, I mean," she continued, pushing aside her thoughts about just how *much* fun she was allowed to have with Orion.

"Actually, I think I might," he said, switching gears so fast Helen wondered if she had interpreted the situation correctly. Orion was staring intently at the slanted lake, biting his lower lip.

"I'm listening," she said, just to remind him that she was still there.

*Had* he been thinking about kissing her, or was she just flattering herself? Helen watched him gently tug his lower lip through his teeth and didn't know which of those two options she hoped was true.

Why did Orion have to be an Heir? Why couldn't he be some amazing guy she'd just met, preferably a full mortal so he was completely removed from this Truce nonsense? It would be so much easier if Orion were just a normal guy.

"You know, in all my reading about the Underworld there have only been a few things that get mentioned over and over," he continued, oblivious to Helen's swirling thoughts.

"It's like they're the only things that the historians agree are really down here one hundred percent of the time."

Helen stated to tick off the list on her fingers, taking an inventory of all the different things that could fit Orion's description.

"Well, we're *in* Erebus right now—this bland nowheres-ville. Then there are the Fields of Asphodel: creepy. And Tartarus: yuck."

"Only been to Tartarus once—when we first, ah, *met*," Orion said, referring to the time he had pulled her out of the quicksand. "And that was enough."

"It's where all the Titans are imprisoned, too. Definitely not a pleasant place to spend eternity," she said grimly. "So, there's Tartarus, Erebus, the Asphodels, the Elysian Fields—aka heaven. I'm sure I haven't found them yet. What am I missing? Oh, yeah, there are the five rivers. The *rivers!*" Helen exclaimed, catching on at the last second. "Everything down here is about the rivers, isn't it?"

Like something recalled from a fever dream—more emo-tion than image—Helen had an uneasy feeling about a river, but she wasn't sure which one. As soon as she tried to turn her mind's eye directly on it, the memory swam away like a pale fish.

"The Styx, the Acheron, all of them. They sort of define the space down here, don't they?" Orion mused as he pro-cessed this new line of thought. "They could lead us, like paths."

"And just how did you come up with this little slice of

genius?" Helen asked with admiration, her former thought lost as if it had never existed.

"From what you said about your favorite lake over there," he said with a wry smile. "It should be a river, but it isn't. That got me thinking that the rivers must be different. The rest of the landscapes down here are always switching around like they're interchangeable. But the rivers stay put. They're always here. I mean, even most full mortals know about the River Styx, right? The rivers are in every reliable account of the Underworld I've ever read, and most of the books say that at some point or another *all the rivers meet.*"

"So, we find *any* river and follow it, and eventually it will meet up with the one we need," Helen said, staring unblinkingly into Orion's eyes, as if moving would ruin the new hope she felt. "Persephone's Garden is next to the Palace of Hades, and the palace is supposed to be near a river. We find that river, and we might find Persephone."

"Yeah, but that's a whole different kind of headache. The river around the Palace of Hades is Phlegethon, the River of Eternal Fire. Not pleasant to stroll along its banks, I'm sure." Orion's brow furrowed in thought. "And then we still need to convince Persephone to help us get rid of the Furies."

Orion suddenly broke eye contact and started looking around in a tense way, as if he heard something.

"What?" Helen asked. She glanced over her shoulder but she didn't see anything.

"Nothing. Come on," he said uneasily. Orion tugged on

Helen's arm, urging her onward.

"Hey, what's the rush? Did you see something?" Helen asked as she trotted alongside Orion, but he stayed silent. "Look, just tell me if it's got fangs, okay?"

"Did you hear about a robbery at the Getty?" he asked out of the blue.

"Ah, yeah," Helen said, surprised by his sudden change in topic. "Do you think that has something to do with what you just saw?"

"I don't know what I saw, but regardless, we've been standing in one place for too long," he said, sounding annoyed. "I shouldn't have let that happen. I can't believe I . . ."

Helen waited for him to finish his sentence, but he didn't. Instead he kept frowning, like something was off, as he walked beside her. Helen kept looking around, but she didn't see or hear any kind of threat.

The tiny bones that littered the ground, the ones Helen had so carelessly kicked earlier, were getting bigger with every few paces. As she and Orion walked a few yards, the skeletons grew from mouse- to cat- to elephant-sized. Soon they were wandering amidst skeletons that were many times larger than any dinosaur's. Looking up at the massive calcified structures sticking up out of the ground, Helen felt as if they were walking through a forest of bones.

Arching ribs soared overhead like the pillars of a Gothic cathedral. Lumpy joints, covered in branching colonies of dead and dusty lichens, lay like massive boulders in their path. Helen noticed that many different types of anatomies were jumbled up, as if hundreds of beings the size of sky-scrapers had died heaped on top of each other. The scale was increased to such an extent that it was as if Helen were looking through a microscope. From her perspective, each pore inside the sequoia-sized bones was so large it appeared as though they were made out of layers of lace. She ran her hand over one of the latticed surfaces and looked over at Orion.

"Do you know what these creatures were?" she whispered. Orion dropped his eyes and swallowed.

"The Ice Giants. I've read stories about this but never believed it was real. This is a cursed place, Helen."

"What happened here?" she whispered, as awed by what she was looking at as she was by Orion's emotional reaction.

"It's an entire battlefield brought directly to the Underworld. That can only happen when every last soldier fights to the death. The Ice Giants are extinct now," he said in a hopeless monotone that was so unlike him. "I've had nightmares about another field like this, transported to the Underworld. Except instead of Ice Giants, all the bones belong to Scions."

His usually smiling mouth was pinched and forbidding, and Helen was reminded of what Hector had said. Orion had lived a rough life. She could sense it in him now, like a sad note in what was otherwise meant to be a joyful song.

She tilted her face under his until she caught his eye.

Pulling him closer to her, she shook his arm gently as if to wake him.

"Hey," she said softly. "You know what always bugged me about history class?"

"What?" Orion was startled out of his morose reverie by Helen's seemingly random question, just as she intended.

"It's all about war and battles and who conquered whom." Helen wrapped both her hands around one of his thick forearms and started to lead him along again. "You know what I think?"

"What?"

His face broke into a smile as he allowed her to lead. Helen was delighted to see the storm clouds that had darkened his face clear so quickly, as if she had the power to banish them at will.

"I think for every battle date they make us memorize in history class, they should make us learn at least two awesome things. Like, how many people get saved every year by firefighters, or the number of people who've walked on the moon. You know what's awful? I don't even know the answer to that."

"Neither do I," Orion said with a quiet smile.

"And we *should* know that! We're Americans!"

"Well, officially I'm Canadian."

"Close enough!" Helen said, waving an enthusiastic hand in the air. "My point is that considering all the amazing things that people are capable of, why do we focus on war?

Humans should be better than that."

"But you're not human, not really, not *wholly* human. Pretty little godling," hissed a slippery, wheedling voice.

Helen heard a ringing scrape, and a bright flash caught her eye as Orion unsheathed one of the many blades he kept strapped under his clothes. He pushed her behind him and dug his fingers into her hip, his large hand pinning her in place in case she tried to do something idiotic, like jump out and start swinging.

"Come and face me," Orion challenged to their adversary. His voice was calm, icy—almost like he had been waiting for this.

Frustrated with herself for being so helpless without her lightning, Helen resolved to learn how to fight like a mortal as soon as she was back in the real world. If she ever made it back.

A thin, warbling laugh echoed through the forest of bones, and a haunting almost-song wove its way toward them.

"Big baby godling! Bigger than most, like the hunter he was named for! Want to fight me, foolish Sky Hunter? Caution! I invented war. War, little beauties, I invented it. But, no, Sky Hunter won't heed. He will fight! And he will forever chase her across the night! For how prettypretty-pretty she is!"

The singsong voice slid off into peals of childlike laughter that made Helen's teeth grind together until they squeaked. As Orion circled defensively, Helen caught a glimpse of a long, gangly figure darting this way and that through the Ice Giants' graveyard. He was scrawny, nearly naked, and painted all over with blue-dye curlicues, like some Stone Age wild man.

"So like my sister, my lover. So like the Face! Oh! The Face that loved, that launched, that spilled so much blood-bloodblood! Again, again! I want to play the Game with the pretty little godlings again!" Giggling, he darted in close, trying to lure Orion away from Helen, but Orion didn't fall for it.

As the wild man came nearer, Helen got a better look at him. Horrified, she pressed herself tighter against Orion's back. The wild man had bulging gray eyes and long dread-locks that looked like they might have been platinum blond or white before they were matted with blue dye and clotted blood. Blood seemed to bubble up out of his skin. It ran from his nose and ears—even from his *scalp*, as if his rotted brain leaked gore from any handy hole.

In his hand was a raggedy sword, its edges orange with rust. Whirling around as Orion intercepted one of the wild man's feints, Helen caught a whiff of him. Her stomach heaved at the necrotic stench. He smelled like sour fear-sweat and rotting meat.

"Ares," Orion whispered to Helen over his shoulder as the god skipped off, giggling hysterically, to hide among the bones. "Don't be afraid, Helen. He's a coward."

"He's insane!" Helen whispered back frantically. "He's

completely and totally insane!"

"Most of the gods are, though I hear Ares is by far the worst," Orion said with a comforting smile. "Don't be afraid. I won't let him near you."

"Um, Orion? If he's a god, can't he pretty much crush you?" she asked delicately.

"We don't have our demigod powers here, so why should he have his god powers?" he said with a shrug, like he was tossing an idea out there. "And *he's* the one running away from *us*. That's usually a pretty good sign."

Orion had a point, but Helen still didn't relax. She could hear the mad god humming to himself as he trotted off in the distance. He didn't sound very afraid of them.

"You there, little godling! Hiding from the others?" Ares suddenly called out, a few hundred yards away. "So inconvenient, when I need all three of you together to start my favorite Game! Soon, soon. For now I will settle. I will watch you play with my uncle's pet instead. Here he comes, little godling!"

"Who's he talking to?" Orion whispered over his shoulder to Helen.

"I don't know, but I don't think it's us. Maybe he's seeing things?" she guessed.

"Maybe not. Earlier, I thought I saw . . ." Orion's sentence was abruptly interrupted.

A great howl sounded through the bone forest. It was so deep and loud Helen could feel it vibrating inside her chest.

A second howl, then a third followed, each one closer than the last. Helen froze out of sheer instinct, like a white rabbit in the snow.

"Cerberus." Orion's voice cracked. He recovered from his fear quickly. "Move!"

He grabbed Helen's arm and dragged her along, snapping her out of her terrified trance. The two of them ran for their lives with Ares' cackling laughter ringing in their ears.

They vaulted over brittle bones, trying to keep the howling behind them while making sure not to run down a dead end. Luckily, the bones kept getting smaller and smaller as they zigzagged out of the forest.

"Do you know where you're going?" she panted. Orion twisted his wrist out from under the sleeve of his jacket and looked at the golden cuff.

"It glows when I'm near a gate," he shouted back at her.

Helen dodged around a particularly sharp-looking pelvis, and then glanced at Orion's cuff. It wasn't glowing, not even a little bit. The howling of Hades' three-headed hellhound was getting closer by the second.

"Helen. You have to wake up," Orion said grimly.

"I'm not going anywhere."

"This isn't up for debate!" he shouted at her with real anger. "Wake up!"

Helen shook her head stubbornly. Orion caught Helen roughly by the arm, forcing her to stop. He shook her shoulders and glared into her eyes.

"Wake. Up."

"No." She glared back at him. "We leave together or not at all."

Another chest-rattling howl split the air. They both turned and saw Cerberus, less than a football field away, bounding through the diminishing cover of the boneyard.

A strange squeak came out of the back of Helen's throat at the sight of him. She didn't know what she was expecting—maybe a pit bull or a mastiff with the head of a Doberman thrown in to round out the trio. The sight of any recognizable breed would have been a comfort. But, no. She should have known that none of those familiar, *tame* dogs existed eons ago when this beast was whelped.

Cerberus was a wolf. A twenty-foot-tall, three-headed wolf with salivating jaws, and he did not have a tame chromosome in his body. As one of the heads snapped at her, its eyes rolled back to show the whites. One head zeroed in on Helen, the other two on Orion. The hackles rose on their shared back, and all three heads dropped into a menacing crouch. One paw padded forward, then another, as a low growl rumbled in all three throats.

"EEEYAYAYA!!"

A piercing cry broke Cerberus's deadly concentration, followed by a shower of bone bits that pelted the left-most head.

All three heads reacted immediately. Cerberus turned and sprinted off after the mystery yodeler, abandoning Helen and Orion. Helen tried to see who had saved them, but she could only make out a faint shadow among the gnarled stumps of bone.

"Go-go-go!" Orion urged optimistically as he turned Helen around. Taking her hand and holding it hard, he ran toward a stone wall that had appeared in the distance. Helen resisted.

"We have to go back! We can't leave . . ."

"Don't waste a perfectly good act of heroism with a *bad* one of your own!" he hollered as he dragged her along. "You don't have to out-valor everyone, you know."

"I'm not trying to . . ." Helen started to argue, but another series of snarling barks from Cerberus changed her mind. The hellhound had apparently finished with the yodeling hero and was on their trail again. It was time to shut up and run.

Helen and Orion bolted pell-mell toward the wall, hands locked as they encouraged each other on. They were both beyond tired. Helen had lost count of how many hours they had been in the Underworld, and how many miles they had traversed in that incalculable amount of time. Her mouth was so dry her gums ached, and her feet felt swollen and bruised inside her boots. Orion wheezed painfully at her side as if every breath were like sandpaper in his lungs.

Looking down at Orion's hand linked tightly to hers, Helen saw the cuff on his wrist begin to glow. With every stride closer to the wall, the golden haze coming from the cuff grew until it surrounded his body in a nimbus of gilded light. Helen tore her eyes away from Orion's illuminated shape to watch a glowing crack form between the dark rocks of the wall ahead.

"Don't be afraid! Just keep going," he yelled as they ran toward it on a collision course.

She could hear the slap of massive paws gaining on them as the hellhound closed the distance. The ground shook and the air grew hot and wet as Cerberus literally breathed down Helen's neck.

The rocks did not part. They did not move reassuringly aside to give Helen and Orion a clear opening. Clinging tightly to Orion's hand, Helen charged ahead without hesitation.

They jumped through the solid wall, soared through a chasm of empty air, and hit what seemed to be another wall. Helen heard a sickening crunch as her temple hit the hard surface. Unable to catch her breath, Helen waited to slide down the wall and hit the ground, but she never did. It took a moment for her to realize that gravity had done a one eighty, and that she was already *on* the ground. She was lying on an icy floor in a very cold, very dark place.

"Helen?" Orion's worried voice splintered off in the dark, and echoed down many separate passages.

She tried to answer him but all that came out of her mouth was a wheezing sound. When she tried to pick up her head, her stomach heaved weakly. There was nothing in her belly to throw up.

"Oh, no," she heard Orion breathe as he shuffled toward her in the dark. She heard a snapping, grinding sound, followed by a bright orange flame as he flicked a lighter. She had to shut her eyes or she knew she'd throw up for sure. "Oh, Helen, your head . . ."

"C-cold," she managed to groan, and she was. It was even colder here than it was in her bedroom, and she couldn't lift herself away from it. She twitched her fingers and they seemed to work, but for some reason her arms wouldn't move.

"I know, Helen, I know." He moved around her frantically, but talked in a soothing whisper, like he was trying to calm a child or an injured animal. "You hit your head pretty bad and we're still at the portal—neither here nor there. You can't heal yourself unless I move you, okay?"

"'Kay," she managed to whine. She was starting to get freaked out that her limbs weren't responding properly.

She felt Orion wedge his hands under her prone body, felt him brace himself for one brief moment, and then she felt shafts of pain shoot from her temple to her toes.

Orion was murmuring to her as he carried her out of the cold zone and into someplace slightly warmer, but Helen had no idea what he was saying. She was too busy trying not to throw up. The whole world was tilting and reeling, and she was desperate for Orion's jarring steps to stop. Every time he planted a foot it felt like he was stepping on her head. Finally, he crouched down, cradling her across his lap, and she heard the snap of his lighter again.

She could feel a warm glow from behind her closed

eyelids as Orion lit a candle. Helen felt him brush her hair back from her temple and try his best to wrap her up inside his jacket, close to his skin. After a moment she started to feel a bit better.

"Why do I feel so sick?" she asked when her voice had grown stronger.

"Never had a concussion?" he asked in return, sounding almost amused. He squeezed her tighter in a brief hug. "It's okay. You're healing fast now that we're away from the portal. You have your Scion powers back in this part of the cave, so you'll be all better soon."

"Good," she said with complete faith. If Orion said she was going to be okay, Helen knew she would be. After just a few more seconds, she felt nearly back to normal and she relaxed in his arms. But as she did, she felt him stiffen.

"I have to leave you now," he said in a gentle voice.

"Huh?" Helen said, lifting her eyes to Orion's. He looked at her sadly.

"We're back in the living world, Helen. They're going to come for us."

As soon as he finished speaking, a pitiful sobbing came from everywhere at once. Orion dropped his head with a pained look and sighed heavily. In a sudden, violent motion, he kicked over the candle next to them, putting it out. He tried to push Helen out of his lap so he could stand and throw her off him in the sudden dark.

Every muscle in Helen's body went rigid, stopping him

from bending forward and standing up. She put a firm hand against Orion's chest, pushed him back, and threw a leg over him to pin him to the ground. A wave of rage broke over her as she squeezed his hips between her thighs.

"You're not going anywhere," she said. Her voice was low and it cracked with hate.

"No, Helen. Don't," Orion pleaded, but he knew it was too late.

The Furies had Helen, and they were commanding her to kill Orion.

# NINE

Zach drove around the island one final time just to make sure that Hector wasn't following him, and then returned to his master's ship. Hector might be an Outcast, but he was still funneling information to the Delos family, and Zach couldn't afford to slip up. Automedon would do far worse than kill him if he accidentally led Hector to their base on the ship with the red sails.

Killing the engine, Zach stared at the dock that led to the graceful yacht, bobbing gently on the night swells. His palms started to sweat and his stomach fluttered at the thought of walking down that row of planks and delivering his full report to Automedon. The face-to-face report was just a formality—Zach had emailed the entire text thread to his master as soon as he had stolen it—but Automedon liked reminding his minion that every second of his day belonged to his master.

There was no way out of this for Zach. And it was all Helen's fault. That bitch.

He had just wanted to know what she had been hiding for all those years. He had tried to talk to her about it in private, but no matter how caring he had acted, she wouldn't let him in. If she had just paid attention to him, maybe gone out with him a few times, none of this would have happened.

Zach ended up getting all the answers he wanted—and much more that he didn't. Automedon came from an era where the only difference between a free man and a slave was timing, and Zach was in the wrong place at the wrong time.

Zach got out of his car and started down the gangplank, reminding himself that at least his master had respected him enough to be honest. He had even been given an important job. He was to spy on his former friends, especially Helen, and give his master any information he could gather about her quest in the Underworld. Dishonorable, but hey, it was a way *in* to this world, at least. Helen was a snob. And the Delos boys? They were all too busy buffing their pretty muscles and sleeping with every hot girl on the island to notice a lowly normal human like him.

Tonight he had served his master well, even though the information he had supplied was not welcome. Zach had proven that there was another surviving Rogue, and if there were two—Helen and this new guy, Orion—then there could be many, many more.

Zach wasn't an idiot. It hadn't taken him long to understand the politics or the ultimate prize involved. Raising Atlantis would give immortality to the Scions, and after thousands of years stuck in a stalemate with the gods, the Hundred Cousins were determined to claim their prize.

There was some debate, coming from the whiny Delos faction, about a great war starting as a result of this, but Zach's master had explained it all to him. War would be a really bad choice for the gods. The Hundred, immortal as soon as they raised Atlantis, would outnumber the Twelve Olympians by *at least* eighty-eight, and everyone knew that there were more than a hundred cousins in the Hundred.

If the Olympians tried to fight, they would be forced to surrender almost immediately. Humanity would finally have gods who could really understand them, gods who had once been mortal. Maybe, for a change, people's prayers would get *answered* instead of ignored.

It made perfect sense to Zach. He knew he was on the right side.

It's just that sometimes Zach heard his master say horrible stuff, like how he wished all of humanity was either gone or turned into mindless slaves, like in an ant colony. On more than one occasion, Automedon had said that he wanted *his* master to "wipe the world clean." Zach had never met his master's master, and from what he had heard, he didn't want to. Ever.

Stepping onto the yacht, Zach heard multiple voices belowdecks and smelled an acidic, rancid scent, like sour milk. His body recoiled from the smell of the visitors, but he told himself to ignore it. Sometimes his master didn't smell right, either. Even though he looked mostly human on the outside, Automedon had an exoskeleton instead of skin and he didn't breathe through his mouth, but through tiny holes hidden all over his outer surface. He didn't smell human— more like musk mixed with dry leaves.

Zach took a seat on the now-vacant upper deck. The other members of the Hundred who'd come with Automedon to the island had all been called back by Tantalus shortly after the confrontation with Hector, Lucas, and Helen in the woods. Zach wasn't sure exactly why, but he thought it had something to do with Tantalus being attacked. Whatever had happened must have been big in order for Tantalus's elite guard to circle the wagons the way they had. All Zach knew was that now an entire battalion of the Hundred Cousins was committed to chasing some mystery woman across the world.

The voices belowdecks rose slightly in disagreement, and then quickly softened as one or the other side backed down. Zach knew better than to interrupt, so he waited on one of the teak benches.

They knew he was there, of course. Zach had learned that his master could hear him no matter how softly he tried to walk. Whoever was down there with him was equally as gifted—either a high-ranking Scion, or something else even more powerful. His master did not use that reverent tone of voice on any being he deemed less than himself, and there were very few beings on the planet that Automedon did not rank as beneath him.

When he heard the group belowdecks begin to ascend, Zach stood respectfully. Following his master up the stairs was a tall woman and a pale young man. They looked like fashion models with their delicate beauty and luminous gray eyes, and they moved like they were floating.

But, on closer inspection, there was too much white in their gray eyes, and they seemed to pant instead of breathe. Zach backed away, and by the displeased look on his master's face knew he had done something terribly wrong. The panting woman waggled her head toward Zach, like a snake zeroing in on its target.

"Kneel, slave!" Automedon commanded.

Zach dropped to his knees but continued staring at the hypnotically *ugly* woman. It had taken him a moment to realize it, but for all her height and sharp features, she wasn't a beautiful fashion model. She was repulsive, and so was the stooping, stumbling boy next to her.

They were the source of that horrid smell—bad milk mixed with sulfur. It made his eyes water, so he shut them. Violent, chaotic emotions began to bubble up inside him. He wanted to hit someone or light something on fire.

"Finally, some reverence," the woman hissed.

"He is ignorant," Automedon said dismissively.

"Is he too stupid to fulfill his duty?"

"Not at all. He is native to this place and quite tied to the Face," Automedon answered smoothly. "*If* these are the

Three Heirs of the prophecy, I expect my slave to behave just the way we need him to. Like an envious human."

"Good."

Zach didn't hear the woman and the young man walk away, but when he opened his eyes, they were gone. Only the hideous smell lingered. The reckless feeling overwhelmed him, and he looked around the deck of the ship for something to break.

The Furies whispered names and hiccupped with pitiful sobs.

Helen told herself to take her hand off Orion's chest and back away. She could feel him between her legs, but she couldn't see him in the pitch black of the cave. That helped. If she could just stop touching him, she would be able to calm down, and she *needed* to calm down. She was so angry that she could have sworn she felt the earth shake.

But she didn't back off. Without ever making a decision, she found herself digging her fingers into him, clutching at his shirt and wrenching him closer to her as he tried to back away.

Another tremor rocked the cavern floor beneath her, and this time she knew it was not her imagination. The quake was so strong that it knocked her off Orion. A great booming noise thundered through the cave as the ground heaved up and came slamming back down. She heard Orion's breath catch in his throat as he tried and failed to say her name.

"*They must not!*"

An insistent susurration flooded the cave, and the sound quickly rose to shouting. The Furies were at a fever pitch, and for the first time Helen could remember, they actually touched her.

Thumping their damp foreheads and their brittle, ash-dusted limbs against Helen's back, the Furies closed in on her. Stumbling forward, they scratched her face and pulled her hair, tearing at Helen with their sharp little nails to break her out of Orion's thrall.

A thousand unavenged murders flashed red in Helen's thoughts.

"*Kill him! Kill him now!*" they hissed. "*He still owes a debt to the House of Atreus. Make him pay in blood!*"

Overwhelmed by the Furies, Helen's heart slipped out of Orion's invisible hand and filled with rage. She reared back and hit him as hard as she could manage—trying to ram her fist down his throat.

Whatever control Orion had been exerting over himself was lost. The Furies were quick to possess him. He snarled like an animal and shot forward, grabbing Helen's upper arms and pushing her roughly onto her back. With his Scion powers restored, he was faster and stronger than she could have imagined. Hector had been right. Orion was enormously powerful. Helen tried to struggle out from underneath him, but it was too late. He had the upper hand now, and with his size and skill he could easily keep her pinned down.

Risking a catastrophic eruption of electricity, Helen allowed a current to run across her skin. She was hoping to knock Orion unconscious, but fatigue made her fall short of the mark, and the painful shock she delivered only made him angrier. Orion screamed and twitched with agony, but he didn't let her go. When he recovered from the electrical storm in his head he leaned down hard on her shoulders, grinding her back into the wet floor of the cave until a gasp of pain escaped from her lips.

Helen realized then that she had misjudged Orion horribly, and that she would pay for it. She still couldn't see him, but she could feel the full mass of him looming above her. She had never noticed how *large* he was until now, probably because she never had reason to fear him before. As she pushed uselessly against his face and throat, she knew that she would not win this fight. She was injured, dehydrated, and beyond exhausted. Orion was going to kill her.

Helen didn't even have to think about it. She knew she'd rather die buried under a thousand tons of rubble than submit to him. She relaxed and began to summon a true bolt—one that would easily kill him and most likely collapse the cave and kill her as well. But she didn't get the chance to release it.

Suddenly, Orion let go of her and pushed himself up, as if he were waking from a dream. She heard him frantically scrambling away from her in the dark. Not knowing where he'd gone made her desperate for some light. Straining her ears against the pounding silence, Helen waited for the

sound of another attack.

Orion's boots creaked somewhere out there. The Furies hissed, calling out to Helen from Orion's hiding place. They were directing her, wanting her to finish the fight.

But now that she was no longer touching him, Helen felt uncertain. Orion wasn't her enemy, was he? In fact, she cared for him—so much that she was starting to worry that she had really hurt him. But the impenetrable dark of the cave revealed nothing, no matter how hard Helen tried to stare through it.

She decided that she needed to know two things. First, was he was okay? Second, if he was, was he about to attack her?

Focusing all her remaining strength on maintaining a balanced charge, Helen conjured a small globe of glowing electricity in her left hand and held it up above her head. Her eyes darted around the toothy stalactites and stalagmites until she spotted Orion. He was backed up against the wall on the other side of the small cavern, his eyes pinched closed. Blood was running down his chin.

"If you're going to kill me, do it now while my eyes are closed." His deep voice rang out sure and steady, echoing down the empty passageways. "I won't fight you."

Generating light had been a mistake. Now Helen could see the Three Furies gnashing their teeth and raking their fingers down their bodies in the shadows. They tore their clothes and left deep red welts on their bleached and clammy skin.

Helen stood up and stalked toward Orion robotically, like a clockwork killer full of cogs instead of thoughts. In an ecstasy of hate, she fell down on her knees in front of him and put her right hand under his shirt.

Sliding her hand along Orion's belt, Helen felt for the knife she knew he kept strapped to his back. He must have known what she was doing, but he didn't try to stop her. Helen unsheathed his knife and held the tip of the blade against his chest.

"I don't want this," she said. Her voice shook and her eyes were blurry with tears that gathered, tipped, and then tumbled down her hot cheeks. "But I need it."

Orion kept his eyes shut, his hands gripping the cavern wall. In the icy, erratic light of her barely controlled electricity, Helen saw him calm himself, as if he'd done this many times before. The ghost-white limbs and ashy hair of the Furies blinked in and out of the corner of Helen's eye.

"I feel it, too. The bloodlust," he whispered, so softly Helen understood his meaning more than heard his words. "It's okay. I'm ready now."

"Look at me."

Orion opened his bright green eyes. The Furies screamed.

A boyish, surprised expression stole across his face. He began to take labored little breaths and his head fell listlessly toward Helen, inch by inch, until his lips grazed lightly against her own. His mouth was very warm and soft. Like a new flavor she couldn't quite place but that she wanted to swallow whole, Helen pulled his lower lip into her mouth

to take a bigger sip of him. Catching his face in one of her hands so she could tilt his wilting mouth toward hers, she noticed something sticky between her fingers. Helen pulled back and looked down.

There was blood on her hands.

Stunned out of her trance, Helen looked down and saw a dark, wet circle expanding across Orion's shirt. His surprised look. She had stabbed him. And then she kept pushing the tip of the blade into him a tiny bit at a time as they leaned toward each other. And he had allowed her to do it without complaint.

Seeing what she had done, Helen yanked the blade out of Orion's chest and sent it clanging against the floor behind her.

He pitched forward with a small sigh and crumpled up at her knees.

Horrified, Helen dug her heels into the slippery ground and scrambled away from Orion's still body, extinguishing her globe of light in the process. Her back hit a stalagmite and she remained motionless, listening for any sound from him. The Furies whispered to her to get up and finish what she had started, but she was too stunned to obey.

"Orion?" she called across the cavern.

She would carry him out, she reasoned with herself. The blade hadn't gone in that deep, so he was just unconscious. Right? *Right,* she told herself firmly. If he was too far gone to heal himself, she'd bring him to Jason and Ariadne, and they could save him, she *knew* they could do it. She didn't care how exhausted she was, how huge he was, or how far

she had to carry him. Orion was going to live, no matter what she had to do.

But the Furies . . . they would make even the compassionate twins want to kill Orion. That is, if Helen could resist the Furies as she brought him back to Nantucket. How could she trust herself with him after what she'd just done to him?

"Orion, answer me!" Helen cried into the dark. "You can't die!"

"Well, someday, I will. But not yet," he groaned. The Furies' whispers rose. "You have to get out of here."

"I don't want to leave you. You're hurt."

"I'm nearly healed. Follow the water uphill. It will lead you out." Orion swallowed painfully. "Please, get away from me!"

The Furies were talking to Orion now, guiding him toward Helen. She could hear them begging him to kill her. He made a desperate sound and Helen sensed him lunging toward her.

Narrowly avoiding his tackle, Helen disengaged gravity and soared up into the air. As soon as she was flying she could sense the faintest movement of air, right down to the minute flow around the stalactites that hung from the ceiling. The air currents helped her figure out which way led up and out of the cave.

She could also feel gusts of air being stirred up by Orion, who was flailing his arms below as he searched for her in the dark. Wounded or not, Helen knew she had to leave him immediately or neither of them would survive the night.

She soared out of the cavern and up through the winding passageways until she could see the dim glow of predawn light at the mouth of the cave.

Helen floated higher to get her bearings. Looking down at the still-dark landscape, she saw that she was near the south shore of Massachusetts and relatively close to the coast. She turned to the first rays of the sunrise, and headed due east out over the open water.

Somewhere over Martha's Vineyard, Helen started crying. She kept picturing the stunned look on Orion's face as she stabbed him—*stabbed* him, she kept repeating to herself in shock.

A sob burst out of her and she covered her mouth with her hand. She tasted something very wrong on her lips and looked at her hand in disgust. It was covered in Orion's blood. She really *had* almost killed him, and the proof of it was stained into her skin. If he hadn't kissed her, he'd be dead now.

Helen swooped dangerously in the air above her house. She tried to clear her eyelashes of the tears that were freezing as soon as they welled up, but they just kept coming. The more she tried to stuff the sobs down, the more violently they seemed to burst out of her. What had Orion done to her heart?

Helen's control over the wind began to falter, and she tumbled in midair like a plastic bag in a storm. She dropped out of the sky and made a beeline for the blue tarp covering her bedroom window.

Tearing the tarp aside, she dove into bed and buried her head under her chilly pillow to muffle the sound of her tears. She could hear her father snoring in the next room, blissfully unaware that his daughter had very nearly become a murderer.

Helen cried herself out as quietly as she could, but no matter how tired she was, she refused to fall asleep. She couldn't bear the thought of descending back into the Underworld so soon, although she knew that it didn't make any difference. This cycle that she was stuck in seemed never ending. If she slept, if she stayed awake, what did it matter? There was no rest for her no matter what she did.

Zach saw Helen lift up the blue tarp over her window and *fly* under it. He'd seen his master do a lot of things that were physically impossible, but seeing a girl he'd known his whole life *flying* was difficult for him to process. She'd always been like an angel, so beautiful she was almost painful to look at, but in flight Helen really did look like a goddess. She also looked upset. He wondered what had happened to her. Whatever it was, wasn't good. Zach assumed she still hadn't been successful in the Underworld.

And how the hell had she gotten out of the house in the first place? he wondered. Then he started to sweat. Somehow, Helen had switched out the lights in her bedroom, and then about half an hour later appeared behind him in midair. Could she teleport now? What was he going to tell his master?

Zach knew he had to make a report. He turned to walk toward his car, parked down the street, and jumped. Automedon was standing behind him, as silent as a grave.

"How did the Heir get out?" he asked calmly.

"She just fell asleep. . . . She didn't leave, I swear it."

"I can smell your fear," Automedon said, his red eyes shining in the dark. "Your eyes are too slow to see her. I can no longer trust you with this task."

"Master, I . . ."

Automedon shook his head. That was enough to silence Zach.

"My master's sister has had word from her brother. They are almost ready," Automedon continued in his blank and emotionless way. "We must make preparations to capture the Face."

"You master's sister?" Zach asked shrewdly. "But Pandora's dead. Don't you mean Tantalus's wife, Mildred?" Zach crumpled onto his knees, all the air rushing out of his lungs. Automedon had punched him in the gut so fast he'd never seen it coming.

"You ask far too many questions," Automedon said.

Zach gasped and clutched his middle, certain now that Automedon had a different master. He wasn't working for Tantalus anymore, and Zach had a feeling it had something to do with that tall, inhuman woman and the misshapen boy with her. Whoever she was, she was calling the shots now for her brother, and it was her brother who was Automedon's real master. Zach knew that Automedon didn't trust him enough to tell him who he was working for, but that didn't mean he couldn't still find out. He just had to be careful.

"Forgive me, master," Zach wheezed as he stood up, still bent over with pain and seething with bitterness. "I will get you what you need. Instruct me."

Automedon's mouth twitched, like he could smell Zach's disingenuous intent. Zach tried to think loyal thoughts. His life literally depended on it.

"Rope, a stake, and a bronze brazier. Do you know what a brazier is?"

"A ceremonial bronze pan. Used to hold burning coals or fire," Zach repeated lifelessly. His master nodded once.

"Keep all of these things on hand. When the time comes it will all happen *very* quickly."

Sitting up, Helen rubbed her throbbing head and noticed that she was still covered in blood and grime. Her skin was oily and tender from lack of sleep and her face felt hot, even though she knew that her bedroom was literally freezing cold. The glass on her nightstand had a spiky film of ice on top.

Forcing herself out of bed, she staggered into the shower and stayed there, trying to forget the way Orion had looked at her, how lost he'd seemed. The word *stabbed* kept echoing around the inside of her malfunctioning mind, confusingly coupled with the memory of how he had touched her.

Helen knew Orion could control hearts, but nothing could have prepared her for what she'd felt when he reached inside her. It sort of hurt, but in a good way—in the *best* way, Helen realized. Her hot face got even hotter and she pinched her eyes shut tightly and turned directly into the stinging spray. For a moment it felt like Orion could have done whatever he wanted to her, and Helen knew she would have let him. Worse, she suspected that no matter what he asked of her, he could have made her enjoy it, too.

"Helen!" Jerry yelled, jolting her out of her vivid thoughts. He only called her Helen when he was really ticked off. "Why is it so *damn* cold in this *damn* house . . . *damn it!*"

*That's it,* Helen thought. *I've finally made my father so angry he's actually forgotten how to speak English.*

Jerry came to the bathroom door and started yelling at her through the wood. She could almost picture him out there, pointing his finger vehemently at the door while he got himself so worked up that he started mixing up words like *irresponsible* and *thoughtless* and said things like *irrespons-less-ness.*

Helen shut off the taps and shrugged into a robe, still wet. She pulled open the door and leveled her father with a look. Whatever Jerry was going to yell next died with a whimper as soon as he saw Helen's face.

"Dad," she said carefully as she dangled precariously from the end of her emotional tether. "*This* is the situation. I already called Mr. Tanis at the hardware store and he came over *on Friday* to measure the window. *Then*, he placed the order with a glass shop on the Cape because this house is so old that *none* of our fixtures are standard size. We have to wait for the shop on Cape Cod to *make* the window, ship it to *back* to us, and Mr. Tanis will come and install it. But until then, *it's going to be freaking freezing cold in my bedroom, okay!"*

"Okay!" he said, leaning away from Helen's sudden attack of the crazies. "Just as long as you're taking care of it."

"I am!"

"Good!" He shifted awkwardly on his feet and looked at Helen with a penitent expression. "Now what do you want for breakfast?"

Helen smiled at him, grateful that of all the proverbial doorsteps Daphne could have left her on, she had chosen Jerry's.

"Pumpkin pancakes?" she said with a sniffle. She rubbed her runny nose on the sleeve of her robe like a little kid.

"Are you sick? What's wrong with you, Len? You look like you've been to hell and back."

Helen laughed, resisting the temptation to tell him how on the mark his guess was. Her sudden laughter only confused Jerry even more. He backed away with a slightly weirded-out look on his face and went downstairs to make her pancakes.

When Helen was bundled up in a thick wool sweater and even thicker wool socks, she joined him in the kitchen and helped. For about an hour she and her dad just hung out, ate, and shared the Sunday paper. Every time the thought of Orion arose, she would try to sideline it.

She couldn't allow herself to become too attached to him. She knew that. But little details kept swimming up to fill her mind's eye—the single beauty mark that hung like a dark tear high on the slope of his right cheek; the sharp, diamond shape of his incisors when he smiled.

Why hadn't he texted yet?

"Are you going to Kate's later?" she asked her dad to get her mind off Orion.

"Well, I wanted to ask you first," he answered. "Are you going to Luke's?"

Helen stopped breathing for a moment, collected herself, and tried to pretend that her stomach hadn't fallen to the floor. For a moment, she tried to reason with the voice in her head that was whispering the word *unfaithful*. She and Lucas were not together. What did it matter if she thought about Orion?

"I'm going to *Ariadne's*, Dad. She and I have this thing; so go to Kate's. I'm not going to be here."

"Another project for school?" he asked so innocently that Helen knew he didn't believe it.

"Actually, no," Helen admitted. She was too tired to keep all the lies straight anymore and decided she would try a touch of truth for a change. "She's teaching me self-defense."

"Really!" he exclaimed, completely shocked. "Why?"

"I want to learn how to protect myself."

Helen realized how true it was as she said it. She couldn't spend the rest of her life hiding behind other people. Eventually, she would run out of champions—especially if she kept stabbing them in the chest.

Orion should have texted her by now. Where was he?

"Oh. Okay." Jerry scowled as he collected his thoughts. "Lennie, I give up. Are you and Lucas dating or not? Because I can't figure it out, Kate can't figure it out, and you look really miserable. I'm assuming you two broke up, but if you did, then why? Did he do something to you?"

"He didn't do anything, Dad. It's not like that at all," Helen mumbled. She was still incapable of saying Lucas's name. "We're just friends."

"Friends. Really? Lennie, you look like the walking dead."

Helen stifled a bitter laugh and shrugged. "Maybe I've got the flu or something. Don't worry. I'll get over it."

"Are we talking about the flu or Lucas?"

Helen's phone buzzed. She dove for it—*Orion!*—but it was Claire, asking where she was.

"What's wrong now?" Jerry asked.

"Huh? Nothing," Helen responded, still staring at her phone. Why hadn't Orion texted her yet?

"You look disappointed."

"I gotta go. Claire's coming up the street," she lied, ignoring her father's comment about being disappointed—which she wasn't, she told herself. She was worried, and that was different.

What had Orion done to her? She knew this wasn't normal. She felt like her brain had been hijacked, and apparently, her skin had gone along for the ride, too. She could still *feel* his hands on her, and she knew she wasn't just imagining it. She could feel points of pressure on the small of her back, like his fingers were pressing into her. She felt him tug on her hips, pulling her closer to him, even though she knew he was miles away on the mainland.

She put a hand out to steady herself and counted to three. The feeling that he was holding her hips in his hands receded, but it didn't entirely go away. Rushing to get away from so many impossible sensations, she kissed her dad good-bye, put on her shoes and coat, and hurried out of the house.

The steps swam in front of her and a familiar scent lingered on the breeze. Helen spun on her heel and twisted her head around to find the source of it. Disoriented, she fell to her knees and held her arms out, groping around like she had been blindfolded. Something was terribly wrong with her eyes. The sky in front of her looked mismatched, as if it had been ripped apart and then hastily stitched back together a millimeter or two askew.

Helen felt heat—wonderful, comforting heat in a sea of cold. Some invisible sun was warming her ever so slightly. She closed her eyes and held out her hand to touch the warmth that hung a shadow's width away, but as she reached out to touch it, it bled into the cold October air and disappeared.

Hot tears stung Helen's out-of-focus eyes. She felt as if she had just been denied something she needed so desperately. Helen swatted at the empty air with her hands, but there was nothing there.

*Come to me, Dreamless One. I miss holding you in my arms.*

Helen froze and looked around. She had heard a man whisper—but from where?

The sound had come from inside her own mind, but the voice had definitely not been hers. It had sounded so soothing. Helen wanted to hear it again.

Getting up off her knees, Helen glanced around self-consciously at the neighbors' windows, hoping none of them had seen her. She didn't know how to explain her momentary freak-out to anyone, least of all to herself. A terrifying thought crossed her mind. Blurry vision, disrupted balance, and hot and cold flashes were all known side effects of sleep deprivation. So was dementia. It was possible that she had imagined the whole thing, including the voice.

Helen knew she couldn't afford to panic. She shook off the fear. Jogging a ways down the street, she made sure no one was watching and then took to the air. Moments later, she landed in the Deloses' arena, right next to Ariadne and Matt, who were already in the middle of a training session. Matt screamed like a little girl.

"What the hell, Lennie!" He scrambled through the sand to regain his lost footing. "You just fell out of the frigging sky!"

"Sorry! I didn't think," Helen apologized.

She'd forgotten that Matt had never really seen her fly, but she had been so surprised that Matt and Ariadne were practicing openly that she had forgotten to come in for an easy landing. She was about to ask if Matt had somehow convinced Ariadne's father that he should be trained when she heard Claire cracking up in the corner.

"Jeez, Matt! I haven't heard you hit a note that high since

the fifth grade." Claire cradled the leather-bound book she was reading to her chest as she shook with laughter.

"Ha. Ha." Apparently, Matt was not up to being teased just then. He turned to Helen with a stern face. "What are you doing out here, Len? Aren't you supposed to be in the library with Cassandra?"

"What's the point? Claire is ten times the researcher I am. I'd just get in her way, taking books out of the library that I don't understand half as well as she could." Helen made an expressive gesture toward Claire, who somehow managed to bow magnanimously while she was still sitting down. "Right now, studying isn't what I need. I need Ariadne to train me."

Ariadne looked at Helen doubtfully. "Helen? You know I adore you and all, but I'm *so* not about to get electrocuted. Why don't you fly to the mainland and find a nice, big tree to set on fire and we'll call it even?"

"You're not understanding me," Helen said forcefully.

All eyes turned to her and she froze. Helen fleetingly realized that she could sound too strong, maybe even a bit scary when she lost her temper. She looked down and saw her hands were blue with static and extinguished the growing bolt immediately. Shaking her head to clear it, Helen redirected her wandering attention and calmed herself. She knew her mind was not entirely grounded anymore and that she needed to be careful.

"Then explain it to me. What don't we understand?" Ariadne said reasonably.

"I need to learn how to fight hand to hand *without* my powers. I need to be able to beat someone at least as big and as strong as Matt without using an ounce of my Scion strength or any of my other talents."

"Is there a reason why?" Claire asked bluntly.

"Last night in the Underworld, Orion and I ran into Ares."

Dumbstruck looks bounced around the arena. Helen's fuzzy brain registered a few hours too late that she probably should have called someone or given someone a heads-up about the whole Ares thing. Meeting a god was a really big deal. She had been so preoccupied with what had happened between her and Orion in the cave that she hadn't even considered the ramifications of what had happened *before* that, when the two of them were still in the Underworld.

What had happened between them was more important to Helen than a god, especially now that she was beginning to suspect Orion was purposely avoiding her. Still, she should have remembered to tell someone about Ares. *Why can't I control my thoughts anymore?* Helen wondered blearily.

*Because you need me. Come. I can give you the sweetest of dreams.*

Helen spun around in a circle and looked for the source of the voice. After one rotation, it became clear that the voice was in her mind again. She took a few breaths and shook her head to clear it of all the skittering cobwebs that were tracing bright, ghostly paths across her eyes.

"Helen? Are you okay?" Ariadne asked, touching Helen's elbow gently with her Healer hands. Helen smiled at

Ariadne's kindness but pulled her arm away.

"Ares ran from Orion because it's obvious that with or without his powers, Orion knows how to fight. But I don't," Helen said, reining in her focus by sheer force of will. "I need to learn how to stand up to Ares on my own."

Especially if Orion hated her now and never wanted to see her again. When she considered returning to the Underworld without Orion, she had to stop herself from tearing up.

"Ares. As in Ares, the God of War?" Claire sounded like she wanted to make absolutely certain that everyone was on the same page.

"Yes," Helen said, nodding regretfully.

"Well, what happened?" Matt yelled in frustration. "Did you speak to him?"

"It wasn't like a normal conversation or anything. He's crazy, Matt—and I mean really *crazy*. He talked like he was reciting poetry or something and he leaked blood from the strangest places. Even his *hair* bled, if you can imagine it, and I don't think any of that blood was his." Helen looked down and saw her fingers vibrate. She was shaking all over.

In the harsh light of day, Helen suddenly wondered if she had imagined the entire encounter with Ares. Everything around her looked so real, but it seemed fake. Colors were oversaturated, and voices raked at Helen's ears like they were all too loud and jarring. It was as if her surroundings had suddenly turned into the set of a Broadway musical, and Helen was the only one standing far enough upstage to see that the world was entirely made out of paint and plywood.

"As near as we can figure, Ares is as mortal in the Underworld as we are." She was trying to outshout all the thoughts in her head. "But he's still a big man and he knows how to fight. I can't defend myself against him without more training. I need you to teach me, Ari. Will you do it?"

"You'll have to be the one to spar with her so I can teach," Ariadne said to Matt quietly. "Are you up to this?"

"Probably not. But let's do it, anyway," he replied.

"Down to the cage," Ariadne said solemnly. "Matt. You'll have to change into a *gi*. I don't want you to get blood all over your street clothes."

While Helen and Matt trained, Claire went inside to tell the rest of the Delos family about Helen's encounter with Ares and maybe try to come up with some kind of plan. Matt and Helen worked for hours, and Ariadne was not kind. More than once, Helen felt as if her sweet, delicate friend was actually channeling Hector in all his drill-sergeant glory.

Hitting Matt was not easy. He was wearing protective gear so he didn't get injured, but even so, Helen balked more often than she should have. Each time she worried about hurting Matt. That thought would lead her back to how she had hurt Orion, and guilt would overwhelm her.

The Furies had made her do it. She hadn't really meant it when she'd stabbed Orion, she reminded herself repeatedly. Even though at that moment when she knelt in front of him, she had wanted to kill him. In fact, there was only one other person toward whom she had ever felt such an overpowering emotion.

*It's the Furies,* Helen thought firmly. *It's instinct, not real emotion.*

But if her instinct was so terrible, how could she trust herself? It seemed like everything she instinctively wanted was immoral, hurtful, or just dead wrong. She had no idea what to do next.

Too tired to lift her arms, Helen let her hands drop. Matt punched her in the face.

"Yikes, Lennie! You really do suck without your lightning," Claire yelled as she came through the door.

"Thanks, Gig," Helen said sarcastically, hauling herself reluctantly off her butt. "What did Cassandra and Jason say?"

"That they would try to figure it out." Claire grimaced. "Honestly? I don't think anyone has a clue about what to do next."

"Great," Helen said while Matt tugged her arm and helped her to her feet.

"Come on," he said to encourage her. "Back to work."

Helen didn't want to work anymore, but she knew Matt was right. Time was short. They all knew that Helen would have to go to bed eventually, and it seemed like she needed everything at once . . . fight skills, plans on how to deal with Ares, theories about what he was doing down there. She needed everyone to come together and figure certain things out for her or it would never get done. Still, Helen felt responsible, like she should be the one to handle this.

A voice in her head that sounded suspiciously like Hector's reminded her that delegating was one of the most important skills a general needed to learn.

*Since when am I a general?* she thought ruefully. At that moment, Helen would have given just about anything to be able to call Hector and ask him for his advice, or text Orion and joke around. And Lucas . . . here Helen stopped. There were a thousand things she needed Lucas for, none of which she would ever get. Why couldn't she just have them in her life? Why was everything so complicated?

"Focus!" Ariadne barked.

Matt saw an advantage and shot in, sweeping Helen off her feet. Her back slammed down on the mat, and Helen stared up at the naked bulb over the cage, thinking about where she had gone astray. In one bright flash, she enumerated all the missteps that had led her to this place.

First: Hector—she knew it was her fault that he was an Outcast. She should have stopped him from killing Creon. But because she had been too afraid of the Shadowmaster's darkness, Hector had been forced to kill *her* enemy for her. Now Hector was banished.

Second: Orion—he had resisted the Furies when he could have easily killed her. In payment she had stabbed him in the chest. Now it was starting to look like she had lost him. The thought hurt so deeply, she gasped and shied away from it.

Last: Lucas. Always Lucas.

Just thinking his name seemed to halt Helen's spinning thoughts. No other thought dared come after. For one brief moment of lucidity, there was nothing but his name, clearing a bright path through her crowded mind.

"Lennie? Are you okay?" Matt asked nervously. Helen realized that she was still on her back, thinking.

"Peachy," she said, dabbing at the fat lip he had just given her. She looked at Matt standing over her with his fists still up and ready. "You know what, Matt? You're becoming quite a badass."

Matt rolled his eyes and walked away with a disgusted look on his face, like he thought Helen was teasing him. But she wasn't. He'd put on some muscle the last few weeks, and he stood like a fighter now instead of a golfer. If Helen squinted and forgot that it was Matt she was looking at, he looked almost tough. And kind of hot, she had to admit, even though it grossed her out to think of Matt as anything but a brother.

"Are you going to get up, or are you done?" Claire shouted cheerfully at Helen's prone form.

"Yeah, I think I'm done," Helen said to the ceiling.

"Good, 'cuz you've got a bunch of texts from Orion," Claire said, unabashedly reading through them. "Wow, he seems really upset. What happened?"

Claire didn't get a chance to finish the question. Helen flew out of the cage and snatched her phone away.

Orion had left her about half a dozen texts. They started

out funny, like he wanted to diffuse the situation, and then they got increasingly more serious. The second-to-last text he sent her said, **We can get past this, can't we?**

And ten minutes after that he had sent, **I guess last night was a deal breaker.**

"What happened last night?" Claire asked, reading over Helen's shoulder. "Did you two . . . ?" She broke off when she saw Helen's eyes flare with anger.

"What? What do you want to ask, Gig?" Helen said, mostly to hide her embarrassment. Helen didn't want to talk about how Orion had touched her, not even with Claire. It was private, but more important, it might turn them against Orion.

They all knew the rules surrounding the Truce. They wouldn't want her to see Orion again if they thought she was too attached to him. But attached or not, Helen didn't know if she could continue in the Underworld without him. She needed him. She just hoped, for all their sakes, that she didn't need him too much.

"Claire didn't mean anything, Helen," Matt said calmly. "We're just concerned. It's obvious from your reaction to his text that you two have grown close."

"You know what? I'm sick of all the little looks I get every time Orion texts me," Helen said defensively. "Of *course* we're getting close! He and I are going through hell together. Actual *hell*, get it? And last night was bad—really bad. After what I did, I didn't know if I'd ever hear from him again."

"What happened?" Matt asked calmly when he heard

Helen's voice break with emotion. She regained control and continued.

Helen told them all about Cerberus, the mysterious person that had caused a distraction, and how she and Orion had run for their lives for the portal. Then, in a dark monotone, she described how they had seen the Furies.

"He was resisting them, but I guess I wasn't strong enough," she admitted. "I looked him in the eye and stabbed him with his own knife. And I did it slowly."

*While I was kissing him,* Helen added in her mind but would never say aloud.

Everyone stared at Helen in utter shock. Guilty tears sprang up in her eyes and she brushed them away angrily, wishing she could as easily brush away the image of Orion's face. He had looked so surprised and hurt. And it was because she had betrayed him.

"Yeah, I know. I'm a horrible person. Now will you all give me a sec to text him back?"

The three of them tried to tell Helen that they didn't think any less of her, that it wasn't her fault that she had attacked Orion, but Helen turned her back on them and focused on her phone. She needed to reconnect with Orion much more than she needed to have her guilt assuaged by her well-meaning friends.

**I'm so sorry,** Helen wrote. **Please, please, please, forgive me?**

She waited. Nothing came back. She started scrolling through the other texts he had left, and from what she read, she didn't think he seemed angry, but maybe he'd had some time to think about what had happened and changed his mind. She might never see him again. In desperation, she sent a flurry of texts:

**If you don't forgive me, I swear I'll never sleep again.**

**Orion? At least answer me.**

**Please talk to me.**

Helen stared at her screen after each text, waiting for a response, but none came. After a few minutes of dead air, she sat down on the floor, utterly exhausted. Her whole body was hot and shaky, and her head felt like someone with massive hands had grabbed her by the face.

"Still nothing from Orion?" Ariadne asked. Helen shook her head and rubbed her eyes. How long had she been staring at the screen? Looking around, Helen noticed that Jason and Cassandra had joined them in the practice room. She rubbed her face and shivered, suddenly very cold.

"We need you to tell us about this distraction you mentioned; the one that sidetracked Cerberus," Cassandra said.

"We didn't see who it was," Helen answered. "But I'll tell you, whoever it was can really yodel."

"It just seems impossible," Cassandra said doubtfully.

"Maybe it was one of those harpies?" Jason offered gently.

"It wasn't a harpy, Jason. It was a *person's* voice, a living person who risked being eaten by a very large, three-headed wolf to help us. I know, it sounds crazy—but Orion heard it, too. It wasn't an illusion."

*I'm no illusion, either, Beauty. I'm waiting for you.*

Helen sat up straighter, her head cocked to the side, trying to locate the source of the voice. It was obvious no one else had heard it.

"Will you come with us to the library, Helen?" The way Cassandra asked made it seem almost like an order. "Jason and I want to talk to you."

Jason nodded curtly at Ariadne as he passed her. His lips were pinched tight in annoyance. Helen noticed that he didn't even look at Claire or Matt; he just walked by them coldly. Glancing back over her shoulder, Helen saw Claire staring at Jason as he walked away from her. She looked like she wanted to either call out to him or start crying. Helen could tell something had happened between the three of them, and she had a feeling it had something to do with how openly Ariadne was training Matt now.

They went upstairs to the library. Through the large glass doors that overlooked the ocean, Helen could see that it was dusk. Another day was dying, but to Helen it was just a change of light.

She looked out at the pewter horizon as it turned darker then lighter and darker again, shifting in bands from sea to sky, and thought how similar the gradient hues of gray were to her experience of day and night. Everything looked like a blah blend of black and white.

She'd have to go to sleep soon. Even if Orion refused to see her again, eventually Helen knew she would close her eyes and go back there. Alone.

"Helen?" Cassandra sounded worried.

Helen realized that her mind had wandered off again and

wondered how long she had been staring out the window.

"You wanted to talk to me?" she asked, trying to sound normal. Her nose was stuffed up and starting to run again. Jason and Cassandra looked at each other, like they hadn't decided who was going to speak first.

"We were wondering how you were feeling," Cassandra finally said.

"I've felt better." Helen looked between the two of them, sensing something fishy.

"Would you like me to check you out?" Jason said tentatively. "I may be able to help."

"That's great, but unless you can take a nap for me, I don't think there's much you can do."

"Why don't you let him try?" Cassandra asked a bit too sweetly.

"Okay, what's going on?" Helen said in a no-nonsense way. Again, they shared a conspiratorial look. "Hey. I'm sitting right here. I can see you two looking at each other, you know."

"Fine. I want Jason to check you over because we want to know if descending has caused any damage to your brain." Cassandra had clearly had enough of being polite.

"What she means is that we've noticed you seem distracted, and your health has been failing," Jason soothed.

"Enough, Jason. She wants us to be blunt, so I will be, even if you're too squeamish." Cassandra's imperious gesture made her seem like a woman decades older than she was. "Scions are susceptible to only one kind of illness, Helen.

*Mental* illness. Demigods don't get the flu or the sniffles. They go mad."

"Or you can just come right out and say it, Cass. Just like we planned on *not* doing," Jason said, rolling his eyes in frustration. "Helen, we're not saying that you're crazy. . . ."

"No, but you think I'm getting there. Don't you?" Helen and Cassandra traded stares, each measuring the other.

Cassandra had changed. Whatever was left of that lovable little girl that Helen once met was either gone or buried so deep Helen didn't think she'd ever see her again. Helen had to admit she wasn't a fan of the woman who was replacing Lucas's little sister. In fact, she thought this new Cassandra was kind of a bitch, and she was moments away from saying so.

"What we need to know is if you are capable of finishing what you started in the Underworld," Cassandra continued, undaunted by Helen's challenging look.

"And if I said no, what would you do? What can anyone do?" Helen said with a shrug. "The prophecy said that I'm the only one that can get rid of the Furies and every night I descend whether I want to or not. So what difference does it make if I can handle it or not?"

"Honestly? None. But it does change how we view the information you bring us," Jason said reasonably. "We're *trying* to believe that what you told us about your descent last night is true, but . . ."

"You have *got* to be kidding me!"

"You said you saw a god—a god who has been imprisoned

245

on Olympus for thousands of years! Then, you said that there was another *living* person in the Underworld with you and Orion, someone who appeared out of nowhere and miraculously saved your lives," Cassandra said with a raised voice. "How did this other person get down there?"

"I don't know! Look, I even doubted that was real for a second there, but I wasn't the only one who saw all of this, okay? Ask Orion. He'll tell you exactly the same thing."

"Who's to say that your delusions aren't affecting Orion's experience of the Underworld, as well as your own?" Cassandra shouted at Helen. "You are the Descender, not him! You've told us many times that if you go to bed feeling miserable, you end up in a miserable place. And if you go to bed *hearing voices* that aren't there, what then?"

"How do you know I'm hearing voices?" Helen whispered. Jason looked at her sympathetically, like everyone else could see something that Helen couldn't.

"All we're saying is that you seem to be able to control the landscape of the Underworld to some extent. You have to consider the possibility that you might be able to create entire experiences."

Helen shook her head fearfully, unable to accept what they were saying. If they were right, then what was real? She couldn't allow herself to give in to this insidious thought. She needed to believe in some things, or she might as well give up. And she couldn't give up, even if she wanted to. Too many people were counting on her. People like Hector and Orion. People she loved very much.

"Cass, you're the Oracle," Helen said, grasping at straws. "Why can't you just look into my future and tell me if I'm going insane?"

"I can't see you," Cassandra said a bit more loudly than was necessary. She made a choked sound in the back of her throat and started pacing around. "I can't see you and I've never been able to see Orion. I don't know why. Maybe it's because the two of you only meet in the Underworld, and I can only see the future of this universe, or maybe . . ."

"What?" Helen challenged. "You started this conversation, Cassandra. You'd better finish it."

"Maybe you and Orion go insane and don't have coherent futures that I can read," Cassandra said tiredly, glancing uncertainly over at Jason, who was glaring back, warning her with his eyes.

"No." Helen stood up. She felt a pressure inside her head give way and her nose start to run again. "I hear what you're saying, but you're wrong. I'm being pushed to my limit, and I know that it's taking a lot out of me, but I'm not going crazy."

Jason sighed and dropped his head into his hands like he was as weary and as fed up as Helen. A sudden burst of energy overcame him. He took three fast strides over to his father's desk and pulled a handful of tissues out of the box that was resting on top.

"Here," he said in an intense voice as he gestured to Helen's face with the tissues.

Helen raised a searching hand and touched her nose.

When she pulled her hand back it was covered in blood.

"Scions don't get spontaneous nosebleeds." Cassandra's expression was unreadable. "Jason and I think this problem is much worse than anyone else is willing to admit."

Helen cleaned herself off as best as she could and looked first at Cassandra, then at Jason. Neither of them would meet her eyes.

"Jason," Helen said, a note of pleading creeping in on her otherwise frustrated tone. "Just spit it out. How *much* worse?"

"We think you're dying," he replied quietly. "We don't know exactly why, and because of that, we have no idea how to help you."

# TEN

Matt wrapped a towel around his waist and sat down on the wooden bench outside the boys' showers in the downstairs torture chamber, or as the Delos family liked to call it, the "exercise" room. Hanging out with demigods was not easy, but he couldn't just stick his head in the sand and pretend that the world was a safe and predictable place anymore. Matt's whole life, his whole future, had changed the second he hit Lucas with his car less than a month ago.

He looked at his right hand and grimaced. He was pretty sure his knuckles weren't supposed to be this big, or this purple. He tried to ignore them. The last time he had told Ariadne that he'd broken something she'd fixed it, and then she turned a terrifying shade of gray. Matt didn't ever want to see Ariadne like that again, especially not for his sake.

Matt just needed a minute to relax in the residual steam of his shower, and then he'd go over to the little freezer in the corner and put some ice on his hand. It'd be fine, and if it wasn't—well, he was left-handed, anyway. His phone rang and he winced as he reached for it, clutching his side.

"Yeah?" he answered distractedly as he walked to the mirror. There was a large red welt rising up on his ribs. *Great,* he thought. *Now I'll have something black and blue on the upper half of my body to match that lovely bone bruise on my shin.*

"Hey, man."

"Zach?" Matt hissed. Immediately forgetting his aches and pains, he spun around and made sure that Jason or Lucas hadn't walked in. "What the hell!"

"I know, I know. I just need—"

"*Don't* ask me for a favor," Matt warned. "I've done enough of those for you over the years already."

"I'm not asking for a favor, I only want to . . . Can't you at least meet up with me?" Zach sounded desperate. "You know, to talk? I just want to talk to you!"

"I don't know, man." Matt sighed with true regret. "We're sort of past that point. I mean, we've chosen our sides, right? After you ratted out Hector, every single member of the Delos family is looking for a reason to kick your ass. Just stay away, all right?"

"All right," Zach said so softly Matt could barely hear him. His voice shook, like he was scared witless. "I just needed a friend."

"Zach . . ." Matt began to say, but the line went dead. He didn't call Zach back.

**R u in bed?**

Helen almost dropped her phone when she saw that the text was from Orion, which would have been really bad, considering she was hundreds of feet in the air and he had no other way to contact her. Recovering from the nearly disastrous fumble, she hovered in midair and told herself to calm down as she typed a reply.

**Almost. Are you going to meet me?** she wrote, wondering if her phone had an emoticon for "hopeful."

**y. Need to c u. Driving 2 caves now.**

**See you soon.**

Helen was unbelievably happy that Orion had finally gotten back in touch with her, but she still felt uneasy. It didn't feel like he'd forgiven her. She would have given a lot to be able to see his face or hear his voice instead of settling for what had to be a text written hastily while he was driving.

She came in for a quick landing in her backyard and ran into the house.

"Do you have any idea what time it is?" Jerry hollered as she bounded past him, heading for the stairs.

"Four minutes to eleven," Helen hollered back as she ran up the stairs and straight into the bathroom. "Punish me tomorrow, okay? I really need to get into bed!"

She could hear her dad mumbling angrily to himself

downstairs about how nice things had been when Helen was nine. In a rather loud voice, he remembered how thoughtful she'd been at that age, how she did everything she was supposed to do, and then he asked the ceiling why daughters couldn't just *stay* nine forever. Helen ignored him as she washed her face and brushed her teeth.

Helen couldn't stop to think about anything but meeting Orion. She had no idea what she was going to say to him, but that didn't matter. She just had to see him.

Before entering her room she put on warm socks and boots that she kept in the hallway, just in case it was as cold in there as it was outside. The door stuck. She pushed it open forcibly, making the wood of the lintel groan as she burst through the entryway. Her first steps crunched, like she had stepped on a carpet of corn flakes. Looking around, Helen saw why.

The entire room was covered in hoarfrost. The dresser, the bed, the floor, even the walls glinted sliver-white with layers of feathery ice. Her breath puffed out in front of her like a billowing cloud of smoke. Tilting her head back in disbelief, Helen saw the small fingers of icicles hanging down like crystalline buds above her bed. It had to be at least ten or fifteen degrees *colder* in her room than it was outside. *How could that even be possible?* She suspected it had something to do with the Underworld. Helen remembered that the cave that led to Orion's portal had been freezing cold.

Shutting the door behind her and desperately hoping that her room would melt by morning, Helen shivered and pulled back the covers on her bed. Ice flakes rose up and danced around the room, like handfuls of glitter tossed in the air. The clock on her bedside table read 11:11. Zipping her jacket up as high as it would go, Helen gritted her chattering teeth in determination and climbed between the stiff, cold sheets.

When Helen appeared next to him Orion was already walking down the infinite beach that never led to any sea.

"Hi," he said shyly, like it was the first time they had ever met.

"Hi, yourself," Helen said back in what she hoped was a spunky way. She was really nervous, and desperate to lighten the mood between them. "So, are we pals again or did you just come down here to tell me where I can shove my quest?"

Instead of laughing, Orion smiled sadly at her. Helen swallowed down the tight feeling that was building in her throat. She didn't know what she would do if Orion stopped helping her. She might not ever see him again.

"I'm *sorry*! I'm really, really sorry, okay? I didn't mean to stab you!"

That sounded terrible. Helen felt her eyes start stinging. Orion got downright panicky at the sight of her tears. If Helen wasn't so upset, the expression on his face would have been funny.

"Whoa! Back up, I'm not mad at you at all. In fact, *you* should be mad at *me*."

"Why would I be mad at you?" Helen asked, bewildered. She wiped at a leaky eye with the back of her hand and tried to see his face. He wouldn't look at her.

"I forced you, Helen. I was trying to—" He broke off and took a moment before starting over. "There have been Scions from the House of Rome who could control hearts so well that even members of enemy Houses could be together and talk to each other like the Furies weren't even there. I know I'm strong enough to do it too, but I've never had anyone to teach me how. I was trying to do it in the cave with you, but instead I did something I promised myself I'd never do to another person. I manipulated you. I made you kiss me, and I'm *so* sorry."

"I'm not," Helen responded so quickly she nearly cut him off. He opened his mouth to argue with her, but she talked over him. "If you hadn't, I would have killed you. I don't think I could have lived with myself if I did. I almost *killed* you," Helen repeated. She was choking up again, feeling how close she had come to doing something that she knew her conscience couldn't handle.

"Hey. I'm fine, so no crying, okay?" He took her shoulders and pulled her into a huge, warm hug. Helen relaxed gratefully against him. "Believe me, I've done things that are far worse. That's why I want you to stop and really think about whether or not you want to have me along."

"You're kinda slow, huh?" she said, her words muffled in his chest. She pulled back in his arms, laughing now the worst had passed. "Of course I want you here. I *need* you. I don't want to get attacked by any monsters tonight."

"Helen, this isn't a joke. I could do much worse than just kill you."

"What do you mean?" Helen thought about him reaching inside of her, how it had kind of hurt, even though it felt so good. He was so gentle. She imagined how horrible it would have felt if he *hadn't* been. "Is this about your invisible hand?"

"My what?" Orion asked, confused. Then he suddenly blushed and looked down.

He eased himself away from Helen and put some distance between them. She shuffled around for a moment, unsure of what to do with her arms.

"I'm sorry, I didn't know what else to call it," she stammered apologetically, thinking she might have said something silly. "It felt like you reached into my chest. I pictured a hand."

"No, don't be sorry. Call it whatever you want. I've just never heard it described that way, that's all. Not that I've done it that much," he added quickly. "I've always known that's not the kind of love I want. Forced."

"No, I wouldn't want that, either. That's quite a talent you got there," Helen said cautiously. She didn't want to offend him, but the truth was, it frightened her a little. "Can everyone from the House of Rome do that?"

"No," Orion assured her. "But they can sway you—and don't think that isn't bad enough, because it is. Sometimes the difference between doing the right thing and the wrong thing takes less than a nudge, but I'm the only one that I know of that can fully turn a heart. Or break it forever. And that's not the worst I can do."

Helen couldn't imagine many things that were worse than having a heart that was broken forever, but something in the way his eyes widened and sunk in with fear told her that *he* could.

"So, what's the worst you can do?" she asked gently. Orion clenched his jaw and spoke through his teeth.

"I'm an Earthshaker."

He said "Earthshaker" like most people would say "ax murderer."

"Okay," she said blankly. "Wait, I don't understand. What's so horrible about that?"

He stared at her disbelievingly for a moment. "Helen . . . have you ever heard of a *beneficial* earthquake? One where everyone went around afterward saying, 'Gee! It's real lucky we had that devastating earthquake! I'm so glad everyone I know is dead and the whole city is a pile of rubble now!'"

Helen didn't mean to laugh, but it slipped out, anyway. Frustrated, Orion tried to turn away from her, but she wasn't about to let him go. She grabbed on to one of his thick forearms with both of her hands and tugged until he turned back and faced her.

"Don't walk away. Talk to me," she insisted, wanting to kick herself for laughing. "Explain this whole Earthshaker thing."

Orion dropped his head and took her hand. As he spoke, he

fiddled nervously with her fingers, rolling them between his own, as if the pressure soothed him. The gesture reminded her of another time when Lucas had taken her hand. She almost pulled away, but she didn't. Orion needed her, and she realized that she wanted to be there for him. Always. Truce or no Truce, Helen couldn't convince herself that caring for Orion was wrong.

"You know that my father's side, the House of Athens, is descended from Theseus, a Scion of Poseidon," he began carefully. "Well, it's very rare, but I was born with *all* of Poseidon's talents, including the ability to cause earthquakes. When a Scion is born with this particular talent, the law of our House is that the baby is to be exposed. But my father wouldn't do it."

"What do you mean by 'exposed'?" Something about the dark way he said the word gave her goose bumps.

"Left on a mountainside to die of exposure to the elements." Orion raised his eyes to meet her gaze. "It was considered a parent's sacred duty to do this to babies born with the power to cause earthquakes in order to protect the community as a whole."

"*Sacred* duty? It's barbaric! Your House actually expected your father to leave you to die on a mountainside?"

"My House takes this law very seriously, Helen, and my father broke it. When I was ten and they found out I was still alive, they came after us. Three of my cousins are dead because of the choice my father made. What about them? They all had fathers who loved them, some of them had wives and sons who loved them, and they're dead now—because of me."

He had a point. His father had killed to protect him, but those men that came after them—they lost exactly what Daedalus had killed to protect. And another cycle of killing and revenge had started anew.

"Is that how your dad—Daedalus, right?—became an Outcast?" She asked the question quietly, careful not to push him too hard. When Orion nodded but wouldn't look up from the ground, a shocking thought occurred to her. "You *agree* with them! You think your father should have left you to die."

"I don't know what he should have done, I only know what he actually did. And I know how it turned out," Orion said darkly. "Before you judge the laws of my father's House, just think about how many mortals—not just Scions but innocent, normal people like your father, Jerry—could be killed by me. Did you feel the tremors in the cave? Do you know how many people felt that quake I made the other night, or if anyone got hurt? Because I don't."

Helen recalled their struggle in the cave, how the earth had rolled under her. She started to get an inkling of how powerful he really was, and it was scary. But it was also exciting. Orion *was* dangerous, but not in the way he thought.

"And I could have done much worse than that." His voice was low and shaky. "Helen, I can bring down whole cities, drop entire islands into the ocean, or even knock the edge of this continent if I really put my mind to it."

Helen saw a desperate light spark in his eye, and she put a hand on his arm to stop him. His whole body was trembling. She could see that he was completely terrified of what he could do, and that he found even the *thought* of causing so much pain abhorrent. That told her everything she needed to know about him.

"You're capable of monstrous things, so you must be a monster. I don't even know why I hang out with you," Helen said harshly.

Orion looked up at her, wounded, until he saw the smile spreading on her face. She shook her head sympathetically, like she thought he was foolish for even thinking her cruel words were said in earnest. He made a frustrated sound and rubbed his forehead with the heel of his hand.

"I'm dangerous when I'm out of control. And you and me together with the Furies . . ." He trailed off uncertainly, desperate to find the words that would make Helen understand him. "I could hurt a lot of people, Helen."

"I get it." And she did. "In the cave you could have hurt me in a million ways, and maybe killed a million people while you were at it. But you didn't. You're a better person than you think you are. I trust you completely."

"Really?" he asked in a hushed voice. "You're really not afraid of me?"

"Maybe I should be. But I'm not," she answered softly. "You know, when the Delos family first saw my lightning, for a second there they looked at me like I was a weapon of mass destruction. But I haven't burned down any major cities. It's not our talents that make us safe or dangerous, it's our choices. You of all people should know that."

Orion shook his head. "There's this prophecy," he said.

"Ugh! Not *this* malarkey again!" Helen said vehemently. "You want to know what I think? I think all those ancient prophecies are so full of poetic nonsense that half the time no one understands what they mean. You're not the big bad Tyrant, Orion. And you never will be."

"I hope you're right," he mumbled so quietly Helen barely heard him.

"You are *so* afraid of yourself," she remarked, truly sad that he couldn't see what a crime that was.

"Yeah, well. I've got reason to be."

"Okay, I wasn't going to ask, but now I sort of have to. You said earlier you'd done way worse things than me, and this was right after I owned up to stabbing one of my best friends in the chest. So what would you consider worse than that?"

Orion smiled pensively as he walked, thinking over her question carefully. Helen watched his face and smiled. He was such a thoughtful guy, and when something was important to him he took his time to think it through before he opened his mouth. She really liked that about him. It sort of reminded her of Matt.

"Can we have that conversation later?" he said finally. "I promise to tell you someday, just not yet, okay?"

"Sure. Whenever you're ready."

He looked over at her with tight lips, trying to be tough,

but his eyes were vulnerable and that made him look very young.

"Am I really one of your best friends?" he asked quietly.

"Well, yeah," Helen replied, feeling jittery, like maybe she shouldn't admit to caring for him so much. But she was only admitting to friendship—not making any commitments that could harm the Truce, right? "Aren't I one of your best friends?"

Orion nodded, but there was a pained look on his face. "I haven't had many friends," he admitted. "I never knew when I'd have to disappear, so I never saw the point, you know?"

He smiled cheerfully enough, but underneath he still looked troubled, like he was thinking a thousand things at once. Helen didn't push him. He must have been terribly lonely his whole life. Her heart pinched at the thought.

She knew she was supposed to maintain some sort of barrier between herself and Orion. But every time she saw him she felt closer to him. And she didn't *want* to block him out anymore.

*What does it matter, anyway?* she thought rebelliously. *I'm not going to be alive long enough to commit myself to anyone, anyway. The Truce is not in any danger.*

They kept walking in no specific direction, wherever their feet decided to wander. It wasn't like they had a time limit or a deadline to meet. Technically, they could stay down there as long as they could bear being parted from food and drink, and although Helen already felt the beginnings of a serious thirst, she had gotten very good at doing without.

As they walked, Helen did most of the talking, telling Orion all about Claire and Matt and her father, Jerry. She should have felt more pressured to make progress, but she didn't. She trusted that eventually she and Orion would find the blasted river they were looking for, and it would lead them to Persephone's Garden.

Helen considered telling Orion about how she was sort of dying, but she couldn't bring herself to spoil the moment. She was enjoying herself too much. And besides, what could Orion do to stop her from dying, anyway? What could anyone do about it? She had no guarantee that finding the Furies would end her descents into the Underworld and save her life. Helen had to accept the fact that this task might be the last she ever completed.

*At least it's something worth dying for,* Helen thought.

She looked over at Orion and knew that there were worse things that could have happened to her. Hades was no picnic, but at least she'd found Orion down here. *It just goes to show that Fate is nonsense,* she thought wryly. *Even if someone tells you the future, you never really know what you're going to find until you get there.*

A whimsical idea crossed Helen's mind, and she laughed out loud.

"What is it?" Orion asked as he shot her a look.

"No, it's nothing," she replied, still snickering. Not looking where she was going, she tripped over some loose rocks in the sand and had to grab on to Orion's arm to regain her balance. "I was just thinking, wouldn't it be great if you and I randomly stumbled over what we were looking for?"

"Yeah, that'd be pretty great," he said as he helped steady her. "Most people would want to get out of here as quickly as possible."

"It's not that," she said, subdued. "I'm not thinking that I want our quest to be over *right this second*. But I do want Persephone's Garden to magically appear in front of us."

The scenery changed.

There was no warning, no gust of wind, and no freaky dissolve like in an old movie. One second they were walking down the infinite beach during the day, and the next they were someplace else. Someplace dark and terrifying.

Just to their left, a massive structure, made entirely out of a strange black metallic rock, soared up into the dead, starless sky. The parapets glared down on them like baleful eyes, and the outermost wall seemed to shift and change position in the haze of the far distance, as if it resented being looked at directly.

Behind the black castle, a thin curtain of fire shot straight up, illuminating the barren plain around it. Following the licking flames down to their source, Helen realized that she must be looking at Phlegethon, the River of Eternal Fire that encircled the Palace of Hades.

Directly in front of Orion and Helen stood what looked like a wrought-iron dome the size of a football stadium. It was made of the same black material as the castle, except instead of being formed into huge, solid blocks, the substance was tortured into decorative curlicues. Under the arching dome was a vast garden. It was as if the builder was trying to hide the fact that he or she had built a giant cage over the garden by making it look elegant.

The black material swam with colors. Blue and purple and even warm tones like red and orange surfaced and subsided on smokelike waves. It was like looking at a rainbow buried in soot—a wonder of light, forever trapped inside darkness.

"Wow," Orion breathed. He was looking around, as astounded by the menacing castle and the cage next to it as Helen was. Then he looked down at her hands, still gripping his arm, and grinned mischievously. "Thanks for taking me with you."

"Don't thank me yet," Helen whispered.

She was staring at the main gate of the cage in horror. The lock on it was bigger than her torso, but there was no keyhole.

"That's not right," Orion whispered when his eyes finally registered the lock that Helen was staring at so intensely.

"No, it isn't," Helen said angrily.

The whole thing pissed her off. This beautiful structure was nothing more than a prison to trap a young woman who had been stolen from her home and then tricked into a detestable marriage. Helen stormed up to the lockless gate and kicked it with all her might.

"Persephone!" Helen shouted. "I know you're in there!"

"Are you insane?" Orion ran up behind Helen and tried to

clamp a hand over her mouth, but she threw him off.

"Let me in!" she screeched imperiously, like she was channeling some prerevolutionary French queen. "I *demand* to be allowed into Persephone's Garden *this instant!*"

The gate clicked and swung open with an ominous groan. Orion turned his head to look at Helen, his jaw dropping open in shock.

"If you say what you want, you can make it happen."

Helen nodded in agreement, still trying to figure out how she'd done it. She thought back to the beginning of the conversation and how she had said jokingly to Orion that she "didn't want to get attacked" that night. They had walked for a very long time without encountering any monsters. Then she asked for Persephone's Garden to magically appear, and it had.

"But I have to know *exactly* what I want, and then I have to ask for it out loud," she said.

Her face twisted up in a rueful grimace and a pained groan erupted out of her as she remembered her tortures. Hanging from the ledge. Imprisoned in the tree. Trapped inside the hell house. Worst—drowning in the pit. The strength swept out of her legs, but she would *not* fall. Not now.

"So many times I've suffered down here and I could have ended it whenever I wanted," she continued in a bitter monotone, needing to say it to believe it. "All I had to do was say what I wanted to happen out loud and it would have. It's almost too easy."

"How young you are!" A musical but melancholic voice

came to them from somewhere inside the giant, gilded cage. "Knowing what you really want and having the confidence to say it are two of the hardest things to do in life, young princess."

Helen thought that over for a moment, and grudgingly admitted to herself that she agreed. If she asked for Lucas, and got him, she'd be guilty of something that would make her feel far worse than any cut or broken bone.

"Come in and visit with me. I promise, you won't be harmed," the voice continued, gently inviting them.

Helen and Orion shared a look and walked together through the open gate and into Persephone's Garden.

Dappled light stretched from floor to ceiling in lacy rays. The dim light that filtered through the cage and the upper canopy of strange vegetation hit on dark green leaves that sparkled and glinted all around, and the dancing light gave the illusion of a gentle breeze.

Helen brushed close to a cluster of what she thought were lilacs, and caught her breath in shock when she felt them. Leaning in close to inspect the cluster, Helen saw that they were actually purple jewels, delicately carved and threaded together to create near-perfect replicas of real flowers. On closer inspection, Helen saw that the leaves were not real either, but spun out of silken threads. Nothing was real. Nothing grew here.

"So beautiful," Orion said under his breath.

At first, Helen thought he was talking about the flower-shaped jewels, but when she glanced over at him she saw that he was looking down the path at the most elegant woman Helen had ever seen.

She was almost six feet tall, graceful as a swan, with skin such a deep shade of black it was nearly blue. She didn't look that much older than Helen, but there was something about the way she moved, patient and precise, that made her seem much older. Her long neck was wrapped in ropes of huge, sparkling diamonds that were, quite frankly, put to shame by the size and luster of her eyes. On top of her glossy, knee-length hair was a tiered crown made of every type of gem that Helen could name, and quite a few she couldn't. She wore a gown of fragrant, living rose petals that glistened with dew. The petals were white at the top and then deepened in shade to blushing pink and then darker still, until her feet seemed surrounded in a cloud of rich, red roses.

Under her bare feet, which twinkled with many toe-rings, a never-ending carpet of wildflowers budded, bloomed, and then withered. Every step she took caused a flood of flowers to spring to life, only to shrivel and die as soon as they touched the barren soil of the Underworld. It was like watching hundreds of gorgeous flowers throwing themselves off a cliff like lemmings, and Helen wanted it to stop.

"Awful, isn't it?" Persephone said in her musical voice as she looked down at the dying flowers beneath her feet. "My essence creates them, but in the Underworld I don't have the power to sustain them. No flower can survive down here for long."

She looked directly at Helen as she spoke, her eyes

communicating more meaning than her words. *She knows I'm dying,* Helen thought.

Helen glanced quickly over to Orion, who seemed oblivious to the silent girl-talk. Helen smiled at the queen, conveying her gratitude. She didn't want Orion to know that she didn't have much longer. If he knew she was dying, he might change the way he acted toward her.

As if obeying a time-honored protocol, Orion stepped forward and inclined his head and shoulders in a respectful bow.

"Lady Persephone, Queen of Hades, we come to beg a favor," he said in a formal voice. It sounded strange, but right for the situation. Helen was surprised to realize that, like the Delos kids, Orion had been raised as a Scion, and he could easily switch between modern slang and old-world manners.

"May we join you?" he asked.

"Come, sit, and be welcome," she said, gesturing to an onyx bench by the side of the path. "For you are welcome here in my garden if nowhere else, young Heir of two enemy Houses." She performed such a smooth curtsy that it would have put a prima ballerina to shame.

Orion's mouth tightened. At first, Helen thought it was in anger for bringing up his less-than-ideal childhood, but as she looked closer she realized that it was because he was overwhelmed with emotion.

Helen finally understood something about Orion that she hadn't fully grasped before. Orion had never been accepted by anyone. Half of his family hated him because he hadn't been left to die on a mountainside, and the other half hated him because the Furies compelled them to. His mother was dead, and the mere sight of him sent his father into a Fury-induced rage. Apart from Daphne, who had an ulterior motive for everything she did, had any Scion ever invited Orion to actually sit next to them with such kindness?

Studying Orion's serious expression, Helen sensed that the only place he had ever been formally welcomed into a Scion's presence was right here, right now, by Persephone.

*He's only welcome in hell,* Helen thought. It made her chest ache to even consider the notion.

Realizing that Helen was standing there gawking, Persephone extended a hand, generously inviting her to join them on the bench.

Helen blushed and bobbed her head in an awkward way. She'd been caught spacing out like a crazy person again, and she couldn't remember when she'd felt like a bigger hick. She dearly wished she'd paid attention to all those stanzas on courtesy that she'd skipped over in the *Iliad.* Persephone seemed to sense Helen's discomfort and gave her a warm, welcoming smile.

"No need to stand on ceremony. Come to think of it, maybe I should be the one to bow to you," Persephone said with the barest hint of a tease in her tone.

"Hey, I'm not the one wearing a crown," Helen said with a laugh, sensing that it was okay to make a joke. Persephone smiled graciously, but then her expression became serious.

"Not yet," she said cryptically, and then continued in an assured voice. "You seek a way to kill the Furies."

Orion and Helen looked at each other, shocked by such an overt statement.

"Yes," Orion said with conviction. "I want to kill them."

"No you don't." Persephone turned her sparkling chocolate eyes on Orion, melting him instantly. "You want to *help* them. They desperately need you to save them from their suffering, my darling. Do you know who the Furies are?"

"We don't," Helen said, not liking how familiar the gorgeous goddess was being with Orion. "Please explain it to us."

"The Furies are three young sisters—born from the blood of Uranus when his son, the Titan Cronus, attacked him. The Furies were stolen away by the Fates at the moment of their creation and forced to play their role in the Great Drama. The pain they feel is real, and the burden they carry . . ." Persephone broke off and stared pleadingly into Orion's eyes. "They are still little more than children and they've never experienced even one single moment of joy. You know my meaning, prince. *You* know what they suffer."

"Hatred," he said, glancing over at Helen. She recalled how horrible it was to feel hatred toward Orion in the cave, and she knew that he was thinking the same about her.

"We have to help them," Helen whispered to him, and he smiled in answer. The two of them were entirely in tune. "We have to set them free."

"The Furies and the Scions," Orion said, determined.

"Yes," Helen agreed. "And I promise, I'll set you free, too, Your Highness."

"No, don't!" Persephone suddenly exclaimed. She rushed to speak. "Hurry, Helen, you won't survive much longer without dreaming! You must bring the Furies water from the River—"

The name of the river was drowned out by a great, booming voice.

"HELEN, YOU ARE BANISHED."

Helen felt her whole body being hurled up and out of the Underworld as if it were being scooped up and thrown by mile-wide hand. For a moment, she thought she saw a huge face dominating her vision. It seemed familiar. His bright green eyes were so sad. . . .

Helen woke in her bed. Sitting up, she dislodged the fine layer of ice crystals that were dusted over her covers like sifted flour, sending some of the glittering flecks to dance in the dry, subzero air. Her face felt stiff, so she pulled a hand out from under the blankets and raised it to her numb cheek. Although her fingers were nearly senseless with cold, she could tell that her entire face was covered in a spiky layer of frost. She moved her hand to feel her hair and she found that it, too, was frozen in thick ropes of ice.

Breathing fast and sending clouds of steam out in front of her, Helen looked around, trying to control her shivering. Everything in her room looked slightly blue, but the deep chill was worst around her bed. Helen picked up the clock on her nightstand and had to rub away a layer of ice with her thumb to see its face. The time turned from 11:11 to 11:12 as she stared at it.

Although she and Orion had been down in the Underworld for what felt like days to them, in the real world she had closed her eyes mere seconds ago and already she was nearly frozen through. The cold was definitely getting worse. Helen wondered if her body would freeze solid the next time she descended.

Then she wondered if she would ever descend again. She'd been banished by Hades himself. That didn't sound very promising.

Helen got out of bed and slipped her way across her icy floor to get her phone, but there was no text from Orion yet. He was probably still coming up from the caves. Time didn't pass while they were in the Underworld, which meant that the second Orion entered the portal would be the second he exited, no matter how long he had "spent" on the other side. If they were lucky, Orion was coming back right now after being allowed to stay in the Underworld long enough to hear what Persephone had to say. Helen could only hope that Orion had succeeded where she had so obviously failed.

Helen shivered violently and realized that she had to get out of her room and warm up somehow. She remembered Hector's lecture on the beach, right after he had nearly drowned her. Helen might be impervious to weapons, but she was not completely invulnerable, and extreme cold could kill her as surely as drowning.

Muscling her icy door open as quietly as she could, Helen poked her head out of her bedroom and looked around. Luckily, her dad was still downstairs watching TV. She shut the door firmly behind her, pushed the bean-bag heat stopper up against the crack on the bottom to hide the unreal cold in her bedroom from her father, and shouted down to Jerry that she was going to take a bath to help her sleep. He grumbled something about how she should just close her eyes and give it more than one second, but he didn't ask any questions or object.

As she headed into the bathroom, Helen smacked herself on the forehead with her phone a few times as punishment for her terrible blunder in the Underworld. She couldn't believe she had been so stupid. Hades was probably not the best place to talk about freeing the captive queen, as "the boss" was probably listening the whole time. And Helen had openly threatened to take away the one thing in the entire multiverse that Hades cared about—his queen. *Stupid!* Now Helen was banished. How the heck was she supposed to accomplish her task if she couldn't descend?

As she stripped and filled the tub up with hot water, she thought through her meeting with Persephone. It struck her as odd that Hades hadn't intervened one way or the other when she and Orion talked about freeing the Furies. It was only when Helen opened her big yap about freeing his queen that Hades had put his foot down.

Helen gingerly lowered herself into the hot water, phone

still in hand, and filed that bit of information away. Then she sighed and soaked, trying to figure out how she was going to thaw out her room before her father found out about it. Her phone vibrated.

**Are you up?** Orion texted.

**OMG, did you hear the name of the river?** Helen sent back.

**What r u talking about? I got booted right after P said you were going to die.**

**Oh. There was more,** Helen replied, ignoring the whole dying thing and hoping Orion would, too. **She told me that we need to give the Furies water from the River . . . I didn't hear the name b/c I got booted, too.**

**Still good intel. I'll find the right one eventually.**

**Wait, "you'll" find? What about "we'll" find?**

**What part of "won't survive" did you not get?**

**That's only if I don't dream.**

**You don't dream?**

**Not when I descend.**

**Then you're not descending anymore.**

Helen thought that was a little bossy.

**NOT really your decision,** she texted back.

**NOT going to argue** came his defiant reply.

**Hang on. You don't control this.**

**N.O. Now go away. I have to drive.**

For ten minutes, Helen sloshed around the tub, muttering to herself. There was something he was missing—a point that she knew she had to make—but she couldn't see it just yet. She tried to get him to come back to the argument with all kinds of texts. She even threatened to lie down and descend immediately. After that, he came back with a long reply, one of those texts that you have to pull over to type.

**If you get back into bed, I swear to you, I'll swim to Nantucket, kick in your door, and tell Jerry everything. You can explain to him why you want to die. Stay out of the UW. I'm not joking around anymore.**

Threatening to tell her dad was just plain low—she'd told Orion that Jerry was a "no-fly zone," and he'd promised never to violate that. But she had to admit, if she was really considering doing it, telling her dad was the only threat that would have stopped her. Orion knew her very well. She wondered how he'd managed that in such a relatively short amount of time. Helen smiled at the phone for a moment, and then forced herself to stop. She didn't like being told what to do, but she *did* like that he cared enough to try.

**I can't descend, anyway,** she finally admitted after a long lull in their exchange. **Hades banished me and booted us both out of the UW because I threatened to take P away. Can you still go down?**

**Pretty sure. You're banished? Wow. There really is such a thing as a good god. Strange that it's Hades.**

She knew he was just worried about her safety, but there was something really wrong with his logic. Helen started typing before she even knew what she was going to say. Her scattered brain finally hit on why she was so upset about being banished, and why she had argued with Orion so belligerently to begin with.

**But remember the prophecy,** she typed frantically. **I'm the Descender—the only one who's supposed to be able get rid of the Furies. If I don't do this, how many more will suffer? You'd never see your dad again.**

Helen bit her lip, agonizing over whether or not she should tell him what she was really thinking.

**We'd never be able to see each other again. I don't think I could handle that,** she finally sent, adding in her thoughts, *for what little time I have left, anyway.*

There was a long pause where Orion didn't respond, and Helen wondered if she'd just made a huge mistake. To take her mind off him, she sent an email to Cassandra and the rest of the Greek Geeks, explaining everything that had happened in the Underworld. Then she stared at the face of her dark phone until she heard her dad come upstairs, get in bed, and start snoring. Still, Orion didn't text back.

Helen got out of the tub and dried off. She didn't really know what she was going to do next, but she knew that she couldn't go back to her frozen room. There was always the couch downstairs, but she decided that whether she lay down or not, it really didn't matter. She'd lost track of how many weeks she'd gone without true rest, anyway.

She spent a very long time in the hot bathroom catching up on the grooming ritual that she'd neglected for ages. She clipped things that needed clipping and rubbed all of her bendy parts with gooey oils. When she was finished, Helen wiped the steam off the mirror over the sink and for the first time in ages, she took a good look at herself. The first thing she noticed was her mother's necklace. It stood out in sharp relief against her flushed skin, glowing on her throat as if it had sucked power from all of her self-pampering. Then she looked up at her face.

It was the same face that so many people had died for eons ago, that so many were still dying for. Scions were still killing each other to avenge deaths that went back all the way to the walls of Troy—all the way back to the first woman to wear the exact face that Helen was looking at in the mirror.

Was *any* face worth all that? It didn't make any sense. There had to be more to the story. All this suffering couldn't be about one girl no matter how pretty she was. Something else had to be going on that wasn't in the books.

She heard her phone buzz and rushed to grab it, knocking over half the toiletries on the sink as she did so. She snatched the assorted bottles and tubes out of the air before they had a chance to clatter noisily against the floor and wake her dad. Suppressing a nervous giggle, she put them silently back in their proper places, then looked at the message.

**I've thought it over. If this is what it takes to keep you alive, then I'm ready for it,** Orion answered, almost half an hour after they'd stopped texting. **I'll let you go, I'll let this whole quest go, but I can't let you die.**

Helen slumped down on the edge of the tub in disbelief. Giving up would damn Orion to a life on the run, without a home or a family. He was willing to suffer all that—for her.

Or was it for her stupid face? After all, they barely knew each other. What could inspire that kind of self-sacrifice?

Daphne had called their nearly identical faces cursed, and Helen had always assumed that her mother had meant that their faces had cursed them. For the first time, Helen considered the possibility that her mother had meant that it cursed the people who *looked* at them. The thought of Orion sacrificing everything he'd ever wanted just because it was dangerous for her didn't sit right with Helen. There was so much more at stake than just one person's life, even if that life was her own.

Helen felt something give way inside—so what if she had a crush on him, or if he had one on her? Orion couldn't give up now. Not just because of what it would cost him, but because of what it would cost them all. If no one got rid of the Furies, what would happen to Hector and the other Outcasts? What would happen to all the Scions? Helen remembered Orion telling her about his dream of a field of Scion bones in Hades, and realized that it had been more than just a nightmare. Orion had received a warning in that dream, Helen was sure of it. The cycle had to end or their kind would eventually become extinct, just like the Ice Giants.

**You jackass.** She stabbed at the keys with her fingers, like she was trying to push her words directly into his big, fat, self-sacrificing, and unbelievably brave head. **If you give up on our quest I will hunt you down myself! I'll find a way to fix this dreaming/banished-by-Hades problem, and when I do we'll free the Furies together. In the meantime, you KEEP GOING. Got it?**

She pressed SEND and waited. There was a long pause. Several times Helen started to write a text, but she ended up erasing each one. She was so tired her eyes were watering and her ears kept getting blocked up, forcing her to yawn repeatedly to clear them.

Mid-yawn Helen felt something pop behind her eyes, and noticed her upper lip had suddenly become very damp. She touched her mouth and found blood on her fingers. She put a tissue to her nose before she had a chance to stain any-thing and pressed down hard, waiting for the bleeding to stop. Finally, after mopping up her bloody face and glaring at her phone as if that would make Orion respond faster, it lit up again.

**You can hunt for me all you want, Hamilton, but you know you'll never find me, right?**

He was joking around again, which was a very good sign. Helen knew this decision had been hard for him, so she needed to be sure. She needed something that resembled a promise, in case she didn't make it to the end of their quest.

**Do we have a deal? You'll keep going no matter what?** she texted. He didn't respond immediately, so she added, **Hello? Deal?**

**Sorry. Getting into bed. Yeah, I'll keep going.**

Helen smiled and slid off the edge of the tub to lean against the wall. She wrapped herself up in her robe and stuffed her feet in her slippers as she scooted down into a makeshift nest of warm, damp towels. She imagined him climbing under the covers in his dorm, taking his phone with him. He'd fall asleep like that, she thought, with their conversation cupped in his hand.

**Knew I could count on you**, she sent, cradling his messages close to her.

**Always and forever. Where are you?**

**Bed**, she wrote, even though it was more like "floor."

**Good, me too. You can finally rest. And so can I! Exhausted.**

Helen didn't want to stop texting with him. She could have stayed up all night trading little stories in the dark, but she was finally warm again after what seemed like years of shivering. Her eyes were beginning to close on their own.

**Good night, Orion.**

**Sweet dreams.**

# ELEVEN

Helen's eyes opened. She didn't feel like she was waking up, and she suspected it was because she hadn't really been sleeping. It felt more like she'd been hit on the head and lost consciousness for a few hours, and was now coming around. Like a jump cut in a movie, one moment Helen was looking at Orion's last text and the next she was looking at the bath mat on the floor. The sun was up, her hair was dry, and she could hear her dad getting out of bed.

Helen could tell from the jittery, clammy feeling all over her body that although her brain had checked out for a few hours, she hadn't gotten what she needed. She hadn't descended, which was a relief, but she also hadn't dreamed. That was very bad. Persephone had told her that she didn't have much time, and Helen didn't know how much longer she could last without dreaming.

Hearing Jerry opening his closet spurred Helen into action. She jumped up and dismantled the nest she'd made herself the night before, then hastily began brushing her teeth to give her father the illusion that she'd just beaten him to the bathroom.

It was Monday, a new week, and Helen's turn to do the cooking. She rushed into her frozen room dreading what she was going to find, but was pleasantly surprised that it had mostly thawed. Something clicked in her head. The intense cold must have something to with how she had been turning her bed into a portal to the Underworld. Since she hadn't descended the night before, the cold had dissipated a bit. It was still a meat locker in there and everything was damp with melt water, but at least she didn't have to take a hair dryer to her dresser to get the drawers open, like she'd had to the day before.

So far she'd been able to hide just how cold it had gotten in her room from her father, but she knew she wouldn't be able to keep it from him much longer. Helen decided that there wasn't anything she could do about that. She just hoped he stayed out of her room. She had other things to worry about, not the least of which was the Myrmidon that was probably watching her at that moment. Helen shrugged off this disturbing thought as best she could, but still went into her closet before she took off her clothes.

She got dressed as quickly as possible, shivering the few seconds she was forced to spend exposed, and then ran downstairs to warm up at the stove as she cooked breakfast. For a while, she turned up the gas on the stove like it was a campfire. When the air all around her wavered with the heat, she sighed happily and closed her eyes, but something wasn't right. She didn't feel like she was *alone*. Her eyes snapped open, and she looked around. The air continued to dance in front of her for a few moments, and then it settled.

Doubt began to creep in. She wasn't hearing voices, but she still felt like there was another presence in the kitchen, and that was obviously impossible. Helen knew she was losing it. She didn't have much time left, but there was nothing she could do about it until that night. She turned back to the stove and got to work on breakfast.

When she was done making pumpkin pancakes she glanced at the clock. Her father was running a bit late, so she put in a bit of extra effort and sprinkled powdered sugar over the top of the stacks through an old bat-shaped cutout, like they used to do when Helen was a kid. When she was finished she looked up at the clock again. She was just about to go to the bottom of the stairs to call up for Jerry when she heard him come down.

"What took you so . . ." Helen stopped dead when she saw her father.

He was wearing a tattered black dress with red-and-white-striped stockings, a black wig, and his face was painted green. In his hand was the traditional pointy witch's hat with a fat silk sash and a silver buckle on the front. For a moment she just stared at him with her mouth hanging open.

"I lost a bet with Kate," he said sheepishly.

"Oh, man. I gotta get a picture of this." Her shoulders were shaking with laughter as she grabbed her phone. She snapped a quick shot of her dad before he could run away, and sent it immediately to pretty much everyone she'd ever met. "Is it Halloween today? I've lost track."

"Tomorrow," he said, sitting down to eat his pancakes. "I've got two whole days in drag and then I'm never celebrating Halloween again."

Halloween was always a busy time at the News Store, and despite Jerry's grumbling about having to wear a dress, Helen knew he loved to celebrate all the holidays. Helen asked her dad if he needed help at the store, but he told her there was no way he was letting her come in.

"You look greener than I do," he said with worry. "Do you need to stay home from school today?"

"I'll be all right," Helen said with a shrug and looked down at her breakfast to hide the guilt she felt. She honestly didn't know if she was going to be all right or not, and she couldn't look at her father and lie.

Claire cruised up to the house in her nearly silent car, rolled down the passenger window, and blasted the song on the radio rather than honking.

"I'd better go before the neighbors call the cops," Helen said to her father as she gathered up her stuff and ran out of the house.

"Come right home after school; you need your rest!" Jerry shouted after her. Helen waved in a noncommittal way from the door, knowing that she couldn't. She had to train with Ariadne for her return to the Underworld. The clock was ticking for Helen, and she had a lot of promises to keep before it stopped.

Lucas watched Helen run out her front door and jump into Claire's car. She looked exhausted and skinny, but even so, her smile for Claire was bright and beautiful and full of love. That was Helen. No matter what she was going through, she had this nearly magical way of opening her heart for others. Just being near her made him *feel* loved, even if he knew that her love wasn't directed toward him anymore.

She'd almost caught him again that morning, and he was starting to suspect that he was scaring her. Somehow, she could still sense him. Lucas had to figure out why, because he certainly wasn't going to stop guarding her. Not until he was certain that Automedon was gone for good.

Claire and Helen started shrieking as they drove off, murdering one of Lucas's favorite Bob Marley songs. Helen had the *worst* singing voice. It was one of the things he liked the most about her. Every time she warbled like a cat that just got stepped on, he wanted to pick her up and . . . yeah.

Reminding himself that Helen was his cousin, he dropped his light-cloak and soared up into the air so he could switch on his phone and start his day. He had a text message waiting.

**I know you were down there w/us. And I think I know how u did it,** read the text. **We need to talk.**

285

**Who is this?** Lucas replied, already knowing who it was. Who else could it be, after all? But he didn't want to give the guy an inch. He couldn't. He was too angry.

**Orion.**

Making him text it was even worse. Seeing that guy's name and picturing Helen say it just ate him up inside. The rage was getting worse every day, and he had to take a moment to stop himself from chucking his phone across the Atlantic.

**Great. What do you want?** Lucas replied when his hands had unclenched enough to type. It was bad enough he had to let Helen go, but did he also have to get texts from the guy who got to spend every night with her?

**You need to be a dick—I get it. But there's no time. Helen is dying.**

"You're in a good mood!" Helen chirped.

"I am!" Claire practically screamed.

"Ooh, don't tell me! Flushed cheeks, dewy eyes . . . *Could you be love? Oh, yeah!*"

Helen sang the final part of the Bob Marley song that Claire had been howling. It perfectly summed up Claire's ecstatic mood, and Claire joined her for the "oh, yeah" part, answering Helen's tacit question.

"What can I say? He really is sort of a god." Claire sighed and giggled gloriously as she careened down the street.

"What happened?" Helen screeched, vicariously giddy. It felt so good to laugh again, Helen forgot about everything else in her life but Claire's glowing face.

"He FINALLY kissed me! Last night," she practically sang. "He climbed up the side of my *house*! Can you believe it?"

"Um, yeah?" Helen grinned and shrugged.

"Oh, right, I guess you can," Claire said, waving it off good-naturedly. "So, anyway, I opened my window to yell at him and tell him that he was going to wake my grandma— you know how she can hear a dog fart two houses down. But he said he *had* to see me. That he *couldn't* stay away from me anymore, and then he *kissed* me! Is that not the best first kiss ever?"

"Finally! What took him so long?" Helen laughed. The laugh turned into a yelp as Claire stomped on the brakes to obey a stop sign. Horns honked at them from either side of the street.

"Oh, I don't know." Claire drove on, ignoring the fact that she'd nearly caused a horrendous traffic accident. "He thinks I'm too fragile, that I don't know the danger I'm in— blah, blah. Like I haven't spent my entire life around a Scion. Ridiculous, right?"

"Yeah. Ridiculous," Helen said as she grimaced in fear at both Claire's nonchalant attitude toward Scions and her daredevil driving. "You know what, Gig? Love doesn't make you immune to car wrecks."

"I know that! God, you sound just like *Jason*," Claire responded, her entire being melting a bit as she said his name. She pulled into her parking spot in the school lot, shut off her car, and turned to Helen with a sigh. "I am so in love."

"Apparently!" Helen grinned. She knew she wasn't Jason's

favorite person anymore, but regardless of how he'd been treating Helen, she could see that Claire needed her support in this. "Jason really is a great guy, Gig. I'm so happy for you two."

"But he's not Japanese," she said, her face falling. "How am I supposed to bring him home to my parents?"

"Maybe they won't mind so much," Helen said with a shrug. "Hey, they got used to me, right?"

Claire gave her a dubious look, held out her hand palm down, and tipped it left and right as if to say "fifty-fifty."

"Really?" Helen exclaimed. She couldn't believe it. "We've been friends our entire freaking lives and your parents *still* don't like me?"

"My mom *loves* you! But, Lennie, you have to understand, you're really tall and you smile a lot. That's kind of not cool with Grandma."

"I can't believe it," Helen muttered crankily as she got out of the car and headed across the parking lot. "I've spent more time with that old bat . . ."

"She's traditional!" Claire said in defense.

"She's racist!" Helen countered, and Claire backed off because she knew Helen was sort of right. "Jason is perfect for you, Gig. Don't you dare let the fact that he isn't Japanese ruin this! That guy was willing to die for you."

"I know," Claire said, her voice getting hoarse with emotion. She stopped dead, even though everyone else was rushing into school to avoid being late. Helen stopped with her, moved by Claire's rare show of vulnerability. "I was so scared down there, Len. So lost and thirsty, you know? And then . . . there he was. I still can't believe he actually came to get me in that horrible place."

Helen waited for Claire to calm down. The rawness of the emotions surrounding Claire's near-death experience reminded Helen of how awful the Underworld actually was. Orion had changed the Underworld so drastically for her that she didn't consider it punishment to be down there anymore. As long as she was with him, she could almost enjoy it.

"But I don't love him just because he saved me," Claire continued, breaking Helen out of her thoughts about Orion. "Jason is one of the best people I've ever met. I would admire him regardless."

"Then forget what your grandmother thinks," Helen said with a firm nod.

"Ugh, I wish I could! But the old boot never shuts up," Claire groaned as she tugged on the door and walked in with Helen, both of them laughing again. Helen had forgotten how great it felt to just goof off with Claire. She began her day in high spirits.

The rest of the morning, however, was like a slow dive into a state of exhaustion. Helen had to keep shaking herself awake, and several times her teachers reprimanded her for nearly dozing off. Somehow she managed to stumble through the morning and met back up with Claire at lunch.

Sitting at their usual table, Helen saw Matt on the other side of the cafeteria and signaled for him to join them. As he made his way over, Claire elbowed Helen and pointed out all the girls staring and whispering as Matt passed.

He had a cut on his lip and scrapes on his knuckles that were obviously from fighting. His shirt, which had been a bit too loose a month ago, looked a little tight now. Through the slightly strained material it was easy to see that his chest and shoulder muscles were positively *shredded*. He'd lost the baby fat in his face, making him look more chiseled and grown-up; he even walked different, like he was ready for anything.

"Oh my God," Claire said with a look of disbelief on her face. "Lennie, is Matt a stud?"

Helen nearly snarfed her sandwich and had to hastily swallow her bite to answer. "Right? Matt's, like, a total babe all of a sudden!"

Claire and Helen paused, looked at each other, and said, "EEEWWW!" at exactly the same time before bursting out laughing.

"What is it?" Matt asked when he got to the table, giving them both weird looks. He pointed to Helen's sandwich and took a guess. "Cucumber and vegemite?"

"No, ding-dong, it's not the sandwich," Claire said, wiping her eyes and still winding down from the laugh. "It's you! You're officially a hottie now!"

"Oh, shut it," he said as a blush instantly colored his face and neck. His eyes darted over to where Ariadne had stopped to chat with another classmate, and then quickly looked away.

"You should make a move," Helen said in a low voice to Matt while Claire was busy waving Ariadne over.

"And get shot down?" he replied sadly, and shook his head. "Hell no."

"You don't know—" Helen began, but Matt cut her off firmly.

"Yeah, I do."

When Ariadne joined them, Helen had no choice but to let it go, but she honestly couldn't see what Matt's problem was. She knew for a fact that Ariadne cared about him, and maybe all Matt needed to do was take a chance and just kiss her, like Jason had with Claire. Again Helen was reminded of Orion and the memory of how his lips felt.

"Helen?" Ariadne said.

Helen looked up and saw everyone staring at her. "Yes?" she said, bewildered and a bit startled.

"You didn't hear a word any of us just said, did you?" Cassandra asked.

"Sorry," Helen replied defensively. *When did Cassandra get here?* she wondered.

"Did you dream last night?" Cassandra asked, like she was repeating herself. Helen shook her head. Cassandra sat back in her chair and folded her arms, her naturally bright red lips pursed in worried thought.

"Why didn't you say anything?" Claire said to Helen, looking both concerned and guilty.

"I don't know," Helen mumbled. "I haven't dreamed in so long I guess I forgot to mention it."

"Well, Orion didn't," Cassandra said in her eerily calm way. Then her face changed dramatically and she leaned toward Helen, looking exactly like a normal girl for a second. "Is Orion always so . . ." She broke off, unable to frame her question properly.

"Funny? Pig-headed? Huge?" Helen fired off in rapid succession, trying to answer Cassandra's question with whatever Orion-ish word popped into her cluttered head.

"Is he really big?" Ariadne asked curiously. "Like the original Orion?"

"He's enormous," Helen answered quickly, trying not to blush. A few more descriptive words bubbled up inside of her head as she thought about Orion, but she kept those to herself. "Help me out here, Cass. Is he always so *what*?"

"Unpredictable," Cassandra finally decided.

"Yeah. That's actually a great word to describe him. Wait, how can you know that?"

"I didn't see him coming," she said, more to herself than anyone else.

"What are you talking about? Did he text you or something?" Helen asked, growing more and more confused. "I never gave him your number."

"Lucas did." Cassandra acted like everyone knew this.

"What?"

"Orion texted my brother first thing this morning."

"How did Orion get . . ." Helen stumbled horribly, and stopped breathing. She couldn't say both Orion's and Lucas's names in the same sentence for the life of her.

The bell rang, and everyone else gathered their things while Helen stared off into space, unable to get past the thought of Lucas. Helen knew she was so sleep deprived that she had become cerebrally impaired, but even so, she knew that it was Lucas's name and not Orion's that had dealt the knockout punch to her nervous system.

"Why didn't you say something, Len?" Claire asked in a hurt voice. She automatically grabbed Helen's dangling arm and dragged her along to her next class when Helen didn't respond to the bell.

"Say what?" Helen mumbled, still in a daze.

"This morning! You didn't say one thing about how you're, you know . . . you let me go on and on about Jason, like it was nothing."

"Gig, don't," Helen said gently. "I'd so much rather hear about how happy *you* are than talk about how messed up *I* am. Really. It helps me to hear that good things are still happening in the world, especially when they're happening to you. I want you to be insultingly happy for the rest of your life, no matter what happens to me. You know that, right?"

"God, you're really dying, aren't you?" Claire gasped quietly. "Jason said so, but I didn't believe him."

"I'm not dead yet," Helen said through a weak laugh as she backed into the room. "Get to class, Gig. I'm sure I'll survive social studies, at least."

Claire waved sadly at her and then trotted down the hall while Helen went in and sat at her usual seat. She watched in shock as Zach came and sat next to her. He tried to say something but she cut him off.

"I can't believe you actually have the nerve," Helen said. She got up and took her stuff, but Zach grabbed her arm as she walked past.

"Please, Helen, you're in danger. Tomorrow . . ." he said in an urgent whisper.

"Don't touch me," Helen hissed, pulling her wrist out of his grip.

Zach's face fell and his eyes looked up at her desperately. For a moment, Helen felt bad for him. Then she thought about how he'd almost gotten Hector killed at the track meet and her softening heart turned back into stone. She might have known Zach since grade school, but those days were long gone. Helen moved to another desk and didn't look at him again.

After school, Helen and Claire ran track and then went to the Delos compound together. When they got there no one was around. Not even Noel, who had left a message taped to the refrigerator informing any hungry person who came into the kitchen that there was nothing to eat and she'd be back in a few hours with groceries. Claire and Helen grimaced at each other when they read the note, then they raided the cupboards for anything they could find to quiet their rumbling post-run tummies. Over their pilfered snack, they sorted out why the house was so darn empty.

Pallas and Castor were still in New York, deep in the never-ending bickering of Conclave. According to their last letter, there was still no decision about permanently getting rid of the Myrmidon, although they had ruled that he wasn't allowed to take up residence on the island. Which was useless, anyway, because it turned out that this whole time he'd been living on a yacht. Jason and Lucas were at football practice, and since Cassandra's cello was missing from the library, Helen and Claire assumed that she and Ariadne were at school rehearsing for the play.

Somehow, the two Delos girls had gotten roped into playing the music for the winter production of *A Midsummer Night's Dream*. Neither of them had the time, but Cassandra was especially peeved about it. She no longer saw the point in trying to appear normal when her underdeveloped body and her uncanny stillness so obviously signaled that she wasn't. Helen knew that maintaining appearances was important, but she had to agree. No amount of volunteering could make Cassandra seem like a normal fourteen-going-on-fifteen-year-old, so why torture the poor girl with theater?

"Hey, Gig?" Helen mused while she and Claire polished off the last of Jason's hidden stash of chocolate chip cookies. "How much do you weigh?"

"Right now? Probably about a thousand pounds," Claire said, brushing cookie crumbs off her lap. "Why?"

"I want to try something that might be kind of dangerous. Are you game?"

"I'm so game I should change my name to Yahtzee," Claire replied smoothly with a hell-raiser grin.

Horsing around the whole way, Helen led her out to the arena while Claire continually tried and failed to hip-bump, trip, and or shoulder-throw her much larger and supernaturally strong friend. When they finally got out to the middle of the sand, after much staggering and giggling, Helen grew serious, telling Claire to hold still. She stood close to Claire, and concentrated on her petite friend's mass.

"Len, that tickles!" Claire giggled. "What are you doing?"

"I'm trying to make you weightless so I can finally show you what it feels like to fly," Helen murmured, her eyes still closed. "Maybe put your hands on my shoulders?"

Claire eagerly did as Helen asked. She'd always wanted to know what Helen and Lucas experienced when they soared effortlessly into the air, but until now, Helen had been too uncertain of her ability to agree to try it with Claire. Lucas had warned her that carrying a passenger would be difficult, but that didn't scare Helen so much anymore. She figured if she didn't try it now, she might never get the chance again.

As soon as Claire leaned into Helen, the two of them floated up about ten feet in the air. Claire gasped with awe.

"I feel . . . It's *amazing!*" Claire's voice wavered with elation, and although Helen was still concentrating on all the variables that kept the two of them aloft, she had to smile.

Flying really was amazing, and despite what Lucas had said, Helen was surprised to find that lifting Claire was complicated, but not draining. She knew Lucas wouldn't mislead her about something like this, so she had no choice but admit to herself what he'd been telling her all along. She *was* stronger than he was. Emboldened, Helen rose even higher.

"What the hell are you doing?" Jason screamed from the ground below them, startling them both.

Claire screeched, and Helen's concentration faltered. Before she could recover, the two of them started to drop quickly. Looking below, Helen could see that they had soared up higher than she'd thought. Even though she and Claire had fallen a long ways, they were still nearly thirty feet above Jason, Cassandra, Ariadne, and Matt, who were all staring up at them with panicked faces.

"Let her down now!" Jason commanded furiously.

"Jason, I'm fine," Claire called in a soothing voice, but he wouldn't listen.

"*Now*, Helen," he growled. Even from so high up, Helen could see that Jason was bright red with anger. She decided she'd better do as he said before he popped a vein or something, and she began to gently lower Claire down to him.

She was still about ten feet off the ground when Jason jumped up and snatched Claire out of the air, forcing Helen to release her entirely. He was so angry he couldn't even look at Claire as he put her down on her own two feet. He rounded on Helen as soon as she touched down in front of him.

"How could you be so selfish?" he asked in a strangled voice.

"Selfish?" Helen squeaked incredulously. "*I'm* selfish?"

"Did you ever consider how badly you could have hurt Claire if you dropped her?" He got louder and more wound up with every word. "Do you have a *concept* for how long a broken leg hurts a full mortal even after it's healed? It can cause them pain for the rest of their lives!"

"Jason," Claire tried to interrupt, but Helen was already yelling back at him.

"She's my best friend!" Helen howled. "I would never let anything bad happen to her!"

"You can't promise that. *None* of us can promise her that because of what we are!" he howled back.

"Jase . . ." Ariadne put a calming hand on her twin's arm. He shook it off roughly and then turned on her.

"You're no better, Ari. You won't date Matt, but you think *training* him is going to help?" Condemnation seethed out of him. "How many times do we have to see it before we finally accept the truth? Full mortals don't live for very long around Scions. Or hadn't you noticed that we don't have a mother?"

"Jason! Enough!" Ariadne exclaimed. Shocked tears sprang to her eyes.

But Jason was already done. In one quick motion, he whirled around, shied away from Claire's reaching hands, and headed straight for the darkening beach. Claire backpedaled after him, giving Helen a pleading look. Helen mouthed the word "sorry" and in response, Claire sighed and shrugged, like there was nothing either of them could do. Then she left to chase Jason, who was rapidly retreating into the gathering shadows of the beach.

"This is my mom, Aileen, and Aunt Noel when they were in college together in New York City," Ariadne said. She removed a picture that was sandwiched between the pages of a book on a shelf over her bed, and jumped down to hand it to Helen.

The photo showed two stunning young women behind a packed bar, pouring drinks. They had a sassy way about them that Helen admired right away, and they were laughing together uproariously as they served multicolored cocktails to the smeared waves of people in front of them.

"Look at Noel!" Helen burst out in surprise. "Is she wearing leather pants?"

"She sure is," Ariadne said with a painful grimace. "I guess she and my mom were a little on the wild side when they were younger. They used to work in nightclubs and trendy restaurants all over the city to pay their tuition. That's actually how they met my dad and Uncle Castor. In a *nightclub*."

"Your mom was very beautiful," Helen said, and she meant it. Aileen was slender, but still curvy and ultrafeminine. She had the black hair and the deep golden-brown skin of a Latin American. "But she doesn't . . ."

"Look anything like us? No. Scions look like other Scions from history. We inherit nothing from our mortal parents," Ariadne said sadly. "I think it would have been easier on my dad if he could look at us and see something of her living on. He loved her very much—still does to this day."

"Yeah, I know," Helen mumbled, and she was surprised to realize that she did know. Somehow she could sense how deeply this stranger in the photo had been loved. Looking at the way Aileen and Noel were cracking each other up,

Helen couldn't help but think of herself and Claire. "They were really close, huh?"

"Best friends since they were babies," Ariadne said pointedly. "There's a pattern, a cycle, to everything in our lives, Helen. Certain themes pop up over and over for Scions. Two brothers, or cousins who were raised like brothers, falling in love with two sisters, or *almost* sisters, is one of those cycles."

"And only one of these women is still alive," Helen said quietly, finally understanding Jason's overprotectiveness. "Well, Jason has nothing to worry about. I'd die before I'd let anything happen to Claire."

"Unfortunately, Scions don't get to choose things like that," Ariadne said with narrowed eyes. "My father would have died for my mother, but it doesn't always end up in some heroic battle to save the person you love, you know. Sometimes, people just get killed. Especially around our kind."

"What happened to your mom?" All this time, and Helen had never asked any of the Delos kids this question. Maybe Jason was right, Helen thought. Maybe she was selfish.

"Wrong place, wrong time," Ariadne replied as she reclaimed the photo of her laughing mother and tucked it tenderly back between the pages of *Anne of Green Gables*. "Most Scions would do just about anything to avoid killing a full mortal. But more often than not, a full mortal will get killed completely by accident just because he or she is *near* a Scion. That's why my father and my brother think we should stay away from anyone who could get hurt."

"But you're training Matt."

"I never knew my mother. Everyone tells me she had a big mouth and a fiery Latina temper." Ariadne shook her head with remorse. "But being tough isn't enough. My father never taught my mother anything about how Scions fight, and I think that must have had something to do with why she died. I'm not delusional. I know Matt could never *beat* a Scion, but that's not what this is about. If I don't at least give him a skill set, then I'd never be able to forgive myself if he gets hurt. Does this make any sense?"

Helen nodded and took Ariadne's shaking hands between her own. "Yeah, it does. I had no idea things were that serious between you and Matt."

"It's not like that," Ariadne said quickly, but then she tossed her head back in exasperation and sighed at the ceiling. It was a gesture Helen had seen from Jason many times when he fought with Claire. "Honestly? I don't know what's between us. I can't decide if I'm insulted he hasn't tried anything or if I should be happy he hasn't tempted me."

It was obvious how torn Ariadne was. Helen didn't know what to say, and eventually decided that maybe Ariadne didn't need anyone else telling her what to do. Instead of trying to give advice, Helen just sat there, holding her hand while she thought it through for herself.

"Ari, do you know where . . ." Lucas said as he opened the bedroom door. He froze when he saw Helen. "Sorry. I should have knocked."

"Who are you looking for?" Ariadne said, almost like she was testing him.

Lucas dropped his eyes and closed the door without answering her question. Helen told herself to breathe and forced herself to move her body in some way so she wouldn't seem so dumbstruck, but Ariadne noticed, anyway.

"You too? Still?" she asked in a slightly disgusted way. "Helen. He's your *cousin*."

"I know that," Helen said in a strained voice, holding out her hands in a pleading gesture. "You think I want to feel this? Do you know that I actually *prefer* being in the Underworld now because at least there I know I'm away from this sickness? How *wrong* is that!"

"All of this is really, really wrong," Ariadne said compassionately, but almost begging Helen. "I'm so sorry for you both, but you have to stop this. Incest, even if it is unintentional incest where the two Scions don't know they're related, is another theme that gets repeated again and again. It always ends in the worst possible way. You know that, right?"

"Yes. I read *Oedipus Rex*—I know how this story ends—but what are my options? Do you have any ancient home remedies that will make me fall out of love with him?" Helen asked, being only partly sarcastic.

"Stay away from each other!" Ariadne snapped.

"You were right there when he lost his mind and told me I wasn't even allowed to *look* at him," Helen shouted back. "And that lasted for what? Nine days? We *can't* stay away from each other. Circumstances always bring us back together, no matter what we do to each other."

A big bubble of desperation was rising and swelling in Helen's chest, and Ariadne's pitying look was enough to make it burst. She stood up and started pacing. "I've literally gone to hell and back looking for a place to dump these feelings that I have for him, but I haven't found a hole wide enough or deep enough. So, please, tell me you have an idea, because I'm out of theories, and if what Cassandra says is true, I'm out of time, too."

Helen felt a pop behind her eyes and raised a hand to cover the gush of warm blood soaking her lips. Ariadne sat in stunned stillness on the edge of her bed while Helen ran to the window, wrenched it open, and jumped out.

Helen accelerated straight up. She wanted to see the thin blue line of air around the earth as it faded into black sky one more time. She wanted it fresh in her mind when she laid her head down that night. She was pretty certain that if she didn't have some sort of miraculous epiphany, she would never pick her head up again.

Cleaning the freezing blood off her face as best she could with the edge of her shirt, Helen stared at the slowly spinning earth. It was nightfall on her side of the planet, but she could still make out the gossamer layer of atmosphere. It was just a fragile sliver of nearly nothing that kept life on one side and frozen oblivion on the other. Helen marveled that something that looked so delicate could be so powerful. *Another gift from Lucas,* she thought, smiling at the humbling sight.

Helen shut her eyes and let herself float. She was up high, higher than she had ever gone before, and the tug of the earth was so slight that for a moment she wondered if she could cut the final thread of gravity that tied her to the world and drift all the way to the moon.

A steely hand clamped onto the back of her jacket, yanking her down and nearly tearing her clothes off. Helen twisted around as she tumbled back to earth, and saw Lucas's tortured face as he pulled her against him.

"What are you doing?" he gasped into her ear, clamping her tight to his panting chest as he rapidly sank them both back down. His throat was so pinched with emotion his voice broke repeatedly as he tried to talk. "Were you trying to drift off into space? You know that would kill you, right?"

"I know, Lucas. I . . . it feels *good* to just let go." She realized that she had said his name aloud for the first time in ages. It was such a relief to finally have his name in her mouth again that she laughed. "I like to do it sometimes. Haven't you ever?"

"Yeah. I have," he admitted, still clutching at her and digging his face deeper and deeper into her neck as he floated them down from the cold night sky. He whispered in her ear. "But your eyes were closed. I thought you had blacked out."

"I'm sorry. I thought I was alone," she whispered back.

She knew she should ask, but she honestly didn't care how Lucas got there. She held on to him tighter and tighter, as if she were trying to push him inside her chest and wrap her skin around him.

*This* was Lucas, and she wanted to hold on to him, hold on

to the person he was in this moment, before he had a chance to turn into the angry stranger again. He sighed deeply and said her name before pulling back from her hug and searching for Helen's widow's walk.

"Where's Jerry?" he asked as they hovered over her house. The Pig, Jerry's ancient Jeep Wrangler, was conspicuously absent from the driveway and none of the interior lights were on.

"Probably still working," Helen said, never taking her eyes off him. "Will you come in? Or is this about to get ugly again?"

"I promised you, no more fighting. It didn't work, anyway," Lucas said, and tugged Helen down to land with her on her widow's walk.

"You *did* do it on purpose, didn't you?" For a moment they stood there staring at each other through the heavy silence. "Did your father have anything to do with it?"

"It was my choice," he said heavily.

She waited for him to explain himself, but he didn't. He didn't try to make any excuses or push the blame off onto someone else. Instead, Lucas left it up to Helen to decide what was going to happen between them next. She punched his chest in frustration, not as hard as she could, but hard enough to make him feel something. He didn't try to stop her.

"How could you *do* that to me!" she cried, just short of howling.

"Helen." He caught her tight fists and pressed them to the

place on his chest that she had hit. "What else could I do? We were together all the time again. Sitting together, telling each other our deepest secrets, and it was confusing you. You have more important things to think about than me."

"Do you have any idea how much that hurt?" she asked in a strangled voice, wanting to hit him again, but finding that her hands relaxed of their own accord and smoothed over him instead.

"Yes." He spoke so tenderly Helen knew that he was just as hurt by their separation as she was. "And the consequences will stay with me for the rest of my life."

Her brow wrinkled with worry. She knew that he wasn't exaggerating—Lucas had changed. His face was so pale it reflected the moonlight, and his eyes were a dark blue that bordered on black. It was like looking at the midnight twin of her sunshine Lucas. He was still beautiful, but so sad it was painful for her to look at him.

After everything he'd put her through, Helen knew she should want to punish him, but she didn't. Somewhere along the way she had laced her arms around his neck and he had started running his hands up and down her back, and she wasn't the least bit angry anymore.

Staring into his eyes, she could see an odd gloom creeping around in there, trying to snuff out the glow she'd always found inside of him. But before she could figure out how to ask him what he meant by "consequences," Lucas changed the subject and pulled away from her.

"I had a long exchange with Orion today," he said, opening

the door on the widow's walk that went downstairs into the house and holding it open for Helen. "He had a feeling that you weren't telling us everything about what was going on in the Underworld. He asked me to help. He cares about you very much."

"I know that." Helen led him into the house and down to her cold bedroom. "But he's wrong. I'm not keeping anything from anyone. It's just that I figured there's no help for me, so why go into the details? I'm not *dreaming*, Lucas. How does Orion think you or anyone else can fix that?"

Lucas slumped down on the edge of Helen's bed, shrugged off his jacket, and kicked off his shoes while he thought. He was so comfortable in her room, it was like he belonged there. Helen's every instinct screamed that Lucas *did* belong in her bedroom, despite the fact that they both knew he shouldn't be there.

"I descended into the Underworld the other night. At first, it was to see if I could help you in any way—without interfering, of course. And then after a few hours it was just to watch the two of you together. For a lot of reasons," Lucas finally admitted, laying all his cards on the table. "Anyway, I got sloppy. Orion saw me there and worked out how I did it. He got in touch with me today to tell me *why* you were dying, and together we realized that I might have the one thing you need to get well again. So I guess I did find a way to help you after all." He swung his legs up onto her bed and settled back against the pillows.

Helen stopped dead. She wanted to stare at him all night,

lying in her bed like that, as perfect as could be, but she couldn't get past what he'd just told her.

"You descended into the Underworld? When? How?" she asked, trying not to squeak.

"Saturday night. Ares saw me hiding in the boneyard and talked to me. I was the other 'little godling.' Remember? Then I distracted Cerberus when she chased you."

"The yodeler?" Helen asked in disbelief. "Wait, she's a *she*?"

"Yes," he said through a chuckle. "I was the yodeler and Cerberus is a she-wolf. Now go wash up. I'll be right here."

"But . . ."

"Hurry," he urged. "I had to wait until you were away from our family to bring you this, but I can't stand to see you so sick for much longer."

Helen bolted into the bathroom and nearly washed her mouth out with soap and brushed her face with toothpaste, she was shaking so badly. She stripped and scrubbed and flossed and combed pretty much everything at the same time before jumping into clean pajamas and running back into her bedroom.

He was still there, just like he'd promised, and Helen's last nagging doubts evaporated. The unnatural separation was over, and they weren't going to start yelling at each other or pushing each other away anymore.

"Oh, good. I'm not hallucinating," she said, only half kidding. "Or dreaming."

"But you need to dream," he said softly across the room,

staring at her. Helen shook her head.

"This is better," she said certainly. "Even if it kills me, staying awake and seeing you in my bed is better than any dream."

"You're not supposed to say things like that," he reminded her.

He closed his eyes for a second. When he opened them he smiled resolutely and lifted up the edge of the covers. Helen ran and dove into them, beside herself with happiness. She didn't care about right or wrong anymore. She was dying, she reasoned; shouldn't she at least die happy? Helen turned over onto her back and lifted her arms up to him invitingly, but he captured her face between his palms and made her settle back into the bed. He hovered over her, on top of the covers, pinning her safely beneath them.

"This is an obol," he said, holding up a small gold coin. "We Scions put them under the tongues of our dead loved ones before we burn their bodies on the pyre. The obol is the money the dead use to pay Chiron, the Ferryman, to leave the shadow lands, cross the River Styx, and enter the Underworld. But this obol is special, and very rare. It wasn't made for the Ferryman. It's for another dweller of the shadow lands."

Lucas held up the coin so Helen could see it clearly. On one side there were stars and on the other side there was a flower.

"Is that a poppy?" Helen asked, trying to remember where she had seen this little gold coin before. A newspaper headline flashed into her thoughts. "You stole these from the Getty! Lucas, you broke into a museum!"

"That's part of the reason why I can't let my family know I'm here, trying this. But you know my real reason . . . cousin," Lucas said.

He suddenly leaned down and brushed his lips across her cheek, but he didn't kiss her. It was more like he was inhaling her. Feeling his warm lips so close to her skin made her shiver.

Helen knew exactly why he had to hide this from his family. Theft was nothing compared to the immorality of what they were doing. Helen knew she should be disgusted that she was in bed with someone who was so closely related to her, but she couldn't seem to convince her body that it shouldn't want Lucas. Matt felt like her brother, Orion felt new and strange and so intense it was a little dangerous, but Lucas felt *right*. If other men were houses, Lucas was her home.

How could she be so mixed up? She pushed against him gently to make him lean back and look at her. She still needed answers, and she couldn't think with his face so close to hers.

"Lucas, why did you steal them?"

"This obol isn't for Chiron. It was forged for Morpheus, the god of dreams. This will bring your whole body down to the land of dreams when you fall asleep."

"The land of dreams and the land of the dead are right next to each other," Helen said, finally understanding why he did it. "You stole them to follow me down, didn't you?"

He nodded and ran his fingers across her face. "There's an old legend, that says if you give Morpheus a poppy obol he may let you visit the land of dreams *still in your body*. I thought if I offered him a trade he might let me cross his lands and go all the way to the Underworld. I didn't know if it would work, but what choice did I have? When I saw you Saturday morning in the hallway . . ."

"You jumped out a window," Helen reminded him. A smile crept across her face as she realized that she had just done pretty much the same thing to Ariadne.

"To go steal these," he said, smiling down at her. "I knew you were sick, I knew that pushing you away hadn't helped, and I couldn't sit back anymore and watch. I had to go down into the Underworld and find out why. Orion got a glimpse of me following the two of you and figured out on his own who I had to be. Then he mostly figured out how I was able to get into the Underworld."

"Mostly?" Helen asked.

"He thought that since I'm a Son of Apollo, it had something to do with music. Which wasn't a bad guess," Lucas admitted begrudgingly.

"You do have a beautiful voice," Helen said. She wanted to keep Lucas talking, just to hear that voice and feel him stretched out next to her in her bed for as long as she could. "But why music?"

"Orion originally thought I was doing what Orpheus did when he followed his dead wife into the Underworld to try and sing her back to life. But eventually, he put the stolen obols together with me, changed *Orpheus* to *Morpheus*, and guessed how I did it. Then he told me why you were so sick and asked me to try this with you," Lucas said in such a way that led Helen to suspect a lot more had gone on in those text conversations than Lucas was letting on. "He's a smart guy."

"What? Are you two best friends now?" Helen asked with raised eyebrows. Lucas swallowed painfully like she'd hurt him. Concerned, Helen reached out and ran her hand across his face, trying to wipe away the sadness that had appeared there so fast.

"I respect him. Even if he won't do what I ask." His voice came out rough and thick. "It's time for you to sleep."

"I'm not tired," she said quickly, winning a little laugh from Lucas.

"You're exhausted! No more arguing," he admonished sternly, although his playful look robbed the words of their sting. "Ask Morpheus to give you dreams again. He was very kind to me. I have no doubt he'll help you if he can."

"Will you stay?" Helen asked. She stared at him, adoring him. "Please, stay with me?"

"As long as I can stand it," he promised, shivering. "I never get cold, but damn! It's freezing in here."

"Tell me about it," Helen said, rolling her eyes. "Come and keep me warm." Lucas gave a small laugh and shook his head, like he didn't know what to do with her.

Staying on top of the covers, he settled in, allowing Helen

to scoot down into a comfortable position. He folded her arms into an X across her chest and smoothed her hair back like he was laying her in her grave. He looked down on her intensely.

"Open your mouth," Lucas whispered.

Helen could feel him shaking and watched a myriad emotions play across his face as he tucked the heavy gold wafer under her tongue. It was still warm with his body heat, slightly salty, and the weight of it in her mouth was remarkably comforting. Lucas reached out and gently closed her eyelids. Keeping his hand cupped over her eyes, Helen felt him brush his lips across her cheek as he leaned close to her ear.

"Don't let Morpheus seduce you. . . ."

Starry skies and inky strips of silk surrounded Helen. She was inside a tent that had no top, just undulating walls of dark, slippery sheets that seemed to breathe slowly as they caught and released a gentle and ever-changing breeze. Here and there between the swaths of material were austere Doric columns carved out of black pearl marble. Dim follow-me lights danced down the passageways, hovering in the night air. As one neared Helen, she saw that up close they looked like tiny candle flames glowing inside iridescent bubbles.

The grass beneath her feet was covered by a field of poppies, their heads nodding drunkenly with the passing winds. Despite the darkness, Helen could feel the cool dewiness of the flowers and see the golden pollen that sparkled inside the bloodred blooms.

About a dozen steps away from where she had emerged into this night-world, silk sheets and voluminous pillows of midnight blue, charcoal gray, and deepest purple spilled over the edges of the largest and most luxurious bed Helen had ever seen. The stars twinkled overhead and the piles of silk seemed to wink back at them like glittering oil slicks in the ghostly blue-moon light. A pair of ivory white arms, followed by a man's naked chest, rose up from the dark mass of cradling material as he took a nice, long stretch.

"I've been calling out to you, Beauty. I'm so glad you're finally here." His voice was familiar. "Beauty and Sleep. Sleeping Beauty. We were made for each other, you know. All the sayings say it. Now come and lie down with me."

His infectiously playful tone drew Helen to the edge of the bed. There was something about that voice that was so reassuring and sweet that Helen knew he had to be the gentlest soul in this or any other universe.

She looked down into the gigantic bed, and saw Morpheus, the god of dreams. He had the whitest skin Helen had ever seen, shiny masses of wavy, black hair, and long slender limbs of delicately carved muscle. Stripped to the waist, he wore silk pajama pants of such a deep wine red that, like all the other colors of his sleeping palace, bordered on black, but never quite reached it.

Morpheus looked up at Helen with startling white-blue eyes that looked almost like liquid mercury. He snuggled into the not-quite black of the silk sheets. *For thou wilt lie upon the wings of night, Whiter than new snow upon a raven's back*, Helen thought as she took in the contrast of his skin on the sheets, wondering where she had heard those lines of poetry. Whoever wrote them, she thought, must have spent many nights with Morpheus.

"It's *your* voice I've been hearing in my head. Little sneak," Helen said, smiling down at the exquisite, half-naked man. "I thought I was going crazy."

"You were, Beauty. That's why you could hear me so clearly. I called and called to you, but you ignored me so I finally went away. Now come and lie down," he complained prettily, holding out one of his milk-white hands. "It's been far too long since I've held you."

Helen didn't even have to think about it. She had never laid eyes on this god before, but she knew him. After all, she had spent nearly every night of her life cradled in his arms. There was nothing Morpheus didn't know about her, no wicked little secret that she had been able to hide from him, and he appeared to love her, anyway. In fact, from the way his starlit eyes gazed up at her, Helen could tell he adored her.

She smiled with relief, slipped her hand into his, and sighed as she let her head fall against his smooth, moonbeam-bright chest. Every muscle in her body let go as wave upon wave of soothing relaxation rolled through her exhausted limbs. For the first time in months, Helen experienced true rest. Just moments in the god's arms made up for all those weeks of dreamlessness.

Morpheus made a sound in his chest, a deep rumbling hum of pleasure, and stroked her face. Gently coaxing her lips apart, he slid two fingers into her mouth and claimed his coin.

"But you didn't need to bring payment to visit me. In the many hours you spend with your eyes closed before or after you descend into the Underworld, you are free to dream. You could have floated in with any of the other sleeping minds whenever you wanted," he said, gesturing to the playful winds that constantly buffeted the tent, occasionally drifting in to ruffle his long, soft hair. "You have more control than you know, Helen. You can even visit me here in body without an obol if you want."

"But I can't visit you," Helen protested, slightly confused. "Even when I don't descend into the Underworld, I haven't been able to dream."

"Because you're afraid of what you'll find in your dreams, not because any outside force is stopping you. You feel so much guilt for what you want, you can't even face it in your sleep." Morpheus lifted Helen, and placed her on top of him so she was looking directly down on him. He dug his fingers into her hair and made it fan around them like a golden curtain that closed them in together.

"I can dream whenever I want?" Helen asked, already knowing the answer. The moment Helen had learned that Lucas was her cousin, she had stopped dreaming by choice. She'd just never admitted it to herself before.

"My troubled Beauty. I hate to see anyone suffer, you

most of all. Stay here with me and be my queen and I will fulfill all your dreams."

The face and body beneath her shifted and changed into a more familiar form. Helen gasped and pulled back. It was Lucas who sat up and gently gripped her arms.

"I can be this one as often as you like, and you needn't feel guilty because I'm not actually him," Lucas said. Helen felt him pull her close and didn't resist. It was all a dream, right? She ran her hands across his chest and allowed him to kiss her lightly as he spoke. "Or, I can be others. The other one you want so much. Maybe more . . ."

Helen felt the mouth against hers grow fuller and softer, and felt the bare shoulders under her hands thicken. She opened her eyes and found Orion kissing her. Pulling away, Helen wondered anxiously what Morpheus meant by this. He knew her deepest dreams, so why had he turned Lucas into Orion?

Orion pushed her onto her back, and she couldn't help but laugh when he jumped on top of her with a naughty grin. He was so much *fun*, and being with him was so uncomplicated. With Lucas, she could be completely herself, but with Orion she could be whomever she felt like being at the moment. The thought was intoxicating.

Orion slid her hands up over her head, pinning her under him. The giddy mood dissipated as quickly as it arose, and Orion's face grew serious.

Helen suddenly understood Lucas's last warning. She could not allow herself to be seduced or she would never leave this bed. Although she didn't want to, Helen shook her head, preventing Orion from leaning down to kiss her. Morpheus took his own shape again and propped himself up on his elbows over her with a boyish sigh.

"You are downright addictive," Helen said sadly.

She allowed herself to consider what it would be like to live forever in this dream palace with this god. She combed her fingers through his hair, making a midnight tent out of his long locks around their faces, the reverse of what he had done with her sunny blonde hair moments ago.

"But I can't stay here," she said, pushing him back and sitting up. "There are too many things I have to accomplish in the world."

"Dangerous things," he countered with genuine concern. "Ares has been seeking you in the shadow lands."

"Do you know why he's looking for me?"

"You know why." Morpheus laughed softly. "He's watching your progress. What you do here in the Underworld will change many lives, including quite a few immortal ones. But for better or worse, no one can say."

"How did Ares get down here, Morpheus? Is Hades helping him break the Truce?" Helen knew somehow that Morpheus would be honest with her.

"The Underworld, the dry lands, and the shadow lands are not part of the Truce. The Twelve Olympians can't go to Earth, and that's the only rule they swore to follow. Many small gods wander the Earth at will, and all the gods come and go from here to Olympus and . . . other places."

Morpheus frowned at his thoughts and then tackled Helen, rolling her onto her back again and holding her in his arms. "Stay with me. I can keep you safe here in my realm, but not outside of it. I see all dreams, you know, even the dreams of the other gods, and I know that Ares is little more than an animal. His only goal is to cause as much suffering and destruction as he can, and he wants very much to hurt you."

"He's foul, I agree. But I *still* can't stay here and hide in your bed." Helen groaned, knowing she was probably going to kick herself for this later. "No matter how dangerous it is, I have to go back."

"Brave Beauty." The god of dreams looked down on her with an admiring smile. "Now I want you even more."

"Will you help me, Morpheus?" Helen asked, stroking his shining hair. "I need to get back into the Underworld. Too many have suffered for too long."

"I know." Morpheus looked away as he considered Helen's request. "It is not for me to say whether your quest is good or bad, I can only tell you that I admire your courage in agreeing to undertake it. I hate to lose you, but I love your reasons for choosing to leave."

Knowing that she might be pushing her luck, Helen decided to take a chance and ask for one more favor.

"Do you know what river Persephone meant? The one I need to draw water from to free the Furies?" she asked. Morpheus cocked his head to the side, like he was trying to recall something.

"Something tells me I *used* to know," he said with a puzzled frown. "But no longer. I'm sorry, Beauty, but I've forgotten. You'll have to discover that for yourself."

Morpheus kissed the tip of her nose and rolled out of bed. He turned back and easily lifted her from the twisted sheets before placing her down on the cool grass with a look of regret. Hand in hand, they walked at an unhurried pace through his palace.

They passed many wondrous rooms filled with fantastical dream imagery. Helen caught glimpses of waterfalls that gushed sparkling liquids of every color, armored dragons atop hoarded riches, their nostrils smoking with barely banked fires, and winged elfin people dancing with the follow-me lights. But the most spectacular room was a large, twinkling cavern, filled with pile after pile of heaped coins.

Above each pile a large cylinder hovered weightless in the night sky. The cylinders were made out of brick, stone, or concrete. Some seemed to be thousands of years old and were crumbling with moss; others looked newly constructed and very modern. One or two even had buckets hanging from ropes dangling out of the bottoms, which Helen found strangely kitschy.

"What is this place?" she asked in awe. The space seemed to go on and on—so far into the dark distance that she couldn't see an end to it.

"Ever throw a coin down a well and make a wish?" Morpheus asked. "All wishing wells, past and present, end here in the land of dreams. It's all a misunderstanding, really. I can't make dreams come true in real life, no matter how much money people shower me with. The only thing I can do is give them vivid visions of their deepest wishes in their sleep. I try to make them as real as possible."

"Very thoughtful of you."

"Well, it doesn't feel right to take people's money without giving them something in return," he said with a sly smile. "And all this could be yours, you know."

"Honestly?" Helen said with a raised eyebrow. "Your warm bed was more tempting than all the cold coins in the world."

As if on cue, Helen heard a pinging sound and saw a far-off glint as one of the enormous piles shifted to welcome another shiny wish.

"I'm deeply flattered."

Morpheus led her away from the room of wishing wells and out of the palace. Standing under an awning, Helen looked across the palace grounds and saw a great tree that stood alone in the middle of a vast plain.

"Beyond that tree is the land of the dead. Stand under the branches and tell Hades that you will not try to capture his queen. If you mean it, he will not hinder your descents into the Underworld."

"How will he know if I mean it?" Helen asked, surprised. "Is Hades a Falsefinder?"

"Yes, in a way. He can see into people's hearts—a necessary talent for one who would rule the Underworld. The one who would rule must be able to judge the souls of the dead and decide where those souls are to be sent." Morpheus's answer came with a quixotic little smile.

"What?" Helen asked, bemused by the quirky look on his face. But Morpheus would only shake his head and smile to himself in answer to her question. He walked her across the grounds, right up to the edge of the arching branches of the great tree, and turned to her.

"When you are standing directly under the tree, no matter what you do, don't look up into the branches," he warned solemnly.

"Why not?" Helen said, dreading the answer. "What's in them?"

"Nightmares. Pay them no mind and they can't hurt you." He gently released her hand. "I have to leave you now."

"Really?" Helen asked with a fearful glance over her shoulder at the nightmare tree. Morpheus nodded his head and started to back away. "But how do I get home?" she asked before he could get too far.

"All you have to do is wake up. And Helen," he called out, almost like he was warning her, "in the coming days, try to remember that dreams do come true, but they don't come easily."

Morpheus disappeared into the blending of stars and shimmering lights on the dark lawn, and without him Helen felt very alone. She faced the nightmare tree and balled her fists to steel herself, knowing that the sooner she got it over with, the better. Keeping her eyes down, she strode under the branches.

Immediately, Helen felt a mass of moving *things* above

her. There were strange squeals and she could hear the scratching of claws across bark as the shadowy creatures ran around. The branches would rustle, then shake, then creak ominously as the nightmares jumped up and down on them in an ever-increasing frenzy to catch her attention.

It took all of Helen's nerve to not look up. For a moment, she felt one lean down right next to her face. She could sense its presence loom close, staring at her. Helen told herself not to look and gritted her teeth to keep them from chattering with fear. Taking a deep breath, she faced the Underworld.

"Hades! I promise I won't try to free Persephone," Helen yelled across the barren land.

While she hated the idea of abandoning anyone, Helen knew what she had to do. Persephone was one princess who was going to have to figure out how to get out of the castle tower without a knight in shining armor to rescue her. That didn't mean that Helen had to like it.

"But I *strongly suggest* you do the right thing and let her go yourself," she added.

The nightmares fell silent. Helen heard footfalls in front of her as someone approached, but kept her eyes on the dusty ground of the Underworld side of the tree in case it was a trick.

"What do you know of right and wrong?" asked a surprisingly gentle voice.

Helen dared to raise her eyes, sensing that the nightmares had fled. She saw a very tall, robust figure standing in front of her. The clinging shadows that chased around him were like large, grasping hands. Helen had seen this darkness before. It was the same malevolent pall created by Shadowmasters. It dispersed and Helen could see Hades, the lord of the dead.

He was cloaked in a simple black toga. A cowl obscured his eyes and under that, the cheek plates of his shiny black helmet covered all of his face but the bottom of his nose and his mouth. Helen remembered from her studies that the helmet was called the Helm of Darkness and it made Hades invisible at will.

Her eyes quickly skipped down from what she couldn't see to take in the rest of him. Hades was commandingly large and he moved and stood with easy grace. His toga was draped elegantly over his bare, muscled arm, and his lips were full, flushed red, and quite beautiful. Although his face was mostly hidden, the rest of him looked healthy and youthful—and unbelievably sensuous. Helen couldn't take her eyes off him.

"What can one so young know of justice?" he prompted while Helen gawked.

"Not much, I guess," she finally answered in a wavering voice, still trying to process the enigmatic god in front of her. "But even I know it's wrong to keep a woman locked away from the world. Especially in *this* day and age."

Surprisingly, the full mouth parted in something that was almost like a laugh, and Helen relaxed. The gesture made him seem approachable and human.

"I'm not the monster you think I am, niece," he said sincerely. "I agreed to honor my oath and be the lord of the dead, but this place is entirely against my wife's nature. She can only survive here a few months at a time."

Helen knew this was true. His position as lord of the dead had been forced on him by chance. Hades had drawn the short straw, and while his brothers claimed the sea and the sky as their realms, he had been doomed to the Underworld. The one place the love of his life could not survive for long. It was tragic, a terrible irony, but it was still his choice to imprison Persephone—regardless of how bad a hand the Fates had dealt him.

"Then why do you force her to stay here at all, if you know it causes her pain?"

"We all need joy in our lives, a reason to keep going. Persephone is my only joy, and when we are together I am hers. You are young, but I think you know how it feels to be separated from the one you love because of your obligations."

"I am sorry for you both," Helen said sadly. "But I still think you should let her go. Allow her the dignity of choosing for herself if she wants to be here with you or not."

The funny thing was, Helen could sense that Hades had followed every twist and turn of her emotions as she spoke. She knew that he could read her heart, and she didn't know if she should be afraid or happy that he would be waiting to judge her heart again on the day of her death.

"You may descend at will, niece," he said in a kindly way. "But I *strongly suggest* you ask your Oracle what she thinks of this quest."

Helen felt herself being scooped up by his mile-wide hand and then gently placed back in her bed. Later, she awoke in her room, freezing cold and dusted with ice crystals, but alert and refreshed for the first time in a long time. The space in the bed next to her was empty.

Lucas had gone, but in a way Helen was relieved. Waking up next to him would have been too hard on them both, especially after what she had experienced with Morpheus.

As Helen thought back, guilt overpowered her, even though she tried to tell herself that feeling guilty didn't make any sense. She couldn't be cheating on Lucas with Orion because she wasn't even supposed to be with Lucas in the first place. It didn't matter who felt like a house or a home or a frigging motel to her. She and Lucas could never be together. Period.

She had to toughen up, she realized. Some people weren't meant to live happily ever after, no matter what they felt for each other. Hades and Persephone were a perfect example of that. Hades had told Helen that he and Persephone were each other's joy, but they were both miserable. Their "love" kept them locked inside prisons that made one of them half dead when they were together and the other half dead when they were apart. That wasn't joy. Joy was the opposite of a prison. It opened the heart instead of locking it away. Joy was freedom—freedom from sadness, bitterness, and hatred. . . .

Helen had a brain wave.

Throwing the stiff blankets off her, she ran clumsily on dangerously chilled legs to her dresser and grabbed her phone.

**I think I know what the Furies need,** she texted Orion. **Joy. We need to get to the River of Joy. Meet me tonight.**

Daphne poured the wine and reminded herself to stand on both feet, like the big, beefy woman she currently looked like, instead of on one leg with a cocked hip, the way she normally would. She could feel the heavy body weighing on her, making her lower back ache slightly. She was over six feet tall and about two hundred pounds, and readjusting her internal awareness to account for all that extra muscle and bone was complicated.

She tried not to yawn. Conclave was never fun, but doing it while wearing the shape of Mildred Delos's ape of a bodyguard was downright exhausting—not just because of all the extra weight, but because Mildred Delos was a straight-up bitch. She overreacted to *everything*, like an anxious little dog that barks and growls constantly because it knows it's surrounded by much stronger animals that would gladly eat it as a snack.

"Scylla! Did you open the pinot gris?" Mildred snapped testily. "I said *grigio*, not *gris*. Pinot grigio. It's an entirely different grape."

"My mistake," Daphne-as-Scylla answered calmly. She

knew the difference between the two wines, and had done it on purpose. She couldn't resist baiting Mildred. "Shall I open the grigio?"

"No, this will do," Mildred said dismissively. "Go stand over there somewhere. I can't bear how you *loom* over me all the time."

Daphne went and stood up against the wall. Mildred could growl all she wanted, but she wasn't fooling anyone. She was useless now that Creon was dead. She had no Scion child to give her any say among the Hundred, and if she didn't have another child by Tantalus she would remain powerless—no more than a forgettable footnote in the long history of the House of Thebes. Mildred was an ambitious woman, and Daphne trusted that she would try to get pregnant again soon. That required the presence of her husband.

If there were any other way to find Tantalus again, Daphne would have gladly taken it, but infiltrating Conclave as Mildred's bodyguard killed two birds with one stone. Daphne needed to be present in case there was anything she could do to help Castor and Pallas in their attempt to get Automedon away from her daughter.

Castor and Pallas didn't know she was there, of course, or that Hector was staying a few nights a week in one of Daphne's safe houses in lower Manhattan, but that didn't matter. Free of the Furies for over a decade now, and capable of wearing any woman's face she needed to, Daphne had always been able to sway the other Houses from the inside to accomplish her goals. Once Castor and Pallas got

Automedon's boot off her daughter's throat, Daphne would finally be able to kill Tantalus.

Mildred's cell phone rang. She looked at the screen and then answered it hastily.

"Tantalus. Did you get my recordings?" Mildred said in a slightly higher than usual voice.

She had been sending recordings of the daily meetings to Tantalus, and even though phone calls were forbidden, he would call with detailed instructions for her every night. Daphne could hear both ends of their nightly conversations because Tantalus had to speak loud enough for his human wife to hear, which was loud enough for any Scion to *over-hear*, even from the other side of the room. As yet, Tantalus hadn't revealed his location to his wife, and she hadn't asked. Apparently, neither of them trusted anyone with that information, not even Mildred's bodyguard.

"I did," he replied coldly. Daphne imagined herself digitized so she could dive through Mildred's phone and jump out of Tantalus's—her hands re-forming solid out of ones and zeros to choke him. "They still call me Outcast. You were supposed to fix that."

"How? The Hundred won't listen to me anymore. Everyone listens to Castor now, and since he found out you're an Outcast he's been saying it openly. You've lost a lot of support," she replied in a clipped, accusing voice. "And there's nothing I can do about that, as things are."

"Not this again," he sighed. "Our son hasn't been dead a month and already you want to replace him."

A long, uncomfortable silence followed.

"Automedon has been slow to respond to my calls," Tantalus said tersely, breaking the chilly stalemate. "And when he does, he always has a less than satisfying excuse."

"No," Mildred said, half rising out of her seat. "What does this mean?"

Daphne had to work to keep her face impassive. Myrmidons were the consummate soldiers. They *never* ignored their masters.

"I'm not sure," Tantalus sighed. "It could be nothing, or it could be that he's working for someone else. Maybe he was already pledged to another master before I hired him. Either way, I don't think I control him anymore, and if that's so I can't stop him from killing Helen if that's what his other master wants. This *cannot* happen, or I'm a dead man. Daphne has pledged herself . . ."

"Must you always find a way to bring her up?" Mildred said, a bitter sneer curling her lip. "Do you do it just to say her name?"

"Keep your eyes and ears open, *wife*," Tantalus warned, his tone grim. "Or I won't be alive long enough to give you the Scion baby you need to get your throne back."

# TWELVE

Halloween morning was overcast and gloomy, just like it should be. The menacing storm clouds overhead added just the right shade of pearl gray to the air, making the autumn colors pop like smears of oil paint on a perfectly primed canvass. It was cold out. Not so cold that being outdoors was intolerable, but just cold enough to make everyone want soup for lunch and candy for dinner.

Helen sent the Greek Geeks a mass text, telling them that Hades had agreed to let her back into the Underworld and that she was out of danger. She didn't mention Lucas's obol and she didn't give any of the details of her meeting with Morpheus. She wanted to let Lucas decide what they were going to tell the family.

She got a few texts back, asking her to explain how she

managed to descend after being banished, but she ignored them and posed a question of her own. She wanted to know where the Shadowmaster talent came from.

**It developed in the medieval times, and it's been a part of the House of Thebes ever since,** Cassandra replied.

That meant the talent was only about a thousand years old. A thousand years was a long time, but not to Scions who traced their ancestors back almost four times as long as that. **Okay. But where'd it come from?** Helen persisted.

No one had an answer.

Helen dressed and got ready for school, then went downstairs to cook breakfast for her father, the witch. Having spent the previous day in a dress, Jerry had quickly learned that the only shame in his costume was that it wasn't elaborate *enough*. After fielding multiple suggestions from customers for how he could improve his holiday spirit, he had decided to pull out all the stops. He had added a corset to the dress, and wore blue lipstick, clip-on earrings, and pointy-toed boots to add some extra oomph.

"Dad. I think you and I need to have a little chat about your cross-dressing," Helen said in a mock-serious tone as she poured some coffee. "Just because all the other kids are doing it . . ."

"I know, I know," he said, grinning into his bacon. "I just *can't* get beat by Mr. Tanis at the hardware store. He's a pirate this year, and you should see his wig! He must have spent a fortune on it! And don't even get me started on the movie theater around the corner. They're handing out thirty bags of candied popcorn for one of the night showings. Kate's is much better, of course, but we have to charge."

Helen ate her pumpkin pancakes—the last batch of the year—and sipped her coffee, listening to her father complain, even though she knew he was loving every minute of it. She felt almost good. Her head wasn't throbbing, her eyes weren't watering, and for the first time in weeks she wasn't sore all over. While she wasn't exactly happy, she did feel a sense of peace.

This feeling was partly to do with the fact that Helen was convinced there was another presence in the room. It didn't scare her or freak her out anymore. In fact, it soothed her. She had forgotten to ask Morpheus if he was the "invisible sun" she had been feeling, but the last time she'd felt this presence she had also heard his voice, so who else could it be?

"Helen?" Jerry said, looking at her expectantly.

"Yeah, Dad?" She'd spaced out again.

"Can you work at the store after school today?" he asked again. "It's okay if you can't, it's just that Luis really wanted to take Juan and little Marivi trick-or-treating. It'll be her first time . . ."

"Sure! No problem!" Helen replied guiltily. "Tell Luis to have fun with his kids. I'll be there."

She had been daydreaming about Morpheus. Or was she just thinking about him *as* Lucas . . . or Orion? Her cheeks throbbed with a blush, and she stood up abruptly and started to gather her things for school.

"Are you sure you feel better?" Jerry asked doubtfully as he watched her stuff books in a bag and check her phone. Claire had left her a text.

"Yeah, I'm fine," Helen replied distractedly, reading. Claire wasn't coming to get her, as she'd been roped into going to school early to decorate for Halloween. "Damn it. I'll have to take my stupid bike." Helen moaned as she did an about-face and headed for the back door.

"Are you sure you can—"

"Yes! I'll be there," Helen cut him off peevishly. She reluctantly wheeled her ancient rig out of the garage, noticing that it had grown more rust over the past month than was scientifically possible.

"Have a good day," her father called after her.

Helen rolled her eyes, thinking *yeah, right*, and pedaled off. She wasn't more than a block away from school when she was nearly run off the road by a speeding driver. She had to veer off the shoulder, bump across the unpaved ground, and splash through the grandmother of all muddy puddles to avoid getting hit.

Great gouts of oily, turgid water splashed up onto her legs and soaked her from the waist down. Helen hit the brakes, and had to take a moment to let the catastrophe sink in, stunned that so much freezing-cold yuck had spewed all over her.

She looked back at the puddle. There was a dead animal floating in it. She smelled her clothes, and sure enough, they smelled vaguely of putrefying squirrel.

"Unbelievable," Helen mumbled to herself. She wasn't usually a clumsy person, at least not when she had a full night of dreaming behind her, and she couldn't believe this had happened.

She read the time on her phone, and saw that she couldn't go home and change. If she did, she'd get a detention from Hergie for being late for sure, and she had already promised that she would work for Luis right after school. Helen decided that spending a day smelling like dead squirrel was better than spending the rest of her life knowing she had robbed two impressionable children of their father on Halloween. Besides, she really liked Luis's kids. They were so *tiny*, and Juan had the most adorable husky, little-boy voice.

Sighing at her rotten luck, Helen got ready to pedal to school, only to find that she couldn't. Her front tire had gone flat. She swung her leg over to get off her bike, and heard a ripping noise.

Somehow, the hem of her jeans had gotten caught in the chain and she had nearly ripped the whole leg off. Readjusting her stance to stop herself before she could tear her jeans any more, Helen slid on some pebbles underfoot and fell headlong into the muddy, dead-rodent-infested puddle, with her ancient bicycle still attached to her pant leg. The bike collapsed on top of her before she could stand, the frame getting twisted and bent as it tangled with Helen's strong body.

"What the hell is going on?" Helen yelled aloud. She heard a tittering laugh and looked across the road to see a tall, thin woman grinning at her.

Right away, Helen knew there was something not quite right about the woman. She had high, arching cheekbones and wave after wave of long, white-blonde hair that reached the back of her knees. At first Helen thought she was a movie star or something, because with her features and all that hair she *should* have been beautiful. But the sneer on her lips and the hollow, serpentine look in her eyes made her downright ugly. No matter how beautiful her body was supposed to be, her polluted spirit made her hideous to look at.

"What are you?" Helen shouted. Goose bumps puckered her skin, more in reaction to the uncanny encounter than to the cold.

The ghoulish woman shook her head at Helen, waggling it forward left to right, like a cobra blankly zeroing in on a hapless mouse. Then she broke eye contact and skipped off. Helen stared after her in shock, thinking to herself, *Who the hell skips?*

Very carefully, in case there also happened to be a bear trap she was about to step in or something, Helen pulled herself up from the nasty-ass puddle and sat down next to her trashed bike. She knew that what she had just seen was no costume, and that her little run-in with Murphy's Law was not a coincidence. Something strange had just happened, but she had no idea what.

Picking up her demolished bike and putting it over her shoulder, Helen walked the rest of the way to school. She dumped her ex-bike somewhere in the vicinity of the rack and wandered into homeroom exactly as disgusting and torn up as the puddle had left her.

There were a bunch of people wearing costumes, and more than one wearing ripped clothes and fake-dirt makeup. Even so, it was obvious that Helen was soaking wet, shivering, and covered in real mud. Looks of shock followed her as she walked across the classroom. Matt and Claire sat up straighter in alarm. She mouthed the words "I'm okay," and Matt sat back in his seat, less alarmed but still scowling, wondering what had happened.

"Miss Hamilton? Am I to assume that the malodorous emanation I detect is an integral part of your Halloween costume?" Hergie asked with his usual nonchalance. "Something of the zombie persuasion, I expect?"

"I'm thinking of calling it 'eau de dead fart,'" she replied, just as cool as he was. Usually Helen was much more respectful, but she felt like pushing Hergie a bit.

"Please visit the powder room and remove it. Although I commend your holiday spirit, I cannot allow such a distraction. There are some students at this institution who wish to *learn*," he chastised in his heroic way. Helen grinned at him. Hergie really was one of a kind. "I shall write you a hall pass. . . ."

"But, Mr. Hergesheimer, I don't have a change of clothes. I'll need help . . ."

"I would expect nothing else. One pass for you, and one for your cohort, Miss Aoki." He tore off two precious slips of paper that pretty much gave Helen and Claire free rein over the hallways for the next two periods.

Claire looked over at Helen excitedly, trying not to scream out of her eyeballs, and the two best friends stood up from their desks and took their passes with humbly bent heads. Getting a hall pass from Hergie was like getting a knighthood. It didn't make you any richer, but it gave you bragging rights for the rest of the year.

"Lennie, you stink," Claire mumbled as they made their way to the door.

"You have *no* idea what just happened to me," Helen whispered back, and went on to explain her entire run in with the ghoulish woman by the side of the road. Claire listened intently as she led them to the theater. "Wait, why are we here?" Helen asked when she saw their destination.

"You need something to wear," Claire said with a shrug as she let them into the prop room. She went directly to a rack of diaphanous, glittery fairy costumes and began holding one after another up to Helen, comparing size. "Are you sure it wasn't just some crazy tourist in a Halloween costume? This'll fit you. It's got wings, though."

"I'm cool with wings. And there is no way that woman was human. She was, like, seven feet tall and she *skipped*," Helen replied, easily shifting conversational gears. "Won't we get in trouble?"

"I'm on the costume committee. Besides, we'll give them back." Claire gave Helen an impish grin as she took one for herself. "Now, locker room. You're unholy stench is making my eyes water."

Helen showered and washed her hair while Claire changed into a pilfered costume of her own and stood at one of the mirrors putting on sparkly makeup to go with it. Claire asked Helen to describe the ghoul very carefully, but she couldn't add much beyond her original first impression.

"It was difficult to get a good look at her, Gig. I was busy doing the breaststroke in a puddle with a dead rodent floating next to me." Helen toweled herself dry and wiggled into an iridescent wisp of a dress while trying not to poke her eyes out on the spiky wings.

"I'll tell Matt and Ari about it in class today, see if they have any ideas. Now come out and let me see!"

"Which characters from *Midsummer* are we supposed to be?" Helen's jaw dropped when she saw Claire's costume. "Ooh, I love that! The spiderweb design is amazing!"

"I'm Cobweb, obviously, and you're Moth. They're good, right? My grandma did the sequin bits."

"These wings are *insane* pretty." Helen floated up into the air and pretended to be surprised that she was flying. "And they work, too!"

Claire grabbed Helen's foot and tugged her back down to earth with a sulky face. "Jason made me promise never to fly with you again. And now that I know what I'm missing, it sucks even harder to watch you do it."

"I'll have a talk with him," Helen offered. "Maybe if I show him how easy it is for me to carry a passenger, he'll see it's not so dangerous and change his mind."

"I doubt it," Claire said. She shook her head and scowled.

"Not that it matters. I think today we're technically broken up, but how would I know?"

"What's that supposed to mean?" Helen asked, jabbing a fist onto her hip and frowning.

"It means that one second he's telling me that he can't see me anymore, and the next he's outrunning my car and begging me to come back. Then ten minutes later, he's dumping me again."

"Last night?" Helen guessed.

"Then, just as I was storming off, he kissed me." She sighed and clenched her fists in exasperation. "Jason keeps *doing* this to me. I think it's making me a little crazy."

Claire dismissed her confused thoughts with a wave of her hand, grabbed Helen by the shoulder, and started nudging her over to the hand dryer. She pressed the button on the hand dryer and made Helen lean her head over the nozzle, drowning out Helen's attempt to ask more questions about Jason. Helen took the hint that Claire didn't want to talk about it and let her angry friend "style" her hair.

The result was a crazy, teased bouffant that Claire insisted on coating with gold-sparkle hairspray. Helen usually would have said no to all that glitter, but she had to admit it kind of worked with the costume. And besides, it was Halloween.

There were tons of people at school that day wearing even more ostentatious getups. Helen had never seen so many people in costume before. The energy in the air bordered on recklessness. Kids were actually bouncing off the walls, and teachers were letting them.

"Is that Parkour?" Helen asked Claire as one sophomore ran up a wall and did a backflip off it.

"Yeah," Claire replied uneasily. "Um . . . isn't anyone going to stop him?"

"Guess not," Helen said, and the two of them looked at each other and burst out laughing. What did they care? They had a Hergie hall pass. They were freaking bulletproof.

By the time they were done retouching this and adding another layer of glitter to that, going to and from the prop room, their lockers, and the soda machine as they came up with more and more excuses to wander the halls, it was almost lunchtime. Hours later, they were sauntering past Miss Bee's social studies class in their kick-ass costumes when the bell rang. All the AP kids poured out of what would have been Claire's class if she had bothered to show up.

"Whoops. I guess we're late," Claire said with a cheeky grin.

Helen was in midlaugh when she felt someone grip her upper arm tightly and pull her back. The air around her blurred and refracted, like she had been shrunk and put inside a diamond. When her pupils adjusted, she saw that she was on the other side of the hallway, and Lucas was using his body to barricade her up against a locker.

"Where have you been?" he asked in a low voice, close to her ear. "Don't move or they'll be able to see us. Stay very still and tell me what happened to you this morning."

"This morning?" Helen repeated, stunned.

"Matt said you looked like you'd been attacked. Then you and Claire just disappeared for *the rest of the day*. School's almost over. We've been worried sick."

"I had to shower and change. We lost track of time." Her excuse sounded lame, even to herself. She had no idea why neither she nor Claire had thought to go back to class.

She glanced over Lucas's shoulder, trying to figure out what was going on, and saw a scared look on Jason's face. He took Claire's hand and led her down the hallway, pulling her close to him. No one seemed to pay any attention to Helen and Lucas at all. They were standing so close—literally on top of each other—but Matt walked right by them like he hadn't noticed, and so did Ariadne. Something was wrong. There was no way Ariadne could look at Helen and Lucas pressed up against each other and not shoot them a disgusted look.

"What's going on?" Helen whispered.

"I'm bending the light so no one can see us," Lucas said softly.

"We're invisible right now?" Helen breathed.

"Yes."

A dozen confusing moments finally clicked in her head. Helen's blurred vision, the uncanny sense of another presence in the room, Lucas's disappearances, and how he could just suddenly come out of nowhere—it was because *he had been there all along.*

"You're my invisible sun, aren't you?"

She felt his stomach, pressed tightly up against hers, tense in a silent, startled laugh. She saw his lips move soundlessly around the words "invisible sun." She forced her gaze away from his mouth to meet his eyes.

"Lucas," Helen chastised gently. "You really scared me. First I thought there was something wrong with my vision, and then I thought I was going insane."

"I'm sorry. I knew I was freaking you out and I tried to stop, but I couldn't," he admitted, embarrassed.

"Why not?"

"Look, just because I pushed you away from me, that doesn't mean I can stay away from you," he said, laughing at himself a little. "It started with me learning how to bend light, but it's turned into something else now. Something I *never* thought I could do." He broke away with a pained look on his face. "I learned how to become invisible so I could stay close to you and let you move on with your life at the same time."

"Have you always been there?" Helen asked in a worried voice, thinking about a thousand private things he could have witnessed.

"Of course not. I miss you, but I'm not a pervert," he said, looking away and blushing a little. "You've always *known* when I've been there, Helen. Unlike everyone else, you can still sense my presence when I'm invisible. No one knows I can do this, except for you."

Helen didn't know how to respond. The only thing she wanted to do was kiss him, but she knew she couldn't. All she could do was stay still and stare at him.

The bell rang and dozens of doors shut simultaneously, but neither Helen nor Lucas made a move. A few random kids were still roaming the halls, looking for trouble. Strangely, no teachers seemed to be stopping them. It was like a day without rules. Helen certainly didn't care if she got in trouble. Suddenly, she felt like destroying something. She couldn't recall ever feeling like that before.

Over Lucas's shoulder, Helen caught a glimpse of the ghoulish woman she had seen by the side of the road, walking down the hallway.

"Right behind you," Helen gasped quietly. Lucas moved very slowly to turn and look. "I saw her this morning, and it was like everything went wrong at the same time. That's why I looked like I'd been attacked."

"She's not mortal," Lucas whispered to Helen as the ghoulish woman moved past them.

"Can she see us?" Helen asked, but Lucas just shook his head distractedly. Helen saw his nostrils flare, and barely a moment later she smelled why.

The she-ghoul reeked like rotten eggs and spoiled milk. It was the smell that Helen had mistaken for dead squirrel— the stench that had clung to her until she had scrubbed it off in the showers that morning.

The smell seemed to permeate the walls, and commotions began inside every classroom that the she-ghoul walked by. There were loud voices and yelling at first, and then crashes and squeals followed, like everyone had suddenly started throwing the furniture around. Notebooks and book bags were being tossed into the air. Soon enough, the doors started opening and students started pouring out, closely followed by the teachers. But the teachers weren't trying to restore order. They were just as unruly as the kids.

Wrapped in their cocoon of invisibility, Helen and Lucas watched in awe as Miss Bee, their stolid, logic-loving social studies teacher, savagely kicked in a locker door with her sensible shoes. Helen looked up at Lucas and could tell he was fighting the urge to join in the destruction. She felt it, too. She had been feeling it all day, she realized. It was why she'd agreed to the costume and the glitter, and why she had been so willing to blow off five classes instead of just one or two. Helen felt like raising some hell.

"Don't even think about it," Lucas whispered with narrowed eyes.

"What?" Helen whispered back. She bit her lower lip, feigning innocence. "Don't you feel like doing something *bad*?"

"Yeah, I do," he said, and pulled Helen a little tighter to him. She felt his body generate a wave of heat, like she had just opened the door to a hot oven, and pressed harder against him. He held his breath and made himself look away from her. "We have to get out of here."

Lucas grabbed Helen's hand and pulled her into a sprint. She understood why right away. If they moved fast enough, they could remain invisible as they went from hiding behind Lucas's light-cloak to moving faster than a mortal could see. It was such a thrill to run through the hallways of her high school at Scion speed that she nearly hooted with glee.

Once outside, Helen and Lucas took to the air and shot up high over the island, away from the influence of whatever was turning their school into the monkey cage at the zoo. Floating high above the ocean, Lucas turned to her and stared with a half smile on his face.

"Maybe adding wings to those paintings wasn't such a bad idea."

She knew immediately what he was talking about. The first time he'd taught her to land after flying, she'd hovered above him while he stood on the ground. She told him she'd seen a painting that looked just like them, only the one in flight in the painting was an angel. He'd told her the angel wings were nonsense. Now he didn't look so convinced.

Helen felt like it had been forever since the day Lucas had taught her to fly, but every second of that perfect time came flooding back in complete detail. She marveled at how much it still hurt.

Helen decided that the saying about "time healing all wounds" was a bunch of bull and probably only worked for people with very poor memories. The time she'd spent apart from Lucas hadn't healed anything. The distance had only made her miss him more. Even the few feet between them in that moment were excruciating. Unable to bear it, Helen soared closer and tried to hold him.

"Lucas, I . . ." Helen reached out, but he jerked away from her with a half-panicked look on his face before she could finish her sentence or lay a hand on him.

"Text Orion, tell him what happened," he said in a loud, nervous voice. He took a moment to dial down the volume before continuing. "He's been around, seen a lot of things. Maybe he knows who that woman is, or at least what we're dealing with."

"Okay." Helen let her hands fall awkwardly to her sides. She told herself not to act as devastated as she felt. "I should go. I promised my dad I'd work at the store today."

"I should find my sister, make sure we're all okay," Lucas said through tight lips. He wouldn't even look at her. "I'll tell everyone what we saw in the hallway and see if we can come up with a theory. And Helen?"

"Yeah?" she responded in a thin voice.

"Let's keep the invisibility thing quiet for now. We'll just say you and I hid in all the commotion."

"What about the obols?" she asked in a remote way, trying to separate herself from him by acting much calmer than she felt. "I've been dodging everyone's questions about how I got into the Underworld last night, but I can't put Cassandra off forever. She can't see my future right now, but sooner or later she's going to foresee something about you and those obols."

"I guess I'm going to have to come clean about stealing them," he said, sighing. "But we should probably not tell our family how I gave you one in bed last night."

Helen knew he'd added that last bit just to remind her that he'd done the right thing by pulling away. Helen knew he had just saved her from a potentially disastrous situation, but it still stung.

They parted ways and Helen went back to school to get her stuff, trying to put Lucas out of her thoughts. *He's my cousin,* she chanted under her breath until the feeling of rejection was replaced with guilt. She felt like an idiot for reaching out for him like that. What was she expecting to happen?

Helen had the vague feeling that Lucas told her to text Orion just to make her think about him, like a guy asking a girl if her boyfriend knew they were alone together. The more she thought about it, the more miffed she became. Did Lucas think she and Orion were dating or something? Helen wondered exactly what the two of them had been saying about her.

Throwing her destroyed bike in the Dumpster with a bit more hostility than was necessary, Helen went in the side entrance of the school and walked quickly down the deserted halls. There were broken tables, overturned chairs, and upended trash cans everywhere. The whole place was a jumbled mess, and it stank like that she-ghoul. Helen hurried to her locker, grabbed her bag, and draped a sweater over her arms to fight off the chill as best she could without crushing her borrowed costume, and then went right to the News Store. She didn't want to hang around and take the chance of seeing that wretched woman again.

Out on the streets, Helen felt a raucous, almost dangerous mood simmering. Amber-hued autumn light added a crackling vibrancy to the already festively decorated streets.

In the town center, orange-and-black Halloween banners snapped in the chilly wind and glowing jack-o'-lanterns flickered, casting spooky shadows in the doorways of the old whaler-style houses and on the cobblestone roads. Helen clutched at her sweater and glanced around suspiciously, looking for the source of the menace she felt.

Dozens of groups were already out trick-or-treating. At this early hour it was mostly parents with small children, but one or two of the costumed hordes were certainly not out looking for candy. These groups had a heightened, aggressive energy, as if their monster masks gave the people wearing them the soul of the characters they depicted. For the life of her, Helen couldn't recognize any of the young people in these groups, which was really strange. Usually, she would have passed half her high school by this point, but the streets seemed to be filled with strangers, which was nearly impossible. It wasn't tourist season anymore.

Something was definitely off. Helen was not afraid for her own safety, but she was still concerned. It was so early, and there were so many little kids still out looking for treats, she wished the people more interested in tricks had waited a bit longer. She went into the News Store with a worried frown, wondering if she should call Luis and tell him to take Juan and Marivi home early this year.

"Nice wings, Princess," a man drawled.

"Hector!" Helen exclaimed as she tossed herself right into one of his fantastic hugs, despite the fact that he was using her least favorite nickname. He caught her effortlessly and she hung from his neck for a bit. "One of these days, I'm going to get you to stop calling me that."

"Not in this lifetime." He tried to sound like he was joking, but she could tell right away that something was wrong. He seemed tense. She pulled back and took a good look at him.

"What's happened to you?" she asked, and ran her finger along a thin, pink scar that was still healing across his cheekbone.

"Family," he said with a sad smile.

"The Hundred are still chasing you?"

"Of course they are," he said, shrugging. "You're the only person I'm certain I'm safe with. Tantalus won't risk harming his one and only chance to be free of the Furies."

Helen frowned and wondered if she should be happy about that or not. A part of her didn't want to do anything that made Tantalus and the Hundred happy, but what else could she do? *Not* help Hector because it also helped Tantalus? She was stuck and she knew it.

"You're freezing!" he said, chafing his hands over her skin to warm her up. "Usually I prefer it when women wear as little as possible, but not you. Where are the rest of your clothes, little cuz?"

"Long story," she chuckled. "So get comfortable, because I've got to fill you in."

"I have something to tell you, too," he said seriously as she dumped her stuff behind the counter. She looked up at Hector, and was struck again by how worn he looked.

"Are you okay?" she asked, really concerned for his health.

"Go on," he said. "We've got a little time, but not that much."

Helen ran off to greet Kate and her father, and then had to count her register before she could come and talk. Kate set Hector up with hot cider and as many hazelnut sticky buns as he could eat, while Helen checked her bank and organized the credit card slips in the relatively deserted front part of the store.

When everything was in order and Kate had bustled off to take care of the noisy customers in the back, Helen caught Hector up on everything that had happened recently in the Underworld. She altered the stolen obols story slightly to make it seem like Lucas had stolen them strictly for her use and not his own, and ended with the riot at school. He listened without interrupting, a brooding look on his face.

"Her name is Eris," he said. "She's the goddess of discord, or chaos, depending on which translation you use. Wherever she goes, disorder, arguments, even riots erupt. Everything that can go wrong will. She is sister and companion to Ares, and she is very, very dangerous."

"Hector. What's going on?"

"I came here to warn you. About two hours ago I saw Thanatos walking down Madison Avenue in New York, right outside the building where the House of Thebes is holding Conclave."

"Who's Thanatos?" Helen asked, although the name sounded familiar.

"Thanatos is the god of death," Hector explained. Helen

nodded, remembering Cassandra had told her that. "He's the original Grim Reaper—black cloak and all bones, but minus the scythe. That bit of farm equipment got added during the Middle Ages. Luckily, most people on the street thought it was just a guy in an amazing costume, although there were a few of the more *sensitive* types out there who keyed into what was really happening and ran screaming."

"What was he doing there?"

"Didn't stop to chat. Thanatos just has to touch you to kill you, so I left that one to your mother and her bolts." Hector gave an expressive shrug. "We don't know why the minor gods are out and about. Daphne sent me back here immediately to have you ask the Oracle if she's seen anything."

"I'll call her right now." Helen took out her phone.

"There's one more thing," Hector said reluctantly. "We don't think Automedon is working for Tantalus anymore. We don't know who's pulling his strings now. It could be that he watched you for a while, saw what you can do, and decided it wasn't worth it. He hasn't attacked you, so don't panic yet. Just keep your eyes open."

"Great," Helen said with a mirthless laugh. "Anything else you want to tell me? Because I just started dreaming again and I could really use some more nightmare material."

Hector laughed with her as she dialed Cassandra's number and listened to the phone ring. She reached out and laid her hand over Hector's, giving him a sympathetic smile. She noticed that he had avoided saying Cassandra's name, and opted instead to call her by her title. He missed them all so much. Hector smiled back at Helen ruefully and dropped his eyes.

"It won't be much longer," Helen promised him softly, listening to the phone ring and ring. "You'll be back with your family soon."

"You found something, didn't you?" he said, perking up. "Why didn't you tell me right away?"

"Orion and I are pretty sure we know what we need. The only problem is I still don't know how to find the Furies once we get it," she replied as she hung up and dialed Matt's number instead. "I didn't want to say anything, just in case this all falls through, but we're going to make our first try for it tonight."

Matt's phone went directly to voice mail. She tried Claire, Jason, Ariadne, and finally Lucas, but in every case she either got shunted directly to voice mail or the call was dropped entirely.

"No one's answering?" Hector asked with growing alarm as call after call failed to connect.

"It's the weirdest thing!" Helen huffed, and began typing an email. Hector reached out and prevented her, taking the phone and deleting the email.

"Helen, go home," he said in a low, tense voice. He gave her back her phone, stood up, and began looking around in alarm. "Go home right now and descend."

A lab table from the science department at Nantucket High came soaring through the front window of the store, shattering the glass and sending the displays tumbling across the floor. The rancid smell of Eris came wafting in after it. Helen fought off the urge to light something on fire, knowing that her emotions weren't real and that she was being manipulated by a malevolent goddess. She heard customers scream in the back room and that snapped her out of her dangerous mood. She vaulted over the counter, but Hector held out an arm and stopped her from sprinting into the back.

"I'll protect Kate and Jerry—from themselves if necessary. You descend," he said in a firm but blessedly calm voice. Helen gave him a level look and nodded once to show she understood his orders.

"Don't be a hero," she ordered him back. "If the Hundred or your family comes, you run."

"Hurry, Princess," Hector said, and kissed her on the forehead. "We're counting on you."

Helen ran out of the News Store. Behind her, she heard Hector explaining to her father that she was going for the police. Avoiding the raucous mob, she darted down a dark alley where she couldn't be seen and soared into the air. Flying under the blue tarp that still covered her window, Helen landed directly in bed, hoping she would eventually calm down enough to fall asleep.

Her feet slammed down hard between row after row of sterile, white flowers. It was the first time Helen could recall ever having a hard landing in the Underworld, and it was most likely because she had been so desperate to get there.

Helen spun around in a circle and discovered that she was in the dreadful Fields of Asphodel. Thankfully, she was not alone. She hadn't realized it until she saw Orion's solid shape a few feet away, but she had been worried about him.

"Orion!" Helen said with relief. She ran the last few steps toward him through the tombstone blooms. He turned and caught her up in his arms with a worried frown.

"What's the matter?" he said into her neck as he hugged her. "Are you hurt?"

"I'm fine," she said, laughing a little at her overly emotional reaction but still clinging to him tightly. Finally, when she felt calm enough, she eased away and looked Orion in the eyes. "I have a lot to tell you."

"And I want to hear it, but can you do something first? Say out loud that you don't ever want anything to attack us again while we're down here?" he asked expectantly.

"I don't ever want anything to attack us again while we are down here!" Helen repeated emphatically. "Good thinking."

"Thanks. I like your dress. But, you know what? I actually think you'd be warmer in those little shorts with the hissing cats. They covered more."

Helen whirled on him with a shocked look on her face. She couldn't believe he remembered seeing her in her pumpkin pajamas.

"You have no idea what happened to me this morning! I *had* to wear this," she said defensively, trying not to blush.

"You look beautiful. Not that that's anything new," he said softly.

Helen stared at him, completely thrown, and then pulled her eyes away and stared at a boring asphodel flower like it was really interesting. She felt Orion move closer to her and told herself to relax. She hadn't kissed Orion last night, she reminded herself. That was Morpheus *as* Orion. Big difference. And the real Orion didn't even know anything about it, so there was no reason for her to feel shy around him. Except that she did. In her head, Helen heard Hector say that she could have a lot of fun with Orion if she wanted, and she lost her train of thought.

"Now, tell me what happened to you this morning," he said, concern creasing his forehead.

Helen snapped back to reality and quickly recounted her accident, the student revolt that Eris had caused at school, Thanatos walking the streets of Manhattan, and the bedlam that erupted in the News Store right before she descended. Orion listened silently, clenching his jaw more and more tightly as Helen went on.

"Are you okay?" he asked in a controlled voice.

"Yeah, but I feel awful!" Helen blurted out. "I left Kate and my dad in the middle of a riot! How could I do that?"

"Hector won't let anything happen to them," Orion said with certainty. "He'll guard them with his life."

"I know he will, but in a way that's even worse," Helen said, almost pleadingly. "Orion, what if the Delos family comes to check up on me at the store and they find Hector?"

"You mean what if *Lucas* comes to check up on you and finds Hector. You're not really worried about Jason or

Ariadne," he clarified, frustration edging his tone.

"The twins are different. Even before Hector became an Outcast, he and Lucas used to fight a lot, and sometimes it got really bad," she said in a shaky voice. "It's like they've always been headed toward something violent, and I keep thinking maybe it's another one of these Scion cycles that's doomed to happen."

"Lucas and Hector are practically brothers, and brothers always fight," Orion said, like it was obvious. "Not everything in our lives is part of a cycle."

"I know. But the Furies! They won't be able to stop themselves."

"That's why we're down here. We have all the time we need now, and hopefully, we'll take care of the Furies tonight," he said. He made her stop and brushed her wrist with the tips of his fingers. It was a slight touch, almost non-existent, but it commanded her attention.

"*If* I can even find them," Helen admitted with a pleading look. "Orion. I have no idea where the Furies are."

Orion leaned away from Helen and adjusted his backpack, assessing her.

"You're just about to panic, aren't you? Don't." He was deadly serious. "This is where you need to be, right here in the Underworld, not back in the real world fighting a hysterical mob. Any member of the Delos family can do that, but you're the only one who can do this. Let's get the water first and take it from there."

He was right. They had to do what they could here in the

Underworld or nothing back in the real world would ever get any better.

"Okay. Let's do this." She reached out and put her arms around Orion's neck, and felt him lay his heavy hands on her hips. "I want us to appear by the banks of the River of Joy in the Elysian Fields," she said in a clear, commanding voice.

Soft, sun-streaked light filtered down through a canopy of gigantic weeping willow trees. A lawn of thick, green, *living* grass cushioned their feet, and Helen could hear the sibilant rush of water over rocks nearby. Not too far off in the distance, Helen could see a large, open field of knee-high grass and pastel-colored wildflowers that served as little stars to the orbiting bees and butterflies.

There was no sun directly overhead. Instead, the light seemed to radiate from the air itself, creating the feel of different times of day in each area. The light in the stand of willow trees that shaded Helen and Orion appeared to be the ripe, long light of late afternoon, but in the meadow it was the light of early morning, still innocent and dewy.

Orion let go of her hips, but took up one of her hands, keeping it loosely clasped in his as he turned and looked around. A breeze played across his face and brushed his loose curls back from his forehead. Helen saw him turn his face directly into the gentle gust, close his eyes, and breathe in deeply. She copied him and found that the air was crisp and energizing, like it was full of oxygen. Helen could not recall anything so basic ever feeling so pleasurable.

When she opened her eyes, Orion was staring at her with

a tender look on his face. He touched the edge of her costume, shaking his head.

"You planned the wings for this, didn't you?" he said playfully. Helen burst out laughing.

"Sorry, but I'm not that clever."

"Uh-huh. Come on, Tinker Bell. I think I hear our brook babbling." Orion led her toward the sound.

"How will we know if it's the River of Joy?" she asked. Before she was done speaking she realized she already knew.

When they reached the banks of the crystal-clear water, Helen felt a giddy bubbling in her chest. She had to fight the urge to start dancing, wondered why she was fighting it, and gave in. She put her arms out and began to twirl around; Orion put his backpack on the ground.

He knelt down and unzipped the top and then stopped suddenly. He put a hand over his own chest and pressed down hard, like he was trying to push his heart back in where it belonged. Glancing up at her, Orion laughed silently, but to Helen it looked more like he wanted to cry. She stopped dancing and joined him.

"I've never felt this before," he said, almost apologizing. "I didn't think I ever *could*."

"You didn't think you could ever feel joy?"

Helen knelt across from him, staring at his overwhelmed face. Orion shook his head and swallowed, and then suddenly reached out with both arms and hugged Helen tightly.

"I get it now," he whispered, and then released her as quickly as he had gathered her up. She didn't know what it was that he "got," but he didn't give her a chance to ask. Handing Helen an empty canteen, Orion went over to the riverbank and dipped the other two he had taken out of his backpack into the sparkling river.

As soon as his fingers touched the water, tears as big as raindrops spilled down his face and his chest shuddered with a startled sob. Joining him at the water's edge, Helen lowered her canteen beneath the surface and touched joy. It wasn't the first time for her like it was for Orion, but after so much sadness and loss over the past several weeks, she cried as if it were.

When they'd filled their canteens, they both sealed them up. She didn't even consider drinking the water, and she could tell from the unwavering way he screwed the caps onto the tops of his two canteens that Orion wasn't considering it, either. Helen knew, deep in her heart, that if she took even one sip she would never leave this place. As it was, she felt a deep longing beginning to build, knowing that this perfect moment had almost passed. She wished could stay like this forever, dipping her fingers in the River of Joy.

"You'll be back someday."

Startled out of her reverie, Helen looked up at Orion and saw him smiling at her, extending a hand to help her up. The filtered light shone down on him and made a halo out of his hair. His green eyes were bright and fringed with eyelashes that were spiky and dark from crying. She slipped her waterlogged hand into his and stood next to him, still sniffling a little after the storm of ecstasy had passed.

"So will you," she told him through a teary hiccup. He dropped his gaze.

"It was enough for me to experience it, even just once. I'll never forget this, Helen. And I'll never forget that you were the one who brought me here."

"You really don't think you'll be back, do you?" Helen asked incredulously, watching Orion stow the canteens in his backpack.

He didn't answer her.

"I'll see you here again in about eight or nine decades," she said resolutely. Orion laughed and threaded his arms through the straps of his bag with a wry smile.

"Eight or nine? You realize we're Scions, right?" he said as he tugged on her hand and led her out into the morning meadow. "We've got notoriously short shelf lives."

"We'll be different," she said. "Not just you and me, but our whole generation."

"We'll have to be," Orion said quietly, tilting his head down in contemplation.

Helen glanced over at him, expecting to find that he had fallen into one of his brooding moods, but he hadn't. He was smiling to himself with a look that Helen could only think of as hopeful. She smiled, too, happy to just walk through the meadow and hold hands with him. The happiness she felt wasn't like the rapture of the river, but rapture would have been too much to bear for much longer. She realized it would have broken her heart if she'd stayed.

The farther they moved from the River of Joy, the more

Helen's head cleared. She looked down at one of her hands. It had been in the water so long it had grown wrinkled. How long had they been kneeling there?

With every step, she was more and more grateful that Orion had pulled her away. He had probably been as entranced as she had been. Yet somehow, he had controlled himself, and then found the extra strength to help her break away as well.

"How did you do that?" Helen asked quietly. "How did you pull yourself away from the water?"

"There's something I want more," he replied simply.

"What could anyone want more than endless joy?"

"Justice." He turned to face Helen and took both of her hands firmly in his. "There are three innocent sisters who've suffered for eons, not because of anything they've done, but because the moment they were born, the Fates decided that suffering was their lot in life. That isn't right. None of us deserve to be born into suffering, and I intend to stand up for those who have been. That's more important to me than joy. Help me. You *know* where the Furies are—I know you do. Think, Helen."

His spoke with such conviction, such passion, that Helen could only stare at him with her mouth hanging open. Her mind went absolutely blank for a few heartbeats, and then a small voice in her head started yelling at her, enumerating all the places where she came up short as a person.

She wasn't as doggedly persistent as Claire was, or as patient as Matt. She didn't have impeccable instincts like

Hector, or even half of Lucas's raw intelligence. She certainly wasn't as generous as the twins or as compassionate and selfless as Orion. Helen was just Helen. She had no idea why she was the Descender, instead of one of these other, far worthier people.

How the hell had she even gotten the job and ended up here in the Underworld to begin with? she wondered. All she knew was that one night she had fallen asleep and found herself wandering through a desert.

*A desert so dry, with rocks and thorns so sharp I left a trail of bloody footprints behind me as I walked,* she remembered clearly. *A desert with a single, tortured tree clinging to a hillside, and under that tree were three desperate sisters who looked ancient, and like little girls at the same time. They reached out to me, sobbing.*

Helen gasped and gripped Orion's hands tightly in hers. She had always known where to find the Furies. They had been begging her to help them from the very start.

"I want us to appear by the tree on the side of the hill in the dry lands," she announced, looking directly into Orion's surprised eyes.

# THIRTEEN

Lucas had hovered over the water and watched Helen soar away from him as she headed back toward the center of town. That dress and those damn wings had almost done him in. He wondered, not for the first time, how all the full mortals that Helen had grown up with didn't suspect that there was something supernatural about her. No matter how down-to-earth she was on the inside, Helen's beauty really was inhuman. Especially when she had held her arms out to him and said his name like she just had.

He'd almost lost it. And the thought of what he would have done if he *had* lost it turned his stomach, if only because he wanted it so badly. They were inches away from crossing a dangerous line, and unless she stopped tempting him in her maddeningly innocent way, Lucas knew it would happen eventually.

Lucas had lied to Helen. The truth was there were nights, more than just one, where he had ducked under that blue tarp covering her broken window and watched her sleep. He always felt bad after he did it, but he couldn't seem to stop. No matter how hard he tried to stay away from her, he would eventually end up in her room and hate himself for it later. Lucas knew that one of these days he was going to be too weak to walk away, and he was going to crawl into bed with her and to do more than just hold her. That's why he had to make sure that if that day ever came, Helen would kick him right out again.

Lucas had tried everything else, even scaring her away, but nothing worked. Orion was their last chance. He squeezed his eyes shut for a moment and hoped that Orion would just do what he was good at. Lucas had asked Orion to make Helen stop loving him. Then she would never try to touch him again, never look at him again like she just had. Lucas tried to convince himself it was better if she moved on, even if that meant that she moved on to another guy. But here he stopped.

Helen couldn't be with Orion, either—at least not forever. That was the only thing that was keeping Lucas from losing his mind. They could never have a life together. But that didn't mean they couldn't . . .

He abruptly shut off his thoughts before they could overpower him. Already the dark tendrils were swirling out of him, inking up the sky. He tried to calm down and *not* picture Orion and Helen together, because he *could* picture it—all too easily.

Even though Lucas had never laid eyes on Orion in person, he still had a pretty good idea what he looked like. He was a descendant of Adonis—Aphrodite's all-time favorite lover. Because Aphrodite favored this one guy above all others, the House of Rome handed down close approximations of the Adonis archetype on a regular basis, much the same way the House of Thebes repeated the Hector archetype again and again. Half the paintings and sculptures that came out of the Renaissance looked like him, because the old masters like Caravaggio, Michelangelo, and Raphael had painted and sculpted Orion's ancestors obsessively. Florence was literally littered with images of the sons of the House of Rome.

But it was more than just good looks that made a legend, especially in the genetically gifted Scion gene pool. There was a reason why both Casanova and Romeo, arguably the two most famous lovers in history, came out of Italy. Calling Orion a "handsome bastard," while accurate, didn't even begin to cover the effect he could have on a woman. The children of Aphrodite were irresistible sexually and most of them could sway people's emotions to a certain extent, but Orion had told Lucas that his gift was much more powerful than that.

Orion had a rare ability. He could make Helen fall out of love with Lucas with a light touch. If that wasn't bad enough, after Helen's feelings for Lucas were severed, Orion could control Helen's heart so that he could have the kind of casual relationship that wouldn't violate the Truce—no

366

commitment, no strings, just sex. That asshole could do whatever he wanted with Helen, and there was nothing Lucas could say against it.

The thought made Lucas want to beat the crap out of something, but instead he reminded himself that his family was probably worried about him and forced himself to head home.

Fortunately, Orion seemed squeamish about using his talent for any reason—even self-defense. He'd been deeply offended when Lucas had suggested that he had touched Helen's heart in the cave for a cheap thrill. And after seeing the two of them in the Underworld together, Lucas knew that Orion would never force Helen into anything. In fact, Lucas was sure he'd protect her with his life. That made him hate Orion less, which only made things harder. Lucas wanted to hate Orion, but since he couldn't, there was no one left to hate but himself.

Heading down the eastern coast, Lucas stayed out over the water so he didn't have to fly too high and freeze his ass off. He'd left his jacket in his locker, but it didn't really matter. He could think himself warm whenever he needed to. In fact, Lucas was beginning to believe he could think himself hot—really hot—almost as if he were on fire. But he didn't have time to deal with that odd new talent right now. It only took him a second before he was landing in his backyard.

The guilt hit him as soon as he touched down, and he started looking around for his little sister. He shouldn't have left her alone at school for Helen. Now that the Fates plagued her nearly every day, Cassandra was even more fragile than a fully mortal child. It took all of her strength to just survive each possession, and the fact that she *did* survive when so many past Oracles had died made Lucas suspect she was probably stronger than he was. But as strong as she was, after a possession she barely had enough strength left to breathe.

The other day he had found Cassandra sitting halfway up the stairs, slumped over and panting. After half a dozen steps, she'd been so worn out that she'd had to rest a minute and catch her breath. Lucas had carried her to her room, but it had been a struggle for him to go near her. She still had the aura of the Fates clinging to her, and although Lucas loved his little sister dearly, the Fates sent a chill down his spine.

Even Cassandra was scared of them, and she had to suffer their presence inside of her several times a week now. Lucas couldn't know exactly what that kind of physical and mental intrusion felt like, but from the way she looked afterward, he assumed it had to be like rape.

The fact that this was happening to his baby sister, and that there was nothing he could do to stop it, made him *very* angry.

Striding across the back lawn toward the house, Lucas struggled to control his rage, reminding himself that he needed to be more careful. So many things made him angry these days. Since that disastrous dinner when he'd struck his father, he had developed a "side effect" that was tied to his anger.

He discovered it in full at Helen's track meet when he saw

her surrounded by the Hundred, but it didn't start there. It had started with his father, just a small seed at first. But it was growing.

Part of him wondered if it would be easier if he talked to Jason or Cassandra about it, but he couldn't bring himself to do that just yet. It would only worry his family more if they knew. Hell, it worried *him*.

Lucas had almost told Helen in the hallway earlier that day, but he couldn't spit the words out for the life of him. Helen had been so afraid of Creon, and Lucas didn't know if he could bear it if Helen started looking at him like that. He still hadn't decided if he should talk about it with anyone, even though the reality was that eventually his all-knowing, all-seeing little sister would find out.

"Cassandra?" Lucas called out as he entered the kitchen. "Jase?"

"We're in here," Jason called from the library.

Jason's voice didn't sound right. He was tense, but Lucas assumed it was because he was still angry with Claire for disappearing with Helen all day and making them worry. The way Jason was handling the situation with Claire really frustrated Lucas. He wanted his cousin to wake up and realize that he'd been given a gift. He'd fallen for someone he could actually have.

The heavy double doors to the library were tilted open, and even before Lucas entered the room he could feel the tension and hear the barely controlled anger in everyone's polite voices.

"Where were you?" Cassandra asked with narrowed eyes. She'd been grilling him about his whereabouts a lot lately, even though half the time she already knew the answer.

"What's going on?" Lucas asked instead of answering her.

"Matt finally decided to share something with us," Jason said tightly. He was so furious his cheekbones were flushed. Lucas had seen that particular shade of red before, and he knew firsthand how hard it was to get Jason that angry. He looked at Matt and raised his eyebrows questioningly.

"I've been in touch with Zach. He called me the night before last, and warned me that something was going to happen today, but he didn't know what, exactly," Matt replied heavily.

"Why didn't you say anything, Matt?" Ariadne asked in a hurt voice. "Even if Zach didn't know the specifics, why didn't you warn us?"

*There's another problem just waiting to happen,* Lucas thought. But there was no way around it. Scions tended to fall in love young because they tended to die young. At least Lucas couldn't find any fault in Ariadne's taste. Matt had proven his loyalty to the House of Thebes many times over. Which was what made this current situation so puzzling. Matt usually made better choices and showed more sense than this.

"You wouldn't understand," Matt replied sullenly.

"Try us," Lucas said, his internal temperature rising. He hated it when full mortals acted as if they were so different from Scions, as if they didn't have all the same feelings.

"If I told you what he told me, what would you have done to him? Questioned him? Beat him up?" Matt exploded. "The guy's a compulsive liar. Most of what he says is bullshit, and that's what I thought his warning was. He has no idea what he's gotten himself into!"

"And that's supposed to make it all okay?" Jason said.

The argument continued, getting more and more hurtful with every exchange. Lucas hadn't been on Nantucket for very long, but he still had every single class with Matt at school. He spent more time with the guy than he did with his own father, and he couldn't remember ever seeing him get angry before. Like Jason, Matt was levelheaded, but right now both of these usually calm individuals were so angry they could barely see straight. Everyone was riled up.

*This much discord isn't natural,* Lucas thought. *Discord.* The riots, the uncontrollable anger—even angelic, goody-two-shoes *Helen* had wanted to do something bad. It all added up.

"Eris," he said out loud. He felt like kicking himself. "Listen, everyone. If Ares tried to instigate some kind of conflict with Helen in the Underworld, then it only makes sense that his sister would try to do the same in the real world. The Truce doesn't include her—she isn't one of the Twelve. She can use her powers here on Earth."

"Oh, gods! Of course!" Cassandra passed a hand across her face and smiled up at him. "How did I miss that?"

"Well, I had more to go on than you. I actually saw her," he explained. "In the hallway with Helen while we were hiding. Eris and Ares look very similar, like they're twins or something, except Ares is covered in blue dye. That's what threw me."

"How can you know what Ares looks like?" Claire asked, her eyes drilling into Lucas. "The Greeks loathed him so much that they barely wrote any myths about him at all—let alone one that describes his appearance in an authoritative way."

*Figures Claire would be the one to spot that,* Lucas thought. He sighed and came clean.

"I've seen Ares. I found a way down to the Underworld and I was there when Ares confronted Helen and Orion."

When everyone stared at him with dropped jaws, he went on to explain about the Getty robbery, what the obols could do, and how he had given one to Helen. He didn't apologize for any of it.

"And you didn't tell us about this, why?" Ariadne asked through clenched teeth.

"You wouldn't have understood," he said, consciously echoing what Matt had said a few moments ago. "All that matters is that Helen can dream again."

"Look, we're all committed to protecting Helen, and if you'd come to us with this idea, you *know* we would have agreed to the robbery to save her life. So why'd you do it alone? Luke, what if you'd been seen?" Jason asked seriously. "The Getty is blanketed with surveillance cameras."

"Not an issue," Lucas replied with certainty.

Jason gave him a doubtful look, but Lucas shook his head once in warning. Jason knew him well enough to know that

Lucas was trying to tell him something. He took the hint and dropped it for the time being, but Lucas knew his invisibility secret probably wouldn't last the night now that Jason was suspicious. He was willing to let that one go as long as no one suspected his other, much more frightening secret.

"Kids!" Noel shouted anxiously from the front door. Everyone reacted to the alarming tone in her voice.

"Mom?" Lucas shouted back as he rose from his chair. A moment later, she appeared in the doorway, out of breath and looking around wildly as she counted heads. She didn't get the number she was hoping for.

"Where's Helen?" she asked, her tension mounting.

"I left her at work," Lucas replied quickly.

"Oh, no," Noel whispered to herself, fumbling with her cell phone as she dialed a number. His father's number, Lucas realized. Castor was still in Conclave with the Hundred. Leaving the meeting could be seen as a breach. Every decision the Conclave had come to up to that point could potentially be scrapped, and his mother knew it.

"Mom! Are you sure you want to do that?"

"Screw Conclave! Castor and Pallas need to come home *now*. There's a huge riot in the center of town, Lucas. Right outside the News Store!"

Heat swarmed Helen's skin, making it sting and prickle with sweat. The bone-dry air smelled like struck matches and wiggled like the surface of a lake. Light blinded her, although there appeared to be no true sun.

Orion released Helen's hands so he could turn and face the only tree in the dry lands. Three small girls stood in its shade, their thin shoulders quivering as they cried. Orion gestured for Helen to join him so they could approach the Furies together. The three sisters reached out for each other fearfully. As Orion took a step closer, they wrapped their arms around each other in a miserable huddle.

"Wait." Helen put a hesitant hand on Orion's arm. "I don't want to frighten them."

"Have you come to kill us, Descender?" the one in the middle asked. Her voice was still childlike, even though it was rough with tears. Now that Helen could see them clearly without feeling their influence, she wondered how she could ever have thought they were grown women. They were just children.

"We know how you Scions hate us and want us dead," whined the one on the left. "But it won't work."

"We don't want to hurt you. We came to help." Helen held her hands up in a peaceful gesture. "Isn't that what you wanted the first time you led me here? For me to come back someday to help you?"

The Furies sniffled and cringed as they clutched at each other, still terrified. Orion slowly took off his backpack and laid it on the ground, glancing up at them soothingly as he did so to make sure none of them were startled. Helen thought it looked as if he were approaching a herd of skittish deer, but his tactics seemed to be working. The Furies watched him carefully with wide eyes and pursed lips, but they did seem to be more at ease.

"We've brought you something to drink," he said gently as he unzipped the backpack and took out the three canteens.

"Poison?" asked the whiny one on the left. "A trick to send us to Tartarus, no doubt. I *told* you already. It won't work."

"Sisters. Maybe this is best," the smallest one on the right said in a thin, wispy voice that could barely be heard. "I am so tired."

"I know you are," Helen said, her heart going out to the three girls. "And I know what it is to be really tired."

"We only want to help ease your suffering," Orion said. He sounded so kind that the one on the left wavered and took a half step toward him.

"There is no end to our suffering," said the leader in the middle, restraining her sister. "You Scions may find peace, even happiness from time to time, but we *Erinyes* are tormented always. We were born of blood spilled by a son who attacked own his father. We are fated to avenge the wrongful death."

The leader glared at Orion accusingly, and he looked up at the Furies with pleading eyes. Helen took a reassuring step closer to him. He was starting to lose focus on the reason they were there. That wasn't like Orion at all.

"I didn't kill my father, no matter how much the Fates would have liked that," he declared in a strong voice. "I was born to bitterness, but I don't choose to be bitter."

"But it's not a choice for us, prince," whispered the smallest one. "The murders are always inside our heads."

"We Erinyes can never forget the blood that your kind has spilled. We remember every moment," the leader said with deep sadness. The three girls began to weep again.

"And that's why we are here. My friend and I think you've suffered enough for the Scions' sins," Orion said in his soothing voice. "We only want to give you some water to drink. Aren't you thirsty?"

"We've not had a single drop of water in over three thousand years," said the one on the left.

All three of them were tempted, that was obvious. It was so hot and dry, even in the shade of their miserable tree, that Helen, who had grown used to deprivation, was desperate just to wet the inside of her mouth for a moment. Finally, the littlest sister stepped forward on legs so skinny and frail they nearly folded up underneath her.

"I am very thirsty. I wish to drink," she said in her tiny, whispering voice.

Her thin arms shook as she held out her hands. Orion unscrewed the lid and helped her steady the canteen and raise it to her lips. She swallowed a small sip, and then looked up at Orion in shock. She grabbed the canteen and tilted it back, swallowing the entire contents in a series of loud gulps before swooning against Orion. He caught her and held her, glancing at Helen reassuringly.

"You've killed her!" the whiny one gasped.

"He can't kill any of us," the leader said. "Look. She stirs."

The littlest one clutched at the hem of Orion's shirt, burying her face in his chest. He stroked her hair with his free hand and spoke softly in her ear as her shoulders started to shake. Helen could tell from his tone that he was telling her that it was okay and that she was safe. The littlest Fury suddenly threw her head back and revealed that she wasn't in pain or crying. She was laughing.

"Sisters," she sighed. "It's . . . heaven! The Heirs have brought us heaven to drink!"

Helen quickly handed the other two Furies their canteens, and watched as they joined their sister in euphoria. The littlest one kissed Orion on the cheek in gratitude and then threw herself into the waiting arms of her two bigger sisters. The three girls cried with joy as they hugged each other, bouncing and squealing and laughing all at once. They looked like three young girls, jumping around at a slumber party.

Glancing over at Orion, Helen saw him staring at the three girls with intense, but seemingly conflicted, emotions. She went and stood close to him, trying to offer him whatever reassurance she could. He seemed shaken up by the mention of his father, and she wanted to let him know that none of that mattered now. The Scions were free of the Furies, and soon he and his father could be together again.

"You were right," Helen said. He looked down at her with a questioning smile. "Setting them free was way better than eternal joy."

They both turned their attention back to the girls, and watched their rejoicing. Then Helen shrugged and made an "eh" noise, pretending like she was still debating it. Orion laughed at her joke, but he didn't say anything. He just draped an arm over her shoulders as they watched the three sisters hug and dance.

The littlest one was the first to break away. At first, it seemed that she had grown tired from all the excitement and needed to go sit for a moment. She staggered away from the group and covered her eyes with a hand. Orion quickly released Helen to go to her aid when she wavered as if she was about to collapse. She bent her head. Red drops stained her white dress as she wept bloody tears. Her sisters took her from Orion, asking what was wrong. Not long after, the other two began to weep as well.

"What happened?" Helen asked Orion.

"I don't know. All she said was that she couldn't get their faces out of her head," he replied with a worried frown as he watched the girls huddle together and speak privately. They seemed to come to some sort of a consensus, and the leader approached Helen and Orion.

"It appears this joy was not meant to last," she said.

The other two girls continued to cling to each other as they cried, and Helen desperately wanted to help them. Orion crouched down and picked up the discarded canteens, frantically checking them for any leftover drops of water but they all were empty.

"We'll get you more," he promised, but the leader shook her head.

"As much as I want to feel that again, I'm afraid it will never last," she said sadly. "We cannot repay this gift, but we wish to give you something in return for the few blessed moments you gave us."

"A gift for a gift that we'll remember forever," moaned the whiny one.

"We release the both of you from all of your blood debts," the leader said, and waved her hand in the air in blessing. "We will never torment either of you again."

She stepped back and joined her sisters, then the three of them began to retreat into the shadows of their tree.

"Wait! Don't give up yet," Orion pleaded. "Maybe we didn't bring you enough. If we get you more . . ."

"Orion, don't," Helen said, putting her hand on his arm to stop him from chasing after them. "They're right. We could spend forever bringing them water, but in the long run joy is just an experience—it's not supposed to last. I see that now. Persephone must have meant a different river."

"And what if she didn't?" Orion asked, frustration cracking his voice. "What if this is our best hope at helping them?"

Helen stared up into his bright green eyes and shook her head mutely. She didn't know what to do next. The littlest one poked her head out from somewhere deep in the shadows.

"Thank you," she whispered before ducking back into the extreme dark on the other side of the tree trunk.

"We have to help them," he said urgently. "We can't let them suffer like this forever!"

"We won't! And I swear to you, we'll keep trying until we get the right river!" Helen's eyes suddenly went out of focus, and she grabbed a handful of Orion's shirt to keep herself from falling over.

"What's happening?" Orion asked, bracing himself. The landscape blurred and Helen felt the world slow, like she was about to wake up.

"I think they're making us leave," she told him. She wrapped her arms around Orion's neck and held on tight. . . .

Matt and Claire ditched the car when they discovered that the traffic was stopped dead for the night, and instead started running down the post-sunset dark of the deserted street, toward the center of town.

Technically, they weren't supposed to be doing this, but neither of them was willing to sit safely at the Delos compound while the Scions went out to fight. Matt was more than a little insulted that Ariadne had begged him to stay behind, like he was a child who couldn't defend himself. He'd tried to argue, but Ariadne, Lucas, and Jason had simply run away so fast Matt could barely see them move, let alone get a word in edgewise. It really annoyed him when they did that.

Cassandra warned them not to go. Common sense had told her it would most likely tick everyone off. Matt much preferred it when Cassandra used her unusually deep wellspring of common sense, as opposed to her talent as an Oracle, to suss out the future. He couldn't even force himself to watch anymore when the Fates pushed their way out of her, like they were digging their way up from under her skin.

It was one of the many things that made Matt question the value of Scion "gifts" and the so-called gods that gave them to the Scions to begin with. What good were the Fates if they only used people like cups to be filled and then emptied, and eventually tossed away? As much as Matt abhorred violence, the thought of what the Fates did to Scions made him want do something athletic, preferably while wearing a pair of brass knuckles.

As he and Claire neared the town center, they could hear shouting and more than a few screams, but the voices were disconnected. In one spot, there were shrieks of fear, and in others there were shouts of rowdy enjoyment. It sounded as if different parts of the crowd were watching different movies.

"Hold up, Claire," Matt said as they rounded a poorly lit corner. "The streetlights are out down that way."

"But the News Store is that way," she protested.

"I know, but let's circle around back and go in through the alley. I want to get an idea of what's going on before we go charging down the middle of the street."

Claire agreed, and she and Matt slipped around the back of the News Store. It was quiet in the back alley, although they could both hear the raised voices of the crowd, like sneaking down the side hallway of a stadium while a rock band performed. They got the sense that something big was happening close by, but they felt strangely separated from it.

"My God, it's dark," Claire said, her voice wavering with fear.

"Yeah, and it's not a normal darkness, either," Matt murmured nervously as they went in the back entrance to the News Store.

"I think I've seen this before," Claire whispered as she rubbed her arms in either cold or fear. "When Hector was attacked by Automedon and the Hundred at my track meet, this same menacing blackness covered everything. I think it means a Shadowmaster has been here."

Inside, the store was a mess. Tables were overturned, crystal jars of candy had broken on the floor, and everything was covered in a layer of flour that must have been deliberately flung out of several torn bags. Matt and Claire picked their way through to the front, looking for injured people who might have been left unconscious, hoping like crazy that they wouldn't find Jerry or Kate. Thankfully, the News Store was entirely empty.

The darkness seemed to be getting thicker as they made their way to the front, and Matt and Claire stumbled blindly out onto the street. They paused as their eyes adjusted to the fog-like darkness left by the Shadowmaster. Coming down the street was a mob of people in costume, led by a tall woman. As the gloom dissipated, Matt instinctively cringed.

"That has to be Eris," he said in a lowered voice to Claire.

"Then who's that?" she asked, facing the opposing street. She was pointing at a tall, skinny boy who seemed to be made up of spare parts. His arms were too long for his body, and he walked with a bandy-legged stride, even as he hunched his rounded shoulders. Despite his towering height, he seemed to *creep* rather than walk. Still pointing in mute fear, Claire backed up against Matt. He could feel her entire body trembling, and the gasping breaths she took threatened to turn into screams in her throat.

Matt had known her since kindergarten, and if there was one thing he was absolutely sure of, it was that Claire Aoki did *not* scare easy. Looking around at the behavior of the crowd, Matt could see people running around, frightened far beyond any normal measure. It was as if each person were being chased by his or her own worst nightmare.

"It has to be another god, like Eris." His voice shook as he spoke. "Think, Claire! Eris is Ares' sister, and she is the personification of chaos—she makes people feel like creating havoc. So what do we feel when we look at that creepy kid?"

"Panic?" Claire wheezed, trying not to hyperventilate. "But I thought the god Pan was a goat!"

"No, no, it's not the damn satyr! There was another," Matt groused, digging thorough his memory. The convoluted, inbred family tree of the gods popped into his mind. "Ares, the god of war, walks with Eris, the goddess of discord, and with them is his son, Terror. That freaky kid has got to be Terror."

"Matt," Claire gasped, using one arm to point one way and the other arm to point another. "The two mobs are headed right toward each other!"

Matt's heart sank. Eris and her nephew were herding their crazed groups down adjacent streets that met at a large intersection kitty-corner to the News Store.

With every step, the horrible gods drew their helpless followers closer to an inevitable clash. Even Matt and Claire, who were making a conscious effort to control their reactions, felt more crazed as the gods drew near. Finally, like a cork blasting out of a shaken champagne bottle, the group surrounding Terror met with the bedlam around Eris, and a full-blown stampede began. In the midst of it all, Matt saw Eris laughing and her misshapen nephew sneering with satisfaction at her side.

Terrified people clashed with rioters in costumes, tearing each other apart in a frenzy of destruction and fear. There was nothing Matt and Claire could do but get out of the way. Gripping Claire's hand tightly, Matt pulled her behind a parked car, ducked down, and used his body to shield her from the flying glass and debris.

The two of them held on to each other, trying to control their emotions so that they didn't join in the fray. The air stank with the smell of rotten milk and burning plastic, and Matt noticed that the scents seemed to play on people's emotions—the more intense the scent, the greater the swell of feeling both in himself and in the crowd.

The glow from the streetlight above them dimmed and then disappeared as a dark pall fell over the intersection. Matt found he couldn't see more than two feet in front of his face.

"What are you two doing here?" growled a voice from inside the nexus of darkness.

*Lucas's voice,* Matt realized with a jolt.

"Come on," Lucas said, holding his hand out to them from the billowing folds of his cloak of shadows, motioning for them to follow him. "I'll hide you in here until I can get you someplace safe."

Matt and Claire hesitated, neither of them wanting to go near him. As they balked, the shadows broke up and moved away from Lucas. There was something menacing about the sound of his voice and the way the tattered ends of darkness clung to him. His blue eyes were black and he seemed so *angry*.

"Ah, Lucas?" Claire asked in an uncharacteristically timid way. "Are you, like, a Shadowmaster?"

Lucas's face fell and he nodded sadly.

"Just how many secrets have you been keeping from the rest of us?" Matt asked, stunned to a hush.

Lucas opened his mouth and looked back and forth from Matt to Claire pleadingly, but whatever he was going to say got interrupted. Moving faster than Matt could focus his eyes, Jason and Ariadne appeared next to them, already asking a dozen questions at once. Lucas held up his hands and tried to explain that he had only recently discovered his talent as a Shadowmaster, when they were all interrupted a second time.

"Kids! Where's Helen?" Kate shouted frantically. They all spun around to see Kate, half running, half limping back toward the vandalized News Store. Her clothes were torn, her hair was disheveled, and she was covered in dirt and flour like she'd been rolling around on the ground, fighting.

Hector was next to her, carrying Jerry who was unconscious and bleeding badly from a head injury.

Hector's eyes were wide and his mouth was parted in surprise. Matt turned back around and saw Lucas, Ariadne, and Jason bristling with tension. He couldn't hear what they heard, but Matt knew from the looks on their faces that all of the Scions were being taken over by the Furies.

"Jason, no!" Claire screamed, throwing herself in front of him before he could attack his brother.

"I've got Ari!" Matt yelled as he tackled her.

Ariadne hissed at him and scratched at his neck and chest, but quickly stopped herself when she saw Matt's blood begin to flow. Ignoring his injuries, Matt covered her eyes with his hand and tucked her close to him as she shook with rage. Glancing up, Matt saw Lucas tilt his head like a lion on the hunt and take a step toward Hector.

No one was left to restrain him.

# FOURTEEN

Helen's eyes opened and she saw the icy pillow next to her, so she knew she had to be back in her room. It was dark, but it was the navy-blue dark of evening, not the pitch black of late night. She was lying facedown on top of something uneven and warm— something that definitely wasn't her mattress.

Propping herself up on her elbows, Helen looked down on Orion's sleeping face. She told herself to get off him, but hesitated. He was frowning slightly in his sleep and for some reason Helen found that adorable.

In the Underworld, his face had been merely gorgeous, but back in the real world, it was downright hypnotic. Everything about the way he looked worked together in harmonious balance, like a visual symphony. The curve of his cheek played off the length of his neck, which led to the sweeping swell of his chest. He was a son of Aphrodite, and as much as Helen knew that irresistible attraction was one of his Scion gifts, knowing that fact didn't make him any less magnetic. He still needed a haircut, but even so, he was truly an Adonis, the pinnacle of male beauty. He always *had* been, she realized, and the longer she looked at him, the harder it was for her to even think about looking away.

Unable to stop herself, Helen ran a curious finger across his lower lip. She only wanted to see if it was as soft as she remembered it, as soft as Morpheus had played it.

Orion's body spasmed underneath her, and his eyes flew open in reaction to her touch. Before he was fully aware of his surroundings, he grabbed Helen and nearly chucked her off him.

"It's me!" Helen squeaked, clinging to his shoulders so he didn't send her sailing through the nearest wall.

Scrambling up onto his knees, Orion glanced around for a moment with a shocked and slightly bewildered look on his face. He released his tight grip on her and reached out with his fingertips to touch the melting ice that lay on top of the bed. An amused smile tugged at his lips as he rubbed the last of the dissolving crystals between his fingers.

Helen could tell just by looking at him that he was making the connection in his mind between the rapidly diminishing cold in her room and the constant, unearthly cold of the portal cave. She was amazed that she was so familiar with Orion's expressions that she could practically read his thoughts. It was like she'd known him her whole life. *Or longer,* she thought with a little shiver.

"This is your bedroom?" he asked. Helen smiled and nodded. He gave her a dubious look. "So . . . what's with the bed-wetter sheets?"

They both burst out laughing.

"I had to get them! I was trashing my regular sheets with mud from the Underworld!" she said, smacking Orion on the leg. He captured her hand and kept it there against his thigh.

"Helen, be honest," he teased. "You still pee the bed, don't you?"

She smiled and shook her head, giving him a look that warned him not to push it. The playful laughter died down quickly, and the fun was replaced by a delicate tension. For some inexplicable reason Helen was still touching Orion's thigh. She snatched her hand away but found that she ended up immediately replacing that same hand on his calf.

Orion leaned back against the pillows and reached out to touch her upper arm at the same time, as if he needed to reassure himself that Helen was really there.

"I'm not attacking you," he whispered with a faraway look in his eyes. He ran his fingers down her arm and cupped her elbow in his palm. "The Furies really released us."

"They did," she whispered back. "Now you can go home."

The awed look on his face crumbled. "You and I might be out, but it's not over, you know," he said.

"Not yet," she agreed, her voice breaking just above a whisper. "But I understand if you have more important things you want to do now."

"What are you talking about?" he asked with a curious look on his face.

"You're free. You can be with your dad." Helen couldn't look at him. Glancing around for something to do with her hands, she realized she was still wearing the fairy wings. She shrugged out of them and spoke in as calm a voice as she could muster. "I understand if you don't want to go down to the Underworld with me anymore."

Orion's lips parted in surprise and he narrowed his eyes at Helen. "Unbelievable," he said under his breath. "After everything I've told you about myself."

Orion flung the bunched-up covers out of his way with an angry snap and tried to stand, but Helen grabbed his arms and stopped him.

"Hey. You haven't been able to see your father since you were ten, and this isn't really your burden to begin with. It's mine. I had to at least bring it up," she said seriously.

"I already told you. I'm in this with you to the end, no matter what."

"I was hoping you'd say that," she whispered, smiling up at him gratefully. His stern look softened into a smile, and he allowed Helen to gently nudge him back into her bed.

She couldn't seem to stop touching him. Orion had probably spent his whole life beating girls off with a stick, and it was embarrassing to know that she was no different from any them.

"So don't put this away just yet, okay?" she said, lowering

her hand to touch the Bough of Aeneas, still in the guise of a gold cuff around his wrist. She allowed herself one tiny, trailing caress across the backs of his fingers and then forced herself to remove her hands from his body altogether.

"I don't think it comes off, anyway," he said softly.

His breathing sped up as they stared at each other. He seemed to relax into her bed and get more alert at the same time, and she wondered if he could see her heart beating in her chest. For just a moment, Helen was certain he was going to lean forward and kiss her.

She panicked, wondering what she would do if he did. This was no dream, and Helen wasn't sure if she was really ready for anything physical, no matter how much she wanted him right then. Orion's eyes flicked down to her chest, and his expectant expression fell away.

"It's okay. I'm not in a hurry, Helen," he told her in a thick voice. "In fact, I'd rather we take our time."

At the mention of time, a wave of panic tightened every muscle in Helen's body. She leapt out of bed, ran to her window, and lifted the blue tarp. She could hear unusually loud noises on the street coming from the center of town.

"Oh my God, I can't believe I forgot!" she yammered hysterically, doubling back to grab Orion's arm and pull him with her as she jumped out of her broken window. "I left my family in the middle of a riot!"

They landed together and took off running with Helen leading the way. A moment later they arrived in the town center and stopped. Helen could barely believe her eyes.

People she saw every day, people she chatted with as she served them muffins and lattes, were trying to tear each other to shreds. Even uniformed police officers and firefighters were running around, smashing car windows and brawling in the street.

"What do you want to do?" Orion asked, ready for a fight. "I don't know this place or these people. Who's the bad guy?"

Helen shrugged helplessly as she watched the free-for-all. Pivoting around in a circle, she tried to decide who to protect and who to fight against. But they were all her neighbors, and from what she could see, the vast majority of them were hurting each other out of sheer panic. She noticed a path being cleared through the random swarm and headed for it.

Automedon, closely followed by her old pal Zach, was carelessly flicking helpless people out of his way. With his inhuman strength, he sent anyone who stepped in his path soaring through the air like kites that had been snipped from their strings. The Myrmidon wasn't intentionally seeking to hurt people—he just didn't care if anyone around him lived or died.

A man was lying on the ground, directly in Automedon's path. A little girl in a princess costume and a boy dressed as a bear were beside him, standing in a pile of spilled Halloween candy. The little girl was bawling inconsolably and pushing on the man's back, trying uselessly to wake him. The brave little boy turned to face Automedon, his fists clenched inside the furry bear paws, ready to defend the fallen man and the defenseless baby girl. The man was Luis, Helen realized as she drew closer, and the children were Marivi and Juan.

Automedon hardly even glanced down. He batted Juan out of the way as an afterthought, and sent his tiny body soaring limply over the crowd. Orion turned into a blur at her side, but Helen stayed rooted to the ground in shock. Zach's face froze into a mask of fear, and he dove for cover as a bolt of ice-white lighting arced out of Helen's chest and connected with Automedon.

She didn't think. She didn't consider whether or not people were watching, or if she wanted to spare the insect for strategic purposes. In her mind's eye, Helen could see nothing but the image of Juan in his darling little bear costume, floating limply through air. She raised her left hand, focused the stream of pure energy, and turned Automedon into a flaming, vaguely man-shaped torch as she strode toward him.

Automedon writhed in agony like a half-crushed bug. As his skin went from fiery orange to dull red, he fell to his knees, and then onto his side, and then—charred to black— he finally went still.

"Helen, stop!" Orion yelled at her. "He's dead!"

Cutting off the stream with a crisp, snapping sound, Helen retracted her left hand and looked down on the charcoal husk that used to be Automedon. Zach scrambled to his feet and took off. Helen let him go, turning instead to face Orion.

He was holding Juan. In such large arms the little boy looked like a toy teddy bear. Helen covered her mouth with a hand, unwilling to ask out loud how bad it was.

"It's okay, I caught him before he hit the ground," Orion said comfortingly as he strode toward her. "But we should get these kids out of the street."

They looked down at Marivi. She was staring up at Helen, her eyes wide and her mouth hanging open in awe.

"Do you remember me?" Helen asked. Marivi nodded, her expression frozen in shock. "Will you come with us?" Marivi nodded again, her eyes still wide.

Helen held out an arm to the little girl and she jumped up, clinging to Helen's neck and wrapping her legs around Helen's waist as tight as a barnacle. Orion balanced Juan carefully on Helen's other hip and then he bent down to study Luis, who still seemed to be breathing.

"He's out, but he'll be all right," Orion said, picking him up without delay. "Is there a safe place near here? The hospitals will be overflowing tonight."

"Ah . . . the News Store?" Helen said, at a loss. "There's a first aid kit, and maybe my family will be there."

"Perfect," Orion replied, motioning for Helen to lead on.

As they headed off, Automedon's blackened body moved. They heard a brittle, cracking noise, and a large rent opened up down his back, exposing damp pink skin underneath. It *breathed*. Marivi buried her face in Helen's neck, hiding her eyes.

Orion and Helen exchanged shocked looks. Suddenly, the shell around Automedon split in half, and he climbed out of his own burnt skin like a crab shedding its outer casing. Covered in mucus, and crouching next to his castoff remains, Automedon looked up at Helen with milky, film-covered eyes and smiled.

"That hurt," he told her in a detached, nearly robotic way as he drooled stringy spit. He looked at Orion and then down at the gold cuff on Orion's wrist, narrowing his oozing eyes. "The Third Heir. Nice to see you again, General Aeneas."

A long, sticky tube uncurled from underneath Automedon's human tongue and seemed to throb in Orion's direction. Then it rolled back up and retracted in a swallowing motion into Automedon's mouth. For a moment, Helen thought she was going to be sick.

"Come on! Before it's strong enough to stand," Orion growled in her ear, and the two of them ran away as fast as they dared while carrying injured passengers.

Before the News Store even came into view, Helen knew something was terribly wrong. She could feel the ground trembling, and glanced over at Orion.

"It's not me!" he said. "Those are impact tremors."

Turning the final corner, they were enclosed in a dark pall.

"Shadowmaster!" Helen yelled at Orion. "The Hundred must be here somewhere. They have a new one. I saw it at my track meet. . . ."

Helen's feet slowed as the darkness began to dissipate ever so slightly. She knew this darkness; she had seen it more than once. Through the clinging shadows that reached like smoky hands, she saw Hector slamming someone—the source of the darkness, Helen realized—against the sidewalk repeatedly. It was Lucas. In a flash, Lucas changed positions, got the upper hand, and tackled Hector, punching him savagely. Snapping herself out of her stunned daze, Helen screamed something unintelligible, and ran the rest of the way with Orion close behind.

"Helen!" Kate yelled, and Helen pulled up short.

Following the sound of Kate's voice, Helen looked and saw her crouched down over Jerry, who was unconscious and bleeding badly. Next to them, Claire and Matt had Jason and Ariadne wrapped up so they couldn't see or hear. Helen gave the kids to Kate while Orion put Luis down next to Jerry. Helen spared her father one worried look, and then threw herself at Lucas.

As she knocked Lucas off Hector, she saw Orion dart in behind them to wrap an arm around Hector's throat in a chokehold. Helen used her superior strength to shove Lucas to the ground. She tried to pin him under her, but he had always been better at grappling and easily slipped out from under her, reversing their positions. He secured her hands over her head, and even though she was stronger, she knew she was trapped. Helen considered shocking him, but she was dehydrated from frying Automedon and knew she couldn't fully control her bolts.

"Please, Lucas, don't do this!" Helen pleaded as a last resort. At the sound of her voice, he paused and seemed to wake from his trance. A confused look flashed across his face and he jumped off her.

"I'll get Hector out of here," Orion shouted as he struggled to keep Hector from pulling free. "Come on, big guy. Time for a swim!"

In a blur of speed, Orion managed to break Hector's stance and carry him off toward the ocean. As soon as the Outcast was too far away to affect the Delos family, their demeanors changed from anger to painful regret. Claire and Matt released Jason and Ariadne, and Lucas dropped his head into his bloody hands, covering his eyes. Helen wanted to reach out and comfort him, but she knew she shouldn't touch him. Instead, she just stared at Lucas with her heart in her throat.

"I always knew there was *more* in you. Something hidden, but I never . . . What is going on?" Kate asked, her voice a hoarse whisper. Helen turned to look at her, and saw that she was barely keeping it together. "Does your father know?"

"No. Kate. Please," Helen stammered. Looking down at Jerry's bleeding head, she was overcome with worry. She had no idea what she needed, or wanted, to say.

"Let's get everyone inside," Matt said calmly, looking over the shell-shocked faces around him to the riot that was still consuming the town. "First things first. We need to get indoors."

They carried the wounded to the couches in the café area at the back of the News Store, and the twins immediately went to work assessing the severity of everyone's injuries. Luis only had a concussion, but little Juan had four broken ribs, a broken arm, and a cracked skull. The twins looked at each other solemnly and prepared themselves for their work.

"Just stand back," Claire warned Kate and Marivi when they gasped at the twins' glowing hands. "It's okay, really. Healing is one of their talents."

"What do you mean, talents?" Kate pleaded. "Helen, you have to tell me what's going on!"

Helen didn't know what to say. She looked down at her father and then back up at Kate, overwhelmed. "I'm a demigod," she finally spat out. "I'm so sorry, but I don't have time to explain this to you just now."

"Alrighty then!" Claire said loudly when she saw Kate's petrified reaction. "I got this one, Helen. You are *so* not good at breaking the news gently, by the way. Kate, brace yourself. This is going to get messy."

Claire started to give poor Kate a crash course in ancient mythology while Helen mouthed the words "thank you" and gestured for Matt and Lucas to join her. She told them about her encounter with Automedon, describing how she had fried him and how he'd shaken it off, molting his burnt skin right in front of her in the process.

"Is Zach okay?" Matt asked Helen.

"Last I saw he was headed down Surfside," Helen answered, not really caring. "He was *with* Automedon, Matt, not getting mowed down *by* him like Luis and his kids, so I think he'll be fine."

Matt turned to Lucas. "Can Myrmidons usually withstand lightning, or throw bolts?"

"No," Lucas said. "They don't have talents like Scions do, but they *are* strong. Stronger than most Scions."

"Even if he was ten times stronger than you, he couldn't have survived that," Helen said darkly. "Automedon must have become immortal somehow. Maybe he became blood brothers with a god, like Cassandra said. Lucas, I hit him with a bolt that could melt *lead*."

Lucas frowned in thought. There were a million things she wanted to ask him, most of which centered on his being a Shadowmaster, but a bright flash caught her attention and she decided it would have to wait. She, Matt, and Lucas went over to check on the injured. The twins had decided to heal the little boy first so Juan could wake up without then being frightened. Ariadne and Jason spent a few moments monitoring Luis, and decided he was okay.

Wobbly, but not permanently damaged, Luis grabbed his kids and rushed out of the News Store, desperate to see if his wife was still at home. Before her father carried her out the back door, Marivi held her pointer finger to her lips as if to say "shhh," promising never to tell.

Already exhausted and turning gray from doing so much work on Juan, the twins turned their attention to Jerry. After a quick assessment, they shared one of those looks that Helen was convinced meant that they were reading each other's minds. But before Helen could begin to ask them how bad the damage was, Orion returned from the sea. Obviously troubled, he thudded as he walked toward them, shaking droplets of water from his hair. He went from being soaking wet to completely dry in a few seconds.

"How's Hector?" Lucas asked, his voice shaky.

"He's upset, but safe," Orion answered.

Lucas dropped his head and nodded.

"How can you be here?" Jason asked him incredulously. "Why aren't we attacking you?"

"Well, the short version is that Helen and I guessed wrong—but in the best possible way. We ended up getting— I guess you could call it a pardon from the Furies. Right, Helen?"

"But we didn't solve the bigger problem. Yet," Helen said, unable to meet anyone's gaze. She felt guilty that she and Orion were free of the Furies, but the rest of her family still had to suffer.

"You're Hector's little sister?" Orion asked, smiling at Ariadne warmly. "He told me to tell you in particular not to worry. He said you worry about other people too much."

Ariadne tried to smile at Orion, but instead began to choke up. She turned back toward Jerry, wiping her tears away with the back of her hand. Helen looked over at Lucas's devastated expression.

He was the only one who had attacked Hector. The others had resisted when he couldn't. The burden would always be heaviest on him. Lucas was this generation's Paris, and he was destined to be the scapegoat in this epic. The deck had always been stacked against him, and now that he also had to bear the stigma of being a Shadowmaster, it would only get worse.

There was a darkness growing in him. Helen wondered if it had always been there—waiting to come out—or if what had happened between them had planted it. She could see he was barely holding on. He used to be so confident, so alive. He used to *shine,* and now he was in shadow.

Something snapped in Helen. She was sick of watching the people she loved suffer for things that were out of their control. There was nothing she could do to help her father, but there was something she could do to help the rest of her family.

"I'm done with this. Are you?" she asked Orion.

"Oh, yeah. *So* done," he answered, understanding Helen's meaning right away. Her eyes drilled into his, simultaneously swearing an oath and demanding one from him.

"We go down. We *stay* down until we find the right river," Helen said with absolute certainly. "No matter how long you and I have to spend in the Underworld, this ends for the rest of our kind *tonight.*"

The corners of Orion's lips tilted up in the faintest of smiles and his tight jaw relaxed.

"I can't run at Scion speed through the caves, or I risk collapsing them. It'll take me a few minutes to get to the caves on the mainland, but then it takes half an hour for me to get down to the portal," he said, lowering his chin like he was getting ready to storm a citadel. "I'll meet you then." Orion turned and sped off.

"Take care of my dad," Helen said to the twins and Kate, and then she headed for the door.

"Where are you going?" Lucas asked, grabbing her arm as she walked past him.

"Home. To bed. To the Underworld," Helen ticked off in order, like she was giving him a list of deadly weapons.

"You're just going to go lie prone in a bed, in a bedroom that has a broken window, after pissing off a Myrmidon?" His eyes flared with frustration. "That sounds perfectly *safe* to you?"

"Well, I . . ." Helen stammered, wondering how she'd overlooked those major details.

Lucas cut her off, muttering to himself about how she was going to give him a nervous disorder. Still firmly gripping her upper arm, he turned her around and led her to the door.

"I'll guard Helen while she descends," he called back to Jason. "If anything happens, reach me on my cell."

"Right." Jason was clearly trying his best to rally. "We're moving everyone to our house. We can care for Jerry better there while we protect the rest."

"Good idea," Lucas responded.

"Keep us posted, brother," Jason added, purposely using the word *brother*. Lucas averted his eyes but smiled gratefully before turning back to the door.

Helen and Lucas plunged onto the chaotic streets and took to the air, looking down on the swarms of people. She felt Lucas pull up short, and directed her eyes to what had caught his attention. Eris was running down a deserted backstreet, chased by two big men with swords.

"My father and uncle," Lucas shouted above the cold wind.

"Should we help them?" Helen asked through chattering teeth. Lucas wrapped an arm around her and began rubbing her bare shoulders with his warm hands. Not for the first time, Helen wondered how he always seemed to radiate heat.

"They can handle it," he said, pulling her against him to keep her warm and leading them onward toward her house. "Stay focused on your task, not on theirs."

Helen had no idea how he could compartmentalize his emotions like that. His father was down there fighting a goddess, but still he stuck to his job. *Like a soldier*, Helen thought. It struck her just how much self-discipline Lucas had, and she tried to follow his example, but she couldn't. Her mind kept straying to Jerry, to the twins, to Hector, but most of all to the fact that Lucas had his arm around her.

Helen followed Lucas under the blue tarp and landed in her bedroom. He led her straight to her messy bed and tried to get her to lie down.

"I don't know what to do," Helen said, unwilling to get in bed.

"Why don't you start by sitting?" he suggested quietly.

"All that brave talk about finishing this tonight, and I'm completely clueless. I have no idea how to end this." She was trying not to burst into tears.

"Come here," he said, taking her hand and pulling her down next to him.

"You know what the worst part is?"

"What's that?"

"I kind of don't care about any of it at the moment," she said, tears trickling out the sides of her eyes. "I don't care that you're a Shadowmaster, and that you've been keeping secrets *again.*"

"I tried to tell you in the hallway today, I really did. I just couldn't. I guess I couldn't face it myself, and telling you would make it real."

"But I don't care what you are!" she said, barely able to keep her voice down. "I don't care that you're a Shadowmaster, or that you're my cousin. I don't even care that I'm supposed to descend and save the Scions in about ten minutes. Lucas, the whole world could be on fire right now, but the only thing that I'm thinking about is how happy I am to be alone with you. How sick is that?"

Lucas pinched his eyes shut and sighed heavily. "What are we going to do?"

"I don't know," she mumbled in a lost way as they reached out and wrapped their arms around each other. "Nothing helps."

"You *have* to move on, Helen," he said desperately.

"I know that!" she cried, resting her chin on his shoulder. The more she thought about letting him go, the tighter she squeezed him. "But I can't."

"Forget about me," he insisted. "That's the only way either of us is going to survive this."

"How am I supposed to forget you?" Helen asked, laughing weakly at such a silly suggestion. "You're too big a part of me. I'd have to forget who *I* am to forget *you.*"

Holding Lucas the way she was, she caught a glimpse of their reflection in the vanity mirror opposite her bed. It startled her. Just as she was saying the word *forget*, she was staring at the word REMEMBER.

She'd totally forgotten she even had a vanity.

She hadn't looked at it or even acknowledged that it was in her room for over a month now. Written on the mirror in viper-green eyeliner were the words THE RIVER I CAN'T REMEMBER and I SAW IT AGAIN. That's funny. She and Orion were looking for a river, right?

"Wait," Helen said, pulling back and looking at Lucas. "Is there a river in the Underworld that makes you forget *everything*?"

"Lethe," Lucas answered immediately. "The souls of dead Scions drink from the River Lethe to forget their former lives before they are reborn."

"The Furies define themselves as 'the ones who can never forgive and never forget,' right? But what if they were forced to forget everything, even who they are?"

"They would forget all the blood debts. The Scions would be free," Lucas said, so softly it was like a sigh.

A moment later they were both looking around the room, confused. Helen's entire train of thought had derailed and went skidding off the tracks.

"*What* river was that again?" she asked through an embarrassed grin. "It's this thing with how I navigate down there. I have to be really specific, or I'll never get there."

"Ah . . . I *know* it. . . ." Lucas wavered for a moment, laughing at himself for being so absentminded. "Lethe! You want to get to the River Lethe!"

"Lethe. Right! Okay . . . so. What do I do once I get there?"

"I don't know," he said, a hint of fear creeping into his voice. "Do you see what's happening?"

"Yeah," Helen said, balling her fists and trying to stay on point. "This river won't let me remember anything once I start thinking about it. That means I shouldn't try to think about it, right?"

"That's right. Don't think about it, just do what you need to do." Lucas turned and fished through Helen's nightstand, taking out an old pen. He scribbled the words *Lethe* and *Furies* on her forearm and then he sat and stared at her in confusion. "I have no idea why I just did that."

"Okay. Great. I'm going to descend now," Helen announced tersely, already getting confused and deciding that she should act before she had a chance to think about it too much. "And in case I forget everything, including to come back, I want you to know that I still love you."

"I still love you, too." A smiled tugged at his lips. "Are you late for something?"

"I think so. I'd better go."

Helen lay back, looking up at Lucas, who was smiling peacefully down on her. There was nothing here to fear, but Helen had a sneaking suspicion she should be afraid.

"Don't tell Orion!" Lucas said urgently, like it had just occurred to him. "It'll make him forget. You just remember where to go and then let him remember what you need to do once you get there."

"Okay," Helen sighed as she snuggled down into the

covers. She was so cold. "Compartmentalize. That's the key to winning the battle."

"It is," he said in a distant voice. He stared at her face, smiling softly.

"Why are we even trying to stay away from each other?" Helen wondered aloud, trying to keep her heavy eyes open. "We're perfect together."

"We are," he mused. Lucas shivered suddenly. "It's getting colder, like the temperature just dropped suddenly."

"It's always so cold in here." She pouted, brushing at the ice crystals forming on her blanket. "Why don't you get under the covers and keep me warm?"

"Okay," he said, and although he frowned like something about getting into bed with Helen bothered him, he did it, anyway. He spooned against her back, and Helen sighed as he pulled her tightly against his chest. She tried to turn around and kiss him, but he stopped her, his teeth chattering as he spoke. "You're tired. Go to sleep, Helen."

She was tired—really tired. She was already half asleep. As much as she wanted to stay with Lucas while he held her, Helen's eyes began to droop under the soothing pressure of his arms. The world melted away, and she stumbled headfirst into the Underworld.

*Wasn't I supposed to meet someone?* she thought. *Oh, yeah! Orion . . .*

# FIFTEEN

utomedon crawled up from the ocean floor, skittering spiderlike on hands and feet as fast as he could to keep up with the third Heir. Underwater, the big Scion was fast, the fastest Automedon had ever seen, and it was all he could do to not lose him. He had his scent, and now Automedon could track him anywhere over land, but underwater his scent washed away in an instant. He couldn't let Orion escape.

Automedon needed to find the portal he used to fulfill his master's order—no matter how whimsical it seemed to Automedon. His master had a thing for situations that struck him as "poetic." From what Automedon overheard at the store while the Heirs were so valiantly pledging themselves to complete their mission or die (about time, in Automedon's opinion), the young prince was on his way there now.

They were so young, so trusting, that they'd had their entire conversation about their partial success with the Furies out in the open. They hadn't even checked to see if anyone was listening. The Face was so open and unaccustomed to guile, very unlike her wily mother. That one changed her appearance, her scent, everything, at the first hint of danger. She was impossible to track—doubly so now that she had the new Hector to train. It was as if having a cub heightened her tiger instincts.

The new Hector was formidable, and for the first time in three and a half thousand years, Automedon did not scoff at the Scion who bore the great warrior's name. He was the first to deserve it, although he still had a lot to learn.

The prince was not to be taken lightly, either. And the lover. Well. Like the dead lord, he had the hand of Nyx on him, and as such he wielded magic older than the gods, older than the titans, even. He was dangerous, that one. The more Automedon watched this crop of heroes, the more he became convinced that his master was right. This entire generation had to be dealt with before they came into their full potential. They were like none that had come before them, especially the Face.

She was far more talented than the others. The tiny fraction of power this new Helen had used on him just minutes before had been a marvel of agony—truly a moment of awakening for Automedon. He hoped to return the sensation shortly.

Sprinting up onto the sandy beach of mainland Massachusetts, on nearly the exact spot where the Europeans built their settlement and began *their* invasion, Automedon found Orion's scent and then immediately lost it again. The trail simply ended. Automedon tried to stay calm as he searched.

*This one couldn't fly, could he?* Automedon leapt into the air, and after a disconcertingly long time, finally tasted traces of the young prince on the breeze. Extending his leap for as long as he could, Automedon found that the trail sketched a wide arc that eventually led back to the ground.

Orion had jumped into the air as soon as he came up from the beach. The only reason he would have done that was because he knew he was being followed. *Very clever,* Automedon thought, impressed. *He's obviously been chased before. But never by me.*

Once on land again, Automedon found himself having to struggle to keep up, but at least the trail was easier to follow than it had been underwater. The young prince made many attempts to double back and confuse whoever might be behind him. A bloodhound might have fallen for any one of Orion's tricks, but Myrmidons were not bloodhounds. They were far better at tracking than any dog ever could be.

The young prince led Automedon down into a dark cave, letting the water guide him, and Automedon had to hang back so as not to be heard in the echoing passages. He wasn't concerned with the dark. He tasted his way, following the chemical trail that the prince had stamped into the ground.

The air suddenly became unnaturally cold, signaling that a portal was near. Automedon surged close to Orion and held perfectly still, silently calling to his master with an ancient prayer. His mind filled with the squabbling of vultures, and he knew that his master had heard him.

The Heir opened the portal and jumped into the dead lord's land. The split second before it closed again, Automedon darted over and pulled his master through, into the neutral zone.

Helen landed with a thud next to Orion. They were walking down a deep beach that seemed to go on forever—never meeting the ocean or the land in either direction. She looked around, hoping for some clues that would tell her what she needed to do next. Something about a river kept popping up in her mind. It struck her that she had no idea what she was doing, walking on a deserted beach with a guy when there was no one else anywhere in sight. *Lucas* was the only one who walked on deserted beaches with her. It was their "thing."

Was she cheating on Lucas?

Impossible! Not even the hot guy next to her (his name suddenly slipped her mind, although she was vaguely aware that she knew him) could make her feel like Lucas did. Although she couldn't exactly remember how Lucas made her feel at that particular moment, because she couldn't quite picture his face.

And where the heck was the sun, or the moon, or the stars for that matter? Wasn't there supposed to be *something* in the sky?

"I think someone followed me, but I don't think he made it through the portal," her beautiful companion said. "I didn't get a good look at him, but whoever this guy is, he's scary good."

*I'm in the Underworld,* Helen remembered, just before she completely freaked out. *And I'm here because I have some very important compartmentalizing to do.*

"Hi," she said uncertainly.

"Hi," Hot Guy replied uneasily. "Helen? What's the matter?"

"I don't know what I'm doing here with you," she said honestly, relieved that at least he recognized her and called her by her name. "But *you* know, right?"

"Yeah, I do," Hot Guy said, slightly offended. "We're here to—"

"Don't say it!" Helen exclaimed, jumping up to cover his mouth with her hand before he could say another word. "We have to compartmentalize, or something. I sort of know where we're going, but you have to remember what we need to do when we get there, or we'll never accomplish whatever it is we're supposed to accomplish. I *think* that's what Lucas said, anyway."

"Okay, I can do that. But why are you acting like this? Did something bad happen to you? Please tell me. . . ." Hot Guy pleaded. "Are you injured?"

"I can't remember!" Helen laughed, vaguely aware that she sounded terribly foolish, while he sounded deeply concerned. He was really worried about her, and that struck Helen as so sweet. "It's all going to be okay. You remember your part—but don't tell me what it is—and I'll do the other thing. You know, the thing that I'm supposed to do because this is my special little quest?"

"Because you're the *Descender*?" he guessed.

"Yes I am!" Helen said with happy-camper enthusiasm. "But what *exactly* is it that I can do that no one else can?"

"You can make us magically appear by the river we need to get to just by saying the name out loud," he said cautiously.

"Right!"

Following an instinct, Helen wrapped her arms around Hot Guy's neck, but she had no idea what to do next. Glancing away from his distractingly attractive mouth, she saw, right in front of her face, the words *Lethe* and *Furies* written on the inside of one of her forearms. On a whim, she decided to just go with it. She figured, heck, it was a fifty-fifty chance.

"I want us to magically appear by the River . . . Lethe?"

Helen found herself on a riverbank in the middle of a barren wasteland, staring up at a stunning man. She had her arms around him, and he had his hands on her waist, but she couldn't remember how they had gotten this way.

"You are so beautiful," she told him, because she couldn't think of a reason not to.

"So are you," he replied, surprised. "For some reason

I think I know you, but I can't remember where we met. Have you ever been to Sweden?"

"I don't know!" Helen laughed. "Maybe I have."

"No, that's not it," he said, a troubled frown tightening his brow. "There's something we need to do. The water!" he exclaimed, releasing Helen and taking off his backpack. Helen knew she had seen that gesture before, even though she couldn't remember the boy who'd made it.

"I feel like I'm having the strongest case of déjà vu ever," Helen said anxiously. "It's like I know you, or something."

"You do know me. You just can't remember because that's what all of this is about. Forgetting," he said in a gruff, worried voice, as he took three canteens out of his pack. "You know, Helen, if this idea of yours wasn't so terrifying I would be saying that it was the most brilliant thing I'd ever heard of." He looked up at her intensely. "I'm Orion and you're Helen and we're here to collect this special water and bring it to three very thirsty girls."

"I don't know why, but that sounds *exactly* right. Hang on," she said, reaching for the canteens. She held out her hand until he gave them to her. "I think I'm supposed to do this."

"You're right, this is your task. My part's coming up." He clenched his jaw in concentration. "I just have to *remember* it."

Helen looked down into the river's turbid water dubiously. Pale fish bumped around under the surface, like clumsy ghosts. They didn't seem smart enough to be afraid of her, and Helen knew she could reach down and pet one with her bare hand if she wanted, but the thought of touching that water was abhorrent to her.

She knew she had to fill the canteens, she just couldn't imagine anyone wanting to drink from them, no matter how thirsty they were. Holding the canteens by their straps, Helen lowered them into the water and let them fill before raising them. Hot Boy reached out his hand to take one from her so he could screw the lid back on, but she pulled it out of his reach.

"Don't touch it! Don't touch the water!" Helen practically screamed as a droplet nearly made contact with his hand. She saw the startled look on her companion's face and felt a bit foolish for her outburst. "Sorry. I just don't think it's sanitary," she said in a more reserved tone.

"We need to travel, Helen," he said in a very reasonable voice. "We have to close the lids."

"I'll do it."

She screwed the tops on and put them in the backpack that he held open for her, rubbing a drop of water away between her fingers. He zipped up the backpack, threaded his arms through the straps, and then put his hands on her waist expectantly. She shied away from him.

He was unbelievably good looking, but *still*. Shouldn't he at least introduce himself first?

"I'm sorry, but who are you?" she asked suspiciously.

"Orion," he said, like he was expecting to have to introduce himself, and then his eyes grew sad and intense. "Quick question. Do you know who *you* are?"

The girl paused, startled.

"How strange," she said. "I think I've forgotten my name."

"Claire, go help Kate," Matt said, shifting Jerry lower so he carried more of his weight. "She's having trouble."

Claire went and took one of Jerry's legs from Kate, sharing the burden. It was farther to Claire's car than Matt remembered. If they were lucky, it was still parked where they'd left it. He sincerely hoped that no one had set it on fire or slashed the tires. If it wasn't drivable, he knew he would end up having to carry Jerry back to the News Store all by himself. Kate and Claire were flagging, and the twins were so exhausted they could barely walk.

Ariadne and Jason had worked a bit on Jerry, enough to get him stable, but things didn't look good for Helen's father. They needed to get him back to the Delos compound where the twins could work on him gradually instead of trying to heal him in moments, which drained them terribly.

Ariadne's face was already a scary shade of puce. Matt wanted to help her so much it felt like a cramp inside, but he didn't know what she needed. If he were a Scion, maybe he could be more useful.

During the twenty-minute walk to Claire's car, the twins leaned against one another, talking softly as if they were encouraging each other with small, private phrases that only they could understand. It seemed to take forever to load everyone in, and then Matt had to walk around to the front and shut Claire's door for her because she could barely lift her arms.

"Call me if you need anything," Matt told her.

"What the hell are you talking about?" Claire slouched over the steering wheel, utterly exhausted. "Aren't you coming back with us?"

"No. I'm going to find Zach."

"What?" Ariadne protested weakly from the backseat. "Matt, he's a traitor!"

"A traitor who reached out to me, trying to tell me that this was going to happen, and I turned my back on him. Zach is my friend, Ari," Matt said evenly. "I can't let him get in any deeper. I have to help him."

"This isn't your fault," Ariadne began to argue, but Jason pulled her back gently.

"Save your strength. You know we need to be careful right now," he whispered to her, their heads lolling close to each other. Ariadne met his eyes and immediately settled down. Jason looked back up at Matt. "Go get your friend. Good luck, Matt."

Nodding a quick good-bye as he lightly tapped the roof of Claire's car, Matt turned and ran back into the center of town. *His* town, not the mad god's, he reminded himself fiercely, before looking through the frenzied, masked throngs for Zach.

"Put your arms around me," the tall young man said.

"Why?" she asked nervously, trying not to giggle. He grinned at her.

"Just put your arms around my neck," he cajoled. She did. "Now. Repeat after me . . . I want us to appear . . . um," he broke off, biting his lower lip in thought.

"I want us to appear . . . um," she parroted back to tease him.

"I can't remember what I was supposed to say," he said through an embarrassed laugh.

"Then it must not have been very important, right?" she said logically. "What are we doing here, anyway?"

"I don't know. But whatever the reason, thanks." He moved his hands from her waist up her back, pressing her closer to him as he felt her shape under his hands.

"Are we dating?" the girl asked.

"I don't know, but it seems that way," he said, gesturing to their tight embrace. "Let's check it out." He lowered his mouth to hers and kissed her.

Her knees melted. This guy was *that* good a kisser. The only problem was, the girl had no idea who he was. She pulled back and blinked a few times to clear her vision, sensing that something was off.

"Wait. Is your name Lucas?" she asked.

"No. I'm . . . hang on. I know this one. I'm Orion," he finally decided.

"I'm probably going to kick myself for this later, but I don't think you're my boyfriend."

"Really?" he asked doubtfully. "Because that felt damn good."

"Yeah, it did," she mused. "You know what? I'd hate to be

wrong about this, so maybe we should check again?" She kissed him, and this time she completely let herself go with it just to be sure. A tiny voice in her head kept saying, *That's not him*, but the rest of her was really enjoying kissing this Orion guy.

He guided her down to the ground, careful not crush her underneath him. The tiny voice started yelling. She tried to ignore it because this guy felt amazing, but no matter what the rest of her body was saying, the damn voice wouldn't shut up until she pulled away from him.

"I'm sorry, but I don't think this is right," she said reluctantly, unable to stop herself from running her fingers through his soft curls one last time. The gesture felt strangely familiar. She looked up at his confused face and noticed he had something strapped to his back, which the girl thought was odd, considering they were making out and all.

"Why are you wearing a backpack?"

"I don't know," he said, reaching back to touch it, like he was just noticing it himself. His eyes flared and he sucked in a breath as his hand felt the shapes through the outside. The contents made a sloshing sound. "The water! Helen, let me see your arm!" he said, leaning back and reading the inside of her arm. She heard the name *Helen* and remembered that it was hers.

"I'm sorry. I nearly forgot myself," he said in a shaky voice as he got off her and helped her stand. He placed her arms around his neck and then put his hands on her hips in a perfunctory way, all the seduction gone. "Say this. I want us to appear near the Furies."

Helen saw a twisted tree in her mind, and a hillside of sharp rocks and thorns. Something told her that this was important and that she should include it.

"I want us to appear on the hillside under the tree of the Furies," she said clearly.

The heat was unbearable, but the flat, blinding light was even worse. Helen shaded her face with her hand and blinked repeatedly, trying to relax the squeezing feeling in her eyes as her pupils rebelled against the insulting brightness. The air was so dry it tasted bitter and caustic—like it was trying to scour the moisture out of Helen's mouth.

She licked her dry lips and looked around. A short walk away was a tree that was so old and starved that it looked more like twisted rope than a plant. Under the shade of this tree stood three trembling girls.

"We told you not to waste your time," the one in the middle said. "We are a lost cause."

"Nonsense," Orion said cheerfully. He took Helen's hand and led her to the tree. The Three Furies backed away from them.

"No, you don't understand! I don't think I can bear to feel that joy, only to lose it again," the littlest one whispered urgently, her voice quieter than rustling leaves.

"Nor can I," said the leader sadly.

"Or I," agreed the third.

"I don't think we should drink, sisters," decided the smallest. "Our burden is heavy enough already."

The Furies began to shrink away from Helen and Orion, back into the dark shadow of their tree. Helen realized that they were shrinking away from something that could make them happy, even if it was for only a few moments.

She recognized herself in this abnegation, and something inside her lit up. Lucas. Would she *really* rather forget Lucas entirely? The floodgates opened, and all of Helen's memories came rushing back in 3-D. She saw the lighthouse on Great Point, her meeting place with Lucas. She also saw another lighthouse, the size of a skyscraper, and shaped like an octagon. Lucas was waiting for her there, about to beg her to run away with him. Standing in the slanted light of winter, he shone like the sun in his armor. *Armor?*

"I know exactly what you mean. I do," she said to the littlest one, trying to shake out of her head the image of Lucas taking off a bronze breastplate. "And as far as I'm concerned, the jury's still out on the whole 'it's better to have loved and lost' argument. But this is different. It won't swallow you whole and then abandon you, like joy always has to. We brought you something that will hopefully last forever."

"What is it?" the leader asked with cautious hope.

"It's bliss."

Orion looked over at her sharply, and she nodded him on. Still uncertain, but following her lead, Orion stepped forward and took off his backpack. As he took out the three canteens the Furies could hear the liquid moving around inside their containers, and it was too much for them to resist.

"I'm so thirsty," the third one whined, stumbling forward desperately to take a canteen. Her two sisters quickly gave in and followed suit, and the Three Furies gulped the water down.

"Do you really believe that? Ignorance is bliss?" Orion said under his breath to Helen. From the complicated look he gave her, she could tell he had all of his memories back as well.

"For them? Definitely."

"And for you?" he persisted, but Helen didn't have an answer. He looked away from her and tensed. "I don't want to forget anything about tonight. Or about you."

"No, I didn't mean that," Helen began to say, realizing that she had hurt him. She was about to explain that she wasn't talking about forgetting their kiss, even though just the thought of it made her whole body heat up in a head-to-toe blush, but Orion shook his head and gestured to the Furies. They had finished their canteens, and were looking around shyly, laughing and shrugging at one another like they were waiting for something to happen.

"Hi," Helen said. The Furies glanced at one another with mounting fear.

"It's okay," Orion said in his wild-animal-tamer voice. "We're your friends."

"Hello, friends?" the leader said, and then turned her palms up in a questioning gesture. "Forgive my confusion. It's not that I don't believe that you are our friends, I just don't know who *we* are."

Her sisters smiled and looked at the ground with relief now that the reason for their anxiety was out in the open.

"You are three sisters who love one another very much. You're known as the Eumenides. The kindly ones," Helen told them, remembering what little she could of the *Oresteia* by Aeschylus. It was the first thing in Greek literature that she'd read, before she even knew she was a Scion. It seemed so long ago. "You have a very important job. Which is . . ."

"You listen to people who have been accused of terrible crimes and if they are innocent, you offer them protection," Orion finished for Helen when she stumbled.

The three Eumenides looked at one another and smiled, sensing that this was the truth. They hugged and greeted each other as sisters, still not fully understanding everything that had happened to them, and that troubled Helen.

"I sort of skipped over a lot of this play. I don't know that much about the Eumenides," Helen admitted under her breath to Orion.

"Neither do I," he whispered back. "What are we going to do? We can't just leave them like this."

"I can take you to someone who can explain this better," she said, raising her voice to include the girls. "Everyone join hands. I am going to take you to the queen."

The three girls blushed shyly at the thought of going before a queen, but they obeyed Helen and the entire party linked hands in a circle. Helen had never tried to move so many people at once, but she knew she could do it.

Persephone seemed to be waiting for them. Or maybe she

was just sitting in her garden, staring off into space—Helen couldn't be certain. Whatever Persephone was doing, she was unsurprised by the arrival of Helen and Orion and the three newly made Eumenides.

She welcomed them all with her characteristic gentility. Without missing a beat or needing much of an explanation from Helen and Orion, Persephone took charge of the three sisters and promised to prepare them for their new life as something like supernatural defense attorneys. The first thing she offered the Eumenides was refuge in her palace, and the second was a bath. The three sisters nearly sighed with happiness at the idea of ridding themselves of the dust of the dry land.

Persephone led the party back to the edge of the garden where it ended at a grand staircase that led into the black Palace of Hades. At the bottom of the adamantine steps, Persephone stopped and politely informed Helen and Orion that they could go no farther. Halfway up the stairs she turned to address them in a formal manner. Helen had the feeling that this was some form of ritual, like a blessing, or maybe even a curse.

"Over the millennia, many have found that it was their fate to attempt to do what you have done. They all failed. Most Descenders and their Shields only wanted to kill the Furies, or to break the curse by using magic tricks and even blackmail. You were the only two who were humble enough to listen to my suggestion, and then brave enough to use compassion as a cure, rather than force. Hopefully, you'll remember these lessons in the days to come."

She suddenly raised her voice, like she was making an announcement to a large audience.

"I have witnessed this incarnation of the Two Heirs, and I say that they have been successful. As queen of the Underworld, I find them both worthy."

Persephone's words fell like stones.

Helen had the uncanny feeling that millions of ghostly eyes were watching and witnessing this oath. Taking her cue from Orion, Helen crossed her arms in an X over her chest and bowed to the queen. A rush of flowing minds surged past them like a whispering wind, leaving fragments of the deads' fears, doubts, and hopes hanging in the air like half-finished questions. The ritual was complete.

"Worthy of what?" Helen whispered to Orion, but he shrugged distractedly, his attention captured by the dark door that led into the palace. A cloaked figured appeared from behind the locked door at the top of the stairs. Although he had been forbidden entry into the palace, Orion began to climb the stairs as if he was drawn to the apparition.

"No, Orion!" Helen scolded fearfully as she grabbed his arm and pulled him back. "It's Hades. Don't go anywhere *near* him."

She clung to Orion, certain that something terrible would happen if the man and the god came face-to-face. Hearing the desperate note in Helen's voice, Orion relented and came back down the stairs to join Helen at the bottom.

"Descender," Hades said in a kindly voice, unruffled by

Orion's aggressive behavior. He spoke softly, yet the sound carried everywhere and his tone was disapproving. "You have not done as I suggested."

"I apologize, sir." Helen racked her brain for what it was that he had suggested. There were a lot of confusing images swimming around in there. A ride on the ferry from Nantucket to the mainland was blending with the wooden deck of a giant battleship and the sound of creaking oars. A walk on a white-sand beach turned into a beach stained red with blood under her feet. She blinked and tried to get rid of the mental pictures. She knew that she had seen them before, but didn't know how or where.

"Be sure to remedy that, niece. The Scions are running out of time," Hades warned her sadly as he and his queen disappeared into the shadows of their palace.

"What does that mean?" Orion asked, turning to Helen urgently. "What about the 'Scions running out of time'?"

"I—I don't know!" she stammered.

"Well, what did Hades suggest to you?" Orion was trying to stay calm, but she could see that he was really frustrated with her. "Helen, think!"

"I was supposed to ask the Oracle something!" she blurted out in a high-pitched voice. "Something about the quest."

"What *was it*?"

"Something about asking Cassandra what she thought about freeing the Furies. I'm supposed to ask if she thought it was a good idea. But that's silly because she's been helping me do this, so of course she's all for it!"

Orion frowned darkly, and Helen knew she had really messed up. Now that she thought about it, not taking a god's advice seemed like an unbelievably dumb thing to do.

"I'm sorry," she mumbled, feeling like an ass.

"Well, it's too late, anyway. Besides, I don't put that much faith in Oracles. Don't worry about it," he said dismissively. But he still wouldn't look at her. Helen apologized again and promised to ask Cassandra as soon as she could, but Orion continued scowling at the ground, deep in thought. She reached out to touch his arm and get his attention.

But before she could do so, Helen felt herself getting picked up by a mile-wide hand. She lurched against Orion, grabbing on to him.

Matt lifted the unconscious woman off the street, opened an abandoned car door, and left her on the seat. Hopefully, she'd be safer in there than lying on the ground. There were a lot of people who had come to their senses after being trampled by the stampeding hordes, and they called out to him for help. Matt did what he could, but as soon as the most vulnerable were taken care of he ran off, feeling like he was betraying everyone he left behind.

He wanted to help them all, but he knew that first he had to find Zach, and he had to do that while he still had some strength. Every muscle in his chest and arms was aching, and some of them were beginning to twitch, just to let him know how unhappy they were with the boss's new hobby of lugging unconscious people around.

Matt rubbed one of his many sore spots and spun in a circle. He had no idea which way to go. He remembered that Helen said she had last seen Zach heading down Surfside. Grasping at straws, Matt took off in that general direction, and ended up following a hunch that led him straight to the school grounds.

Someone was on the football field, throwing perfect spiral passes into a soccer net. Matt jogged through the stiff, frosty grass in time to see Zach bury one in the back of the net.

"Did you see that?" Zach asked, barely even glancing at Matt. "That was just pretty."

"Yeah, it was. But you always had a great arm. You could throw like that freshman year," Matt replied, close enough now to see Zach in the bright moonlight. He looked awful—pale, sweaty, and haunted. If Matt didn't know him better, he would have thought Zach was doing serious drugs. "Is that what this is all about? Football?"

"How do you do it?" Zach asked with a bitter scowl on his face. "How do you hang out with them? Watch them do the things they can do and not hate them?"

"It's hard sometimes," Matt admitted. "Damn. I wish I could fly."

"Right?" Zach said through a laugh. There were tears behind that sound, though, and Matt heard them threatening to break out. "It's like you wake up one day and there are all these invaders, taking your opportunities away. They aren't from here but we're supposed to try and compete with them? It isn't fair."

There was a dangerous note in Zach's voice. He sounded calm when Matt knew he was anything but. Matt spread his stance, just in case Zach did something crazy.

"I know a bunch of Scions that would say the same about what's happening to them," Matt said evenly. "I understand how you feel, Zach, I do. There are so many times I've envied them, even resented them a little. But then I remember that they didn't choose to be Scions, and I haven't met one who didn't suffer for it. I can't blame them for being born what they are, especially when all of them have lost so much because of it."

"Well, you always were the better person, weren't you?" Zach scoffed, and turned to leave.

"Come back with me. Come to the Delos compound. We'll figure something out," Matt said, grabbing his arm and making Zach face him.

"Are you insane? Look at me, man!" Zach said, shoving Matt away from him violently and yanking up his shirt so Matt could clearly see that his ribs were covered in huge black bruises. "This is how he treats me when I'm *loyal*."

"They'll protect you. We all will," Matt promised, horrified by what had happened to his friend but trying to keep his voice calm. Zach's eyes narrowed and he flicked his shirt down.

"Oh, so now you feel bad. Now you want to help me. Let me guess, you need something."

"I just want to keep you alive!" Matt was so insulted, he wanted to hit Zach but settled for yelling at him instead. "I was wrong. I should have been there for you the first time you came to me. I get that now, and I am truly sorry. But even if you never forgive me and you're still throwing this in my face fifty frigging years from now, I still don't want you to *die*, you dumb bastard! Do I really need another reason to want to help you?"

"No," Zach replied, humbled. "You're the only person in the world I believe would be willing to help me. But it's no use. Sooner or later he's going to kill me." He turned and began to walk across the field.

"Then we'll just have to kill him first," Matt raised his voice after Zach.

"You have no idea how," Zach fired back derisively over his shoulder.

"Why? Because he's blood brothers with a god?"

Zach's back stiffened and his stride slowed.

"Which one?" Matt pressed, taking several steps closer to Zach. "Tell me which god and maybe we can find a way to get rid of him!"

Zach turned around but held up his hands in a stop gesture, warning Matt not to follow him. He backpedaled as he spoke, and the look he gave Matt was hard and hopeless.

"Go home, man. And stop *helping* the Scions! Tonight's riot is nothing compared with what's coming, and I don't want anything bad to happen to you. The gods have a special place picked out in hell for the full mortals that fight against them, you know."

"How can you know what the gods have planned?" Matt

shouted after him. "Doesn't Automedon work for Tantalus? Zach, answer me! Which god is Automedon's blood brother?"

But Zach had disappeared into the dark.

# SIXTEEN

"Helen?" Orion said from far, far away.

"Gods, you're heavy," Lucas groaned.

Helen couldn't figure out why they were making such a racket when she was trying to sleep. It was rude.

"Sorry, but I wasn't expecting it to be so *crowded* in here," Orion replied in an annoyed voice. Helen tried to recall where "here" was.

"It's not what you think. I came to guard her while she descended," Lucas grunted. "You know what? If she won't wake up, toss her off."

"Why are you two being so noisy?" Helen mumbled peevishly, finally opening her eyes.

She saw that she was lying facedown on top of Orion, and he, in turn, had Lucas pinned underneath him. All of them were stacked in her tiny bed, tangled in the blankets and dusted with ice, like frosting on the layer cake. After all that had happened in the Underworld, it had slipped Helen's mind that she had descended while Lucas held her in his arms, and even though a lot had transpired in that other universe, just milliseconds had passed in this one before she reappeared back in her bed with Orion in her arms.

Helen looked down at the Scion sandwich and tried not to blush. There was no reason for her to be embarrassed about any of this, right?

"Why are you so damn heavy?" Lucas asked breathlessly as the air was pressed out of his lungs. "I've lifted school buses with less effort."

"I don't know," Helen mumbled, and tried to release gravity. It didn't entirely work, although she did feel herself lighten a bit. "What the hell is going on?"

"What's wrong?" Orion asked.

"I can't float!" She shivered as the ice in her hair melted and turned into cold water that ran down the back of her neck.

"Calm down and try again," Lucas said gently.

She did, and after a few moments it worked. She hovered over Orion as she unwound the constricting blankets, and then wafted away from him.

"That is so amazing," Orion said, looking at Helen in awe as he got off Lucas and out of bed.

"You've never seen Helen fly?" Lucas said, and then he nodded as the reason why occurred to him. "No powers in the Underworld. Huh," he mumbled to himself, staring at the fast-melting ice on Helen's bed, deep in thought.

"Lucas, we did it," Helen said. He glanced up at her, quickly discarding his absorbing thoughts. "We're all free—the Scions, the Furies. All of us."

"Are you sure?" he asked, almost daring to smile.

"Only one way to find out," Orion said. He took out his phone, dialed, and waited until someone on the other end answered. "Hector. We think it's over. Get to Helen's as fast as you can." He ended the call and looked at Helen and Lucas impassively. Lucas's eyes widened with worry.

"Are you sure that was a good idea?" Helen asked Orion uncertainly.

"No, he's right," Lucas said, and seemed to brace himself for another encounter with his cousin. "It's better to test this with just the four of us. Safer."

"Okay. But can we do this outside?" Helen asked sheepishly. "My dad really loves this house."

As soon as Helen said it, she was overwhelmed with worry for Jerry. She'd put the thought of him on the back burner so she could focus on what she needed to do, but now that she wasn't running around like a crazy woman for the first time in what had to be the longest day of her life, Helen was desperate to find out what had happened to her father.

She led Lucas and Orion down to her front yard and then pulled out her phone to call Claire.

"How's my dad?" Helen asked as soon as she answered.

"Ahh. Alive," Claire said tentatively. "Look, Lennie, I'm not going to lie to you. It's bad. We're on our way back to

434

the compound now. Jason and Ari are going to work on him there, but other than that, I don't know what to tell you. I'm driving, so I'd better go. I'll call later if something happens, okay?"

"Okay," Helen tried to say, but it came out a whisper. She hit the END button and wiped her wet cheeks quickly before she looked up. Orion and Lucas were staring at her.

"Is Jerry . . . ?" Orion began.

"He's not good," Helen said in a strangely high voice.

Helen began to pace, and she didn't know what to do with her hands or her feet. She touched her nonexistent pockets, ran her fingers through her snarly hair, and tugged at her clothes. It was as if all of her extremities had just picked up and started flapping on the breeze, like one of those fan men dancing outside a car dealership. Without Jerry, she was just one big loose end.

"Jason and Ariadne are very talented, Helen," Lucas said in a low voice. "They'll fight for him. You know that, right?"

"Yeah," Helen said in a distracted way, still pacing. "And if they can't save him, I'll go down there and I'll . . ."

"Don't say it Helen," Orion interrupted urgently. "You may be the Descender, but Hades is still lord of the dead. Remember what happened when you said you'd free Persephone? How easily he dealt with you? Don't even *think* about trying to steal from him."

"He can't have my father," she said, suddenly very still. She looked up and stared at Orion, daring him to defy her. "I'll turn the Underworld upside down and shake it until

435

Jerry drops out if I have to, but he *can't have* my father."

"Helen," Lucas said, his face masklike with fear, "no mortal can cheat him or beat him. Please listen . . ."

"Luke?" the questioning voice came from across the dark yard.

Lucas spun around to face Hector, who was striding toward them across Helen's lawn. Whatever he was going to say to Helen was immediately forgotten. Hector stopped a few paces away from Lucas, and they stared at each other tensely, both waiting for the Furies. Who didn't come.

"Son of a bitch," Lucas whispered, too stunned to move for a moment. He looked at Helen, shocked. "You really did it."

The cousins came together and clasped each other in a fierce hug, both of them apologizing at the same time. While Helen looked on, she felt Orion staring at her. She glanced over at him and found him watching her with worry.

"Princess!" Hector said as he released Lucas and scooped Helen up into one of his big hugs. "I knew you could do it."

"I had a lot of help." Helen giggled as Hector lifted her off her feet and squeezed her.

"I heard," Hector said, putting her down to face Orion. He pulled Orion into one of his manly back-thumping hugs, and then turned back to Lucas. "Where's the rest of the family?"

"Almost all of them are back at our house, but less than an hour ago I saw our fathers fighting Eris in the riots. Looked like they had her cornered, but I didn't see anyone fighting

Terror. He could still be on the loose." Lucas gave this report with soldierly precision.

"I just wish I knew why all these small gods are making cameos today after so many decades of silence." Hector bit his lip. His eyes darted up and met Helen's, and her shoulders slumped when she got his meaning. Why was everything always her fault?

"Wait. Where else have the small gods been seen today?" Orion asked, sharing a confused look with Lucas. Hector filled Orion and Lucas in on Thanatos crashing the Conclave in New York, and the fact that Automedon might have broken his contract with Tantalus.

"Where's Daphne?" Orion asked, concerned for her.

"Last I saw she was electrocuting Skeletor. Why? You looking for a fight of your own?" Hector asked Orion with a devilish smile.

"Hell yeah," Orion replied immediately, grinning back at Hector. Helen thought they were enjoying the prospect of a showdown with the small gods a bit too much.

Helen had to shake her head to clear it. For some reason she kept seeing Orion and Hector in armor. When Hector turned to include Lucas, her déjà vu got even worse. For a moment it looked like Lucas was wearing something that looked like a toga.

"Wait, guys. Helen's dad was injured. And I'm not sure I like the idea of her being in the middle of riot with Automedon on the loose," Lucas interjected before they could charge off. He glanced over at her and his brow wrinkled with concern when he saw her face. "Ah, Helen? Are you okay?"

"Yeah," she said, shaking herself out of it and rubbing her temples. "I'm just so tired I think I'm starting to see things." *Like a marble palace lit by torches and everyone decked out in leather and bronze.*

"Then go to your father," Hector told her. "Personally, I think you can take the Myrmidon, but whatever. Stay safe. The three of us can handle this without you."

"No, I should help."

"Go," Orion said, rolling his eyes at her. "If we get into trouble, you can come rescue us with your almighty lightning, okay?"

"Are you sure?" she said with a grateful smile, already taking to the air.

"That is just fricking awesome," Orion breathed, forgetting everything to marvel at Helen as she floated above him. Acting on impulse, he reached up and ran the backs of his fingers along the back of her calf. Helen swallowed hard around the lump in her throat and looked at Lucas, who was purposely looking elsewhere. Orion followed Helen's eyes and dropped his hand, realizing what he was doing.

"Get out of here, Princess," Hector said knowingly. "Go take care of Jerry."

Helen couldn't help but glance at Lucas and mouth the words *Be careful* to him as Hector and Orion turned toward the center of town.

"You too," he whispered back, his eyes warm. Her stomach was already filled with butterflies from Orion's intimate touch, and now they grew to the size of a 747. Lucas turned and broke into a run to keep pace with Hector and Orion, leaving her hanging breathless in midair. As she watched them speed off, she couldn't decide who she wanted to stare at more—Lucas or Orion. Her attention was so torn between the two of them that she felt like she was watching a tennis match.

Deeply confused, Helen flew to Siasconset, landed in the Delos family's backyard, and forced herself to change gears and focus on her father. She rushed into the house and went right to Noel, who was in the kitchen, cooking up a storm.

"Helen!" she said, barely looking up from the twenty-gallon pot she was stirring. "Go downstairs, past the exercise room, and into the cellar. You'll find three freezers. Open the short one and take out the big roast. Hurry-hurry! Everyone will be hungry."

"Short one. Big roast. Got it," Helen said, and bolted off to run Noel's errand. She didn't even try to argue. She may not have been around the Delos family for very long, but she knew enough to know that when she was in Noel's kitchen she'd better do as she was told. She came back in half a second and put a frozen roast the size of an ox in the sink that Noel was pointing at in a hassled way.

"They're working on Jerry in the guest room we normally put you in," Noel said, finally turning to Helen with a sympathetic look. "Go quietly. If one or both of the twins are sleeping, don't wake them. It could injure them."

"Okay. Thanks," Helen said.

She twisted her hands and shuffled her feet, not knowing what to do with herself. She knew she was supposed to go upstairs and check on her father, but she didn't want to see him hurt. She felt her loose ends starting to flap around again.

Looking at Helen's attack of the fidgets, Noel's eyes widened and she immediately put down her scorched wooden spoon, wiped her fingers on her apron, and pulled Helen into a big, soft hug. At first Helen was startled stiff, but then she just let go and really leaned into it. Noel smelled like bread dough and baby powder. Helen couldn't remember anyone but Kate ever feeling so fluffy and relaxing. It was like hugging a warm muffin.

"Better?" Noel asked as she leaned back and looked Helen over appraisingly. "You look exhausted. Did you stop dreaming again?"

"No, I can dream," Helen said, laughing a bit as she smoothed down her now torn and dirty dress and wondered how Noel knew about the whole non-dreaming thing. "It's just been a really *long* day."

"I know, honey. And you've done so much," Noel said, cupping Helen's face in her hands and looking at her intently with wide, loving eyes. "Thank you for bringing my Hector back to us." Noel kissed her on the forehead, the gesture reminding Helen of Lucas. Which reminded Helen . . .

"Wait. How could you know about Hector? That happened, like, five minutes ago."

"All my boys call me *first* whenever they have either really good or really bad news. It's the in-between news that boys are not so good with," Noel said with a grin and narrowed eyes. "You'll see for yourself someday." Then she turned back to the counter, picked up a giant knife, chopped something like it had insulted her, and dumped its sorry bits into a bubbling pot.

Surprising herself, Helen wrapped her arms around Noel from the side and stole a quick hug. Noel absentmindedly kissed the top of Helen's head and stroked her hair while she stirred, like she was used to both giving and receiving random affection at any given moment from any kid in her inner circle. More relaxed now and ready to deal, Helen went upstairs to find her father.

Automedon left his master in the strange in-between land at the bottom of the cave, went above ground, and summoned his slave. The mortal boy was not accustomed to his new life of servitude, but luckily for him, he was moderately intelligent and didn't make many mistakes. As soon as Automedon relayed directions to the cave and inquired after the arranged provisions, he raced back to Nantucket, still not certain if the curse of the Furies had been entirely lifted or not. He was willing to take the chance and move forward with the plan either way, but it took him a full thirty-eight minutes to return and locate the Face.

At first, Automedon had looked for her at home, but found only her scent lingering heavily in the front yard. He could taste that she had not been alone, and that even the Outcast had been with her at her house. A brief glance at the ground told Automedon that there had been no confrontation, no Fury-induced fight. There was only one explanation for that.

The Descender had been successful! After so much waiting and watching, after so many generations had proved themselves unworthy, it was finally time. His master was right. All that she had needed was a little push, a little incentive to figure it out, and she had. This was no look-alike. This Descender was the princess he had been waiting for—the real Helen.

Fired up by this new victory, Automedon tasted the trails. They were still so fresh he could sense the emotions of the Scions who'd made them. There was nothing but brotherhood in the air—brotherhood and undying love. The taste of love rose, and then faded in the turbulent winds of the atmosphere. She must have flown away. The men had definitely run off together to the center of town, back toward the distraction that had been carefully orchestrated to occupy the small army of powerful Scions that guarded this new—and Automedon would swear before the gods—*true* Helen. So far, everything was going according to plan, except for the most important part.

Automedon held very still. He couldn't afford to waste one movement. This was the event that three and a half thousand years had built. Everything was in order, everything was finally as it was always meant to be—except for one thing. He had to find Helen.

She wasn't at the home of her mortal father. She wasn't

with the lover. She wasn't at school. Unless Helen had left the island, which she almost never did, there was only one place left: the satellite dwelling of the House of Thebes in Siasconset.

Both of the twins were sleeping, one on either side of Jerry in the big, white bed that Helen herself had healed in after her fall with Lucas. Jerry looked pale and sunken, like he had been deflated. Lying on top of the covers and curled up like cats at the bottom of the bed, the twins had their eyes closed in restless sleep.

They were panting and their fingers kept tensing into claws, their brows wrinkling in unison as if they were sharing the same nightmare. The air in the room was baked dry as a desert. Helen knew that meant they were following Jerry around the edge of the dry lands, just outside the Underworld, trying to shepherd his frightened spirit back into his body. They were fighting like crazy, that was obvious, but they both were covered in sweat and paler than sheets of paper. Helen knew they wouldn't last much longer.

Kate stood up from a chair in the corner and rushed to embrace Helen when she entered the room. As they hugged, Helen saw Claire sitting on the floor on Jason's side of the bed. Claire gave Helen a wan look and stood up gingerly, like her legs had fallen asleep a long time ago. The three of them silently agreed to go down the hallway to another room before they had their talk, so as not to disturb the trio in the sickbed.

By chance, Kate happened to pick Lucas's room. Helen almost backed out, but then she found that she couldn't resist the temptation of being close to anything that belonged to him.

"What's going on?" Helen asked.

"Jason said that Jerry got lost down there. He said that all of this should have been over before we even got in the car and came here," Claire said calmly.

Kate jumped in, unable to contain herself. "But there was some horrible god interfering. He must have led Jerry's spirit in the wrong direction while we were carrying him to the car," Kate said in a shaky voice. "And now the twins can't find him."

"Morpheus met with Ariadne on the border of his land to tell her that it was Ares who misled your dad," Claire said in a hushed voice, and looked over at Kate for corroboration.

"Helen. Why is the god of war trying to kill your father?" Kate asked, her voice trembling on the verge of hysteria. Kate was a practical woman, and not accustomed to emotional outbursts, but she was still trying to wrap her brain around the fact that everything she knew as myth was really true. Helen took her hand and squeezed it.

"I should have told you," Helen said, barely able to look Kate in the eyes. "I thought I could protect you if I kept you separate, that you and dad could go on with your lives if you just didn't know. It sounds so *stupid* now when I say it out loud, but I really believed it could work, and I'm sorry. Ares is trying to get to me. I don't know why he's doing it, but I know he's using Dad as bait."

"Okay," Kate said, wiping away a leaking tear and pursing her lips in determination. "So what can we do about it? How do we save Jerry?"

"Not we," Helen whispered darkly, remembering Morpheus's warning that Ares dreamed of hurting her. "Me. Ares wants me."

"And you're just going to go running right down there to face him, aren't you?" Cassandra asked from the doorway. Helen turned to see Cassandra standing behind her with her arms crossed in anger. "Even though you know this is probably a trap?"

"Yes. And I have to go right now."

"Lennie, that's just about the dumbest thing I've ever heard you say," Claire said, disbelief wiping all expression off her face. "*Matt* is a better fighter than you are and he isn't even a Scion. And you think you can take on Ares alone?"

"Yes," Helen said, looking around impassively at everyone's shocked faces. "I'm the Descender. I can control the Underworld and Ares can't. I don't know what it says about me, that I have power over that place, but there it is. Up here, I wouldn't have much of a shot against him, sure. But in the Underworld I can beat him—at least long enough to get my father back. I know it."

Helen walked to Lucas's bed and pulled the covers down.

"Helen. Your father wouldn't want you to endanger yourself for him," Claire said firmly as she put a hand on Helen's shoulder and turned her around. Helen couldn't remember the last time Claire had called her by her full name. She, Kate, and Cassandra were all ready to stop her, which they could do easily. Unless she convinced them, all they had to do was keep her awake.

"I know my dad wouldn't want this, but . . . well, too bad!" Helen finally burst out in a rough whisper, trying to keep her voice down and nearly failing. "He'll die if I don't get him away from Ares, and if the twins stay down there much longer, they're going to die, too. You know I'm right, Claire. You know how every second on the border of the shadow lands feels like forever to the soul stumbling around in it."

Claire dropped her eyes and turned her head, nodding painfully. She did know, and the memory still frightened her.

"Just wait for Orion to go with you," Cassandra begged, crossing the room to Lucas's bed as Helen climbed into it.

"I can't. It takes Orion half an hour to get down to where the portal is on the mainland from Nantucket. In the Underworld, time moves differently, but my father's spirit isn't in the Underworld yet. Time hasn't stopped, it's *stretched out* for him and the twins, and every second I waste up here feels like days and days to them down there. Jason, Ari, and my dad won't last in that desert another half an hour. I have to go *now*."

Kate, Claire, and Cassandra looked around at each other sadly. They knew Helen was right.

"I wish I could say everything's going to be all right, but I haven't been able to see your future for a while now. I'm sorry," Cassandra said, leaning forward impulsively to kiss her on the cheek. "Good luck, cousin," she whispered tenderly, clinging tightly to Helen's neck.

Helen reached out her other arm and brought Kate and Claire into the hug as well.

"You'd better leave now and shut the door behind you," she said resolutely as she let the three of them go. "It's about to get dangerously cold in here."

The Oracle was near. That was a problem. Her dear mortal females could die and not disrupt the plans of the Twelve, but the Oracle was almost as important as Helen herself, and unfortunately she was far more fragile.

True Oracles who were strong enough to bear the crushing weight of the future were precious, and although the gods were subject to the Fates just as mortals were, they had never had an Oracle of their own. Procuring one had always been a top priority. This Cassandra in particular was a favorite of Apollo's. He had waited for her for millennia.

Listening in on the conversation between the princess and the Oracle, he could hear her taking the bait. No matter how dangerous it was to her, she would follow her father down to the shadow lands, just as his master had predicted.

Automedon had a very small window of opportunity. He could only strike after she created a portal, but before she descended. If he didn't sting her then, the goddess charm she always wore around her neck would prevent any penetration. Worse than that, she would be able to incapacitate him with her lightning long enough to fly away. She was only vulnerable for a moment—the cold of the Void was the signal—and then he had a split second to act.

Pacing around the outside of the mansion, Automedon tasted the air for the scent of any of her protectors. Luckily, they had their hands full in the center of town. Automedon heard the Heir, the true princess of legend, dismiss her handmaidens with a loving embrace, and relax into the sleeping trance, the mental state from which she preferred to conjure the portal. The time had come.

Automedon leapt forward, knocking down the front door, and sprinting up the stairs on all fours. The mother mortal raised her hand to draw the curse of Hestia down upon him, but she was too slow.

Leaping over the precious Oracle to spare her, Automedon knocked the two pretty but useless handmaidens aside. He shattered the lover's door into splinters, vaulted onto the bed, and cupped the princess's sleeping head in his right hand half a heartbeat before she descended, the very moment she was most vulnerable. Her beautiful amber eyes snapped open. From inside his left wrist, Automedon slid his stinger out of its sheath and pierced the Princess's slack throat. Her eyes fluttered and her lips quivered as his venom flooded her blood. He heard screaming from the hallway and from the bottom of the stairs, but the noise was inconsequential. He had his prize, and none of them was anywhere near strong enough to keep him from taking it.

The princess went still. Automedon picked her up and

carried her paralyzed body out of the lover's window and off the island.

Lucas watched Hector blur as he sped off to find his father, while he and Orion stayed back to help a cluster of injured people onto the sidewalk. A triage center was forming, and people who lived in the area were coming out of their houses with water, bandages, and first aid kits to help the wounded. Lucas and Orion had urged Hector on, but had to stop themselves when they couldn't ignore the cries for help.

"We should check the next block, too," Orion said when they had helped the last of the injured, and the two of them began to run at a human pace down the nearest alley.

"Hold up," Lucas called out to Orion as he fished his buzzing phone out of his jeans.

Lucas looked at the screen and saw that it was his mom. He answered it immediately, already feeling a sick, slithering sensation in his gut.

"Lucas, he took her," she said in a clipped and urgent monotone. "Helen was just about to descend to help her father and the twins when Automedon broke down the door, stung her, and then jumped out the window with her."

"How long ago?" Lucas asked coldly.

Orion's eyes flared as he picked up on Lucas's chaotic emotions.

"A few minutes ago. Claire and Kate got knocked down by that creature, and I just finished making sure they were still alive," his mother responded in a disgusted tone. "I don't understand this, Lucas. *How* could he sting Helen? The cestus . . ."

"I gotta go." Lucas hung up on his mother, not because he was angry but so that he could think. After relaying the information to Orion he went silent.

"Should we go back to your house? Try and find a trail?" Orion suggested.

"There won't be one," Lucas said quietly, wishing Orion would just shut up.

"Then what do you suggest?" Orion continued as he scrutinized Lucas carefully. When Lucas didn't respond he raised his eyebrows and repeated himself. "Lucas. I can read your feelings, you know. Tell me what you're thinking so we can work it out together."

"I'm trying to figure out how the hell anyone would be *able* to capture Helen! Have you ever tried to fight her? Even when she holds back she's a beast!" Lucas was teetering right on the edge of violence. He wanted to hit Orion, but he settled for yelling. "I can barely handle her and I don't think she's shown me even a fraction of what she's capable of. Can you imagine what she'd do to someone if they tried to kidnap her and keep her against her will? Half of Massachusetts would be on fire!"

Orion looked at Lucas's chest with concern.

"You're freaking out. I need you to calm down right now. For Helen." Orion grabbed Lucas by the shoulder, and Lucas felt flooded with warmth. His heart slowed down, and a wave of soothing feelings overtook him.

He knew Orion was a Son of Aphrodite and could manipulate emotions, but Lucas had never actually experienced anything like it before. It was a physical change, like an instant drug working on his body and mind, and for a moment Lucas wondered just how much Orion could affect him, and in what ways. If Orion could make him feel this good, it was reasonable to assume he could make him feel just as bad as well. The implications were astounding.

"I'm sorry," Orion said, releasing Lucas. "I don't like to do that without asking first."

"No, it's okay. I needed it," Lucas said gently, knowing that Orion disliked using his talent to control hearts under any circumstance, even when it could benefit him greatly. He continued in a much calmer voice. "Did you notice the ice on Helen's bed when she brought you back from the Underworld tonight? How she couldn't float right away, and how I couldn't lift the two of you off of me? Is that loss of Scion powers normal when Helen descends?"

"It's normal around all portals into the Underworld. They're dead zones. No heat, no living organisms growing on the walls, and no Scion talents. I think Helen creates a temporary portal when she descends, and it must take a few seconds to dissipate after she dismantles it," Orion said with a thoughtful frown.

"Do you think Automedon would know all this about portals?"

"I wouldn't doubt it. There have been other Descenders, and he's three days older than dirt. That monster's probably seen everything," Orion said. "He wouldn't have much time, though. Remember, after a few seconds, she could fly again."

"Not a lot of time, sure. But if he were *expecting* it, it'd be enough. He was watching her for a few weeks. He'd know she would definitely follow her father down into the Underworld," Lucas said, sensing that he was on the right track. This had to have been planned. "Automedon just had to make sure Jerry got terribly injured—easy enough to do in a riot—and then when every Scion on the island was out chasing Eris and Terror . . ."

"There'd be no Scions around to protect her while she went after her dad," Orion finished. Then he shook his head as he noticed a flaw in their logic. "But Automedon could have done this any time over the past few months. She descended every night, and no one's been guarding her. Why wait?"

"Well," Lucas said, looking away embarrassed. "I've almost always been with her at night, usually on her roof. But no one, not even Automedon would have been able to see me."

"How can you know that?"

"I'm a Shadowmaster. And I can also make myself invisible." Orion's eyes widened. Lucas plowed on impatiently before they could get off topic. "But that's not the point. Automedon had to wait for Helen to complete her task in the Underworld before taking her. Tantalus wouldn't dare make a move against Helen before that."

"But why take her now? Tantalus knows about me and probably the dozens of other Rogues, too. He can't hope to achieve Atlantis unless he kills us all. Do you think he intends to start with Helen?"

The world tilted on its axis for a moment as Lucas considered that. What if Helen were already dead? Was it possible that half of his heart could die without him feeling it? Lucas shoved a hand in his pocket and felt the last poppy obol left in the world, rubbing it between his thumb and forefinger. He already knew what he would do if Helen died.

"I don't know," he whispered, banishing that thought for now. He looked up at Orion intently. "You're right. It doesn't make sense for Tantalus to have her kidnapped now, but remember, he's probably not the one calling the shots anymore. Automedon's new master must have wanted the Furies out of the way as well before he gave the order to take Helen. Regardless of why Automedon waited, there's only one place I can imagine where anyone would be physically *capable* of holding Helen prisoner."

"A permanent portal. My portal is the closest one and I got followed there earlier tonight," Orion said ruefully, like he wanted to kick himself. He started moving toward the west. "Do you want to wait here for your family while I go after her?"

Lucas smirked at Orion, not bothering to answer the question.

He knew that the smart thing would be to contact Hector and make it a three-to-one fight against the much stronger

Myrmidon, but there was no way he could make himself hold still long enough to do that. He charged after Orion, and half a moment later they were at the edge of the island.

"Oh, God, Matt! You have to get here," Zach rasped into the phone. His breathing was uneven and the receiver kept brushing against his chin, like he was running or walking fast. "He's got Helen and he's going to hurt her!"

"Wait. Where's *here*?" Matt interrupted. He waved an arm frantically at Hector, Pallas, Castor—everyone who happened to be standing around the Delos kitchen, trying to figure out where Automedon could have taken Helen. Zach kept talking, the words spilling out of his mouth in a gob, like yolk dribbling from a cracked egg.

"I was supposed to call Lucas and that Orion guy," Zach stammered. "That's what I'm supposed to be doing right now, what I was *always* supposed to do, and I will because he'll kill me if I don't, but I know that's his plan, so I can't follow it entirely, right? I figured if I tell you, then we can figure something out."

"Slow down! What do you mean 'plan'?"

"The plan to start the war! He needs all three of them to do it!"

# SEVENTEEN

Helen's cheek was hot— burning hot.

But the rest of her was freezing, she realized as she clawed her way up from the dragging darkness and back into consciousness. She was colder than she had ever been and something close to her smelled awful, like rust and rot.

"There she is, she's come to play! Two more to come, then bombs away!" tittered a wheedling voice. "Prettyprettypretty godling."

Ares.

Helen held very still and tried not to start shrieking. She needed to think. The last thing she remembered was Automedon's face over hers, a jab in her neck, and then liquid pain pumping through her body until her brain switched itself off in self-defense.

"I see you there, my pretty little pet," Ares said, no longer laughing. "You cannot hide behind your eyelids. Come. Open them. Let me see our father's eyes."

She heard the note of anger creeping into his voice, heard the threat in his move toward her. He'd called her bluff, and her eyes opened in terror. She disengaged gravity to fly away, but it didn't work, and she immediately saw why. Even the air was saturated with ice crystals. The cold was so complete it stretched the senses beyond their limit and twisted them back the other way around until ice burned like fire.

In the flickering light of a bronze brazier, Helen could see that Ares had her bound with thick rope, staked to the ground at the entrance of a portal. Helen looked around desperately, but in her heart she already knew she was in the perfect prison. In the Underworld she could transport herself away from Ares with a few words. On Earth, she could at least put up one hell of a fight, and maybe get away. But at a portal, when she was neither here nor there, she was just a teenaged girl, tied up, and at the mercy of a maniac. This was planned, Helen knew. It had probably been planned for, literally, ages.

"Tears! I *love* tears!" Ares gushed as if he were talking about puppies. "Look how the little godling weeps . . . Still so pretty she is, she is! Let's change that."

Ares hit her across the mouth and Helen felt something snap. She took a deep breath. So this was it. She spat and looked up at him, no longer crying. Now that it had started she knew it wouldn't be long, and in a way that was better than waiting for it. At least if Ares was here torturing her, that meant he wasn't misleading her father's spirit in the Underworld. This wasn't the outcome she'd been hoping for when she'd closed her eyes to follow her father down into the Underworld, but it was better than nothing. Helen looked up at Ares and nodded at him, ready for whatever he had to dish out now that she knew her father was safe.

Ares hit her face again and then stood up so he could kick her in the stomach. The wind came out between the seized-up muscles in her abdomen until she made a strange braying noise, like a donkey. He kicked her again and again. If she tried to avoid the blows by curling up and turning her back to him, he stomped rather than kicked. She felt her forearm snap and tried to bring her leg up to protect her side, but that only made him attack her more viciously. When she stopped trying to dodge the blows and just let them come, he backed off.

Helen rolled around on the ground, struggling to find a position that would make it possible for her to breathe with several broken ribs and her hands tied behind her back. Wheezing and writhing, she finally found that kneeling and bending forward with her forehead resting against the fiery ice of the ground was best. The choking, hacking noise she made as she forced air around one of her punctured lungs sounded almost like laughing.

"Fun, isn't it?" Ares squealed, and started skipping around in a circle. "But I shouldn't have kicked your middle so very much because now you can't yell. And that's what we need, right? So silly of me! Well, we can wait a bit before we play again."

He knelt down next to her folded form and ran his finger through her hair. The exposed back of her neck crawled as he chose a tress from the nape.

*He will yank it out in a moment,* she told herself. *Just relax and don't fight it. It will be easier that way.*

"You are exceedingly quiet," Ares sighed as he began to slowly braid the chosen lock. "That is a problem. How will the other Heirs find you if you don't holler and yell like you're supposed to? You're supposed to shout *SAVE* ME, LUCAS! OH, *SAVE* ME, ORION!" He momentarily adopted the soprano register of a damsel in distress before immediately switching back to his normal voice. "Just like that. Go on. Try it."

Helen shook her head. Ares leaned over her, putting his lips right up against the cringing skin of her neck. He breathed his foul, rotten breath across her scalp and the backs of her ears. Even in the scouring cold of the portal, Ares still overwhelmed her with the smell of death and decay.

"Yell," he said quietly, no longer sounding like a madman. For the first time she could remember, Ares had abandoned his usual singsong way of speaking. He sounded sane, and to Helen that made him infinitely more terrifying. "Call out to them to save your life. Call out to them, Helen, or I will kill you."

"You're trying to trap them," Helen said between panting

breaths. "I won't fall for it."

"How can I trap them? I am as powerless as a mortal in this nowhere place, and they are two against one," he said, sounding logical. "They might even win."

He wasn't lying. His punches and kicks had hurt her insides badly, but she didn't feel the strength of a god behind those blows. She looked at the knuckles on his left hand, the hand he had used to strike her, and saw that ichor, the golden blood of the gods, oozed out of the deep scrapes on his fist. It made her smile to know that although she'd lost some teeth and she couldn't see out of her right eye anymore, Ares had most likely broken his hand in the process.

"Call out to them," he pleaded, like all of this was for her own good. "Why won't you yellyellyell, broken little godling? They *want* to save you."

Helen knew he was right. Lucas and Orion were looking for her, and they didn't need their Scion powers to fight Ares like she did. Both of them were strong men. She was just a skinny, exhausted, tied-up, Myrmidon-poisoned girl going against a gigantic brute twice her size. They were warriors by nature. Let them do the fighting. They *enjoyed* it.

Not too far away, she heard Orion calling out to Lucas, leading him through the labyrinth of the caves.

"Do you hear that, Helen? Your salvation is *so close*." Ares twisted his fingers to tighten his grip and ripped the braided lock of hair out of her head, tearing an inch wide swath of scalp off with it. Helen couldn't stop a high-pitched whistling wheeze from escaping the back of her throat, but she managed to keep the volume lower than a whisper. She wouldn't scream. Ares grabbed another, larger lock—one that was lower and attached to even more sensitive skin.

Out of her one good eye, Helen saw blood from the back of her head running in a stream off her chin and staining the ice below her face. It fanned out in a pool, bright and vibrant, as it climbed its way through the crystal lattice like it was filling the thirsty fibers of woven cloth.

"They aren't going to just happen to find you, if that's what you're hoping for. There are dozens of portals in these caves. Orion knows most of them, but still, it could take them all night to find the right one." Ares sounded like he was growing tired of this game. "Call out to them now and save what's left of your skin."

Staring into a pool of her own blood, Helen saw two armies. She saw them come together in a bright flash of metal on metal. She saw an azure-blue bay fouled by the filth of a siege camp, and then over time, she saw those clear waters muddied and clogged with the ashes of burnt bodies. Finally, she saw Lucas lying lifeless in a burning, smoke-filled room.

*That was what happened the last time I let others do my fighting for me.*

"I will not call out," Helen whispered as hot tears joined the blood beneath her face. "I would rather die."

"You love Orion and Lucas so much you'd die for them? Both of them?" Ares asked quietly. He pushed her over onto her side so he could look at her destroyed face. She worked to focus her one good eye on him and responded without hesitating,

"Yes. I love them both. And I'd die for them both."

Ares went silent. Watching the muscles of his face twitch, for a moment Helen thought he was struggling to come up with something to say. Then he sucked in a breath and burst out laughing.

"One down, two to go!" Ares said, almost like he couldn't believe it. "Automedon was right! So ready to bleed and die—and it's not just you, either. The thing that truly astounds me is that he says your two noble defenders would bleed and die for *you* as well. Do you know what that means, broken little godling? Do you know what it means if I mix all this blood you and the other two Heirs would so willingly spill for each other? Four Houses, conveniently packaged into three loving, brave, and, thank Zeus, *naive* Heirs."

Helen's mind raced. She struggled back up onto her knees and stared at the blood freezing into ice on the floor. She thought about how special the conditions had to be to make her normally impervious skin bleed, and how much Ares must have gone through to get her here so she could do just that. Then she thought about how much had to happen to get Lucas and Orion to work *together* when just hours ago they would have been prevented from even being in the same room because of the Furies. There was only one thing that brought them together, and only one thing she knew for a fact both of them would fight, bleed, and die for. Her. And she had already bled and *pledged on*

461

*that blood* to do the same for them.

"Blood brothers. We'll be blood brothers," she gasped through her split lips. "All Four Houses will be united."

"And we gods will be free from our prison on Olympus," Ares said solemnly. "Three and a half *thousand* years I've waited!" His words ended abruptly as his throat closed off in a choked sound.

"No. I won't let it happen," she stammered, unable to accept it.

"Do you know what the tastiest part of all of this is for me? Except for the part where I get to torture you, of course," he continued, ignoring her weak threat. "It's that, yet again, it's *all for the love of Helen*! I would never have believed that not one, but *two* world wars could be started for the love of a woman. You'd think money, sure. Land, of course. Thousands of wars have been fought over money and land, but LOVE? And yet here we are. Aphrodite wins again! Another war to end all wars starts for your love, and because of your love for two men and three pathetic Furies as well! And lovelovelove will be the reason the world collapses into warwarwar. It is sheer *poetry!*"

As Ares gurgled with insane laughter, the enormity of Helen's multiple mistakes fell on her one by one, crushing her beneath them. Morpheus had expressed misgivings about her quest, but she'd never asked why. Hades had explicitly warned her not once, but twice, that she should ask the Oracle—not Cassandra the little sister, but the *Oracle*, the mouthpiece of the Three Fates—if freeing the Furies was the right thing to do. Even *Zach* had tried to tell her that she was in danger, but she hadn't given him a chance to explain.

And biggest of all was the warning she'd gotten from Hector. He'd told her that the most important thing was that she *didn't* fall in love with Orion. Hector had always known, even though Helen hadn't, that this struggle was about love. When he'd told her not to fall in love with Orion, what he was trying to tell her was that love, real love, always made a *family*—even if it wasn't a traditional one. Love was what mattered, not the laws or the rules or the gods.

Helen could rant and scream that she'd been tricked, that none of it was her fault, but she knew better. She had charged headfirst into this quest without ever stopping to think about what could go wrong. All along she was so convinced she was right because she was doing a good deed that never once did she listen to anyone who disagreed with her. Lucas had warned her that hubris was the greatest danger to Scions, but she hadn't really understood why until just that moment. Being a good person and doing good deeds didn't necessarily make you *right* all the time.

In the next cavern, Helen heard Orion and Lucas speaking to each other in frantic whispers, urging each other on toward the flickering light of the brazier.

"Please," she sobbed quietly. "Just kill me now."

"Soon, soon, pet. Shhh," Ares cooed as he pulled a little bronze dagger out of his belt and knelt down next to her. Helen felt a sliding, throbbing heat trace across her neck. With one efficient motion, Ares had slit her throat. "You'll die, but the cut is shallow enough that you won't die right away. I'm afraid you won't be able to speak, though. I can't let you go sharing the plan with the other two Heirs before they do a little fighting and bleeding of their own, now can I? Don't want to ruin it."

She tried to scream, but instead a thin membrane of blood shot out of her neck and sprayed across Ares' face. He grinned and licked his lips.

"Who's a good girl?" he said in baby talk, making grotesque kissy-faces at her. Then he stood, went to the rock wall, and whispered to it.

Helen had nearly drowned once when she was a child. Since then she had always feared the water, even though she had grown up on an island perpetually surrounded by it. Now it seemed that after all that fussing and fearing over the water she was going to drown on dry land. As blood frothed in her lungs and burned her inner ears, she thought to herself how similar her salty blood tasted to the salt water of the sea. She could hear the little ocean inside her, throbbing and rushing, ebbing out of her with every beat of her heart. Or were those footfalls pounding across the frozen cave floor?

"Uncle! Let me through," Ares hissed more loudly at the rock wall.

Nothing happened. The look on Ares' face grew frantic.

"Helen! No!" Lucas screamed across the yawning cavern. His cry echoed off the walls, filling the dark corners of the caves and multiplying inside of them.

Ares spun around and put his hand on his knife. As he looked down at Helen, she could tell he was contemplating a hostage scenario.

The ground heaved up and came slamming back down, making Ares stumble away from Helen and clutch at the wall. "Get away from her," Orion growled.

Unable to roll over to look at them, Helen stared at Ares' petrified face through her one good eye. His eyes were flying back and forth between Orion and Lucas as Ares backed up against the wall of the portal. Orion was right. The god of war was a coward.

"Hades! You have your orders!" Ares screamed hysterically as he slapped his hand repeatedly against the frozen rock wall. "Let me pass!" The portal sucked him in and Ares was gone. After a brief pause, Helen heard hurried steps behind her.

"Luke. Oh, no," Orion groaned.

"She's not dead," Lucas said through gritted teeth. "She can't be dead."

Helen felt both Lucas and Orion kneel down next to her. She felt hands cup her shoulder and her hip to tilt her gently toward them. She squirmed, trying to shrug them away. She would have gotten up and run away from them if she could. Even their delicate touches felt like whips across her skin, but the pain wasn't the reason she wanted them to stop touching her. She couldn't let them get her blood on their hands.

"Easy, easy. It's okay, Helen," Lucas said in a high whisper.

"I know it hurts, I do, but we have to move you."

No. What they had to do was get away from her. She tried to tell them to go, but all that came out of her was a gush of blood from her neck.

"I have a knife," Orion said, and Helen felt the bonds on her wrists cut away.

Lucas scooped her up into his arm and she fought him lamely, struggling to get him to drop her. She wanted to die in the portal, before the blood brother ritual could be completed. But as she flailed and coughed she only made it worse. She was literally spraying blood from her neck, covering Lucas and Orion. Ares might be a coward, Helen thought, but he knew *everything* there was to know about hurting people. The wound he had given her had made it a sure thing that anyone who came within five feet of Helen got bathed in her blood.

"I'll lead the way," Orion said in an urgent voice.

Helen felt a vague swaying motion, and saw the bobbing beam of Orion's flashlight ahead as they began their ascent. She could hear just fine, and her vision wasn't too bad, but she couldn't move or speak. She tried to wiggle her toes or move a finger. None of her limbs responded. She told herself to blink, but she couldn't even close her good eye. Helen was locked inside herself and completely conscious. She knew she would have to watch as the events unfolded and wondered if this was some special torture that Ares had devised for her. Maybe he'd poisoned the blade to paralyze her?

*Or maybe I'm just dying,* she thought hopefully. *If I hurry, maybe I can still stop this.*

"There's the exit," Orion called back over his shoulder with relief. Helen could make out his beautiful profile, backlit by a bright moon and a thousand stars winking through the dark squeeze of the cave's mouth.

She saw Orion's face fall as something outside the cave caught his eye. He spun around to face Helen and Lucas, crowding them back into the cave as he hunched his big shoulders over the two of them protectively. Helen saw his mouth drop open in a gasp and his bright eyes grow wide as the tip of a sword appeared under his breastbone. The ground shook. Over Orion's shoulder, Helen saw Automedon's shiny red insect eyes staring at her.

"Orion!" Lucas exclaimed. He reached out a hand from under Helen and grabbed Orion's shoulder, trying to hold him up as Orion and Lucas sank to their knees together with Helen pressed between them. The tip of the blade disappeared as it was yanked out, and the shiny metal was replaced by a rush of dark blood. Helen watched as if in slow motion as a drop of Orion's blood fell on one of her many wounds and mixed with hers.

*That's one,* Helen thought helplessly. Thunder rolled across the clear, cloudless sky.

"My knife," Orion breathed.

Lucas nodded almost imperceptibly, understanding Orion's meaning. Helen tried to speak, hoping she had healed enough to at least warn Lucas *not* to fight, but instead all that came out of her was gasping cough.

"Can you take her?" Lucas whispered, looking into Orion's eyes and begging him to be honest. In answer, Orion slid his arms under Helen and took her weight.

Lucas reached under Orion's shirt to unsheathe the long blade. In a blindingly fast motion, he sprang to his feet, vaulted over Orion and Helen, and pushed Automedon away from the wounded pair.

Orion held Helen close to his chest as he panted for a few moments, like he was willing himself to heal faster. With a painful groan, he finally hauled himself to his feet and shuffled out of the cave with Helen in his arms.

Outside, pressed up against the wall next to the mouth of the cave, Helen spotted Zach—his eyes wide and staring. Still paralyzed, she screamed on the inside, but nothing came out. Zach looked at Helen's ruined face and made a desperate sound, catching Orion's attention. Orion glared at him, and Zach stared back at Orion in terror.

Helen felt Orion's head tilt down to look at the sword in Zach's hands, and then back up into Zach's eyes. Without pause, Zach held the hilt of the sword out to Orion, offering him the weapon.

"I'm a friend of Helen's. You fight. I'll stay and guard her," he said in a level voice. Orion looked at Lucas, caught in a clinch and getting kneed in the gut by Automedon, and made up his mind quickly.

Helen tried to struggle when Orion put her down on the ground at Zach's feet. She tried to spit out the word *traitor* but all she could do was stammer the letter *T* a few times and twitch.

"I'll make sure he comes back to you," Orion promised quietly, and kissed Helen's forehead. Pressing on his wounded chest as if that could make it stop hurting, Orion took the sword from Zach and charged into the fray to fight alongside Lucas.

"Don't worry, Helen, I just called Matt. They're all coming. Hector said even your mother is on her way." Zach tried to make her more comfortable by tugging ineffectually at the tears in her dress and smoothing her blood-soaked hair. As he looked her over, his hands started to shake and tears began to gather in his eyes. "I'm so sorry, Lennie. Jesus, look at what he did to your *face!*"

Breathing hard and coughing up inhaled blood, she stared at Zach and focused all her energy on making her frozen tongue move.

"Khl ma," she slurred. Zach narrowed his eyes, trying to figure out if she'd said what it sounded like she said. Helen braced herself and tried again. "K-hill me."

Finally able to move her fingers, she scrabbled at her slit throat, looking to rip off her heart necklace so Zach would be able to kill her. Zach slowly shook his head at Helen, choosing to misinterpret what he'd heard her say. He caught her hands and held them still, took off his shirt, and pressed it against the wound at her throat.

Incensed with frustration, Helen watched helplessly from the ground as Lucas and Orion fought Automedon, all three of them moving so quickly she could barely make out their separate shapes. Automedon stood between the two of them, mechanical and accurate, every motion begun and completed with surgical precision.

Helen knew just enough about fighting to know that she was watching the perfect warrior. He was stronger, faster, and more patient than any fighter Helen had ever seen. If Orion or Lucas darted in to wound him, he took the blade into himself and let it leave again without concern. He leaked a vaguely greenish-white fluid from several places, but Helen already knew that he couldn't be killed that way. He was just waiting for them to get tired.

Still bleeding from the chest, Orion faltered and took another wound to the stomach. As he fell back, Automedon saw his moment. Rather than attack Orion on the ground, he engaged Lucas. With a deft flick, Automedon spun Lucas's smaller blade out of his hand, sending it flying. Then he made a move to go after Lucas while he was unarmed.

"Luke!" Orion yelled, his voice breaking with exhaustion. He tossed Lucas his sword and left himself defenseless. Automedon let Lucas catch it.

Lucas flew over Automedon and landed in front of Orion who was grimacing and clutching his newest injury. He tried to get up, and fell back down with a grunt, blood pouring out of him alarmingly fast. Lucas dug in, making it clear that if Automedon wanted to get to Orion, he would have to go through him first.

Helen saw Automedon smile and felt a panicky thrill

radiate out from her belly and shoot down her arms and legs. This what exactly what Automedon wanted. He was *counting* on them to be brave and selfless. That would be their downfall. Her skin crackled with desperate static, but she didn't have enough strength to generate a bolt. Ignoring the fiery pain it caused her, Helen managed to flop over onto her broken forearms and began to drag herself toward them.

"Helen, don't!" Zach said in surprise. He tried to stop her, but as soon as he touched her he jumped back, getting a mild shock.

"Stop fighting him!" she tried to yell as she crawled, but even though she was healing fast, her vocal cords were still severed. The only sound she could make was a harsh, grating whisper. Automedon hefted his sword confidently and swung it over his head.

"Brace yourself," Orion warned Lucas, and before Automedon could bring his sword down on them, the ground shook violently.

A booming noise sounded out through the dark, and a giant chasm opened up between Automedon and Lucas as Orion yanked the earth apart. Automedon fell to his knees and scrambled frantically as the ground beneath him gave way. Lucas disengaged gravity and floated, while Automedon seemed to magically regain his footing. His sense of balance was so good he could ride an earthquake like a surfer riding a big wave. Seeing this, Orion's and Lucas's hopes flagged.

When the shaking subsided, Lucas landed in front of

Orion, adjusted his grip on the sword, and faced Automedon grimly. They both seemed to know that they couldn't win this fight, but neither of them would quit. Automedon faced Lucas and Orion in turn, and then bowed to them courteously.

"Clearly, you are the Three I've waited thousands of years for," Automedon said across the ten-foot-wide rip in the ground. "I thank Ares I've had thousands of years of battles to prepare myself for you or I would not have been ready. But the time is here, and I *am* ready."

Automedon leapt easily over the gap, landed, and turned to face Lucas and Orion. In three moves, he had disarmed Lucas. In two more moves, he had Lucas on his knees, shielding Orion with his body and bleeding from a deep cut in his shoulder.

Helen heard Lucas scream and her pain vanished. She stood up, her skin glowing blue and coursing with power.

"Don't you touch him!" she whispered hoarsely, her lips curling with rage. She held out her left hand and a blinding white bolt arced out of her palm and connected with Automedon. He crumpled to the ground, convulsing in agony. Helen dropped her arm and staggered to the side.

Finally able to get to his feet again after Orion's earthquake, Zach stumbled after Helen and managed to prop her up as she tipped over, nearly fainting with the effort of generating a bolt. He got another nasty shock, but he gritted his teeth and held on to her as they staggered their way toward Lucas.

She fell down next to him, reaching out and pressing on his shoulder as if she could hold him together with her bare hands. She was vaguely aware of thunder rolling and she knew that his blood was mixing with hers, but she didn't care. She couldn't stop herself from touching him. All she had to do was get him away from Orion before their blood mixed, and the ritual would be stopped.

Helen felt something grab her bare ankle, and looked back to see Automedon as he yanked her toward him across the ground to keep her from interfering.

"It's too late, Princess," he said calmly.

Helen looked and saw Orion holding Lucas up as both of them reached out to her, trying to snatch her away from Automedon. Orion's wounded chest was pressed against Lucas's bleeding shoulder. Thunder rolled across the sky for the third and final time.

"It is done," Automedon said, closing his eyes for a moment in relief.

Helen looked at Lucas and Orion. From their searching, confused expressions, she could tell that they could feel something had happened to them all—they just didn't know the name for it yet.

"And now to deal with you, slave," Automedon said as he jumped dexterously to his feet, completely recovered from Helen's bolt. "You swore on this dagger to serve or die. And in the end you did not serve."

He took a bejeweled bronze dagger out of its sheath on his belt. Before Helen could haul her broken body up onto her knees to shield him, Automedon threw the blade right into Zach's chest.

Helen caught Zach as he fell down next to her on the ground. She had a memory flash of a time in second grade when Zach fell off the monkey bars and sprained his ankle. He'd had the same wide-eyed and baffled look on his face, and for a moment he looked like he was seven again and they were pals, trading treats out of their lunch boxes.

"Oh no, Zach," Helen whispered, laying him down as gently as she could. Automedon turned away from the carnage he had caused and raised his hands to the blue beginnings of the dawn on the horizon.

"I have fulfilled my end of the bargain, Ares," he said rapturously. "Now give me what I ask. Reunite me with my brother."

"Helen," Zach wheezed urgently, while Automedon was addressing the sky. "His blood brother . . . wasn't a god, like Matt thought." He grabbed the blade still sticking out of his chest and started yanking on it, hurting himself more and more.

"No, leave it in. You could bleed to death!" she tried to argue with her cracking, whisper of a voice, but Zach wouldn't quit until Helen helped him pull it out. He wrapped her hands around the small blade meaningfully.

"It was *Achilles*."

Zach let his head fall back and turned his face to Automedon's feet, which were just inches away from his dying eyes. Without giving it another thought, Helen flipped the blade over in her hand, grabbed the hilt firmly, and stabbed it into Automedon's heel.

His head snapped around to look down at Helen. Utter shock and disbelief froze his face in a blank O. In mere seconds, he hardened into a stone statue that began to crack, then crumble, and then disintegrate into a pile of ash. Helen looked down at Zach and saw that he was smiling.

"Hold on," Helen croaked as she looked around for something to put on Zach's wound. She saw his bloody shirt lying a few yards away and began to scramble toward it.

"Don't go," Zach begged, holding on to Helen's arm. With his other hand, he reached into the pile of dust that had been Automedon, and pulled out the pretty dagger, handing it to Helen. "Tell Matt I said he was a great friend."

His body relaxed and his eyes emptied, and Helen knew he was dead.

"See, Eris, I didn't double-cross him—the Myrmidon got his wish," tittered a voice that made Helen's heart stop for a moment. "He is reunited with Achilles. Just not on Earth, where he would have liked it!"

"At least his slave will be there to care for him in the Underworld," hissed a woman's voice.

Helen closed Zach's eyes, promising silently that she would make sure Zach made it the Elysian Fields, drank from the River of Joy, and never had to serve anyone again. Then she turned to look at what she could already smell.

Ares stood on the other side of the chasm, flanked on either side by his sister Eris and his son Terror. Helen dropped her head and panted, knowing it was true. The Olympians were free. She felt a hand on her shoulder and looked up to see Lucas and Orion crouching next to her.

"How?" Orion gasped, motioning to Ares.

"The three of us," Helen responded. "We became blood brothers."

Lucas and Orion shared a pained look, realizing too late how their better natures had been used against them.

"Can you fly?" Lucas whispered, clutching his wounded arm to his side. Orion was next to him, pale and shaking with blood loss. Neither of them was in any condition to fight. Helen looked across the deep rip in the ground at Ares.

She'd felt rage before, but this was different. She thought about how helpless she had felt when she was tied up and completely at his mercy while he beat her. He'd probably done that to countless thousands of people, she thought. And now he was free again. It was Helen's responsibility to make sure he never tortured anyone else. She had loosed this monster into the world. Now she had to put him down.

"I'm not going anywhere." She stood up stiffly. One of her legs still wasn't responding very well, but for what she had planned, she didn't need it to.

"Are you insane?" Orion sputtered, tugging lightly on her arm, trying to get her to duck down. Helen put her hand over his until he stopped.

"Helen, you can't hope to win this," Lucas said resignedly, like he knew he'd already lost this argument. He stood up next to her, took her hand, and looked at Orion.

"How are you doing?" he asked.

"Terrible," Orion winced as he staggered to his feet as well. "And I'm pretty sure I'm about to feel even worse."

Helen tried to smile at the two of them and tell them how much she loved them both, but her face hurt too damn much and she could barely speak, so she settled for squeezing their hands gratefully.

"Do we have a plan?" Lucas asked Helen, like he figured the answer was no, but he may as well ask, anyway.

"Are you really going to try to fight me, little godlings?" Ares shouted across the gap incredulously. Helen ignored him.

"How deep is that rift, Orion?" she asked under her breath.

"How deep do you need it to be?"

"Does it go down into the caves? The ones with the portals?" she continued. Orion nodded, still confused. "And can you make it *wider* when I ask you?"

"Sure, but . . ." Orion broke off as Helen's meaning suddenly dawned on him. He frowned and began to shake his head at her, but he never got a chance to voice his concerns.

Ares raised his rusty, serrated sword over his head and burst into flames. But if Ares expected her to be afraid of fire, he was sorely mistaken. Helen launched herself over the chasm and landed on him in her supermassive state before he could even finish his battle cry.

She ground him two feet down into the dirt, right at the edge of the chasm. He tried to cut her head off, but she knocked the blade of his sword away with the back of her impermeable hand like she was swatting away a fly. The abominable sword went flinging up over the edge of the chasm. Ares watched it moving away from him with his mouth hanging open.

Before he could recover from his shock, Helen clamped her knees around his ribs and dug her fingers into his throat, choking him with all four of her battered and bruised limbs. His fire burned brighter, like he was trying to scorch her, but Helen only squeezed tighter. Her lightning was ten times hotter than any flame, and to show him, she sent two bolts directly into his neck with both her hands.

As Ares convulsed under Helen's relentless onslaught, Lucas and Orion threw themselves at Eris and Terror, tackling the startled gods and hitting them repeatedly. None of the Scions could actually kill any of the immortals, but Helen didn't care. Death was too good for Ares, anyway.

"Orion! Now!" she screamed, clutching Ares in a bear hug and taking on more mass than she had ever attempted before. She felt Ares growing in size, getting larger and larger as he bellowed with fury, and she clamped on to him desperately. For a moment, she thought Orion wouldn't be able to do it.

The ground beneath them rumbled and shook, and then it gave way. Locked together, Helen and Ares fell down into the deep chasm, tumbling and spinning toward the icy portal that glowed faintly at the bottom.

Helen didn't know if it would work or not. She could come and go from all levels of the Underworld while she was sleeping, but this was the first time she had ever tried it awake. She didn't know if she could open a standing portal, or if she could only create new ones when she slept. She concentrated on staying calm, like she did when she relaxed herself into sleep when she descended, and hoped for the best. Right before they hit, Helen spoke.

"Open, Tartarus, take Ares, and seal him up forever with all the evil souls he has double-crossed," she said.

She couldn't kill an immortal, but she was pretty sure if she could get Ares through a portal, she could imprison him in Tartarus forever. Helen knew from experience that it was way worse than death.

The ice split, and she and Ares stopped falling and started hovering. A hundred hands came through the rocks and ice and grabbed a different part of Ares.

"Impossible," he breathed, his eyes locked with Helen's.

"Go to hell," she whispered.

And then she released him. With a deafening squeal, Ares was dragged into the dark pit of Tartarus by the hundred hands. An incalculable number of writhing arms closed over him until finally, Ares, the god of war, disappeared underneath them forever.

The portal closed, leaving Helen hovering at the bottom of the dark rift. The only sound was her, panting with exhaustion.

Her vision blurred. Barely able to float, she used her hands to guide her up the wall of the chasm. Her body began to tremble violently and her head lolled on top of her neck. As she got higher, she heard her name being called repeatedly by several voices. She fumbled her way toward the sound, sobbing with fatigue and pain.

Just as her strength failed, two different but dearly loved hands reached over the edge of the pit and hauled her up into the pink air of a new dawn.

# EIGHTEEN

"I stabbed him, but it was all Zach, really. He was the one who figured out how to kill Automedon." Helen pried Matt's hand off Zach's wrist and replaced it with the beautiful dagger. "He wanted me to give you this and tell you that you were a great friend. Which, of course, you are."

Matt looked down at the ancient artifact and shook his head. "I don't want it."

"Take it," Helen said. "It was his last wish, and my throat hurts too darn much to argue."

Matt gave her a sad smile and a sideways hug. He stared blankly at the dagger for a moment, then tucked it into his belt under his shirt. Both of them felt horrible about the decision to leave Zach's body on the streets in Nantucket, but they knew there was no better way to conceal the true cause of his death than to blame it on the riot.

"I won't leave him in a disrespectful place, I promise. I'm very sorry about your friend, Matt," Pallas said in a surprisingly tender voice. He put a hand on Matt's shoulder and squeezed it reassuringly until Matt looked him in the eyes and nodded, signaling that he was ready to let go. Pallas picked Zach up gently and ran away so fast Helen knew it almost looked to Matt as if they had disappeared.

Without making her ask, Matt took Helen's arm and put it over his shoulders, half carrying her back to the main pow-wow that was taking place at the edge of the chasm. Her leg had been broken in several places when Ares kicked her, and she still couldn't walk on it but, like the rest of her, it was healing. She could see out both her eyes again at least, even though the right one was monstrously swollen. Helen still had plenty to be grateful for. Eris and Terror had run off as soon as Ares was defeated, and as soon as Helen had opened her eyes, Daphne had told her that her father and the twins were still alive. Unlike Zach. Matt placed her in between Orion and Lucas, and went to stare down the hole like Hector and Daphne.

"I already told you," Orion said, gingerly pressing gauze pads to his two wounds. "The portal is closed. Look at my wrist." He held up the Bough of Aeneas. "When it's *not* glowing like that? That means it *isn't* near a portal. Can I close the rift now so the farmers who own this place don't accidentally fall down it?"

Lucas began to laugh at Orion's tone, then quickly stopped laughing and clutched at the shoulder his father was bandaging. Helen could tell Orion was done with answering questions. He tended to get more sarcastic when he was ticked off. She decided it was time to step in and let him off the hook.

"I shut the portal, and I shut it forever," she rasped through her tender vocal cords. "Ares isn't getting out that way, if at all. Go ahead and close the rift, Orion."

"But how can you know that?" Daphne interjected with mild exasperation. "Is there any way for you to go down and check, Helen?"

"Daphne, look at her. She's suffered enough for one night. Stop pushing," Castor said with his usual levelheadedness while he finished wrapping Lucas's shoulder. "If Helen and Orion say it's okay to close the rift, then let him close it."

Daphne threw up her hands and turned away, blowing air through her lips noisily, just to let everyone know that even though she had been overruled, she still didn't agree. Hector rolled his eyes and shared a look with Orion. Apparently, both of them were familiar with this little display of Daphne's, although it was the first time Helen had ever seen it.

"Close it," Hector said to Orion. The ground squeezed together with a grinding moan, and shut with a small boom.

"Well, looks like we'll never know now," Daphne said in a snippy undertone.

Helen really wanted to slap her, but she couldn't stand up without Matt, and he had wandered off somewhere. She craned her head and found him searching the ground for something. He suddenly crouched down, sifted through Automedon's ashes, and pulled out something shiny. The sheath to the blade, Helen realized, wondering why he wanted it.

"Hey. You okay?" Orion asked her, jarring her out of her thoughts. Orion put a finger on her chin to make her hold still and stared into her injured eye. Still staring at it, he leaned to the side and called over her shoulder. "Hey, Luke. Have you seen this?"

"Yeah," Lucas said heavily, looking down and nodding. "Did you notice the shape?"

"Yeah. Very fitting."

"What are you two talking about?" Helen said, her voice cracking.

"There's a blue-white scar running down your right iris, Helen. The kind of scar Scions don't get rid of," Lucas said quietly. "It's shaped like a lightning bolt."

"Is it, like, freaky looking?" she asked Orion, paranoid that no one would ever want to look her in the right eye again. He started to laugh and then stopped abruptly, clutching his wounds and grimacing just as Lucas had moments earlier.

"Actually, I think it looks kind of awesome. Not too happy about how you got it, though," he said in a falling tone.

"Me neither." With or without a scar, Helen knew she would think about this night for the rest of her life. She just hoped Morpheus would be kind and not send her any nightmares about it.

"We'll have to call a summit," Daphne said to Castor. "Of

*all* the Houses. Atreus, Thebes, Athens, and Rome."

"I know," Castor said, nodding. He looked over at Orion and shrugged. "When's good for you?"

Helen, Lucas, and Orion all laughed at that, but the moment of levity died fast when they considered *why* they had to have a meeting of the Houses to begin with. They needed to tell all the Scions that the war had started and come up with a plan to deal with it.

"In the meantime, I think we should call everyone we can. Tell them to watch their backs," Hector advised.

"Do you think the gods would really try to pick us off one at a time?" Lucas asked dubiously.

"No," Matt said, rejoining the group. "I think they want a real war. Something big and heroic."

"More fun that way," Helen said remotely, thinking of Ares and his twisted idea of playtime.

"This isn't a game," Hector reminded Helen and Matt gently. "The gods have seen what Helen can do, and what they face is worse than dying. I don't know about you, but I'd rather spend eternity in the Elysian Fields than in Tartarus. If I were Zeus, I'd make Helen my first target, but I don't think Orion and Lucas are much farther down on the gods' hit list. Like it or not, the Houses are united. We stick together from now on. No one wanders away from the fold."

Everyone nodded at Hector's decree. He was, and always would be, their hero.

For a moment Helen saw Hector wearing a breastplate and holding a spear as he addressed the troops. Jason stood behind him, holding Hector's plumed helmet with pride. At the base of the castle walls, wave after wave of brave soldiers screamed Hector's name, bathing it in glory.

"Getting the right conditions to lock Ares in Tartarus was a lucky break," Helen said, blinking until the vision of Hector, glowing red and gold in the sunshine, went away. "It's not something that happens all the time."

"But it did happen," Daphne said, turning toward Hector with a touch of excitement. "And now all the gods must know that if it could happen to Ares, it could happen to them. They *should* fear us. For a change."

Helen watched her mother worrying her lower lip between her fingers as she paced, deep in thought. It was almost as if Daphne wanted this war, but why? Daphne was a lot of things, but suicidal was not one of them. Helen banished the notion, convincing herself that Daphne was happy only because there was a chance that the gods might try to avoid a war now that they were threatened with Tartarus. That had to be it. Pinching her swollen eyes shut as she tried to clear her throbbing head, Helen felt Lucas take her hand and squeeze it briefly to get her attention.

"My dad said Jerry and the twins are awake now," he said softly. His forehead creased when he saw Helen's eyes swim. "Are you okay?"

Helen smiled at him and shook her head. She wasn't okay. None of them was. She held out her other hand and took Orion's.

"Want to meet my dad?" she asked him.

"Yeah. I guess you should meet mine, too," he said, but he didn't look too excited about it. He looked sad. Orion's head bobbed forward and he blinked a few times, trying to stay conscious.

"Okay. Time to go," Castor said, his face furrowed with worry. "The three of you are in really bad shape. We need to get you back to 'Sconset. Daphne? Hector? Let's go."

Helen, Lucas, and Orion were still too weak to stand, and needed to be carried back to Nantucket. Helen fought it at first, but then moments after Daphne picked her up, Helen was overcome with exhaustion. She hadn't expected it, but Daphne's arms were much more familiar than she could have imagined.

Glancing first at Orion and then letting her eyes land on Lucas, Helen let her head rest against Daphne's shoulder and fell asleep to the soothing rhythm of her mother's heart.

## ACKNOWLEDGMENTS

You know the saying, "It takes a village to raise a child"? Well, that goes double for trilogies. I have a ton of people behind me, aptly known as Team Starcrossed, and they keep this traveling circus afloat. It starts with my manager, Rachel Miller, and my agent, Mollie Glick. They've pushed me, supported me, fought for me, and even kicked my butt when I needed it. They've made me a better writer, and to me, that's what this journey is all about. Next, I have to thank Hannah Brown Gordon and Stephanie Abou. They're like my own personal UN, and they've done so much for me in so many different languages I have to say *danke/ gracias/merci/obrigado* just to cover a few of the bases. Barbara Lalicki, my editor at HarperCollins, worked so hard to help me get *Dreamless* in shape . . . thanks, Babs! To my two Katies, Katie McGee and Kathleen Hamblin— you're both clutch. Alyssa Miele, den mother in training, keeps me in stitches even when I'm *in* stitches, which is no small feat. Amy Plum, Robyn Shwer, and Laura Arnold are just about the best beta readers a girl could ask for, and I am indebted to them for their keen insight and caring support. I have to say thank you to my foreign publishers, especially Dressler, MacMillan and Giunti, for the fantastic job they've done with my books overseas. Lastly, I have to thank the most important person on my team, my helpmeet and love of my life, my husband. *Te quiero.*

In a war that could end it all,
will Helen follow her destiny—or her heart?
The powerful saga concludes in

# GODDESS

# ONE

Helen could see what she guessed was the River Styx just off to her left. It was a roaring torrent, riddled with icebergs. No sane person would dare swim across it. Feeling stranded, she limped around in a tight circle. A quick scan of the horizon showed that there was no one else on the barren plain.

"Damn it," she swore to herself, her voice breaking. Her vocal cords were not completely healed. Less than an hour ago, Ares had slit her throat, and although it still hurt when she spoke, cussing made her feel better. "So typical."

She'd just made a promise to her friend Zach. He was dying in her arms, and she swore that she would make sure that he drank from the River of Joy in the afterlife. Zach had sacrificed himself to help her, and in his final moments, he'd given her the clue that allowed her to kill

Automedon and save Lucas and Orion.

Helen intended to keep her promise to Zach even if she had to carry him to the Elysian Fields and right up to the banks of the River of Joy herself—broken ribs, wonky leg, and all. But for some reason, her usual way of navigating in the Underworld wasn't working. Normally, all she had to do was say out loud what she wanted and it just happened.

She was the Descender, which meant that she was one of the exceedingly few Scions who could go down to the Underworld in her living body and not just as a spirit. She could even control the landscape to a certain extent, but of course just when she needed that talent the most, it found a way to go on the fritz. It was just so *Greek*. One of the things Helen resented the most about being a Scion was that it meant that there was an appalling amount of irony in her life.

Helen pinched her bruised lips together in frustration and raised her hoarse voice to the empty sky. "I *said*—I want to appear by Zach's spirit!"

"I have that one's soul, niece."

Helen spun around and saw Hades, lord of the Underworld, standing several paces behind her. Tall and poised, he was wreathed in shadows that dissipated like fingers of fog relaxing their grip. The Helm of Darkness and the extra yards of fabric from the black toga he wore obscured most of his face, but she could just make out his lush mouth and square chin. The rest of his toga was draped over his body like a decorative afterthought. Half of his smooth chest and his powerful arms and legs were bare. Helen swallowed and concentrated on focusing her swollen eyes.

"Sit, please. Before you fall," he said softly. Two simple, padded folding chairs appeared, and Helen eased her abused body into one while Hades took the other. "You are still wounded. Why did you come here when you should be healing?"

"I have to guide my friend to paradise. Where he belongs." Helen's voice trembled with fear, although Hades had never hurt her. Unlike Ares, the god who had just tortured her, Hades had always been relatively kind. But he was still the lord of the dead, and the shadows around him were filled with the whispers of ghosts.

"What makes you think that you know where Zach's soul belongs?" he asked.

"He was a hero. . . . Maybe not at the beginning when he was still being a jackass, but at the end, and that's the bit that counts, right? And heroes go to the Elysian Fields."

"I wasn't questioning Zach's valor," Hades reminded her gently. "What I asked was: What makes *you* fit to judge his soul?"

"I . . . huh?" Helen blurted out, confused. She'd taken one too many knocks to the head that night, and she wasn't up to a lesson in semantics. "Look, I didn't come here to judge anyone. I made a promise, and I just want to keep it."

"And yet I'm the one who makes the decisions here. Not you."

Helen had no argument for that. This was his world. All

she could do was stare at him pleadingly.

Hades' soft mouth curved into a distant smile, and he seemed to consider what Helen had said. "The way you handled the freeing of the Furies proved that you are compassionate. A good start—but I'm afraid compassion is not enough, Helen. You lack understanding."

"Was that a test then? The Furies?" An accusing note crept into her voice as Helen recalled what she and Orion had gone through on her last mission in the Underworld. She got even angrier when she considered what the Furies themselves went through. If those three girls were tormented for thousands of years just to prove that Helen was a compassionate person, then there was something terribly wrong with the universe.

"Test." Hades' lovely mouth twisted bitterly around the word, as if he could read Helen's thoughts and agreed with her. "If life is a test, then who do you think grades it?"

"You?" she guessed.

"You still don't understand." He sighed. "You don't even understand what this is." He gestured to the land around him, indicating the Underworld. "Or what you are. They call you the Descender because you can come here at will, but the ability to enter the Underworld is the smallest manifestation of your power. You do not understand what *you* are enough to judge others yet."

"Help me then." He seemed so sad, so beat down by his lot in life. She suddenly wanted to see his eyes very badly and leaned closer to Hades, trying to dip her head down to see under the fabric obscuring his face. "I want to understand."

The shadows spun out again, hiding him and murmuring the regrets of the dead. Helen's insides chilled. The words from the Tyrant prophecy came to her mind—*born to bitterness*. She sat back.

"Shadowmasters," Helen whispered. "Do they get their power from you?"

"A long time ago, a woman known as Morgan La Fey from the House of Thebes had the same talent you have—the one that allows you to come to the Underworld. She bore me a son named Mordred, and since then my burden has haunted the House of Thebes." His voice trailed off regretfully before he stood and held out a hand to her. She slipped her hand into his and allowed him to help her stand. "You must go back now. Come to me as often as you like, niece, and I will try my best to bring you to understanding." Hades tilted his head to the side and laughed quietly to himself. His lips parted, revealing diamond-shaped incisors. "That's why I've allowed you, and those with the same talent before you, to enter my realm—to learn about yourselves. But right now you are too badly injured to be here."

The world shifted, and Helen felt his mile-wide hand lifting her out of the Underworld and placing her gently back in her bed.

"Wait! What about Zach?" she asked. As Hades released her, Helen heard him whisper in her ear.

"Zach drinks from the River of Joy, I swear it. Rest now, niece."

Helen reached out to move the shadows away from his face, but Hades had already left her. She fell into a deep slumber, her broken body greedily sucking up sleep as it tried to heal itself.

After Ares was sealed away in Tartarus and the rift in the ground closed, Daphne had carefully collected her daughter's broken body as Castor carried Lucas and Hector carried Orion back to the Delos compound. Daphne had only been running for a few moments when her daughter fell asleep in her arms. For a moment, Daphne was worried. Helen's injuries had been horrible—some of the worst Daphne had ever seen—but when she listened for the sound of Helen's heart, she heard it beating slowly but steadily.

It wasn't much past dawn by the time they made it back to Nantucket from the caves on the Massachusetts mainland. In the early morning light, Daphne carried Helen up the Delos staircase and down the hallway to the first room she could find that seemed to belong to a girl. She looked regretfully at the pretty silk comforter that her filthy, blood-soaked daughter was about to ruin. Not that it mattered. The House of Thebes had a large enough fortune to replace it. A fortune that had, in part, once belonged to Daphne and Helen's House—the House of Atreus.

Tantalus could scream "holy war" and rant about how it was the "Scions' turn" to rule as much as he wanted, but he'd never fooled the Heads of the other Houses. The Purge some twenty years ago was just as much a grab for the other

Houses' wealth as it was a grab for immortality.

The prophecy that started the Purge said that when the Four Houses were made into One House by the shedding of blood, then Atlantis would rise again. The exact wording that Daphne had memorized stated that in the new Atlantis, the Scions could find immortality. The prophecy didn't actually say that the Scions would *become* immortal— it just said they could *find* immortality there. Daphne wasn't optimistic enough to think immortality was a sure thing. But Tantalus was, and he'd used this prophecy to rally the Hundred Cousins of Thebes around him to kill off all the other Houses.

The whole thing was a sham, as far as Daphne was concerned, sanctified by a lot of mumbo jumbo from the last Oracle—who they all knew had gone crazy after making her first prophecy. But it worked.

Lots of Scions left their vast properties behind to be plundered by the House of Thebes in order to play dead and avoid the slaughter—like Daedalus and Leda, Orion's parents. Like Daphne herself. But Daphne had never cared for money. Then again, she'd never had any moral qualms about taking money when she needed it. Other Scions, like Orion and his parents, did have qualms about theft, and they'd struggled for the last two decades while the House of Thebes lived in luxury. Remembering this, Daphne placed Helen on the bed and destroyed the lovely comforter with a little smile.

Before Daphne could turn to get water and gauze to clean

her daughter's rapidly healing wounds, Helen disappeared and life-draining cold took her place. Daphne assumed that Helen had descended. Time ticked by. Daphne waited, her anxiety growing with each moment. She had thought that trips to the Underworld were instantaneous—that time didn't pass. So much time went by that Daphne began to wonder if she should wake up the rest of the house, but before she made a move, Helen reappeared. Her body smelled like the barren air of the Underworld.

Daphne's teeth chattered, not from the cold, but from the fearful memories the smell of that air awoke in her. She had nearly died so many times now that she could guess what part of the Underworld Helen had visited. The smell was not baked enough to be the dry lands, and there was a touch of damp mud clinging to Helen's feet. Daphne guessed that meant she must have gone to the banks of the River Styx itself.

"Helen?" Daphne cooed. She smoothed her daughter's hair and peered into her chilled face.

Helen had been terribly injured in her battle with Ares, but if she were going to die, Daphne knew she would be dead already. Helen must have used her ability to descend to the Underworld on purpose, probably to look for her newly dead friend—the envious one who'd unfortunately gotten himself enslaved by Automedon.

More than once, Daphne had gone on a similar journey looking for Ajax, but she did not have her daughter's ability to come and go in the Underworld at will. She'd had to all but die to get there. After Ajax had been murdered, she had no will to live, but she knew that killing herself wouldn't reunite her with her lost husband. Daphne had to die in battle like Ajax had, or she would never end up in the same part of the Underworld. Heroes went to the Elysian Fields. Suicides went—who knows where? She had thrown herself into every honorable fight she could find. She sought out the other Scions in hiding and recklessly defended the weak and the young—just as she'd done for Orion when he was a little boy. Many times, Daphne had been nearly killed in battle and made the journey down to the Underworld, always seeking her husband by the banks of the River Styx.

But all she had found was Hades. Unrelenting, enigmatic Hades, who would not restore her husband to life and take her instead no matter how much she begged or bargained. The lord of the dead did not make deals. She hoped Helen hadn't descended in the hopes that she could raise her friend back to life. It was a fool's errand—for now, anyway. But Daphne had been working for nearly two decades to change that.

"Can't see you," Helen murmured, and her fingers flexed, like she was trying to grab something. Daphne immediately understood. She, too, had wanted desperately to see Hades and had tried to pull the Helm of Darkness off his head. Eventually, after Daphne half died enough times to pay off all of her blood debts and rid herself of the Furies, Hades had finally showed her his face.

It was recognizing Hades that had set her plan in motion.

The plan that had broken her only daughter's heart by separating her from the one she loved.

"Oh. Sorry," Matt said from the doorway, startling Daphne out of her spiraling thoughts. She wiped her damp face and turned to see that Matt had Ariadne draped limply across his arms. She was a ghastly shade of gray and barely conscious, having exhausted herself trying to heal Jerry. "She wanted to sleep in her own room."

"I'm sure they'll both fit," she said, gesturing to the wide bed. "I didn't know where else to take Helen."

"Seems like there's an injured person on every piece of furniture in the house," Matt said. He carried Ariadne over and laid her down gently next to Helen.

*Strong boy,* Daphne thought, staring at Helen's friend.

"It'll be easier to watch over them together, anyway," Daphne said, still surveying Matt.

He'd shaped up and put on a lot of muscle since last she saw him, but even still. Ariadne was a buxom girl, not a willowy thing like Helen, and Matt wasn't even breathing hard after carrying her down the long hallway.

Ariadne mumbled something unintelligible to Matt before he pulled away, her face crinkled in protest at his departure. He stopped to smooth her hair. Daphne could nearly smell the love wafting off of him and filling the room, like something sweet and delicious baking in an oven.

"I'll be back soon," he whispered. Ariadne's eyes fluttered and then stilled as she fell into a deep sleep. He ran his lips across her cheek, stealing the smallest of kisses. He turned to Daphne and looked down at Helen. "You need anything?"

"I can handle it. Go. Do what you need to do." He gave her a grateful look, and she watched him stride out of the room—back straight and shoulders squared in the new light of morning.

Like a warrior.

Helen saw herself running down a beach toward the biggest lighthouse she'd ever seen.

It was strange at first. How in the world could she be watching herself like she was watching a movie? It didn't feel like a dream. No dream had ever felt so real or been so logical. Still not understanding what was going on, she quickly got wrapped up in the drama and just went with it.

Dream Helen was wearing a long, diaphanous white dress, held together by a richly embroidered girdle. Her sheer veil had come loose from the pins in her hair, and streamed behind her as she ran. She looked frightened. As the giant lighthouse loomed closer, Helen saw her dream-self recognize a figure standing at one of the points of the octagonal base. She saw a flash of bronze as the figure undid the buckles at his neck and waist, and allowed his breastplate to fall into the sand. She saw herself cry out with happiness and pick up speed.

After shedding half his armor, the tall, dark young man turned at the sound of her voice and ran toward her, meeting her halfway. The two lovers crashed together. He caught her up against his chest and kissed her. Helen watched herself throw her arms around his neck and kiss him back, then pull away so she could kiss his face over and over in a dozen different places—as if she wanted to cover every bit of him. Helen's mind drifted closer to the entwined pair, already knowing who the other Helen was kissing.

Lucas. He was strangely dressed and wearing a sword around his waist. He had sandals on his feet, and his hands were wrapped with worn leather straps and covered with bronze gauntlets, but it was really him. Even the laugh he gave as the other Helen smothered him with kisses was the same.

"I've missed you!" the other Helen cried.

"A week is far too long," he agreed softly.

The words were not English, but Helen understood them just the same. The meaning echoed in her head, just as the relief of being reunited with her love echoed through her— as if it was her body that was pressed against his. Suddenly, Helen knew that it was her body, or had been, once. She had spoken this language, and she had felt this kiss before. This wasn't a dream. It felt more like a memory.

"So you're coming with me?" he said urgently, catching her face in his hands and forcing her to look at him. His eyes glowed with hope. "You'll do it?"

The other Helen's face fell. "Why, always, do you talk of tomorrow? Can't we just enjoy right now?"

"My ship leaves tomorrow." He let her go and pulled away, hurt.

"Paris . . ."

"You are my wife!" he shouted, pacing in a circle and tugging his hand through his hair exactly like Lucas did when he was frustrated. "I gave Aphrodite the golden apple. I chose love—I chose *you* over everything that was offered to me. And you said you wanted me, too."

"I did. I still do. But my sister has no head for politics. Aphrodite didn't think it was important to mention that while you may have been tending sheep that day, you were not a shepherd boy as I believed, but a prince of Troy." The other Helen spared an exasperated sigh for her sister and then shook her head, giving up. "Golden apples and stolen afternoons don't matter. I cannot go with you to Troy."

She reached for him again. For a moment, he looked like he wanted to resist, but he didn't. He took her hand and pulled her to him as if he couldn't bring himself to reject her, even when he was angry.

"Then let's run away. Leave everything behind. We'll stop being royalty and become shepherds."

"There's nothing I want more," she said longingly. "But no matter where we go, I would still be a daughter of Zeus and you a son of Apollo."

"And if we had children, they would have the blood of two Olympians," he said, impatience making his voice harsh. Apparently, he'd heard this argument many times already. "Do you really believe that's enough to create the Tyrant? The prophecy says something about mixing the blood of four houses that are descended from the gods. Whatever that means."

"I don't understand any of the prophecies, but the people fear any mixing of the blood of the gods," she said. Her voice dropped suddenly. "They'd chase us to the ends of the Earth."

He ran his hands over her belly, cupping it possessively. "You could be pregnant already, you know."

She stopped his hands. Her face was sad and—for just a moment—desperate. "That's the worst thing that could happen to us."

"Or the best."

"Paris, stop," Helen said firmly. "It hurts me to even think about it."

Paris nodded and touched his forehead to hers. "And what if your foster father, the king of Sparta, tries to marry you to one of those Greek barbarians like Menelaus? How many kings are asking for your hand now? Is it ten or twenty?"

"I don't care. I'll refuse them all," the other Helen said. Then she cracked a smile. "It's not like anyone can force me."

Paris laughed and stared into her eyes. "No. Although, I'd like to see one or two of them try. I wonder if Greeks smell better after they've been struck by lightning. They certainly couldn't smell worse."

"I wouldn't kill anyone with my lightning," she said with a chuckle, twining her arms around his neck and molding her body closer to his. "Maybe just singe them a bit."

"Oh, then please don't! Singed Greek sounds like it would smell far worse than fully cooked," Paris said, his voice growing heavy as he smiled at her. Suddenly, the humor ran out of their shared gaze and sorrow replaced it. "How am I going to sail away without you in the morning?"

The other Helen had no answer. His lips found hers, and he threaded his fingers through her hair, tilting her head back and taking her weight as she gave herself up to him. Just like Lucas did.

Helen missed him so much she ached—even in her sleep. It hurt so much she woke up and rolled over, groaning as she accidentally put too much pressure on her healing bones.

"Helen?" Daphne asked softly, her voice inches away from Helen in the darkness. "Do you need anything?"

"No," Helen replied, and let her swollen eyes drift shut again. The dream that greeted her made her wish she'd stayed awake, despite her injuries.

A terrified woman was struggling against a massive claw that was wrapped around her waist. Enormous wings, fringed with feathers each larger than a person, beat the air as the giant bird hauled her into the night sky. The skyline of New York City flashed past as the woman struggled.

Helen saw the bird tilt its beaked head to look down at the woman in its talons. For the briefest of moments, the menacing eye of the eagle rounded until it was shaped like a man's. He had amber eyes. Blue lightning flashed in the black middle of his pupils. The eagle screamed, freezing Helen's blood and sending shivers through her sleeping body.

The Empire State Building rose up in front of them, and then Helen saw no more.